ICE HAMMER
INSURGENT

Ice Hammer Book 2

ICE HAMMER
INSURGENT

Ice Hammer Book 2

BASIL SANDS

A PERMUTED PRESS BOOK
ISBN: 978-1-68261-692-5

Insurgent
Ice Hammer Book 2
© 2018 by Basil Sands
All Rights Reserved

Cover art by Christian Bentulan

PERMUTED
PRESS

Permuted Press, LLC
New York • Nashville
permutedpress.com

Published in the United States of America

1

Sergeant Karamof scanned the width of the valley through the range-finding binoculars. One of the benefits of being in Spetsnaz, Russia's Special Forces, was getting the best equipment the Army could afford. Through the viewing slot in the mountainside observation post they'd dug, he could see for a dozen miles in most of three directions: south, west, and a good bit of the north. He turned slowly to Junior Sergeant Vasilli who had been sharing the eight by eight by four-foot-deep dugout with him for the past eight days.

"This place reminds me of the country around my grandfather's farm in Mirny," Karamof said. "Except that it doesn't stink of oil and gases from the mine."

"You're from Mirny?" Vasilli scanned the terrain below them through his rifle scope.

"Yeah. Grew up in a cold desolate place, joined the Army to get away from it, and get sent to Alyeska of all places." He pronounced it using the old Russian name for the land that had once been part of the Russian Empire.

"I didn't know that," Vasilli said. "I've known you more than a year and never knew you were from Mirny."

"I try not to think about it," Karamof said. "At least it is cleaner here. Well, at least in the cities. This mountain sucks ass though." He peered through his binoculars again at the tiny village that lay below. A circle of sod-roofed cabins was set around a glen about the size of a football field.

They'd been watching it for more than a week after a satellite had picked it up on a routine search. Since it looked inhabited and seemed to have been built with an attempt at camouflage, regimental intel officers wanted it checked out to make sure it wasn't a rebel training camp of some kind. The two drones they'd sent had picked up little movement, a couple of children, and one or two adults, which seemed to mean it was probably just a native settlement like many small settlements in Karamof's home country of Siberia. But with the large forces building up in nearby Glennallen, orders had come down to make sure the highway would not be coming under attack by organized insurgents.

"All I have seen down there are children, and a few adults," Vasilli said. "I am positive this is a nothing place."

"That has yet to be established," Karamof said. "Since I am from a place like this, I know what kind of fighters it can produce."

He paused and let out a massive fart that rumbled the ground beneath him.

"I also know that I have not taken a decent shit since that bird dropped us off."

He rose and moved to the entry hole, hidden between a large rock and a spruce tree. "This is a load I must release."

"Don't get eaten by a bear."

"Perhaps I will come back with a fur coat."

Vasilli snickered as his sergeant stepped out, shovel in one hand, AK-12, the twenty-first-century reboot of the ubiquitous AK-47, in the other.

"Going vox."

"Good," Karamof said. "You can enjoy my ass music in stereo."

The sergeant moved a dozen yards away, took a knee and froze, listening to ensure nothing was moving nearby that might make a meal out of him. A couple of minutes later, eyes and ears satisfied, he opened his entrenching tool, a compact folding shovel with a steel pick opposite the spade, and dug a cat-hole. Once it was deep enough he turned, dropped his trousers, then squatted over the hole, rifle across his knees. With a tensing of his abdominal muscles, another Herculean fart exploded like a grenade going off.

Vasilli laughed over the headset.

"You don't know how good this is," Karamof said between straining. "Better than an orgasm."

"If your shit is better than sex, you better try a different whore than that fat girl you've been taking," Vasilli said.

"She is nice, soft and warm," Karamof grunted, "but a shit like this is the building blocks of life itself."

2

Scouts

"**S**o do you think they will want to move?" Charlie whispered to Ben as they crouched behind a cluster of large rocks, taking a short rest after cresting the mountain that over looked Scout Town, the name they had settled on for their little village.

Bravo Company had been on patrol for more than three weeks. They had left towards the end of breakup, the Alaskan equivalent of spring, when the ice melts on the rivers and the landscape suddenly transitions from cold white to wet green, through the first part of June. Tommie Dolan, the Irish mercenary who was second-in-command of the boys and men who made up Troop 104 Alaska Defense Force, guided Sergeant Eddie Strang and Corporal Ben Stone's company on a patrol to verify reports of Russian troops nearby.

They'd first heard about the Russian presence from Dr. Alex Tatum. He'd been introduced as the "Philosopher/Bushman" of South Central Alaska, but turned out to be much more than that. Fluent in several Alaskan and Russian dialects of the Yupik and Inupiaq languages, he also had a good understanding of Russian, Mongol, and Mandarin. With that skill, he had been able to translate much of what he'd heard while posing as a local trapper when he'd come across the Russians in chance encounters in the months following the initial invasions. Dr. Tatum, mild-mannered, soft-spoken, his half-sized right arm twisted from a childhood injury, seemed little more than a simple uneducated and pliable bushman to the occupiers. The fact that he was black lowered his esteem even further among the notoriously racist Russian soldiers. Even if he produced the sheepskins to prove it, they would never have believed that he actually held multiple graduate degrees and two earned doctorates. And they certainly had no idea that he carried a Top Secret "Eyes Only" Clearance, had been a senior analyst for the NSA and a personal friend and advisor of three American Presidents. Those facts were easily hidden from the invaders by his fur and tanned leather clothes, his crippled arm, his wild hair and unruly beard. Somehow, the Russians had missed the fire in his eyes.

Ben thought about those eyes. The way they'd looked at him at that first meeting of patrol leaders, and in subsequent encounters. Dr. Tatum's eyes seemed to bore deep inside when they connected with him. He felt like he'd learned something merely by the contact. But the man's words burned even deeper.

"When you are leading men," Dr. Tatum had said on that long ago day. Had it only been a few months? "Their lives, their well-being, sit in the palm of your hand. But their fate is already decided by God. You cannot change that; you can only help them be strong for when it comes."

Ben glanced around at the others, absentmindedly rubbing the snake-like scar that ran around his right forearm. Almost a year before, he'd earned that scar crossing the Tazlina river to save his friend and it still itched from time to time. Tommie signaled for him to come forward to where he was squatting with the company sergeant, Eddie. Ben paid close attention to the way Eddie did things, and how he carried himself. Even though he was only a few years older than Ben, Eddie had been a real soldier in Afghanistan for two years with the Alaska National Guard. Ben tried to emulate his posture, to look and act like him. Like a real soldier. He crouch-ran toward the leaders, staying low and moving silently across the forest floor as they'd practiced ad nauseum over the previous year. Once there, he took a knee and waited for instructions.

"Ben," Tommie said, his Irish accent still crisp as if he'd never left home, "take a couple of your boys 'round this bend of the mountain to make sure there's nothing waiting for us on the other side. If those Ruskies have been about, they might be here too. Get your brother and two others to check it out before we bring the rest around."

"Yes, sir," Ben replied, his voice deep, no longer the light pubescent timbre of the previous year. He sounded like a man, a warrior. He went back to the group and tapped Charles on the shoulder, then found his younger brother, Ian, the best shot of the troop, and Todd, Commander Mike's son. The four of them moved ahead, rounding the bend in the mountain trail.

They stalked in silence, as if hunting prey. Eyes alert. Ears attentive. Sniffing the air for every subtle change. After a year living in Alaska's absolute wilderness, training to hunt and track and live off the land, their senses were tuned to the forest and tundra. Like a banker who trains to detect counterfeit bills by handling thousands of real bills until their fingers are able to instantly identify a fake merely by touch, they breathed the scent of the forest and the people of their village daily to the point that even the slightest foreign odor or whisper of sound that didn't belong stood out like a giant thorn in their senses. Ben raised the small FRS radio to his lips to call back and let them know all was clear when an unexpected sound rumbled somewhere ahead of them.

"Moose don't fart, do they?" Charlie whispered.

"I've never heard one like that," Todd said.

"Ten o'clock," Ian said, peering through the scope on his rifle. "Fifty yards. White guy squatting in the woods. Taking a dump maybe. Russian uniform."

Ben pressed the talk button and whispered, "Contact, stand by."

The sound of a sniggering laugh drifted from a place to the left. Their eyes slid that direction. The telltale straighter-than-natural edge of a man-made structure jutted at a barely discernible angle from the mountain side, a birch pole covered with dirt and rocks. To their trained eyes, it stuck out like a sore thumb.

Conversation in Russian whispered between the man they saw and the one hidden. Ben signaled Ian to keep his sights on the squatting man. He motioned to Todd and Charlie to move toward the shelter, making the hand sign for a grenade. They all nodded in compliance and moved toward their designated positions.

Ben whispered into the radio, "Stand by for contact."

Ben made the sound of a chirping squirrel and all three of his compatriots moved to action. Todd rolled a homemade hand grenade into the hidey-hole. Charlie provided cover in case the occupants came out. The squatting man lurched to his feet, yanking his trousers up with one hand, snatching his rifle with the other. He moved too late. The grenade exploded inside the shelter, accompanied by a short squelch of human misery. Ian's rifle barked. A pink mist burst from the shitting man's head.

A pair of ravens launched from the trees overhead, cawing in fright.

✳ ✳ ✳

"We have to get out of here," Mike said. "Those guys you killed were Russian Spetsnaz. They're the Russian Special Forces/Navy SEAL combo force. When they don't report in, there will be a world of hurt coming our way."

"They were definitely watching us," Tommie said. "Directly above and with good optics too."

He held up the expensive binoculars they'd taken from the dead Russian soldiers.

"We need to get out of the area as fast as we can," Mike pointed to the other leaders. "Get everyone packed up and ready to move. We're leaving in two hours."

✼   ✼   ✼

It took just over four hours, but they did eventually move out. Personal packs fully loaded with as many provisions as they could carry. Over the previous winter, they had captured and domesticated a half dozen caribou as well. It had been surprisingly easy, as the caribou, known as reindeer once they'd been tamed, were very docile, even in the wild. Once trained, they were able to carry the heavy packs of winter clothes, and cases of food, ammunition, and weapons on their backs or dragged on sledges. The troop was very glad for the reindeer, and the fact that one of the adult men, Walt, had been a horse trainer before the war. He was able to adapt that knowledge easily to the wild animals. In addition to other supplies the reindeer would carry, the heavy caribou fur outer garments the boys had made the previous year were the most prized, and it would have been a real bummer to leave those behind, hoping to find a herd again in the autumn and make new winter clothes as the cold bore down on them.

Ben glanced over his shoulder at his brother and the other boys in the group, making sure everyone was moving and had their gear. They'd been lucky that all but one of the boys who had first settled in their camp had survived the winter. The one who had died, had died from what Tommie called a 'terminal case of stupid' after goofing off around the fire, getting badly burned, and suffering for weeks from infection before his body could no longer cope. And it had been a memorable kind of suffering for everyone who witnessed it. Writhing in pain as puss oozed from the third-degree wounds on his arms until the fever boiled his brain and drove him mad. When he finally died, it had been a relief to everyone.

The boys of Ben's platoon filed past, their bags riding high on their backs. The weary boy faces of a year before had been transformed. They wore the look of confidence that came from endless training and a handful of combat encounters. Still afraid, still nervous for what lay ahead, but now they were confident that they could perform when the shit hit the fan. From the previous summer until this point, they'd been constantly sharpening their stalking, hunting, and fighting skills. They'd become expert shots to a man, and could silently approach any beast, human or otherwise, in the forest without detection, until it was too late for that prey. Countless hours spent sneaking up on each other, designing custom camouflage ghillie suits, and memorizing the plants, rocks, and terrain of their surroundings had built a strong skill set. They'd learned how to scout and track, to be able to look at a foot or paw print and tell how old the creature was, how large, and whether it was a hunter or being hunted.

And they'd learned to kill.

Animals at first, hunting for food and fur. Caribou fur snow suits and mukluk boots, rabbit fur mittens, fox and martin hats. Then, after word had come of Russian soldiers at the highway town of Glennallen, they started sending scouting parties. On three occasions, those excursions had ended up in contact. Violent contact. Two of which involved the Stone brothers, Ben and Ian, and a number of dead Russian soldiers with no losses to the scouts as they melted back into the forest. Those encounters had most likely brought the observation post to their neck of the woods. They had been tracked to their lair.

Now that those observers had been killed, there would be no doubt as to the perpetrators of the other fights. And they would likely be blamed for every other attack that had occurred throughout the winter, regardless if the scouts had anything to do with it or not.

Move, escape, rebuild. That was their only hope.

3

Brad

everend Dale Parker had presided over a couple hundred weddings in his nearly fifty years of ministry. But none in conditions quite like this. He took a deep breath and moved to the final oath.

"Brad Stone, before the Lord God and these witnesses," his Oklahoma drawl had not diminished even after decades in Alaska, "do you take Sammi Park as your lawfully wedded wife? To have and to hold? To love and to cherish? To protect and encourage her all the days of her life?"

Brad looked into Sammi's eyes. Dark brown, almost black, almond-shaped Asian eyes set in porcelain skin, the kind of face seen in old-fashioned Korean paintings.

"I do," he said.

"And Sammi Park," the reverend continued, "before the Lord God and these witnesses, do you take this man, Brad Stone, as your lawfully wedded husband? To have and to hold, and to love and to honor, to respect and to encourage all the days of his life?"

"I do," she replied without hesitation.

"Then with these vows you have each written and ascribed to before the God of Abraham, Isaac, and Jacob, and our Lord Jesus Christ, and with the blessing of these witnesses hereto, I now pronounce you man and wife."

Their eyes were locked on each other. Time stopped. A loud silence weighed on the surrounding crowd.

"Uh, son," Reverend Parker said, a smile spreading on his face, "this is where you kiss the lady."

Brad leaned forward, took his new wife into his arms, and kissed her. Cheers and applause echoed against the mountain backdrop as the entire Chiknik community affirmed the marriage of their leader and his beautiful bride.

They released the kiss and Sammi buried her face into his shoulder, tears of joy streaming as she sobbed. Her own life dream fulfilled in the most unexpected of circumstances. He was much older, more than thirteen years between them, but she'd loved this man since she'd been a teenage girl. And while the tragic loss of his first wife had broken her own heart almost as much as his, this moment brought her joy beyond anything she'd ever imagined possible.

She looked up into his eyes and saw the same feeling reciprocated. His eyes shimmered as he looked down at hers, love pulsing from his gaze.

Brad held Sammi tight, feeling the force of her joyful sobs as she buried her face in his shoulder. He fought the flashes of a similar day more than twenty-seven years earlier, blinking back images of Youngmi smiling up at him. Forcing himself to see the new reality. To see only this woman who had been just entering first grade the day he, a twenty-year-old Marine Corporal, married Youngmi Ma, the beautiful Korean college student. Another image rose in his mind. Youngmi's cobalt blue Mercedes with the customized plate, 1004, transliterated as *Chunsa*, or Angel in Korean. The car lay crooked in the ditch, full of bullet holes. Her face was blown out like a flesh rose, a massive exit wound from a large caliber rifle round. The blood-spattered windshield, spider-webbed bullet holes in the glass glistened red, rays of sunlight sparkled white through the cracked glass. Her favorite shirt, with sequins spelling out the words *Hollywood Style,* nearly black with dried blood. He squeezed his eyes shut and forced the images away, wanting only to remember her alive, and then to see only the present. Sammi was not a replacement for the old life. She was a new life, a different life altogether. A new beginning. Wife lost. Sons lost. New wife gained. New children to be made. All things are in God's plan, this was his destiny, his preordained destiny. The darkness evaporated and he smiled into Sammi's eyes, filled with joy at the chance to begin again.

Kharzai, the best man, glanced past Brad and Sammi, to the first row of attendants where Jung Ah stood, the dogs Happy the Black Lab and Penny the Golden Retriever, sitting on either side of her like canine bodyguards. His lips stretched into a broad smile, exposing teeth that stood out bright white against his black beard and brown skin. He jerked his eyebrows up as Jung caught his stare, and he gave his head a quick nod, making his big curly "Perfro" (Persian Afro) jiggle like a stack of thick black Slinky toys. He mouthed the words, "You're next."

She responded with a raised eyebrow and an "Are you serious?" smirk. The look quickly melted into a smile that took ten years off her already attractive fifty-year-old face.

4

The building Brad sat in, while not a completely rustic sod-roofed cabin like many in the little town of Chiknik, was definitely not a mansion like the one he'd spent the previous winter in. The sturdily built board-framed structure measured about twenty by twenty, and was two short stories tall. It was well insulated against the winter cold, which meant it also seemed to retain the summer heat like an oven. Many people outside of the Arctic did not realize just how hot the summers could be. With twenty-four hours of sunlight for almost four months, the interior regions in particular could stay in the nineties for weeks on end. A dry breeze coursed through the open windows with all the comfort of a bellows blowing across a blacksmith's hearth. Sweat ran into Brad's eyes and dripped from his nose as he looked over lists of names of people who had recently arrived in the village of Chiknik, twenty miles north of the Glenn Highway, and nearly fifty miles east of the City of Palmer, which stood firmly in Chinese control.

Every day, dozens, sometime scores, and on one occasion more than a hundred refugees streamed into Chiknik from the surrounding areas. Some had traversed hundreds of miles of open wilderness, from Glennallen, Wasilla, and even as far as Valdez, in search of the rumored safe haven, a virtual paradise, where there was food every day, and even wine and beer to drink. They came all that way, avoiding enemy soldiers and struggling against the hazards of the wilderness only to find a village that had sprouted into a city overnight. A city that could barely take care of its own, let alone a constant influx of new mouths.

"We can't sustain the population," Brad muttered.

Kharzai glanced at him from across the room, Happy and Penny lying quietly beneath his chair, dozing in a swath of bright summer sunlight. "Well, we could always sell Boardwalk and cash in the hotels."

Brad gave him a sideways glance.

"Seriously, Kharzai, we cannot keep up with the people coming in here. We need more food and supplies than the land can provide."

"I know," replied the Persian. "I really do know. Our only real option, in my experience, is to start raiding the enemy."

"Raiding?" Brad's mind went to the previous autumn when a thug named Thor had been doing just that to survive. Then, last spring, he and his band had turned to aiding the Chinese invaders in order to fill their own stomachs.

"Not like Thor," Kharzai said.

"Damn it," Brad blurted out, "how do you do that?"

"Do what?" Kharzai gave him a blank stare, raised an eyebrow, and then said with a smile, "You were thinking about Thor too?"

"You are definitely weird, dude."

"What can I say? The three sisters speak to me," Kharzai replied, referring to the Weirds, also known as The Fates or the Norns in Nordic mythology. Three sisters of ancient lore who weave the fate of every person, drawing the threads of their lives together in an interconnected tapestry. "Regardless of my, or their, weirdness, we do need to start hitting the enemy on both sides and get to taking their stuff to feed our folkses. Otherwise, a whole lot of our people will starve this next winter."

Captain John Charles, military commander of the Alaska Defense Force Sutton Brigade, entered the room. His senior NCO Gunnar, a giant Swede who personified the image of big, scary Viking, followed behind him.

"What's up, gents?" he said, taking off his cap and sitting in a chair next to Kharzai across the table from Brad. Penny sat up and nuzzled his hand until he reached over and scratched behind her ears.

Brad pulled a map from a corner of his makeshift desk.

"John," he spread the map over the table, "where do we get more supplies, food, and weapons, with the least potential losses?"

John looked at him, then over to Kharzai, then back to Brad.

"You think we're ready to go on the offensive?"

"Ready?" Brad sucked in a deep breath. "There is no ready as far as I can see. But we really have no choice." Brad tapped the inventory register he'd received from the supply officer earlier that morning. "From this, it looks like we've got enough food for about two thousand people for the next three months."

"Yup," John said. "Sounds right."

"But we've got over three thousand people here now," Brad said. "Almost double what it was when I arrived a month ago."

"Yup," John said again. "Some of them are coming in with some food supplies of their own, most are not. A lot do have weapons when they come in and a fair amount of ammunition."

Gunnar spoke up, "One guy even came in with a Stoner MG63, an original collector's item from the Vietnam war and six drum magazines full of 5.56. That man was loaded for war."

"Whoa, that is one very cool weapon," said Kharzai. "The SEAL's choice."

"But did he have any food?" Brad asked.

"Yeah," said Gunnar, "one half-eaten MRE and a packet of Ritz Peanut Butter crackers."

"Okay, so to my original question," Brad said, "do you have a plan to take care of these people?"

"Nope," John said, his matter-of-fact tone unchanged. "That's why we came looking for you, figured you might have a better grasp on this kind of stuff."

Brad closed his eyes, sucked in a deep breath, and let it out with a hiss.

"How in the world would I know how to lead a huge group of refugees? I was an IT manager for crying out loud, not a politician," he said. "Besides, I thought you guys had it under control and just needed an image for the people. I thought I was just a figurehead."

"We did have it under control," John said, "until people found out Ice Hammer was real and was here and decided to make you their Messiah."

"Don't say that." Brad, who'd been a church youth leader for over twenty years, pointed an angry finger at John. "Not ever. I don't hold kindly to blasphemy."

"None intended," John raised his hands in surrender, backing away from the accusation, "but that is the honest truth, like it or not. For whatever reason, someone pinned grand leadership status to the image of you cutting down that Chinese soldier, and that's the way so many of these people see you. Hey, it worked for Tito back in dub-dub two; he ruled the whole country of Yugoslavia for almost forty years."

"He was a military dictator and serial adulterer," said Brad.

"Okay, so stick with Messiah then," Kharzai said.

Brad gave him a look.

Kharzai smiled his best disarming grin and continued, "Well, boss, it's better than them calling you Mein Fuhrer or Glorious Leader or something. At least the Messiah is a nice guy."

"We could call you Pope," said Gunnar.

"You guys are *not* helping." A long pause hung between the four of them. Commander of the military forces, symbol of the resistance, and both of their faithful sidekicks/personal bodyguards. "We need to get proactive, and now is the season to do it. Winter prep is a summer job. Let's come up with ideas on who to take our provisions from that will have the least impact on surrounding civilian populations."

John let out a snort. "Are you serious? If we take anything from the Chinese or the Russians, they will immediately punish any civilian population within radio distance of the attack. That's just the way they work. Which is why I haven't done that kind of attack yet."

Brad glanced at him, then to Kharzai.

"He's right, boss," Kharzai said. "I've seen it in more than one conflict during my career in Uncle Sam's Criminally Insane Altar boys." Kharzai loved to pan his previous career in the CIA's shadowy Clandestine Service. "Commies really are bastards in that regard."

"Well, what the hell am I supposed to do to support all these people without punishing the ones that couldn't get out?"

"That is the where the line between soldier and politician becomes even more delineated," John smiled at Brad, "boss."

"Shit," Brad said.

"Yeah," Kharzai said. Happy lurched awake from some kind of doggy dream and rose beside his chair, nuzzling his hand until he reached up and scratched behind her ears. "And you're the commander of the ship trying to row up the so-named creek with a cracked wooden spoon instead of a paddle."

The four men glanced silently back and forth to each other, each waiting for the others to say something wise, or at least meaningful. Kharzai spoke up instead.

"Sometimes I feel like this is an episode of the old Johnny Quest TV series."

"Yeah," said Gunnar, "I've thought that too."

"Wait, you had Johnny Quest in Sweden?"

"Of course," Gunnar replied. "What, did you think we just sat around eating pickled fish and drinking Akvavit?"

"Um…yes?" said Kharzai.

"We had all the American cartoons, probably more than you did in middle of nowhere Iran or wherever you're from."

"Dude," the hairy one replied, "I grew up in Indiana."

"Really?" said John. "Indiana's in Iran?"

"Anyway," Kharzai waved them off, "Brad is Dr. Quest, Gunnar is Race Bannon, John is Johnny Quest, and I am Hadji."

"No, John is the Dr. and Brad is Johnny," Gunnar said, "'cuz everyone has to protect Johnny, even though he's got serious skills."

"Well, either way," John said, "Gunnar is Race and Kharzai is Hadji."

Kharzai smiled his crazy-looking smile as he looked at the man he had put himself under for this war. This was a war he had no number for, no name. He'd long ago lost count of the conflicts he'd been involved in. This war was simply now. It was today. Another day of blood and courage and weeping, crying children. He absentmindedly scratched deep into Happy's black fur, straight to her skin, until the dog was smiling in ecstasy, tongue lolling from her mouth. That kind of happiness was what Kharzai longed for: doggie-joy. To know conflict and terror and violence, but to be able to completely forget it all and let his tongue hang out of his wide-open mouth while Jung Ah scratched his back.

That must be what heaven is like. At least I hope it is.

He felt compassion for Brad. The man was an IT guy, a computer nerd, not a famous general or governor or anything. He was no warrior of great renown like Eisenhower or Washington, or even a combat veteran like Hitler or Stalin or John Kennedy, or even Lee Marvin or Jonathan Winters, for that matter. While he had been in United States Marine Corps' Force Recon, trained as the 'elite of the elite,' he'd nonetheless missed all the wars of his generation and had no combat experience prior to this war that could make him either an evil overlord, a handsome president, or a Hollywood Star. Unlike those famous and infamous leaders who led nations and armies, or had become famous actors, Brad's only claim to fame had been being caught on a drone's camera dispatching two Chinese soldiers with a mountain climbing tool like a medieval warrior. Those pictures and video had somehow, amidst the carnage and chaos of war, found their way into the view of much of the public of Alaska and maybe even folks in Canada and the lower forty-eight states. Survivors had flocked to him. In small numbers at first, such as the group he had met up with at the Hamilton Farm, and then where they found and wintered in a wilderness mansion. Now that John had dragged him out of his doomed paradise to this village turned fortress, they came in droves. Brad had fallen naturally into leadership with minimal guidance from John and his giant sidekick Gunnar, the previous leaders who had shaken them from their nirvana in the forest just before an army of Chinese led by a traitorous gangster had descended, raining death and destruction of their little paradise.

Once at Chiknik, Brad, at John's urging, took control of the local leadership apparatus and all the duties that entailed, thereby allowing John and his military cohort to focus on defense and training, and other military whatchamajigies. Many of those things, of course, were subjects Kharzai knew all too well, after nearly twenty years as a deep cover CIA agent rooting out some of the world's most dangerous men. He had met a handful of Brad's in his time in the trenches. Men who had risen to the challenge to lead, encourage, and focus people on what it takes to survive and maybe even beat back their enemies. He knew this particular Brad had what it takes to guide people, to get them through the trials and suffering that lay ahead of them. He just had to find a way to get Brad to see it for himself, to trust in his quasi-Calvinist theology and accept that this was his destiny.

5

Youngmi

Youngmi stared out the window into the bright June evening. The Alaskan summer's "Midnight Sun" hung in the sky bathing the Arctic in the life-giving light and warmth of a three-months long, two-thousand-hour day that grew hundred-pound cabbages and energized bodies for endless hours of work.

It also made it possible for an invading army to maintain a high operational tempo for a long period of time. The People's Army had crushed western and south-central Alaska under its fist in less than thirty days from the initial attack. Judging by the lack of new US troops arriving to help the beleaguered resistance in the forty-ninth state, the rest of the country had fared little better. From what news she'd been able to glean from conversations with the general and what she'd overheard amongst the soldiers and in the city, she'd been able to put together a picture of the dismal situation in the lower forty-eight and most of Canada. The major cities on both coasts and in both countries had been decimated, many of them destroyed in nuclear attacks as the Chinese army overran the west coast and the Russians the east. With massive atomic devastation in places like Los Angeles, New York City, and Washington, DC, tens of millions of people had died in a single day, and huge swaths of the rest of the country were instantly cowed into terrified surrender. She had learned from Mai that some type of extremely elaborate computer hack had silenced the U.S. military's capabilities to detect the missile strikes and even the ability to strike back until it was too late.

It was the largest invasion in the history of the world, involving not only the two other super power nations but their satellites and subject states as well. With US forces out of the way, the Chinese and Russian armies had easily been able to assert their authority throughout their respective regions since there was no longer anyone strong enough to resist them.

Youngmi thought about the nuked cities, the collapse of the concept of Mutual Assured Destruction that for most of the century had kept countries from doing just what had happened in North America for fear of retaliation destroying the aggressor's country at the same time. She imagined what it must have been like to be in an airplane heading from one city to the next only to discover that your destination no longer existed. Then she remembered the hack Mai had mentioned, and wondered if the thousands of passenger liners in the air at the moment of attack had even stayed airborne, or had they simply fallen from the sky when the communications stopped.

The devastation had struck almost exactly one year earlier. She glanced toward the horizon, the city of Anchorage. The skyline was devoid of the previous summer's columns of black smoke as the fighting had mostly died down. There were still occasional attacks and firefights, or the explosions of bombs left by resistance fighters. But every time a sniper or an IED (Improvised Explosive Device) took a Chinese soldier's life, a dozen or more random citizens would be rounded up and imprisoned, or sometimes shot. The reprisal shootings had recently been reduced by a great amount. In last few months, General Zhang's occupying army worked to ensure they did not kill off significant numbers of the people who could run the city, or provide backs to do needed work. Forced labor sentences had become the preferred method of getting back at the resistance fighters. The threat of community members being held hostage in the camps crimped many insurgent's will to fight, when they knew their own relatives or friends could be worked to death, or if identified killed outright, because of their actions.

Relatives and friends. Those were two things she was not sure she had any longer. She blinked back tears remembering the phone conversation she'd had with Brad just moments before the bombs started falling and people starting dying all around her. In the shapeless segment of history before the world lost its shape and death rained down, they'd been making nerd-sexy talk on the phone. For an IT systems administrator and his web-programmer wife, it was easy to use tech terminology to turn each other on with thinly veiled allusions to hard disks and ram power in an attempt to disguise the conversation from her mom and younger sister who had been in the car with her. Mom had seen through it, and Young-Ja, her younger sister by two years, had nearly had a stroke trying to hold back the laughter. Young-Ja was dead, she was certain of that. She had felt it in her soul minutes after the rumble and noise started to crescendo. It had felt like a part of her own body being torn away. She had no idea what had happened to her mother and step-father, the Sergeant Major, US Army Retired, but presumed they had not survived either. They were fighters, but they were also in their seventies. And most of the fighters who'd stayed in Anchorage did not survive the winter man-hunts and the massacres.

She'd seen no sign of their sons since that day. Jay, the twenty-four-year-old cook who worked on the North Slope for weeks at a time, had just started a new shift up there the day before the attack. Sixteen-year-old Ben and fourteen -year-old Ian were Boy Scouts who had just been dropped off at summer camp, one as a staffer and one as a camper. She'd heard nothing from or about any of them. Brad, she at least knew, was alive. She knew that he was alive only because the general was hunting him like an outlaw. She'd seen the pictures and been in the room when Zhang talked about him, listening in while her platonic-lover discussed finding and publicly killing the man he had no idea was her real-life-husband.

She turned from the window and surveyed the spacious, elegantly furnished apartment. Heavy, dark wood and leather furniture adorned the main room. She walked from the window to the highly polished mahogany dining table with seating for ten that stood under an unostentatious crystal chandelier, taking her customary seat at the side, to the right of the head chair where the general always sat. A deep bong sounded from the far corner of the living room, the tone repeating four more times from a large grandfather clock that ticked the seconds away behind a wide brown leather couch, loveseat, and chair arrangement that reminded her of a men's smoking lounge in a fancy country club somewhere. All in all, the space was warm and comfortable feeling, albeit heavier than her personal tastes, a solid masculine vibe in which she felt out of place at times. Her own room in the two-bedroom suite had been decorated in a more feminine style, with lace and soft white colors that the general's daughter Mai had assisted her in applying. Comfortable indeed.

Youngmi was a prisoner in a mostly comfortable cage, held behind smiling bars, by a gentlemanly, benevolent tyrant. Her survival outside General Zhang Ko Bai's protection had lasted only five days before she'd been captured and gradually found herself transformed into his mistress of sorts. Most people, military and civilian alike, who saw them together looked at her with the assumption that she was his bed-mate. The fact of the matter was that he enjoyed her company in a completely platonic manner. He talked to her in friendly, even intimate terms, but he had never crossed the physical boundary. The general still loved his dead wife, and he seemed to know that Youngmi loved her most likely dead husband as well. She often wondered what he would think if he discovered...no...when he discovered, her husband was the man known as 'Ice Hammer,' the most wanted resistance leader in the state of Alaska.

As for everyone else, all of the Alaskans she'd known prior to 'The Day,' as she'd learned to call it, were either dead or minions.

Minions.

That's how she saw the successful survivors. Herself among them to a degree. Whenever the general took her out for a meal at a restaurant or to a public gathering, which had been happening more frequently over the past few months, she looked at the faces of the people on the streets and in the shops. Some of them looked back at her with undisguised hatred, their eyes burned with a glare that muttered unspoken threats toward her as a traitor. Most people though seemed to try hard to not look at her at all. They shuffled along the streets or through the shops with an aura of barely suppressed terror, a glazed look that made her think of animated mannequins. Terrified animated mannequins. They still seemed to have their wits about them, in a very general sense, but it was as if the deed to their minds had been foreclosed on, or stolen. No longer in ownership of their own lives, they walked the streets and went about their jobs in fear every day that they would offend the new governors and find themselves in the hands of the "Justice Squad." This "Justice Squad" patrolled the city alongside the local police department, not only seeking to solve the more commonly understood crimes of theft, rape, or murder, but also weeding out those that would speak against the regime, the general's person, or especially the communist party. They were the modern-day Chinese communist equivalent of Hitler's Gestapo, the East German Stasi or the Russian KGB. Thugs enforcing their Maoist ideal with an intensely violent zeal. It was common knowledge that few who entered the dark realm of the enforcers of 'peace' emerged from the meeting both alive and whole.

While the public masses probably made the assumption that Youngmi was safe as the general's mistress, she was, in all reality, no different than they were. She too lived in fear of imminent destruction at the hands of some zealous Chinese officer trying to get a leg up at the expense of anyone under their dignity. She knew without a doubt that if her collusion with Captain Chi, the CIA plant in the Chinese People's Liberation Army Intelligence Division, were discovered, she would be dead as fast as any captured low-level resistance fighter, her life probably being taken by General Zhang's own hand on account of her treachery.

Footsteps in the hall outside the quarters caused her to snap her gaze to the surface of the dining table where she and Zhang shared a meal most nights. Her reflection shone back from the highly polished surface as she stared down at it. Although she had been living in his personal space in the headquarters building, albeit with her own private bedroom, for most of the time since he'd taken her captive, she still felt nervous every time he came home, as if each night may be her last with his discovery of her duplicity.

General Zhang Ko Bai, Commander in Chief, Chinese People's Army Alaska Occupation Forces, had been and still was an utter gentleman to her as he managed the death and destruction that continued around them. While Youngmi was the doppelganger for his deceased wife, Zhang had enjoyed her company in a completely platonic way for nearly a year, and showed no signs of wanting to take her physically all that time. At times, due to his lack of physical contact with her, she wondered if he thought of her as less than a woman, since he was Chinese and she Korean, the enmity between the two countries extending back millennia. Her mind drifted to her husband again.

Brad Stone, the Ice Hammer as he had been nicknamed by Chinese military intelligence, reputed to be the leader of the largest militia resisting the occupation. To her knowledge, neither the general nor his staff knew of her connection to the notorious fighter who's extremely violent gutting of several Chinese soldiers with a mountain climbing tool like some ancient Viking warrior had been caught on video and gone viral.

They will know eventually. They will find a record somewhere and I will be finished.

Her heart leapt in her chest as the door to the apartment swung open and General Zhang strode in, his face lighting up when he saw her sitting at the table. She quickly composed herself and responded with a demure smile of her own as he crossed the room to take his seat.

"Good evening, my lady," he said in fluent Korean with an uncharacteristic happiness to his tone.

"Good evening, my general," she said, letting her eyes give a hint of the same pleasure he seemed to be exuding. He sat at the head of the table near her corner seat. She continued in the same language, "May I ask what it is that makes you so happy this evening?"

"Indeed you may," he said, the smile stretching even further. "The answer is composed of two individual components…"

Before he could continue, a white-smocked cook entered and spoke in Mandarin to which the general nodded, his smile never diminishing.

"Of course, bring it in. I am famished."

Immediately, two servers in red smocks entered bearing silver-lidded plates which they carefully set on the table before them. On cue, they raised the lids and Youngmi took in a breath of surprise.

Steak. Rice. A rich brown gravy that smelled of expensive spices and wine. And well-aged Kimchi.

With the exception of special occasions or when he was out at a restaurant with Youngmi, the general ate only what the common soldiers ate at every meal. This ensured both that he knew what his men were experiencing, and that his soldiers ate well. The dish before her tonight looked like something Brad would have made on the barbeque for a special dinner. The smoky odour of flame-broiled meat was delicious, sending her salivary glands into instant over-production.

"My general," she blurted, "what is this? Are the soldiers all eating this well tonight?"

"Yes, actually," he said, "at least, that is, all of the soldiers in Headquarters and Intel commands are. The men in the field, well, I am afraid they'll to have settle for what they get."

"Kimchi for everyone as well?"

"No," he said, a broad smile on his face, "kimchi is a bit too spicy, garlic powered for most Chinese tastes, but I knew that you would find it very rewarding, my love."

She reddened instantly; he'd never spoke to her with such a term of endearment.

"What is the meaning of such a feast?" she asked in a wary voice.

"Two reasons," he said again, looking into her eyes as he spoke. His expression was like that of a little boy with a secret he could not keep.

"Are you going to share those reasons with me?" she asked with a coy smile.

"Maybe," he replied. "Perhaps we should play a round of Kai Bai Bo to see if I should let you in the secret."

Kai Bai Bo was the Korean version of Rock, Paper, Scissors.

"Are you serious?" Her mouth turned in a humorous smirk.

"Yes, ma'am, I am," he said in a mock Texas cowboy accent. She had never seen him in such good humor.

"Okay fine," she said and held up her fist to start the game.

"Kai, Bai, Bo!"

They both hammered their closed fist in the air to the beat of the count, then opened their hand for the symbol they chose.

Kai, closed fist for rock. Bai, open hand for paper. Bo, two spread fingers for scissors.

Youngmi's paper hand beat Zhang's rock and he instantly cried out, "Best of three!!"

Two more times and she beat him at each attempt, paper wrapping rock and rock crushing scissors.

"You are very good at this game, Youngmi! I should consider putting you on my tactical staff," he said with a laugh. "Combat is little more than Kai, Bai, Bo with guns."

She forced herself to laugh at his comment. "Okay, you said you'd tell me what you are thinking about."

"And that I will do, my love," he answered with a flourish of his hand a short stage bow. "First, there is peace in the Kenai Peninsula. All resistance has ended and the fishermen and bush men alike have laid down their arms and agreed to serve the revolution willingly, with no more fighting."

"That is excellent news," she said with a forced smile, simultaneously glad that there would be less killing and angered that her countrymen had surrendered to the conqueror. She hid the latter emotion. "But that is only one reason. What is the second reason?"

"You."

She blushed even deeper than before.

"Me?"

"It is because of you that they did so, Youngmi." He leaned forward taking her hand in his. "You have been teaching my officers and senior enlisted to speak and read English, and have been incorporating American philosophy and the strange ways that your Alaskan people in particular think, the freedoms your people think they have. The way they want to have a voice and would be willing to follow anyone who lets them decide their own fate on a personal level and lets them speak their own minds freely. Some of the officers took this to heart and followed your way of teaching and voilà! It worked!"

He slapped the table with a beefy hand. "The local commanders, under the tutelage of the officers you taught in this very building, let the fishermen speak openly without the threat of guns. They let them vote without fear of reprisals if the vote was against them. And the majority agreed that if we let them continue in their previous trades, and if the People's Army pays

28

them fairly for their products, they will no longer resist but will take up the banner of the revolution and rebuild this land."

Youngmi was flabbergasted. She'd had no idea the general had realized she was trying to indoctrinate the Chinese officers in the way Americans think, in hopes of turning their hearts against their own government. The fact that it had worked so perfectly, and that he was happy with the results, made her swell with pride that she'd had such an impact.

"That is incredible, my general," she replied. "I am very thankful that no more must die to further your cause in the region."

"Well," he said, taking a bite of the steak from his plate and sighing with pleasure as he chewed the succulent morsel. "There is still much to be done, even much more fighting. But to have such a large territory capitulate and allow peace is a very good step to the future."

Youngmi wrapped a leaf of kimchi around a small clump of rice with her chopsticks and delicately placed it in her mouth. She closed her eyes and savored the red pepper and garlic spices and the tingle of the fermented vegetable on her tongue, the flavor signature of her Korean heritage caressing her taste buds, sending a shiver of joy through her whole body. Although she'd lived in America far longer than she lived in Korea, the taste and smell of kimchi was something she had never been far from. Since the invasion, she had not expected to enjoy it again. It was like being reborn. She took a bite of the meat as well, and sighed just as deeply as he had. The meat was tender, with a salty tang on its outer crust, and richly flavoured that made her hear Sam Elliot's voice saying, "Beef, it's what for dinner," in the back of her mind as she chewed. The delicious taste sent her into sensory overload.

"My general," she said after swallowing, "where did you get such fine meat?"

"Ah, this is a gift from our Russian compatriots to the north," Zhang said, cutting another slice and slipping it into his mouth. "They discovered a large herd of the massive, hairy beasts called 'bison' in their territories near Delta Junction. When they heard of our great accomplishments, they shared the meat with us. A feast for kings!"

Youngmi's heart dropped as she stared down at the remaining steak before her. The Delta bison herd was the sole source of bison in Alaska. If they had been decimated, they would possibly be gone forever.

Suddenly, she caught herself in another loop, "Russian comrades?"

"Yes, of course," he said, masticating another bite of the succulent meat. "Didn't you know? I thought I'd mentioned them at some time in the past."

"I knew the Russians were in the eastern United States, but not that they were here in Alaska."

"Indeed, the Russians share this conquest with us. Since this was all their former land, it was part of the alliance with them. Russia has the east and north, and China got the west and south of Alaska."

"I am so sorry, my mind cannot wrap around such great endeavors as you have undertaken my general," she replied, attempting meekness.

"You hide your feelings well, Youngmi," he said. "But not as well as you imagine."

A nervous feeling washed over her, and her eyes went back to her plate. Zhang's kind smile never abated as he looked at her.

"If I were you," he continued as he dabbed meat juice from his lips, "I would hate what has happened to your homeland too."

"I do not..."

"Don't deny your true thoughts." He sliced another piece of meat, put it in his mouth and chewed, letting the silence hang in the air.

Youngmi rolled another leaf of kimchi around a small ball of rice and tentatively put it in her own mouth, the pleasant flavors dissipating, losing their appeal as she chewed.

"Look, Youngmi," the general put down his fork, "both your birth nation and your adopted nation have been conquered by enemies from whom you thought you were immune. You have lost your family, your home. Everyone and everything you held dear is gone or irrevocably changed. And yet in the year that you have been within my protection, you have mentioned none of it. You have never lashed out at me. I have never awakened to find you hovering over my bed with a kitchen knife. But I know, there is more to you than you show."

She said nothing. She set her chopsticks neatly down onto her napkin, and put her hands on her lap.

"I am not such a fool to believe that you, after all this time, do not still harbor some form of hatred for me."

She stared down at the half-eaten meal before her, no appetite remained.

"Youngmi," the general said, his voice still smiling, "you have nothing to fear from me, even now. I want to you know, that you are not my property. It would deeply sadden me and Mai alike if you chose to do so, but you may leave at any time."

"Thank you, my general," she managed. She pictured the general's daughter, a young lieutenant in the intelligence office, who had become like a favorite niece, almost like a daughter, to her.

"Perhaps my son made a mistake in bringing you here." He let out a sigh of his own, the smile gradually falling. "Because in bringing you to me, and in me befriending you, we have inadvertently endangered your life. If, after all this time you were to leave, I fear that you would not live long once people know you have been at my table all this time."

"It is not much of a choice, then, is it, my general?" She raised her eyes, peering straight into his, allowing the anger to flair, to let him see the misery of the trap he'd put her in.

"No." He looked down at his own plate, pushing the remaining food around with his fork. "No, it isn't. And I am sorry, very sorry I got you in to this. Sometimes, I wish I could undo it all."

"Sometimes?"

His lips curled in a sardonic grin and he let out a breathy laugh.

"You don't miss much, do you?"

There was another long pause. Several heartbeats passed, the grandfather clock in the background ticked most of a minute by before she spoke again.

"My general, since as you say, I am now a pariah among my own people and cannot go out from your protection to rejoin them, I have a favor to ask of you that may be useful to both of us."

He looked at her as he took another bite of steak, chewing carefully before swallowing the morsel.

"Ask me, if it is within my power, and is reasonable, I will do anything for you," he said, "truly…anything."

"Food for the common people. They need to be fed, and fed properly. I understand that many died over the winter from both the cold and the lack of proper food, especially children. With your permission, I would like to set up a food distribution network and medical care checkups, provided by your army."

He gave her a look. "We already do pass out food to civilians."

"Yes," she could not let the momentum of her thoughts pause, or she may not ever find the courage again, "but only to those who join the communist party. Those who do not join are left to starve."

"Then let them join."

"But my general," Youngmi tried to remain calm, even as her emotions boiled inside her chest, "when the resistance hears of more deaths because you are starving those who will not join the party, their numbers will only grow and their tenacity increase, and more Chinese soldiers will die. If you feed everyone, whether or not they are party members, then the greater number of common people will grow to respect you and not wish to join the fight that will risk their lives and their families."

Zhang leaned back in his chair, thoughtfully twirling his chopsticks between his fingers with a mesmerizing pattern back and forth across his knuckles.

"Party members must have an additional privilege for having joined then," he said.

"Perhaps give them free electricity, or extra firewood for the winter. Or give them jobs in your new government."

He stared at her, his face contemplative. Her resolve did not waver, and she did not flinch under the scrutiny. His lips slowly broadened into a fresh smile, his handsome eyes sparkling in the light from the crystal chandelier.

"You are a very special person, Youngmi, very special indeed."

6

Gunnar

Gunnar Olafson had been a staff sergeant in the Alaska Army National Guard prior to the war. He and Captain John Charles had served together for over ten years as guardsmen, and had done combat tours as regular infantry in Iraq and then in Afghanistan with Alaska's elite Long Range Surveillance team. After their first deployment, the two had decided to go into business together working at something that was close to their hearts: tracking and hunting. In their case, rather than hunting animals for food or trophies, they hunted the greatest of all game.

Man-Trackers Ltd did just what the name on their business cards stated: tracked men. In their case, bad men. They used their highly unique set of skills to track down, hunt, and deliver some of the hardest criminals and bad men in the United States to local, state, or federal law enforcement agencies. They had brought in every type of criminal from thieves, to gangsters, to rapists and murderers. Usually, they brought them in alive, unless that is the suspect decided to test their resolve. The paycheck was good, but the knowledge that they'd brought down a lot of scum was much more satisfying.

The day the war started, John and Gunnar had been tracking a very evil man. David Speltzner, a forty-two-year-old pediatric physician's assistant, had murdered his most recent victims, a pair of eight-year-old twins, in a Montana State Parks rental cabin.

He had raped and strangled the boys to the brink of death time after time until they finally expired. Unknown to him, Hank, the park maintenance man, had a sideline as a dirty-minded voyeur. Hank had hidden a battery-powered motion detection camera in the one room cabin, to accommodate his collection of video recordings of hiker couples having passionate loud sex unlike anything they could do back in their city apartments. Three days after Speltzner left the cabin, the lesser pervert collected the camera on his monthly trip to the remote site. As soon as he got to his own cabin, one of the structures with regular electricity and internet in the park, he downloaded the videos to his computer and started scanning through his catch. He smiled as, in between super-fast forwarded individual male campers, or ugly old couples, he logged three different couples doing what couples do five miles off the beaten path, where there is guaranteed to be no one to hear the cries of ecstasy. All three of the man and woman pairs were fit, athletes with seemingly endless energy. There was also one guy/guy couple that rented it, but once he realized what was about to happen, he quickly deleted that one. Not his thing. The next to last video from a week and a half earlier was of a group of four young women, mid-twenties and healthy looking. Hank had seen them in the Ranger's office, signing in and turning in a copy of their trip itinerary. They were all very attractive, in that outdoorsy, rustic way of women who are not afraid of the wild.

Much to Hank's consternation, his expectations of a great all-girl orgy were left unrequited. The four of them, if he understood the audio right, were just a group of housewives on a few days break from their children. None of them undressed any further than bra and shorts. They probably wore less clothing at the gym in front of a bunch strange sweaty guys. Boring.

He started into the last video when his phone rang. He got up from his Lazy-Boy and walked into the kitchen to find the wireless handset. He answered and chatted with his supervisor up at the state office for nearly twenty minutes, then hung up and returned to his laptop. He sat down, kicked the leg rest up on his recliner, and went back to watching the show. It took several seconds for his eyes and brain to focus and agree on what they were seeing as he watched David Speltzner rape and strangle two little boys until they were dead, all in 4KUltra High Definition.

Hank made a plea deal to exonerate himself in exchange for the video. By the time law enforcement saw the actual video several weeks later, Speltzner had escaped from Montana. The following June, US Marshals had learned of his likely location in a cabin a few miles off the highway near the Alaska bush community of Sutton, about sixty miles north east of Anchorage. The marshals called in John and Gunnar, who soon found the cabin halfway up a small mountain in a remote area with no road access. Speltzner had been in hiding off the grid for nearly a year, waiting for things to all blow over and his vile crimes to be forgotten.

John and Gunnar had led a team of US Marshals to his location when the invading forces hit. They had taken Speltzner into custody with almost no resistance, which usually happens with his type, especially when surrounded by a dozen men with scary-looking, military-style weapons. They were loading him into their off-road vehicle when they heard the distant rumble of a massive explosion roll across the sky from the direction of Palmer. It sounded like thunder. With a cloudless blue sky above them, they knew it was not a sound of nature. When the team and prisoner rode out of the forest and into a clearing, near the dirt road where they'd parked their pickup trucks, they got a frightening view of Anchorage in the distance, columns of black smoke rising on the horizon.

The sound of many more explosions drifted on the otherwise quiet summer air from that direction. Their cell phones were all dead, and the radio frequencies that connected them with State Trooper headquarters in Palmer were nothing but static. Quickly realizing something was seriously wrong, they changed course to make their way to a nearby Guard Armory to find out what was going on, only to discover it deserted and none of the communications working. The marshals they were with decided to go back to Anchorage, leaving the prisoner for them to lock up in the small holding cell at the armory until they called back with instructions. The call never came.

They waited several days, but less than two dozen citizen soldiers had reported in to the armory to regroup. Many of them told stories of a massive invading army that had barreled through Anchorage and mostly secured all of the highways as far as nearby Palmer and Wasilla. They decided to take matters into their own hands. Speltzner was an issue they had to deal with. It was an easy choice. The man was definitely guilty as hell and there was no way they could set him free to destroy more children, especially with so many about to become vulnerable due to this new war. He was sent on a fast path to hell where he belonged, with a bullet between his bushy eyebrows.

"Command decision," was what John called it when one of the soldiers resisted the execution.

Typically, National Guard Armories would have plenty of weapons stocked in them, but little if any ammunition. Ammunition was kept where it was needed, and issued from main supply depots prior to deployments or training exercises. Luckily, their company was scheduled for summer drill and had just received a mass of ammunition, MREs, and fuel for their vehicles to support two weeks of range training and live-fire exercises for their full complement of two hundred guardsmen. They loaded as many weapons, gear, ammunition, and supplies into their vehicles and onto their bodies, and led the men under their leadership back to their home town of Chiknik.

John, Gunnar, and twenty soldiers gathered another dozen people along the way. When they arrived, they found the town had more than doubled from just over five hundred residents to nearly eleven-hundred. By the final weeks of autumn, that number had doubled again. And the horror stories of those who'd escaped the direct attacks of the Chinese army had sent tremors of terror through those who had been a safe distance away from the immediate assaults.

"Captain," Gunnar had growled in the guttural Swedish accent he'd not been able to shake since immigrating to Alaska as a teenage boy nearly twenty years earlier, "we have to prepare. There will be many people coming here, and it looks like the enemy is not going to leave anytime soon."

John nodded in agreement. "Let's build an army. If the US is broken, we will have to take back our part of it ourselves."

7

Kharzai

For such a large man, Gunnar moved with astonishing elegance, like a three-hundred-pound cheetah on the hunt. Only once before had Kharzai met a soldier of similar proportion and skill. Liam Cleary had been trained in classical ballet as a youth and had a promising future as a dancer until a sudden growth spurt in his late teens and a testosterone explosion gave him gorilla-like proportions. The ballet scene didn't have much use for him after that, but the British Royal Marines and later MI6 were able to cast him in perfect roles. Liam did not survive his military career though, and Kharzai had had to abandon his friend's body in the sand of an Iranian Air Force base as it was blown sky high, thanks to their efforts to stop a nuclear launch. While Liam was a foot shorter than Gunnar, he was a good bit thicker. Their actual mass would've been about the same. The Swede reminded him a lot of his old friend, just taller, blonder, and with the wrong accent.

"Come up," Gunnar growl whispered into his mic. "You'll want to see this."

Kharzai trotted in a crouch, moving like a predatory beast in his own right. Moving up beside his new partner, he felt like a little child in comparison, and wondered if David saw Goliath this way when they were up close. He was happy Gunnar was on his side.

"Whassup?"

The Swede pointed through the trees down the slope ahead of them. Kharzai caught it immediately. Distant shadows moved between dark spruce trunks. Their trained eyes started to pick up details that an average person would not notice until they were far too close. The pair cautiously raised their rifles to their shoulders and peered through the optics that enhanced the view before them.

"I count at least two dozen armed men," Gunnar whispered.

"Ruh roh, Raggy," Kharzai said in a Scooby Doo impression. "Just saw a couple RPG-32s in there. And look at their skin."

"Yeah, they're white."

"Russians."

"Let's get a better look," Gunnar said, then surreptitiously reached down and rubbed something on his chest.

Kharzai noticed the move, raising an eyebrow, but said nothing. He signaled the dozen men that made up rest of the patrol to drop to their bellies and move forward fifty meters. As they drew nearer, the sound of voices rose on the air. They continued to within twenty meters of the Russians. The estimate of their numbers doubled instantly. There was a second camp just beyond the first. At least forty, maybe sixty men in uniform. It was a professionally set up camp, but seemed like they were not expecting company. Kharzai tapped Gunnar on the shoulder and pointed to a small rise off to their right. A breeze wafted past them, grasses and fallen branches gently bent at the disturbance. A tiny dust devil whirled over the rise lifting handfuls of dried leaves off the ground and laying back a flap of something as it spun past the crest of the hill. The front sight post and slotted flash suppressor of a Dragunov sniper rifle was visible where the leaves had been. A hand slowly reached up and spread the end of a camo web back over the gun's muzzle.

Gunnar looked back to Kharzai. "We didn't see him coming in, and he obviously didn't see us either."

"Asleep maybe?"

"Could've been, but he's awake now."

"If we go back, he'll probably see us."

"Let's move forward, get a good head count, then move across their north flank and make our way out."

Kharzai gave a slight nod. But before they could move, a commotion broke out in the camp in front of them.

One cried out in Russian, pointing at a dark shape a few yards away, "Medved!"

"Bear!" Kharzai hissed.

Men shouted, some voices in alarm, some cursing, others laughing hysterically. A handful of soldiers grabbed their rifles and ran after it, firing at the massive beast as it burst through the trees, its paws shaking the ground with every step of its eight hundred plus pound body. The huge, dark shadow galloped toward the resistance patrol, grunting in panic, breaths wheezing out a terrified sound, eyes open so wide that they could see the whites like bright O's around the black iris. Bullets whizzed over their heads, as the bear continued directly toward where Kharzai and Gunnar lay. The soldiers charged after it laughing gleefully, huge smiles stretched their faces like schoolboys playing a game. The bear cried out in pain as bullets struck it. The beast tripped over its forepaws, slammed face first to the earth, and rolled in a ground rumbling somersault, coming to a halt two meters in front of the pair of resistance fighters.

Several soldiers ran to the fallen animal, laughing and whooping in their excitement. There was no way they would not see the militiamen just steps away from the bear. Kharzai and Gunnar both slid their fingers around the triggers of their rifles. A heart beat later, four Russian soldiers lurched up to the bear, saw two pairs of human eyes looking up at them, and died before they even understood what they were looking at.

The gunshots were not immediately recognized as aggression, sounding like more of the same game, and other soldiers continued to run in to the scene, unprepared to find their friends crumpled on the ground in death. The whole of the militia opened fire and another half dozen fell. Gunnar rolled right and took out the sniper on the mound, then called out an order and his men rose and advanced on the Russian camp, rifles up, firing at everyone that moved and everyone that didn't move.

Within two minutes, it was over. A handful of Russian soldiers had escaped, perhaps a dozen. fleeing on foot into the forest, but more than thirty lay dead or dying on the ground.

Kharzai motioned toward a wounded soldier. "See if there is one we can take for interrogation."

The men quickly gathered up weapons and ammunition and ruck sacks.

"Don't put on the backpacks yet," a militia soldier named Franklin said as he approached and took out a small electronic device that looked similar to a pocket GPS and ran it over each of the ruck sacks.

"Why not?" said another soldier.

"Remember the original Red Dawn movie from the eighties?"

"Yeah."

"The Russians tracked down the Wolverines by putting tracking devices in some food they let the kids find."

"That was a movie."

"Yeah," said Franklin, "and it was also almost forty years ago. Technology has improved greatly since then."

He moved the device over the first couple of packs, and nothing happened. On the third, the scanner let out a high-pitched chirp, increasing in intensity as he drew near a particular pocket. He opened the pocket on the side of the large camo patterned bag and emptied the contents, then scanned over them where they lay on the ground. Nothing happened so he scanned that same pocket again and the gadget squealed again. He slid a thin piece of lead into the pocket to block the signal from going deeper into the ruck and scanned it again; same beep. Franklin squeezed around the cloth until he felt a very small, very thin square, barely discernable in the cloth. He took out his knife and sliced into the fabric revealing a shallow pocket that contained a plastic circuit board about half the size of a credit card but half the thickness, with paper thin copper circuits running through it and a flat lithium battery embedded in it.

"Bingo!"

He scanned the rest of the ruck sack, declared it clean, and moved on to the next. Four of the sacks had tracking devices that he removed. Each of the dead soldiers also had devices, a small chip about the size of a dime, embedded under the skin at the nape of their neck.

"Digital Angel," Franklin said, as he lifted the device from the cut he'd made in one of the dead men's flesh. "These are not actual tracking devices, just ID chips, most likely with their medical records embedded as well. To read the data on them, you have to get within an inch or two of the skin. That's why they have the battery powered ones in some of the gear. Those packs were probably the squad leader's or officer's gear."

"So they could be tracking us right now?" said one of the men.

"Not likely," said Franklin. "If they were actively tracking at the moment, my little sniffer here would let me know there was a signal scanning the area. They don't use live feeds unless they are on an active assault, usually only special forces guys. Burns batteries too fast to have it running all the time. They can turn it on to find their gear though, which is why I took the trackers out. If we carried these packs back to our site and they scanned from satellite for these specific MAC addresses, there is a better than average chance that they would find them, and us with them."

"That'd suck," said Gunnar.

"Big time," said another soldier.

"Yup," said Franklin. "They'd be on our camp like a polar bear in a flock of penguins."

"Polar bears and penguins don't live in the same place," said Gunnar.

"Not anymore," said Franklin, holding up the chip for everyone to see.

Kharzai gave him a sideways look, and decided he liked Franklin. "Where'd you get that scanner?"

"Made it." Franklin handed it to Kharzai to inspect. "Before the war, I was a project manager for north slope oil supply operations. We had all of our inventory tagged with similar chips to the one I found in the ruck sack. I didn't like the scanners the vendor supplied us with because they only read a couple frequencies specific to their own equipment. So I built my own from a few other parts I had around. This one reads all of the various frequencies as well as creates reports, and can even crack encrypted codes in chips."

Kharzai looked the device over and saw the logo of the popular company that had designed it for its original intent. "You built this from an old GPS?"

"I had to add a lot of other parts, but yes."

"How many do you have?"

"Just two," Franklin said. "This and one other that was in my truck when the war started."

"Don't get killed for a while," Kharzai said, handing it back with a smile. "We need your brain."

8

Scouts

Ten miles into the wilderness, south east of Scout Town, the boys ducked in surprise as a high-pitched screech ripped the air above the forest. A formation of three drones flashed overhead, their shapes a barely visible blur traceable only by their contrails. Seconds later, two explosions rumbled toward them like an invisible tsunami. They glanced back to see two columns of black smoke rise into the air, join as one, and continue several hundred feet up, gradually dissipating in a greasy streak across the sky. The village they'd called home for most of the last year, most of which they had built with their own hands, had been utterly devastated. The massive explosions echoed back and forth off the mountainsides, one after the other. Even at this distance, the pressure punched their bodies and set their ears ringing. The entire area they'd worked so hard to build from scratch was leveled by multi-ton bombs directed via long distance remote control.

"We saw three drones," Ben said, "but there were only two explosions."

"The third one," Steve said looking up into the sky, "was probably a surveillance unit. Watching to make sure the other two hit their intended targets and left a sufficiently large hole to prove to the brass it was worth the effort."

Tommie took off his cap and wiped sweat out of his eyes. "By the sound of those explosions, there is little if anything left of our little town. It's probably just a big splat mark with a crater in the middle."

"True that," Mike said, his own ears ringing with a familiar high-pitched wail he'd grown accustomed to after years of war. "Modern technology has its ups and downs. The upside is that they can do that from a distance without threatening their own pilots' lives on such a mission. The downside is that it's harder for them to tell if there is activity down there or if anyone escaped when they do it big like that."

Ben shook his head, eyes wide with recognition of how close their end had been (how closely Death had been stalking them?).

"They just missed us by a few hours," Ben said. "If you hadn't told us to hurry up, we'd all be dead right now."

"That's the way it is in war, boyo," Tommie said. "You never know your fate till it hits you."

Eddie spoke from nearby, watching the smoke roll up on the horizon, "We used to call in strikes like that in Afghanistan. Exactly the same thing, except we were on the delivery side instead of the receiver side."

"In the end," Mike took out a small towel and wiped a sheen of sweat that glittered across his forehead, "it's all the same. War sucks for both sides. And now, we'll make it suck more for them. Let's move."

It took just over ten days to make their way across miles of open wilderness before they arrived at what would become their new base camp. Mike and Tommie had pre-planned three other backup sites to accommodate the group. This particular new site, twenty miles south as the crow flies, near Klutina Lake and the river by the same name, would be their operations center for as long as it would last. The land was mostly raw, without even the single cabin Mike had kept on the previous space.

"So do you own this land too," Ron asked, "or are we just squatters this time?"

"As it happens, I actually do own this spot," Mike replied as he dropped his pack in the tent-sized clearing around him. "It was a gift from an old Army friend's tribal elders after some stuff we did together in the Army."

"What kind of stuff?" Ron asked.

"To quote the famous line from the movie STRIPES, 'Arrrrrrmy stuff, sir!'"

A laugh rose from the older men who knew exactly the movie he was referencing.

Mike had been given the land by the Ahtna Athabaskan tribe when the son of one of the tribal elders, a former Special Forces officer and one of Mike's best friends in the Army, had described to the tribal leaders his exploits fighting the Taliban and Al Qaeda. The memory of the hair-raising exploits they'd shared as advisors deep inside enemy territory and how he'd saved his friend's life on three separate occasions was seared into Mike's mind.

Once, he knocked his friend to the ground just as a Taliban machine-gunner had zeroed in on his exposed position. Another time, Mike ran through a hail of bullets to drag the man to safety after he'd been shot. The third time had been in an intense hand-to-hand battle where, after they'd exhausted their ammunition, they used everything from rifle butts and knives to spades and rocks to beat off an enemy ten times larger than their team.

Major Henry John's father convinced the other elders of the Ahtna Tribal Corporation to make him a member, even though he was a white Mormon who had no affiliation with any Alaska Native group. In lieu of the monthly financial dividend that ordinary tribal corporation members receive, he asked that they deed a portion of land to him to use as a hunting ground to take other warriors to for therapeutic hunts. They agreed, and now the scouts were about to rebuild their town on over one hundred acres of raw land that consisted of little more than a cluster of half a dozen dirt tent sites a hundred yards from the lake.

The boys had only the supplies they'd been able to carry out of the old Scout Town on their backs and what the reindeer could drag through the forest. It was early summer, so there was time to build, and hunt, and fish, and to prepare for the winter, as long as they were not being chased.

They also had to make real the plan to take the fight to the enemy, a task the leaders took seriously. Very seriously.

9

Chiknik

efugees continued to pour in by the dozens. Sometimes, over a hundred per day came in. Nearly two-thirds were women and children. Of the men who came in, everyone between the ages of fifteen and sixty were required to serve in the militia, and women could volunteer. The only exemption from service was for severe disability. And it had to be major. The only way a person could get out of serving at least as a basic perimeter guard was to have severe retardation or mental illness, or be a quadriplegic. Even if a man was in a wheelchair, if he could hold a rifle, he was posted to guard duty. For those who were fully functional, there were three levels of military service.

The Village Security Forces, VSF, were charged with immediate close-in security for Chiknik, not to exceed two-hundred meters outside the town. Members of the VSF stood nightly watch rotations, performed day and night security patrols around the village perimeter, and sat in listening and observation posts just beyond the edges of town. Among these were the youngest boys, the oldest men, and those who lacked military temperaments or had disabilities that limited their capacity to operate under the harder stresses of a long-range patrol. They all received general training in security and basic military instruction for the defense of the village and how to repel an ambush or report an enemy sighted.

The second section of the militia was the Tactical Patrol Force, TPF. These were men who were fit enough to go on patrols up to ten miles outside the camp, for days at a time with a full load of gear. The majority of the men in the militia were in the TPF. If the enemy came calling, these men were the sharp end of the spear they would run in to. They were trained in weapons, tactics, ambush, assault, and defense. They also performed light reconnaissance. Within their ranks were a large number of combat-experienced veterans representing every war from the end of the Vietnam conflict to the recent Wars on Terrorism in Iraq, Afghanistan, and other locations. Their training regimen modelled very closely that of the US Army Infantry.

The third section was the Chiknik Rangers. These were all volunteers and performed long-range patrols that roamed an area beyond ten miles from the village and ranged more than two hundred miles out. These men, sometimes for months on end, actively sought the enemy. Their jobs ranged from no-contact deep reconnaissance and surveillance missions, to active hunter-killer teams whose mission it was to find the enemy wherever he was, to destroy him, and to crush his comrade's will to fight. Emphasis was placed on the latter of these two missions.

These were men who understood the term "violence of action" and defined the most extreme of American warrior ethos. Their ages ranged from sixteen to fifty, and their fitness level was uncompromising. They were required to maintain themselves at the same levels of fitness and training as US Marines and Army Rangers. They lived off the land and what they could take from the enemy. They were guaranteed opportunities for combat. This was not a unit in which to play soldier. The Ranger barracks was comprised of a series of dugout structures that housed unmarried members of the unit. At the main barracks building hung a wooden sign into which had been carved a highly summarized version of Roger's Rules for Rangers, originally penned in the

1740s during the French and Indian War. The rules included such missives as:

- Don't forget anything.
- Keep your gear and your body ready to go at all times.
- See the enemy first.
- Never take a chance you don't have to.
- Don't use your gun if you can kill 'em with your hatchet.

And one the most important rules of the group:

- Never lie to another Ranger. You can lie all you please when you tell other folks about the Rangers, but never lie to another Ranger.

Prior to the war, a lot of the public would have found men like the Chiknik Rangers to be too black and white, frighteningly single-minded. They would have been dismissed as less than intelligent brutes good for nothing but manual labor and violence. Of course, now that the survival of modern civilization was wholly dependent on such men, their general standing in the world of majority opinion had risen considerably. And a lot of men strove to join their ranks, but only the best qualified.

That said, there were a certain number of other men who, regardless of the required militia service, had neither talent nor the will for physical war even in defense of their own families. These were the kind of men who, while they had been lucky to escape the enemy with both their lives and balls intact, may have been better off if they'd just stayed put and subjugated themselves to the conqueror.

10

Scouts

The Russian camp at the Tazlina River Bridge south of Glennallen was of moderate size. Its sole purpose as far as Mike and Tommie could discern was to guard the bridge itself, and the Alaska Oil Pipeline crossing that ran parallel to it. A platoon of Russian infantry was split between the ends of the bridge. At the north end of the bridge, one squad of soldiers was deployed in support of a T-14 Main Battle Tank. At the south end, facing the opposite direction, another squad supported a 2S19 self-propelled 152mm howitzer, a full-sized artillery piece mounted on tracks such that it looked like a tank but with a much bigger gun.

The T-14 was a line-of-sight weapon with extreme accuracy within ranges of not more than five kilometers, just over three miles, while the 2S19 was designed as a quickly mobile rearward deployed support weapon best suited for beyond line-of-sight fire missions, up to twenty kilometers away, about thirteen miles. The latter could launch a much larger shell with exponentially more destructive power, but was a lot less accurate. Militarily, while the T-14 was a scalpel, the 2S19 was a bludgeon.

It was intended to perform the kind of mission that would lay waste to a several square acres-sized area, firing shells that could demolish an entire house, or a trench with dozens of men a long way off. It was not created with the idea of defending a bridge where the attackers would be within a couple hundred yards of it. In this case, it was most likely an asset that an officer had and either did not know how to use, or that he did not want to lose to a different unit so made sure to keep it deployed regardless of its usefulness. A mechanic appeared to be working on something at the side of the turret, which would occasionally start a traverse, rotating part way around on its axis, the barrel swinging counter clockwise only to make a screeching metal on metal sound that seemed spelled serious mechanical trouble, the gun unable to pass the ten o'clock mark if the front was high noon.

A dozen man squad was set up at a forward guard post about a mile to the north to provide security against any vehicles coming from that direction. The dozen men set a road block formation around a GAZ Tigr, a Humvee-like vehicle armed with a 12.7mm machine gun to keep blockade runners and/or saboteurs from getting too close. There was no similar guard posted to the south, indicating a possible man-power shortage with the Russians; that, or they were confident no one would be coming from that direction.

Ben had come up with the plan of attack. He presented it to Mike and Tommie and they agreed to let him run it. They would move in at just past one in the morning, as the all-night sun was at its shallowest angle, providing long dark shadows in the forest and scrub, making it easier to stalk close to the bridge. One team of scouts would cause a diversion by staging a sniper and small arms assault on the security point in hopes of drawing a portion of the bridge defenders up to help against that attack.

Ian and Charlie would take out the positions near the primary target, the bridge, while the team under Eddie's command rushed in and put explosives on the bridge itself powerful enough to blow the structure apart and prevent, or at least postpone, the transportation of tanks and large vehicles sent from the Port of Valdez. The already strong current of the river itself would make it very difficult to put a temporary pontoon bridge across the two-hundred-yard span of raging ice cold water. Thanks to a long hot spell, the river was twice its normal depth due to the contribution millions of extra gallons of ice cold, heavily silted glacial melt rushing by with enough force to bend steel.

While the intensity of the river worked in the scout's favor in regard to their mission goals, carrying out the attack itself was hindered by the one thing that was common to all farther north regions: the midnight sun. Twenty-four hours of daylight meant no cover of darkness until late August, which was two months away. Of course, modern technology had made darkness nearly obsolete years earlier with the advancement of night optics. When fighting a modern army, night time made little difference anymore.

"This is exactly like a war movie," Charlie said to Ian as they lay in their sniper post, watching the latter's brother and his team creep toward the bridge.

"No," said Ian, "this is exactly like a war. Movies don't have smell."

Charlie let out a little burp. "Too much wild onions?"

"Yeah, you gotta lay off, man, you'll give us away."

Ben and Eddie and a four-man squad had spent the past two hours slithering invisibly through a couple hundred yards of waist-high alder and willow thickets that grew between the heavier forest and the highway, providing cover all the way to the bridge. Their team members stopped at a pre-selected area from which the four could provide close up cover fire as Ben and Eddie continued into the underside of the bridge. Once in position, Eddie clicked a small walkie-talkie on and off three times to signal the others then hunkered down into a thicket of alders waiting for the gunfight to start to the north.

Ian smiled as the sound of gunfire and hand-grenades sounded like distant thunder rumbling above the roar of the river. A desperate-sounding voice called out in Russian from a radio speaker on the tank and immediately the T14 started forward to support the post. More radio chatter threw some of the soldiers on the north side of the river into action as well, three-fourths of them jumping onto vehicles and sprinting toward the sound of the gunfire. The defenders of the actual target had been nearly halved by a panicked officer's snap demand for support. The self-propelled howitzer's diesel engine fired up and the massive vehicle started across the bridge to take up the T14's abandoned spot.

Ben and Eddie scanned for booby traps, trip wires, or other things that may have been placed under the bridge to hinder attackers like them. They were both relieved and surprised to find none as they moved into the structure of the bridge. The rumble of the 2S19's engine shook the bridge then died in a puff of black smoke, the mechanic jumping back down, cursing angrily. They placed one pound blocks of Semtex where the steel lip connected with the asphalt of the highway proper. Scrabbling across the girders like a pair of monkeys, they shimmied further out, placing more charges every ten yards or so along each side of the structure then adding a final one at the far end in the same bridge-to-road contact surface as the first charge.

Det-cord, a thin, flexible plastic tube filled with pentaerythritol tetranitrate, or PETN, was strung in a loop from charge to charge with a radio-initiated detonator wired into each end. At two points along the circuit, the det-cord had been shoved through holes drilled into the sides of plastic milk jugs filled with homemade Tannerite, ammonium-nitrate aluminum powder. The mixture was made from ammonium-nitrate pellets taken from a road construction site, mixed with powdered aluminum the boys had shaved from scrap metal. Tommie referred to the ammonium-nitrate aluminum powder as ANAL powder, pronouncing the abbreviation with relish as he had explained how to use it. The extremely stable mixture was only explosive when a high-velocity projectile like a rifle bullet was fired through it. The resulting explosion would act as the detonator for the det-cord in the event the radio signal failed.

Someone among the bridge defenders shouted in Russian and a pair of soldiers knelt behind the steel guardrail of the bridge, peering down into the long shadows beneath. Ian squeezed his eyes shut one time; his heart pounded a single sledgehammer beat against the wall of his chest then instantly fell into to a calm, lethal rhythm. He fired two quick shots and both men dropped, hitting the pavement like sacks of cement, dropped beside the tank-like vehicle. He then dispatched the mechanic who had jumped into the turret.

The Tigr's heavy machine gun swiveled on its mounts, pointing in the general direction of the attack. The man behind it let off a stream of fire that lit the twilight sky with muzzle flashes that blazed bright as the sun. A stream of hot bullets snapped over heard, shredding trees and brush hungrily. The other sniper team cracked off a shot that blew the top of the soldier's skull off like snapping the lid off a Tupperware container. His half-decapitated body slid back into the vehicle. The driver jumped out of the side door in an apparent panic only to be riddled with bullets before he realized his mistake.

Once the daisy chain was completed and they were back on the ground on the south side of the river, they signaled their team. The rate of covering fire increased exponentially as they started their journey back to the forest, boogying back out from under the bridge and into the shadowy brush.

The body of the dead soldier in the 2S19's turret rose out of the hatch then tumbled down the side of the vehicle. Before the massive vehicle got another twenty feet, the thing slammed to a sudden stop, rocking on its tracks. There was a loud pop from its exhaust pipe followed by a cloud of black smoke and the diesel clack of the engine went silent. Another figure popped up in the turret, grasped the 12.7mm, and ripped off several bursts from their position in the middle of the bridge.

The air around Ben's head exploded with angry slaps, as if an ancient god were snapping his fingers right by his head. The fiery lead spears sounded like angry, supersonic hornets the size of Volkswagens. He sensed the heat of the tracers as they flashed past. The turret gunner stopped firing, a string of Russian vulgarity spewing from his mouth. Gun jammed, the enraged soldier swung an AK-12 carbine up and loosed a thirty-round magazine of 5.45×39mm. The arc of fire again went mostly over their heads. A grunt behind him drew Ben's attention long enough to see Eddie stumble, as if he'd tripped over a root at his feet. The latter took two quick steps trying to regain his balance, then fell flat on his face in the dirt.

Ben ran back to him, grabbed the collar of Eddie's vest, and dragged him the remaining distance until they were hidden in the trees.

"Do it now!" Tommie shouted as another volley of bullets zinged past, snapping into the foliage around them and sending spruce needles and shards of shredded wood into their faces. Ben dropped behind the cover of thick tree trunks and large rocks, pulling Eddie to safety beside him.

At the bridge, the tank commander looked down then seemed to come to a sudden realization of what was about to happen. He shouted into the crew compartment as he changed the magazine in his rifle. The engine roared back to life with another black cloud exploding out of the rear as the driver reversed the vehicle, the commander's eyes wide as he tried to get off the bridge in a hurry. He dropped back inside the vehicle, and the turret started to swing their direction then once again the grinding sound of destroyed steel gears stopped it at ten o'clock.

Unable to bring the gun to bear by rotating the turret, the driver decided to rotate the whole thing to get a shot off with its big gun. The tracks stopped up against the guardrail and the 2S19 jerked forward, turning and lowering the howitzer until it pointed at the muzzle flashes coming from the woods. A huge blast of smoke erupted from the gun along with a boom that drowned out all the other battle field noise, and made the bridge tremble under the impact. The earth around them instantly shook as a ninety-pound artillery round slammed into the ground fifty yards to the left of their position with the force of an earthquake.

The scouts pressed themselves deep into the dirt against the coming explosion.

Nothing happened.

"They loaded the wrong round," Tommie shouted. "Not enough distance to arm it. Hurry up and blow that bridge before they figure out what they're doing!"

The boy assigned as the detonator, a fifteen-year-old named Jason, twisted the knob on the small radio to the same frequency as the radio wired to the blasting caps embedded in the Semtex and squeezed the talk button on the transmitter. Nothing happened. The bridge did not go boom. He checked the frequency, then tried again.

No go.

He slapped the radio, turned it off then on again, eliciting a high-pitched chirp, then pressed the transmit button one more time.

Nothing.

"Maybe it's line of sight!" shouted Ben. "You need to get it out from behind these big rocks and try again."

Jason quickly stood up and twisted his body out from the cover, stretching the arm with the radio beyond the rocks to get a clear shot at the detonator.

The 2S19's driver was doing another three-point turn to get the boy's position lined up better.

Before he could squeeze the talk button one more time one of the 12.7mm guns ripped off another stream of bullets and Jason's arm and shoulder vanished in a bright red mist, strips of shredded meat raining onto the boys nearby, spattering them in gore. Arterial blood sprayed in an arc that stained the rocks and trees for twenty feet or more.

His mouth stretched into a wide "O" as if to scream, and he stumbled toward the space where his limb had been seconds earlier. The next burst of 12.7mm smacked him directly in the chest. His entire body vanished this time, leaving only his shoes, with the remnants of his feet still in them, shin bones sticking up like bright white markers of the boy that was Jason.

Radio detonator gone, Ben shouted to his brother, "Ian! Hit the Tannerite! Hit the Tannerite!"

Ian sighted down the barrel of his rifle, putting the cross-hairs onto the nearest jug of ANAL, and squeezed the trigger as the 2S19 repositioned. The bullet smacked the jug, high-velocity impact scrambling the atoms of the mixture and causing an instant chain reaction that lit the sky with a bright white flash as if the sun had decided to stand on the bridge.

The sound of the explosion slammed the air a half second later, followed by the creaky, high-pitched cry of steel being stressed beyond its capacity. The 2S19's cannon fired as the surface it was on leaped several yards skyward, bouncing the forty-ton vehicle into the air like a child's toy, then slamming it back to the surface with a bang that sounded like a secondary explosion.

What had been a bridge only seconds before surrendered to physics, the whole lot, self-propelled howitzer, steel frame, asphalt, and half a dozen men plummeted into the icy cold water that raged below. Beams cracked and twisted with an almost animate cry, as if a living soul inside the steel was being tortured.

The hulking steel box slammed into the river, displacing its contents for just long enough to bare the rocks on the river bed, only for the glacier-fed deluge to immediately fill it back in, burying the remnants of those it consumed. No one swam away from the carnage.

The high-explosive round the 2S19 had fired in its death throes ripped a hole in the forest ten miles away on the other side of the river.

Ben hoisted Eddie onto his shoulder in a fireman's carry and ran with the team back to the assembly area. He felt a warm trickle ooze down his back, but Eddie's grunts let him know the sergeant was okay. Once they reached the relative safety of the rendezvous, they angled up the hill until they reached the rest of the troop and silently continued further into the wilderness. Twenty minutes later, hidden well inside the heavily forested area more than a mile into the scrub, Ben lowered Eddie to the ground, panting and exhausted, but happy that no more bullets whizzed by.

"Hey, Sergeant," Ben said breathlessly, dropping to his knees and giving Eddie a light slap on the cheek, "on your feet, man. I can't carry you all the way back."

Eddie stared at the sky, his face pale in the growing early morning light, expression blank.

Ben stared at his friend and mentor. The sound of the firefight had ceased in the background, random shots popping in the distance like the last few kernels in a batch of popcorn as the traumatized Russian survivors fired at shadows and ghosts. He grabbed Eddie's lapels and shook him.

"Sergeant?" His voice demanded a response. "Eddie!"

His friend's eyes stared skyward, unblinking.

"Ben," Tommie had come from nowhere, "he's gone. You're the sergeant now. Grab his ammo and weapons and move your men out of here before those Russian bastards get their act together and come hunting for us."

Ben looked up, tears rolling down his cheeks, "But we've got to help…"

"There is no help but God's for Eddie." Tommie gave a steely glare. "Now move your arse, or I will leave you here and put Todd in charge."

Ben closed his eyes, sucked in a deep breath, opened them again. Eddie's face was white, lips blue, glazed, lifeless eyes growing duller by the second.

He glanced back at the rest of the group.

Todd gave a quick "I don't want the job" shake of his head.

Ben rose to his feet.

"Okay." He reached down and snatched Eddie's weapons, ammo, and aid pouch and quickly rifled through his pockets, wiping tears away with his sleeves as he forced himself to maintain control. He pulled out a compass, map, and other items, including a watch and his wallet.

He stood and turned to the others.

"Bravo Company, on me. Let's get out of here before we're all dead."

11

Ping

Colonel Ping watched as Youngmi wrote on the white board at the front of the classroom for the senior officer's weekly English lesson. General Zhang had insisted that all of his headquarters officers and senior NCOs, even those who already possessed workable English skills, take the classes. The classes were divided by the various ranks, sergeants and warrant officers in one group, lieutenants in another, captains and majors in another, and colonels in a separate class. Only he was exempt, unless he chose to attend.

In Ping's mind, not only was it a waste to spend so much time learning the language and customs of a vanquished enemy, it was an utter insult to have them taught by the general's mistress. His distaste was exacerbated further by the fact that she was a filthy Korean, lowest of north Asian peoples in his eyes. They'd been puppets of the Japanese for the first half of the twentieth century and later puppets of the Americans. In the days before the current war, they had been a prideless race whose highest achievements seemed to be K-Pop music, food-porn videos, and smartphones that no longer worked.

This woman, Ma Youngmi, held an additional curse. She was the mirror image of Ma Xiu Ying, the woman he had loved as a young officer. But she had given him little more than a friendly glance as she fell for and married his long-time friend Zhang instead. Jilted by Xiu Ying, Ping had watched as Zhang, beside whom he had graduated from the military academy and served in battle, quickly climbed the ranks, constantly staying one step ahead, always looking a little down on Ping.

Ping blamed Zhang's success, and his own lack of a general's star, on Xiu Ying. Her family wealth and position within the party had taken what should have been his career and fed it to his rival. But he'd got them back.

Serving as Zhang's Intel Chief since after the general had received his first star, Ping slowly slipped Xiu Ying a steady diet of arsenic-laced food and drinks. The tasteless, odorless poison, in tiny but frequent doses, provided him a slow but effective revenge as it set in motion to the physiological effects that over the course of a decade filled her stomach and intestines with an irreversible cancer that wasted her away. While he was still forced to serve under, and pretend to be the friend of, General Zhang Ko Bai, Ping reveled in the pain he saw on his old friend's face every day. Even more pleasing was the abject sorrow in the general's daughter, Mai, and son, Po. Both of Zhang's children, who should have been Ping's, had all gone as he'd planned, ate bitterness for every meal as they had watched their duplicitous mother waste away.

And then Ma Youngmi was brought in as a captive, and General Zhang began to smile again. Mai, a junior lieutenant in the intelligence command, once again sparkled like a little girl. He had even heard Mai call the Korean whore 'Ayi,' the affectionate term for aunt. Po, a major in command of the Special Detachment that had been the spearhead of the initial invasion, while he was seldom around her, had been the one responsible for bringing her to his father in the first place, as if to rub this woman in Ping's face for what had happened to his mother.

Even Youngmi herself, kept looking at him with that same disdainful look that Xiu Ying had given him. She looked down her Korean nose at him as if she were rightly here, sharing the affections of the general. As if she was the legitimate wife of Zhang. As if she were Xiu Ying, come back from the grave to haunt him.

"Colonel Ping, sir," Youngmi called out to him, "it is your turn to read this sentence out loud."

He looked at the sentence and studied it briefly.

The helicopter landing pad is fifteen meters wide and fifteen meters deep and is marked with a large letter H.

He took a breath and tried it, "Duh hedacopterr randing pad ishu piptin meters oowide anda piptin meters ahdeep and isa marked oowituh a rarjeh retter hayche."

"Ah, that is very good, Colonel Ping," Youngmi said, a smile on her face. "You said it at the proper speed and with all the right emphasis. If you can learn to make the local accent, it will be perfect, almost native."

Ping gave an expressionless nod, accepting the compliment. But the last sentence came at him like an insult.

Almost native, why would I want to sound native? These are the natives that lost their country to me and my people.

The class drew to an end and the half dozen colonels filed out. Youngmi stood beside the door, bowing as each officer left. Ping was last. He stood before her, not continuing on with the other officers. When he did not move on with the others, she rose from her bowed position. He looked straight into her face, eye to eye, as they were the same height.

"Ms. Ma, I am flattered by the praise you gave me during the lesson," he said, his voice deep and full of formal courtesy, his accent thick but still understandable. "Perhaps you would be willing to take me on as a personal pupil and help me improve my accent, with…private lessons."

Youngmi flushed briefly. He could see what he was certain was acknowledgement of his unspoken flirtation in her face.

"Thank you for asking, Colonel Ping," she replied in his own language of Mandarin, in which she'd become quite proficient over the year since her captivity. "I am very honored that you would consider me worthy to even be offered such a direct request from a man of standing like yourself."

Her Mandarin had become amazingly good in a short time, less than a year. Apparently, she was not only giving lessons, but receiving them from someone.

"But only General Zhang could authorize such an arrangement. If you wish, I could petition him to allow you a private lesson with me in his quarters such as that which his daughter receives."

Ping barely held back the rage he felt at her reply. To have her so deftly deflect his advance by invoking the name of his enemy, and then to put him on the same level as a twenty-two-year-old girl, Lieutenant Zhang, his own very junior officer, was an insult that even a mindless Korean could not mistake.

"I understand," he replied through stiff lips. "There is no need to bother the general, Ms. Ma. I know you are busy with many pupils, and he of course is busy with the entire war. Perhaps when things are more at ease we can talk again. And maybe by then, I will have absorbed this barbarian tongue more satisfactorily simply by mere immersion."

"Yes, Colonel Ping," she bowed again toward him, "may it be so."

Ping held his gracious posture, even as the rage built inside him. This bitch was even more demeaning than Zhang's first wife, and Youngmi wasn't even the general's legitimate woman. She would pay a considerably higher price for such an insult as she had dared given him. There was no doubt in his mind. Ma Youngmi's suffering would push the great and powerful General Zhang Ko Bai straight to his grave!

✳ ✳ ✳

"Why can't you lazy sons of whores get me good imagery of the rebel base?" Ping slammed the blurred photos down on the desk. "We hear reports of thousands of people hiding in the mountains and you can only get me blurry pictures of old cabins and moose! Do I need to send you all out there on foot?"

"Sir," a young lieutenant replied, "the winds in the mountains above where we believe they are hiding are too strong for the drones to fly in. And if we get too low, we lose connection with them."

"Lose connection?" Ping's face turned red, his eyes squinting as if he were preparing to hurl fire balls at the young man. "It is not like you're connected with a 56k modem, Lieutenant. We have state-of-the-art satellites in space that can see every square inch of this planet, and you are telling me that you cannot stay connected to your drones?"

The lieutenant started to say something in reply, but the words froze just behind his lips. He merely stood there trembling. Another officer spoke up for him.

"Sir, we believe there may be some kind of mineral content in the mountains, perhaps a radioactive element, that is causing the imagery to fade and warp like that. We have tried many times, and even manned aerial reconnaissance has come back with the same type of anomalies in that area."

Ping ran the fingers of one hand through his thinning hair and grimaced back at the officers.

"You people are worthless," he grumbled.

12

Chiknik

Merrill Treadmore was an asshole. He knew that. He very likely may have been the first to concede that he was not only an asshole, but that he was probably even a complete and total asshole if there were such a ranking structure within assholedom.

With that in mind, he took every advantage of the fact that people expected nothing less from him than what such terms implied, once they got the know him. Of course, he was also really good at making himself look better than his actual heart and soul were until it was too late for the electorate, or sheeple as he liked to refer to them, to recognize him for what he was. That was what gave him power, especially when he found new groups of victims.

He had arrived in Chiknik as a member of a large group of refugees that had accumulated as they traveled from the areas between the Matanuska Valley and Valdez. The timing of the war, as tragic as it had been for so many, had actually saved him from a major political loss as the reporter that was about to expose his corruption was killed in the opening attack on the port city of Valdez. When he saw that the Russian occupiers were not going to accept him into their provisional leadership scheme, he escaped and joined other refugees making their way north. Eventually, they found the camp of the fabled Ice Hammer and petitioned to join the groups of refugees who made up the town of Chiknik.

Merrill attended the first 'Chiknik Assembly' that had been called together by Brad Stone, recently appointed leader of the refugees of South Central Alaska. The intention of the meeting was to call out those interested in taking part in village leadership. Merrill happily stepped forward.

"What was your name again?" John Charles, the military leader of the village, asked.

"Merrill Treadmore," he said. "I came up with the group from Valdez two weeks ago. I had been a city councilman there, and I must say what I see here in Chiknik seems more like a military dictatorship than any kind of American city I have ever experienced."

"That's because that's what it is at the moment," John replied.

"And just how long before that changes?"

"Well, Mr. Treadmore," Brad said, "that depends on just how long it takes to stop the shooting."

"Why does it have to be that way? Wouldn't it be better if we had a more democratic approach to local leadership?"

"In some regards, that is what we're doing here," Brad said.

"In some regards?" Merrill smirked sarcastically as he glanced around the circling crowd. "So it will continue to be a dictatorship? But you'll allow us common folks a chance to kind of feel free?"

"Mr. Treadmore," Brad scrunched his eyebrows together, quickly concluding he did not like this man. He tried to keep his voice calm but could feel anger slowly igniting. "You are just as free as you were before you came here. If you don't like it here, you are free to leave. Heck, you can even start your own refugee camp modelled the way you want."

"Oh, so that's how you respond to a suggestion for change?" Merrill cocked an eyebrow and motioned with a hand toward the door. "Banish a person?"

"He never said banish," John said. "But if you insist on trying to stir up something, you might find just that to be your plight."

"Mr. Treadmore," Brad said, "you seem to be attempting to take things off track from what we wanted to accomplish at this assembly."

"I am not taking things off track; I am attempting to put things on track. I have over twenty years of experience leading communities, more than half of that as an elected official. I think I know a thing or two about how to manage a group of people in need."

"And how many of those years were serving refugees fleeing an army that has sacked all of their towns and cities and has no qualms killing masses of civilians at will? How many armed military encampments have you managed?"

"That is not the point," Merrill answered. "I—"

"No, Mr. Treadmore," Brad interrupted him, "that is exactly the point. We are at war, and we have lost. The American form of governance of the past few decades brought us to this point. Until we can get these enemies off our land, that country is gone. It no longer exists. If you or anyone else has a problem with the way we are leading in this situation, you are welcome to leave and start your own city. Otherwise, work with us as we grow and form, but do not come in here and cause division before you have even gotten to know us."

Kharzai filled their cups from one of the remaining bottles of the fine wine taken from the wilderness mansion. The magnum-sized bottle was already half empty.

"This stuff is really good," said John. "What's it called again?"

Gunnar read the label, "Screaming Eagle Cabernet Sauvignon, 2012."

Brad swallowed a mouthful. "I will admit it is noticeably tastier than the Yellow Tail I usually bought back when, not that Yellow Tail was bad mind you. This stuff is just better."

"It should be," Kharzai said. There was a scratch at the door. Kharzai turned and opened it, letting Happy and Penny back in from doing their business outside. The pair of dogs followed Kharzai to their place on either side of his chair as he continued speaking. "While I am no sommelier, I do happen to know a little about some of the finer wines, you know one of those James Bondish things all spies have to know. And if memory serves me right, Screaming Eagle is a pretty pricey brand, as in this bottle is way top-shelf stuff, like a bottle of the best Yellow Tail Australian Cabernet would implode if it were set on the shelf next to this pricey stuff. And the reason I know this is that I was once tasked with helping a rich Iraqi escape to the west without getting zapped by the Daesh guys."

Daesh is a derogatory Arabic term for the terrorist group ISIS and their allies.

"And this millionaire," he continued, "who was not a very devout Muslim when it came to the pleasures of the world, was on the waiting list for this winery's subscription membership, which is the only way to get it. Screaming Eagle Winery had a list of people waiting for the privilege of being able to purchase from them several years long. Rich guys waited in line for five years or more for a chance to get on the list as soon as someone else got off of it, which was, more often than not, when they died. My guy had just made it to the inner circle and got his first six bottles delivered at a price of nearly fifty-thousand US dollars."

John nearly choked on the wine he had just swallowed. "Fifty-thousand for a six-pack? You have got to be kidding me," he managed as he caught his breath.

"Nope," Kharzai said, sniffing at the wine in his glass. "All true, and not a bit of exaggeration. He paid a premium to get it delivered to Iraq, and since his area was not in conflict at the time of his order, they did. Each bottle, before shipping, was just under eight grand."

The other men paused and stared at their glasses.

"Would you believe he nearly changed his mind about leaving, for fear that in the rush, especially if there was any gun play, the wine bottles might get broken?"

John took another sip then said, "Wow, I feel like I should have frilly cuffs and maybe a Louis Vuitton man-bag in my lap to drink this stuff."

Gunnar held his cup with a pinky extended. "We have some white gloves and premium quality Depends diapers around here somewhere, should I break those out for the occasion?" He took a huge gulp that drained his cup and reached for the bottle for another refill.

"I don't think this tastes that much better than a twelve-ninety-nine magnum of Yellow Tail Cabernet," said Brad, referring to the 1.5 liter-sized bottle he always kept in his pantry at home in South Anchorage.

"So, should we start telling people to eat cake," said Gunnar, "like Mary Anthony?"

"Uh," John held out his own glass for another refill, "I think you mean Marie Antoinette, Queen of France in the way back when."

"Yeah, same lady," said Gunnar. "She was the lady that worked that club in Paris when we got leave from Bosnia that time. The one with the unusually long tongue and the pointy..."

"No," John said, interrupting his friend, "that was just an imposter. She was not the actual Queen Marie Antoinette of cake-eating fame."

"Well, she was pretty good at eating my cake," Gunnar rumbled in reply.

"Speaking of tastes, as in potentially bad bile-like tastes suddenly rising in my mouth," Kharzai said as Gunnar refilled everyone's cups, a wistful look in his eyes, "I have a feeling we're gonna have some trouble with that Treadmore dude."

"Ya don't say," John said, glad for the one hundred eighty degree segue.

Brad took a sip of his wine and put it back down. "I worked for the government for more than twenty-five years including the military and civil service, and I've been around people like him every place I've worked. He seems to be like one of those career bureaucrats that always made life in the trenches so miserable. He seems to be from the most wretched sub-species of rat, who, in my experience, is always stirring things up, irritating everyone, and then feasting on the dead flesh of the destroyed lives and careers they left in their wake."

"What are you going to do about him?" John asked. "You know he's going to be out there whipping up the impressionable in the group, stirring up the lowest common denominator types. And there are just enough knot heads in the bunch that he'll get a following if for nothing more than to make trouble for you, Brad."

"I've got a few ideas from how it was taken care of during my bad old days," Kharzai said, a violent glimmer in his eyes, "but they were decidedly un-democratically-subscribed by the republic of American ideology methods."

"We'll not go there," Brad immediately replied. "While we can't go back to the full-on modern constitutional American way like it was, we're not heading down Saddam Hussein way either."

"I never said anything about Saddam Hussein," said Kharzai, patting Penny on the top of her golden fur. "My dogs are not man eaters. For that matter, they're not even squirrel eaters as far as I can tell. I won't be siccing any dogs to be devouring my enemies like good old Uday and Qusay. I was thinking more along the lines of Vlad Dracul…but not so post-hole through the guts-like."

"What?"

All three of the other men in the room turned their heads in similar question at the fuzzy-headed mad-man.

"You know, Prince Vlad Dracul," Kharzai raised an eyebrow as he glanced around the group of blank stares, "of Dracula fame. Except the real guy was not able to turn into a bat, and definitely did not live forever. But he did sometimes drink the blood of his enemies, mostly Ottoman Turks who'd invaded his country. He was also known as Vlad the Impaler for his proclivity for impaling enemy soldiers, or anyone who opposed him for that matter, on long poles, right up through their bottoms. They didn't die fast either. The poles were rounded instead of sharp so when the victims would be shoved onto it, instead of stabbing and slicing up their guts, it mostly just moved out of the way until it was good and wedged in, and they would hang there for days slowly dying. Some stories say he would ring them about his dinner table when in the field and sop their dripping blood up with his bread, or catch it in his wine cup and drink it." Kharzai raised his glass in a toast and sipped the contents.

"Sounds like a real Class A fella," John said with a grimace.

"Yeah, let's not go down that road either," Brad said. "We'll just let things play out and see what happens, yes?"

13

Youngmi

Mai looked up from her lesson.

"Yes, Mai, do you have a question?"

"No, Ayi," she replied, using the affectionate term for aunt. The young woman looked back down at her English work, started to complete the sentence she was conjugating, stopped and let out a sigh, "I…well…actually yes, I do have a question."

"What is it?"

"You…um…" the young woman stumbled over her words, eyes searching the inside of her skull for the right combination of words. "You…you were marry before?"

"Yes." Youngmi kept her emotions at bay, replying with a smile that belied no feeling as her pulse raced and an uneasy quiver ran through her belly at the thought of her husband. "I was married for longer than you have been alive."

"What was it like?"

"What was what like?"

"To be with only one man, for so long time?"

"You can look at your own parents and see what it was like."

"No." Mai fiddled with her pencil. "It was different for them. Father is a soldier. He was gone most of the time. Your husband, he was not soldier, was he?"

"When we first got married, he was a Marine," Youngmi said, "a special kind of soldier that is part of the Navy."

"I have heard of the American Marines." Mai's eyes brightened. "My grandfather called them 'Yellow Legs' from his time in the Korean War. He said they were very fierce warriors, ten of them could fight a hundred regular soldiers. He said the Chinese soldiers in his brigade were told to avoid the Yellow Legs when they met them and fight the regular soldiers instead."

"Yes." Youngmi pictured Brad in his uniform in the early nineties. The yellowish khaki canvas leggings of the Korean War era were long gone, but the legends of USMC ferocity continued through every war they've been involved in since their formation in a Philadelphia tavern in 1775. "But when my husband was in the Marines, they did not wear the same kind of boots like they did back in your grandfather's time. They were not called yellow legs. They were called 'Leathernecks' or sometimes 'Devil Dogs.'"

"Ah." Mai thought about this. "Was his neck skin rough like leather?"

"No," she smiled, "he was a very smooth-skinned man when he was young."

"Then was he cruel like a demon wolf?"

"Definitely not," Youngmi replied. "My husband was always a very kind and generous man. I always felt safe with him."

"He was not always a Marine when you were married?"

"No." Youngmi remembered the day he left the Corps. He left, not because he wanted to quit the Marines, but due to injuries. She learned later that he could have stayed if he had chosen to, rather than accept a medical discharge. But he had been worried that if he did, he would lose her since military life, especially life as a Recon Marine in the Fleet Marines, was so hard on marriages. "He was only a Marine for a couple of years after we were married, then he left the military. He was a computer technician after that."

She did not know why she volunteered that information to Mai. She did not want anyone in the building knowing any more about her past life than what was absolutely necessary. The less they knew, the less power they could wield over her.

"Why do you ask these questions, Mai?"

"Well," Mai hesitated, seemed to think over her answer, then blurted, "my father cares very much for you. Maybe he cares even as much as he did for my mother, maybe more."

Youngmi flushed. The conversation was heading in a direction she did not like.

"He talks about you a lot when we are in private," Mai continued. "But…"

Silence hung for several seconds. Youngmi felt a red flush creep across her face.

"But…what?"

"He…" Mai froze again, seeming afraid to continue. "I…"

"Say what is on your heart, Mai."

"Please, if you still love your husband, and if you think he is alive, do not break my father's heart." Mai looked pleading into Youngmi's eyes. "I do not think he can bear losing another woman he loves."

14

Youngmi's Food Project had worked wonders on public relations between the common people, the party, and the army. By the end of the first month of general distribution, rebel attacks had dropped nearly in half. Just as Youngmi had predicted when she broached the idea with General Zhang. With their stomachs full, or at least the hunger pangs gone, the drive to fight for survival dissipated dramatically. As many potential recruits realized that they were not going to be driving the Chinese occupiers back to the sea anytime soon, and that help from the rest of America or even Canada would not be coming, working with the conqueror proved to be less of a burden than raising arms against them.

Youngmi stood behind the serving line of the Midtown Subsistence Food Distribution Center set up in the overflow parking lot of the Alaska Regional Hospital. She hefted a plastic box of rations onto the table, wiped a stray lock of hair out of her eyes, then tucked the strands back into the band that held her ponytail. Every day, more and more people showed up to receive their allotments of rice, beans, soy milk, and vegetables, arranged in measured calorie-specific bundles based on sex and age. They were collectible only with a provisional government-issued food card. Each man over 16 received 1500 calories per day, women 1200 calories, and children 1000. It was a starvation ration, Youngmi knew, but it was free for everyone. The general public was also encouraged to supplement their meals with fresh vegetables grown in communal gardens and in household plant boxes as well as whatever could be foraged. That much was made available to everyone, regardless of party affiliation. Party members were granted an extra 400 calories per person, but they were also required to work the food lines to ensure the masses got fed first. To get more food points required additional work, which would earn extra food credits in the amount of 50 calories per hour of labor for the general population, double that for party members. The chip inside their food card was updated electronically each day when they finished work or weekly when the new general rations were issued. They could also earn points to buy firewood, fuel oil, or coal to heat their homes and cook their meals. The work credits could be used to purchase clothing or household items as well. But the credits could not be traded or bartered, or gifted to anyone else.

"Comrade Andrews," Youngmi called to a man wearing the green armband emblazoned with the red Chinese flag that signified party membership, "how many have come through your line today?"

"We have fed over a thousand people today, Comrade Ma," he replied. "Mostly families with children. But some were single men."

"Any violators?"

"One possible, ma'am, but when we questioned him, he immediately left before the soldiers could talk to him further."

Violators were individuals who showed up either with multiple cards, or tried to use a card registered to someone else. Each person's card, when swiped, brought up a photo of the registered owner and the amount of food or other items they were due. Almost immediately after the system was first put in place, some people had tried to hack the computers or create counterfeit cards. The system was secure enough that thus far only a few had gotten away with it, and none more than once. The penalty for cheating the system, in effect stealing other people's food, was public flogging for the first offense, and execution for a second offense. Surprisingly, even with such harsh punishments, some people kept trying.

"Very good, keep up the good work," Youngmi said. "Make sure all-party members are fair to the people who come to get food. But keep your eyes open for violators."

The system was working wonderfully. Almost impossible to cheat, and everyone got an equal portion according to their allotment. If they wanted more, they could work for it and it would be theirs. The lazy and the criminals got barely enough to survive.

In some ways, the system felt like the former American welfare system. If you're poor, sign up and you will be given food. The difference, of course, was that unlike the old welfare setup, Youngmi's system did not provide enough food to get fat, and the cards could buy nothing but the specific types of items allowed. They could not be traded or sold for other goods. And if the card was all you relied on, you would eventually starve. You had to work to survive.

Of course, once the food was distributed, there was little that could be done to stop thieves from breaking into a person's home and taking it from those who had worked for it. Such criminals, if caught, paid a very stiff penalty for a first instance of physically stealing food from another person. The first and only penalty was public execution, being hanged with a sign on their chest stating "I stole food from children."

Even with such dire consequences, some gangs still made a business of such theft. Quite often, they claimed to be feeding the freedom fighters, but everyone knew they were only filling their own bellies rather than working at a legitimate job. As the system grew though, and more safeguards were put in place to protect the citizens, that would change.

Youngmi looked around at the families walking away from the food center with three days' worth of food, the maximum anyone was allowed to receive at one time. They had smiles on their faces, knowing they would not starve today, that they had enough to get by even if only at a minimal existence. She felt like she was finally accomplishing something to help her fellow countrymen.

In the year since the invasion, many people had been allowed to return to their former careers, especially construction workers and road maintenance crews and mechanics. Business owners were only allowed to return to their businesses if they joined the communist party, membership being required to be able to purchase a business license. Doctors and nurses were allowed to return to work as well, but if they chose not to join the party, their pay was roughly half that of party members.

Life in Anchorage was gradually returning to something like normal, like a shadowy memory, a mockup of the past.

15

Farley

"You need to stop spreading that Treadmore guy's crap." Farley the butcher felt his face growing red. He hated it when that happened, but it always did when he was in his confrontational mood. And whenever he had to talk to Weasel Davis, Weasel was the man's actual legal name given to him by his parents, he quickly escalated to confrontational mood.

"C'mon, Farley, think about it," Weasel said. "He's got good points. I mean, what makes Stone any more qualified to lead us than anyone else? I mean, he might've killed a bunch of chinks, but how does that make him a leader?"

"Ice Hammer has what it takes to do the job in my book." Farley jabbed a finger at Weasel's chest. "Your buddy Treadmore is just trying to bring him down because he's jealous."

"Jealous? Jealous of what?" Weasel let out a snort of a laugh.

"Jealous that Ice Hammer is the leader, and Treadmore is just a regular citizen," Farley replied, "that's what."

"Stone doesn't have any qualities that a guy like Treadmore would be jealous of." Weasel's eyes widened as he thought of something. "Now, maybe his way-too-hot wife has some attributes to be jealous about. If I was into that Asian jungle love thing, then I'd definitely want to get my hands on some of her exotic attributes." He let out a nasty sounding chuckle.

"If I ever hear that you or anyone else ever touches Mrs. Stone or gives her a hard time in any way…" Farley's hand gripped the handle of the meat cleaver tight enough that his knuckle's whitened. He let the threat hang in the air unfinished.

"Yeah, but what if she gives me a 'hard time.'" Weasel grabbed at his crotch.

"You're about to cross the line," Farley said, his voice low, threatening.

Weasel waved a hand to dismiss his words. "Anyway, I'm not here to chat about women or politics. I need to get some meat for dinner."

"You've already got your ration of meat the other day," Farley said.

"Meat once a week is not enough, man." Weasel pointed to a stack of freshly cut pieces Farley was packing for the preservation team to take to the cellar. "You've got plenty; all I'm asking for is one extra portion for tonight."

"You want more meat, volunteer for the Patrols, or even better, join the Rangers."

"Now that is crazy talk, man. That military stuff is not my thing. The village guards is enough for me."

"Then don't complain if you're not willing to do the work."

"C'mon, Farley." Weasel implored with hands held like he was looking to collect alms. "We've been buds our whole lives. Help a brother out. I know you're skimming; let me in the game and I promise I won't tell anyone."

Farley's beefy hands curled into fists. His face went from red to purple.

"First off, we were only 'buds' because you were the only kid in Glennallen whose house was close enough for me to walk to, and that only lasted until we were seven years old and you stole my Pokémon cards from my school backpack," Farley spoke through gritted teeth. "Second, if you ever accuse me of being dishonest again, you'd better be ready to back those words up with your life."

Weasel's face went pale as he caught the look in Farley's eyes. He put his hands up defensively and took a step back. He'd seen Farley kill a man with his bare hands when bandits had attacked their party as they made their way to Chiknik, and he realized he'd tread into truly dangerous territory.

"Whoa, dude, just chill, man. I was only kidding."

"You need to leave now, Weasel. I don't want to see you back in my shop until your next ration card is issued."

16

Mai

Mai settled down to the task she had been ordered into. The table just inside the entrance to the room was covered by several stacks of brown cardboard folders stuffed with official documents from all of the municipal and borough records available in both Anchorage and the Mat-Su valley. She and a handful of other junior officers had been assigned the task of going through the piles of records to separate those belonging to people who had applied for benefits versus those who had not. Those who had not applied for benefits, and therefore were not being tracked by the new government's computer systems, were to be verified as living or dead. Those believed to be living were to be further separated into categories of potential threat to the regime. All able-bodied men or women between the ages of fifteen and seventy who had not applied for a food card and were not verified as dead were to be marked as potential resistance fighters, their families singled out and brought in for questioning. If neither the individual nor the family could be found, they would be marked as resistance fighters and their pictures and data, culled from DMV records, would be posted in the wanted database. Anyone who had family members in the wanted database would not be able to collect their food ration unless they came to a police station and reported all they knew about the wanted person and signed a form disowning that individual and swearing to turn them in if they ever saw them again. Failure to report such a meeting would be met with imprisonment and "re-education."

It was a mind-numbing job that could have been done by lower-ranking soldiers rather than junior officers, but Mai was certain she understood why she had been assigned the task. Colonel Ping hated her and was doing everything he could to make her miserable right under her father's eyes. He knew she would not report her suspicions to her father; therefore, all she could do was deal with it. That, and hope Ping had a stroke from all the accumulated evil stored in his twisted little brain. She soothed herself with images of him driving into Anchorage in his armored convoy, only to be hit with an armor-piercing bullet from a resistance sniper. Sometimes, she pictured herself behind the trigger.

In addition to herself, there were five other young officers assigned this duty, three women and two men, all junior lieutenants. She did not know why they were on Ping's bad side. Each of them had been given a roughly equal stack of work divided alphabetically. A-B, C-F, G-K, L-R, S-T, U-Z. S and T combined made a stack larger and any other of the combinations, and that was the one Mai had been assigned. She flipped open the next file on her desk. Paper copies of property tax certificates listing the names of home owners. She scanned through the stacks of records, printed the DMV records for the questioned ones, and put those printouts in a folder together with the property records so they could be entered into the wanted database once their living or dead status was verified.

If Ping just let us enter them directly into the wanted database, it would save a lot of paper and a lot of time. What a wasteful man.

She wondered how they could be sure if a person was a member of the resistance or had been killed in the first weeks before records were being kept. After nearly three hours, she drew near the end of the S folder, rubbing her already tired eyes. Almost a third of the records had new files created as potential resistance members. She found yet another pair of home owners, a man and wife, neither of whom had applied for benefits, and neither of whom were verified in the death registry.

Stone, Bradley M. and Stone, Youngmi M. 8972 Winchester, Anchorage Alaska 99507

She pulled up Bradley Stone's DMV file and printed the record containing his photo along with his pertinent information. She grabbed the page off the color printer and looked at the high-resolution image.

She let out a gasp.

Ice Hammer.

The image in the photo was almost certainly him. The same face she had seen on the drone images, albeit without the death rage. Now they had a name. She had finally discovered exactly who the Ice Hammer was. With this information, she could not only get a promotion, but she could get Ping to ease up in his constant pressure. She kept her face stoic, so none of the others would see that she had stumbled onto something important and try to steal her glory.

She closed the folder and slid it under the stack, then she pulled up his spouse's DMV record. Her heart caught in her throat, and she feared it would stop beating altogether as the image resolved on her screen. Mrs. Stone was her own Ayi, her English teacher, Ma Youngmi.

This is bad, this is very bad.

She slid the paper into the folder with Bradley Stone's and racked her brain for what to do. Ice Hammer was a big reward, but to lose her surrogate mother, a woman who had shown her such kindness. She could not bear the thought.

In a flash, she knew what she had to do. She had administrator credentials to the DMV database. She could delete their records and no one would be wiser.

No, wait. The total number of records in the DMV database shows up on everyone's screen. If I deleted a record, the others would notice the number change on their screen and know something had happened.

Instead, she moved back up the list to a record farther back, one of another Korean woman whose picture would fit in place of Youngmi's. She copied that file in place of Youngmi's picture and changed the name to a random Korean sounding name, Soojung.

Congratulations, Stone, Soojung K. You are now married to Ice Hammer, and Youngmi Ayi is safe.

She slipped the file folder with Brad and Youngmi's data into her satchel between the pages of her English notebooks and finished going through the stack in front of her, her face masked with the image of bureaucratic boredom. Once they had finished, after more than eight hours with only a single break to eat food that had been brought to them, she hurried back to the room she shared with another junior lieutenant.

Lt. Hong, a computer network specialist, looked up from the small desk on her side of the room. "Hi, Mai, how was your shift?"

"There are few things as exciting as sifting through fifty thousand records looking for the ones that might be something special, but no one really tells you what is special about them. But if you let one slip, you'll be standing guard duty in the snow for a year."

Hong laughed. "That is why I fix computers and networks: you know what you are getting into. You analysts…well, your analysis gives me a headache just thinking about it."

Hong rose to leave, slipping on her uniform jacket and tightening the black patent leather belt around her waist. "Time to go give my computer nerds something to fantasize about."

Lt. Hong often joked about how the male-enlisted computer techs under her command fantasized about having sex with her, but all of them were so nerdy they were guaranteed to be virgins until they bought a wife from some country hick in the backwoods of North Korea.

"See you later. I'll be quiet if you're sleeping when I come back in."

"Thanks," Mai said as the door closed. She listened to Hong's footsteps click down the hall, then rose and locked the door. She went to her desk, took the notebooks out of her bag, and pulled the file out from between them. She opened the folder and looked at the pictures again. There was no mistaking either identity. Youngmi was Ice Hammer's wife. Mai wondered if Youngmi knew what her husband had done, and whether she knew that the general's men had been tasked with finding him above all other rebel leaders. That he had become the symbol of the resistance.

She opened her uniform jacket, took it off, and dropped it onto her bed. Her own body odor wafted up to her nostrils and she suddenly felt disgusting. Leaving the folder on the desk, she walked into the bathroom to start the shower. She turned the handle on the tap and the water hissed against the tiles. Her fingers worked the buttons of her blouse when the lock on the room door clicked in its slide and the door swung open. Mai rushed back into the room to see Hong standing at her own desk, right beside the folder Mai had left open.

"Sorry to startle you," Hong said hurriedly. She raised the lanyard with the computer room swipe card that would give her access to her work space and the USB token that gave her admin rights on the network. "Can't do my work without my magic wand," she said of the small device that looked like a thumb drive but actually held her half of the encryption codes to the network.

She turned to leave. Mai watched her glance quickly over the open folder on the other desk as she headed to the door. Hong called back over her shoulder, "You shouldn't bring work home; it's not healthy."

The door shut and Mai listened as Hong's heels receded down the hall with a loud clack-clack-clack. Her heart beat the same rhythm, blood forcefully pulsing the metallic taste of fear through her tongue. She stared at the folder on the desk. Ice Hammer's picture lay on top, the DMV datasheet below the image. Youngmi's picture was just beneath her husband's, the edge of the image sticking out, only a portion of her face exposed. Barely enough to identify her if the viewer was already familiar with the face. Hong was new at the unit; Mai did not believe she had met Youngmi yet.

What did she mean, it's not healthy. Was that a warning?

She crossed the room and closed the folder, then jammed it back into her bag. She stuffed the bag in her wardrobe, and locked the door. How was she going to deal with this?

17

Sammi

ammi came out of the small elementary school after a long day of preparing for classes. She and a few others who had been school teachers and home school moms before the war had organized a K-8 school to make sure the children of Chiknik got at least a basic education. In addition to teaching a combined 3rd & 4th grade class, the teachers and parents planning the school had elected her as vice-principal. Classes were scheduled to start immediately after the harvest of the summer's crops, an event in which everyone was expected to participate.

The late summer sun had already descended below the horizon into an earlier dusk that almost started to match the twelve-hour day-night cycle of areas much closer to the equator. Sammi was the last person to leave the school. She locked the door behind her then turned onto the walking path to make her way back to the small house she and Brad shared a short distance from his office. The evening was mostly silent in this area of the community where there were fewer houses. Her footsteps pressed softly into the gravel beneath her feet, the sound echoing with a light rhythmic crunch off the wall of the school building as she stepped towards home. A peaceful quiet seemed to pulse in the town. She took a deep breath of fresh, clean, mountain air and glanced around, smiling at the way the descending sun angled between the buildings, casting long shadows that contrasted sharply amidst bright beams of horizontal light.

"Evening, Mrs. Stone."

The male voice startled her. She spun around hands up the way Brad had taught her, ready for physical combat.

"Whoa," Merrill Treadmore raised his hands and took a half step back, "boy, you Stones do tend toward violence, don't you."

She allowed her body to take on a relaxed appearance, keeping her guard up beneath the skin, ready to pounce or to run in an instant if the situation called for it.

"You startled me, that's all," she said. "What do you want?"

"My, and I'd been told you and your husband were such pleasant people. I guess you Anchorage types have a different sense of pleasantry."

"Perhaps if you weren't spreading lies about my husband, my attitude toward you would be a little different." Sammi gave him a look that couldn't be mistaken for polite, even on her gentle kindergarten teacher face. "If you have something you'd like to say, say it. My husband will come looking if I am not home soon."

"He keeps you on a leash like the rest of us, eh?"

"That's not what I meant." Sammi hated speaking to Treadmore. He always twisted her words, reforming them into something very different from what she intended. In the weeks since he'd joined the camp, he had left his mark everywhere. The wake from his passing through a group of people seemed to froth over with negativity. Some folks came out of such a meeting quickly despising Treadmore, but others, those who swallowed his slanderous politics wholesale, came out questioning the very reasons they'd dragged her and Brad and the rest of their group out of their comfortable existence before Captain John showed up, the Chinese Army hot on his trail.

Being married to Brad was everything she'd dreamed it would be. Brad being thrust into the role of leader of this hodge-podge of people was sometimes very rewarding as they were able to help and give guidance. At other times though, when they had to deal with people like Merrill Treadmore, it was a nightmare she wished she could wake up from.

"I'm sorry, Mrs. Stone," Treadmore said, almost sounding sincere. "I didn't mean to sound so nasty; sometimes I just need to think my words through better before I open my mouth." He paused for a moment, as if trying to let his change of tone sink in. "I've noticed the hard work you are doing toward building this school, and helping the children of Chiknik. You and I have a lot more in common than you may realize. I too started out as an educator before I moved to Alaska. I understand to some degree the difficulties you must face trying to stand up an entire school system in such times as we find ourselves these days."

"Really? You were a teacher?" Sammi looked at him with that look one gives a politician who has just said something they'd hoped would connect with a possible voter, but was most likely complete bullshit. "Where did you teach?"

"Oh, I was a school administrator in the lower forty-eight many years ago, when you were probably still a little girl." Merrill smiled in a manner that made Sammi's skin crawl.

"What was the name of the school?"

"It was a long time ago, a small school in Arizona, you wouldn't have heard of it."

"You'd be surprised what I've heard, Merrill."

A flash of something rippled through his expression, like a momentary lapse in his guard that revealed a terrible image of the past stowed inside his head. It was as if the lid to his thoughts cracked open and she saw a glint of...guilt?

"Well, it has been nice talking to you, Mrs. Stone. I must be getting back to my cabin. I've got an early guard shift."

He said the last word with an obvious note of sarcasm in his voice, as if he saw no need for, even felt it was ludicrous to have, the village guards.

"Be careful on your watch then. There are a lot of things that go bump in the night out here."

18

Scouts

"There's got to be at least a dozen men in there," Ben whispered to his brother and the other boys nearby as he studied the hunter's cabin through the binoculars he'd taken from the Spetsnaz trooper they'd killed two months earlier. Ben had filled the position of platoon sergeant very well after the loss of Eddie. It was not long after the battle at the bridge before the older men let him run missions on his own. They never regretted it.

"Where are their outer guards though?" asked Todd. "I haven't seen anyone keeping watch on them."

"Maybe they feel safe?"

The sound of someone snoring drifted from the cabin. It was no ordinary snore. It was the sound of a man with severe sleep apnea.

"No, they have guards out," Ben said, "somewhere. It smells like a trap to me."

"Probably is," said Ian. "Let's wait until it gets darker and see if they show themselves."

The leaders of Troop 104, Alaska Defense Force, had set up a new Scout Town twenty miles south of the original near Klutina Lake. While it was quickly growing to near the same quality as their first town, the boys of Ben's platoon seldom seemed to be occupying the sod and log cabins they had built at the new location. His platoon was made up of the most skilled trackers and fighters, the varsity as Mr. Gerber called them. They preferred to spend most of their time roving the wilderness like Viking raiders.

After a year living in the forest, being trained by former Special Forces Master Sergeant Mike Jameson and Irish Mercenary Tommie Dolan, they had begun to take the fight to the enemy. Since shortly after leaving Tazlina Lake, while the majority of the group built up their new homes, Ben's Wolves had spent the summer performing reconnaissance and hit-and-run guerilla operations against the Russian troops in their area.

Focusing on supply convoys and running raiding parties, they'd been able to keep themselves supplied relatively well. While the Russian rations were definitely not tasty enough to write home about, they were packed with carbohydrates and protein. There was never enough food for anyone to get fat, but no one in their camp starved.

The current excursion was intended to be a psy-op mission, as Mike had called it. Psychological Operations. In other words, they were to mess with the enemy's head. To that end, Ben's platoon moved through the occupied territory with the intention of locating the enemy. Once they found a group small enough and in the right kind of terrain or location, they moved to contact. Their tactics came in two flavors: Grape, kill a portion of them, leaving some alive to report the slaughter, and Cherry, kill them all and leave their stripped bodies to be found. Then they would vanish into the woods, leaving the enemy's sense of security crushed. Keeping them on edge and fearful.

Just before midnight, as the late summer night was as close to fully dark as it would get, the lights inside the cabin went out. Ian was the first to see two of the watch posts keeping an eye on the approaches to the cabin. He pointed their positions out to Ben.

"Let me go in alone," he said. "I can get by without alerting the sentries and take care of the men sleeping inside."

"No," said Ben, "let's take the guards out first."

"Let me try to sneak past them," replied Ian. "If they move, you shoot them, and I'll just roll a grenade inside the cabin."

Ben thought about this. His brother, not yet fifteen but the size and build of a full-grown man, had been taking on increasingly risky tasks. So far, he had always come out on top, but Ben feared he may start thinking he was invincible and get himself killed taking too many chances.

"Let's take out at least one of the guards first," Ben said. "Then you go in from the side he was watching."

"Okay," Ian said. "I'll take Charlie with me and we'll get the one on the left. He will stay there and watch for anyone else who might try to get me."

Ben gave his younger brother a long look. Ian was both taller and stockier, nearly six feet tall and probably close to two hundred pounds in spite of their meager diet. But he was still just a boy, only fourteen years old. That said, he had proven his skill in every military task he'd been given. He'd proven his skill in combat and then some.

"Okay," Ben said. "Make it quick and get out of there if anyone wakes up."

"Don't worry, big brother," Ian's face stretched in a smile that would have made a wolf reconsider its options were it to face him, "I got this."

Ian crawled over to his best friend Charlie, tapped him on the shoulder, and the two slunk into the forest. Crawling silently on their bellies, they quickly disappeared into the undergrowth. They took their time as they approached the perimeter guard post. As they drew near, they could see the occupants of an observation hole a few dozen yards from the cabin. The two young soldiers in the hole stared past their machine gun, looking right past Ian and Charlie hidden in plain sight right in front of them. Ian made the motion for a knife and Charlie drew the homemade iron stiletto he carried in a sheath on his thigh, a needle-pointed, razor sharp blade about ten inches long beyond the hilt. Ian drew his own and they slid into the hole behind the two sleepy soldiers.

In a flash of motion, they slapped their hands tight over the mouths of the enemy, young men not much older than they were, and plunged their blades into the base of their skulls, cutting off their lives in a silent instant as their brain stems separated from their spines. The boys lowered the bodies to the ground. Charlie stayed in the hole, turned the machine gun around, and covered Ian's approach to the cabin.

Ian slid back out of the hole and slithered across the ground toward the cabin. He moved like a snake among the high grasses and rough timbers the enemy soldiers had recklessly failed to clear out. Their lazy site preparation was about to become their undoing. At the base of the stairs that lead up to the door, he paused, listening for half a minute. The only sound was the saw-like snoring of the one soldier.

Ian carefully crawled up the steps, blending with the darkest shadows, and felt his way to the door. He glanced up and noted that the door did not even have a door knob, just a latch for a padlock, which the Russian soldiers had apparently smashed off.

He pressed against the base of the door and swung open at his touch. He quickly slid inside through a narrow opening. Once in the near totally dark interior, he rose to his feet and stood in the darkened corner near the entrance, listening and waiting for a reaction.

The snoring was much louder and constant on the inside, almost like a recording on loopback. It drowned out all other sound in the room, and made him wonder how the other men could possibly sleep with their partner making such a racket. They must have been completely exhausted from their hike out to the remote location.

Ian smiled at his fortune. The enemies deviated septum was the sound camouflage he needed. He set to work ensuring they would get all the rest they would ever need, the eternal kind.

Less than two minutes had passed when he slid back out the door. The snoring soldier still sawed logs with every breath as the spirits of his eleven companions hovered over the sleeping mats where their bodies lay. Those who'd been on their sides or bellies had their brain stems severed with a swift shove of Ian's stiletto blade, dying in instant silence. Those lying on their backs died with their throats chopped open by a whack of his tomahawk.

He wondered why some men's throats seemed to be so much softer than others, allowing the blade to nearly decapitate them with little more than one or two good strokes, while others were like hard leather that had to have the stiletto point shoved through their larynx like an awl punching through thick hide.

Regardless of the method, he was efficient in dispatching them all, their death rattle buried beneath their compatriot's ripping gasps as the unwitting soldier struggled through the storm of sleep apnea.

Oh, what he will think when he wakes up in a few hours.

Ten minutes later, Ian and Charlie returned to Ben and the rest of the platoon. They brought one nice new PKM machine gun and two one-hundred round drums of ammunition. Ben stared at his brother's face in the near darkness.

"What did you do?" Ben asked.

Ian's eyes and teeth stood out in a crazy smile against the moon-lit sheen of blood splashed in a sheet across his face like black streaks of crude oil.

"I'd hate to be the guy I left alive in the morning," he said. "His snoring covered for me so well, I got everyone else without any problems."

"How many were in there?"

"Twelve," Ian said, "the only one left is snoring man, and he ain't going to be happy when he wakes up."

Ben stared at his brother for a moment. A monster seemed to slowly shrink back into its cave within the younger boy's soul.

The beast that had been set loose inside that cabin was now constrained, albeit it barely, inside the walls of Ian's mind.

"Don't worry, bro, I am just doing my job," Ian said, clapping his hand against his brother's neck. "Although, I really do have to say, that was pretty fun."

As he pulled his hand away, Ben felt a sticky resistance like glue on Ian's palm. Ian patted his brother's cheek once more. Dead men's blood plastered the side of Ben's face and neck.

"God, I love my job," Ian said as he turned to slink back the way they'd come.

19

Brad

Farming and gardening in Alaska was always a challenging effort. But it was one that if done right, yielded an amazingly bountiful harvest for the cool sub-arctic climate. Only a fairly limited range of produce grows in the arctic without the use of the man-made climate anomaly of a greenhouse. That said, what does grow in the Land of the Midnight Sun, grows very well.

Every year before the war, the Alaska State Fair boasted displays of hundred-plus pound cabbages and turnips and rutabagas the size of a man's head. Potatoes the size of Nerf footballs were very common, a single spud that could feed an entire family. While these record-sized vegetables were not sought for competition purposes in Chiknik anymore, the rich black soil and nearly twenty-four-hour sun that created those prize-winning monster vegetables did wonders nonetheless on the more common harvest. Carrots, potatoes, beets, cabbages, snap peas and broccoli had been successfully grown all around the town in one- to five-acre plots scattered around the edges of the settlement, as well as several larger farm fields that had existed from before.

The plots were spread out in a way that both encouraged inhabitants to work on the spaces near their village sections. Having them separated like that also made sure that if they were spotted by the enemy, a single bombing run would not destroy their entire crop. Nutrient rich rhubarb stalks grew in clumps around many houses providing ample vitamin C and other good stuff, as did wild strawberries and huge patches of raspberries.

Higher up in the hills, blueberries and lingonberries grew on knee-high bushes, alongside clusters of crow-berries, small black berries that grew on tiny evergreen plants. The crow-berries were similar to juniper that grew much farther south on the continent, but did not have quite as strong a flavor.

Plant boxes hung from window sills and stood on the ground on the sunny side of houses, growing bundles of lettuce and green, leafy veggies for eating all summer or drying for use in winter soups. Most of those boxes could be moved into the houses during the winter to keep at least some fresh greens and herbs on the table in the cold months.

Some wild plants were harvested at earlier times of the year, such as fiddlehead ferns and wild spinach in spring and early summer. Those were preserved by pickling, canning, or drying to be eaten year long as side dishes or in soups.

Brad looked out his window as he sipped a cup of hot Labrador tea, made from leaves harvested in the boggy marsh land just east of town. It wasn't caffeinated like most popular teas, but had more of a relaxing effect that still seemed to awaken the senses as he watched the late August sun dawn bright and crisp beyond the fields where the tea had been harvested.

Most of the month of August had been spent harvesting one crop or another. Fields of barley and hay were baled to feed horses and the ever-growing herd of newly domesticated reindeer. Cabbages and broccoli were cut and moved to larders along with root vegetables like potatoes, carrots, and turnips that were dug up and stored underground in boxes filled with insulating saw dust to keep them from freezing in winter's harsh temperatures.

Cucumbers got pickled. Peas were dried. Wild berries were picked and preserved in what jars were available, or dried in the sun or over fires to be reconstituted later with only slightly more tartness than their fresher forms.

And, much to the consternation of some of the stauncher conservatives in the group, a heavily guarded field of marijuana had even been allowed to grow and be stored for medical purposes. The argument that there would be no other anesthesia or pain relievers only barely won the day on that crop.

All of the harvest was stored in several strategically placed large cellars that kept it at a temperature just below forty degrees Fahrenheit.

The sky had cleared and the sun shone down in its full glory. The air had a clean feeling that seemed to allow it to filter down extra deep into the lungs and to open new channels in the mind.

*　　*　　*

"Ice Hammer! Ice Hammer!" a teenage boy ran screaming into Brad's office.

John caught him by the arm and stopped him as he burst through the door.

"Calm down, boy, what's the rush?"

"Bodies," he huffed out between wheezing breaths, "we found bodies at the edge of one of the fields. Someone killed some of the harvesters and took their stuff!"

"Where?" Brad asked. "Take us there."

Minutes later, Brad, John, and a few others reached the edge of a field on the eastern side of the village. Four bodies, two women and two men, lay face down in the dirt, blood crusted around small bullet holes in the back of their skulls.

"Who would've done this?" one of the village men said.

"How did we not hear the shots?" Brad asked.

John squatted down beside one of the bodies and examined the wound. He quickly looked back up and gave his appraisal. "Twenty-two caliber bullet, probably subsonic. Wouldn't have heard it unless you were right beside them."

Brad shook his head and pressed his fingers into his eyes. He turned away from the bodies and let long breath hiss out from between his lips.

"What the," he sucked in a deep breath and shouted, "what kind of sick bastards would do something like this?" He rubbed his hand across his face. When he lowered them, the face of a leader glared from beneath his brows. "John, get trackers on it and find out if there is any sign of them escaping. If you find them, bring them in. If they resist, kill them. That'll be judgment enough for me."

"Consider it done, sir," John said. "This is what I did before the war. We will know soon who and where they are."

John immediately jogged into the brush beyond the field, two other men, Rangers who'd been left behind on the last mission, following close behind. Brad ordered the burial of the victims to be organized. Without modern means of embalming, there would be no time for a traditional wake and funeral as had been known for most of the twentieth century. The bodies had to be burned or buried within the day before they started to fester and potentially spread infection to the rest of the population.

"Increase guards and patrols around all harvesters until we figure out who did this," Brad ordered a nearby militia officer. Then more quietly to those closer by, "We must have some kind of bandits sneaking into the area and stealing the harvest. But to murder people like that is unnecessary. They could have just joined us and shared in the blessing we've had so far."

An hour later, John returned, the men who'd gone with him carrying large baskets of harvested vegetables.

"Bad news, boss," he said. The expression on his face was not one that inspired peace.

"What?" Brad grunted.

"Trail circles out of the village, two men, running first then jogging. But about a half mile out of the village, they hid the vegetables and did a loop right back in. The trail was lost on the hard-packed streets in town."

"So you're saying they're here?"

"That's what the evidence seems to suggest."

"That'd make it easier to find them."

"Eh, could make it easier, or could make it harder."

"Go on."

"If someone saw them come back in, we might get lucky." John wiped sweat from his brow and shook it into the dirt beside him where it splattered on the dust, making dark spots of nearly black mud that stood out against the lighter dry brown powder. "On the other hand, they came back in at the residential area. Almost everyone in that section of town is out in the fields. All the houses near the place we found the footprints were totally empty. No answers when we knocked on doors."

"Could it be one of the residents in that neighborhood?"

"No real suspects there. Several families with small children. A few older couples. The perps," cop speak for perpetrators, "were men, strong, probably youngish, under forty at least."

"What do you suggest?"

"Two things." John held up his finger to start counting them off. "One: we pull in everyone who lives in that immediate area and interview them as potential witnesses. About a dozen people, including kids."

"Kids?" Brad glanced at a young mother walking past with a toddler at her side. "Why in the world would we bring kids in? No way this was done by some child."

"Not as potential suspects," John replied, "but as possible witnesses. Kids can be some of the best witnesses, because they are usually guileless and will say exactly what they saw, at least most 5-12 year olds that is; teens is another thing altogether."

"What was the other option?"

"We immediately send the guard through the village to inspect all .22 caliber firearms. Anyone whose weapon shows sign of being fired recently, or anything that looks like it's been cleaned since this morning gets an interview."

"Too bad we don't have a crime lab here," Brad said. "Good friend of mine worked at the one in Anchorage was a ballistics expert. He'd probably be able to figure it out in a heartbeat."

"Yeah, well," John said, "nowadays, we're just a short hop from dunking witches in the lake with a duck."

Brad let out a sardonic laugh. "Sounds like something Kharzai would say."

"Maybe I shouldn't hang around with him so much, eh?"

"Maybe none of us should," Brad said. "This seems to truly be his element."

After a thorough search of the village neighborhood near the suspect's re-entry, no weapons were found that had either been fired or cleaned recently. No one had witnessed anyone coming back in from the trail John described. The investigation led nowhere. Two days later, three more bodies were found at the edge of a different field. The next day, two more.

"Dammit!" Brad slammed his hand down on the table. "Have we got a serial killer or something on our hands? Thanks to this crap, everyone is afraid to go out to the fields and get the rest of the harvest. We have guards all the way around, but somehow these monsters got through."

"The fields where the bodies were found did not have full-time patrols," John said. "The roving patrols found them just an hour or two after the shootings. And the last two found were a couple of teenaged lovers who'd run into the woods for a tryst near a field that was already harvested."

"The point is, people are now scared to go outside," Brad said, anger forcing deep lines into his forehead. "This is like some stupid horror movie with a psychotic serial killer stalking us. Who the hell does something like this?"

"I don't know." John looked at a schedule on the wall. "Kharzai and Gunnar get back with the Rangers in a few days. We will have more security in town then, not that that will necessarily make a difference if we have a psycho gang doing this."

"We need to figure this out," Brad said. "And we need to get rid of these sickos fast."

✻   ✻   ✻

A group of citizens gathered in the town center, the mass of bodies growing fast. They were not in a pleasant mood, an edge of intense anger blending with anxiety permeated the atmosphere with an almost definable odor. Sweat mixed with the sour stench of utter terror. A light mist of rain drizzled over the assembly, the cold, wet weather moving even the least agitated spirits to a sense of despair.

"Something is going on, and these guys in charge are simply not doing enough to stop it," Treadmore addressed the crowd of a few score citizens. "Dozens of our fellow refugees, our brothers and sisters, have been killed just trying to harvest our food and Mr. Stone and his henchmen have done nothing about it!"

"It's only been nine people, not dozens," someone shouted from the audience.

"Only nine?" Treadmore cried. "Only nine? You minimize the deaths of these people over semantics?"

"You exaggerated the numbers to make it look worse," the man shouted back. "Just tell the truth!"

"Is that you, Farley?" Treadmore replied. "Is that Farley the butcher?"

"Yeah," Farley stepped closer. "It is me. And while this is definitely a horrible tragedy you're trying to sen...sen....uh..."

"Sensationalize?" A young woman in the crowd nearby helped him find the word.

"Yeah, sensationalize it," Farley glanced appreciatively at her and then back to Treadmore. "You're trying to draw attention to yourself at the expense of the dead."

"Oh really?" Treadmore stepped forward, but kept out of the physical reach of the thick-handed butcher. "So, Mr. Butcher man, what do you see our illustrious leaders doing to stop these men who've killed *only* nine of your peers?"

"I…"

"NOTHING!" Treadmore cut him off. "They are doing nothing! Just sitting there in their nice little houses, with their pretty little wives, eating extra rations all on their own and wondering how they can profit from us little people."

"What?" Farley's face was moving toward angry purple. "You are a liar, Mr. Treadmore. The only one with a wife is Mr. Stone. And I know exactly how much rations those men get. It is the same as—"

"The same as who?" Treadmore stalked closer, imposing into Farley's space. Challenging him. "The same as you and me? Is that what you were going to say? Really?"

"Yes, they get exactly what everyone else gets. Only the TPF and Rangers get extra food, and that's because they—"

Treadmore cut him off again, "Are the glorious leader's henchmen. Yes?"

"No, because they—"

"They supposedly work harder than the men and women who work the fields? Than the mother who cares for her children? Than the grandmother who wants only to have this war end and to go home? Are you, Farley the butcher, trying to tell me that Mr. Stone and his wife, and his 'Three Musketeer" bachelor compadres that lead the violent men with the guns and who hold all of the power in this little community deserve more privileges than the rest of us? Are you telling all of us that we are somehow less than them because we don't have the power to take what we want?"

"Huh?" Farley's face was full purple in near rage. "You keep cutting me off!"

"No, Farley the butcher," Treadmore addressed the general audience with every word, "I'm not cutting you off, I am finishing the sentence. Because while you may think these leaders of ours, Stone, Captain John," he said Johns rank with an unmistakable sneer, "and their two veritable Robins, the Swedish monstrosity and the insane Arab," he pronounced Arab with a long "A,"—Ay-rab, "are some awesome blessing from heaven poured out on us mere mortal souls, I think they are just more of the same of what we had before the war. Men who grabbed power and are enriching themselves at our expense."

"Wha—?"

"We need change! No more status quo." Treadmore's voice grew louder and more insistent. "This is still America! We need elected leaders, not military dictators! We need a vote to put in fair and honest leadership to meet the needs of 'we the people'!"

Some in the crowd, stirred by the emotion of the speech, roared their approval.

Farley fell back to the young woman who'd helped him find his words. "He kept cutting me off, putting words in my mouth."

She leaned toward him. "We need to tell Mr. Stone and Captain John about this."

The young woman rushed off to do just that.

"Troublemaker, that's what he is," Derrick Briggs, the village baker, stood in line at Harley's counter, waiting with those who'd queued up to get their weekly ration of meat. He kept clenching and unclenching his fists such that the knuckles on his chocolate-toned fingers turned bright white with each increasingly agitated flex. "That man has not done a single bit of good for this community since he got here. He just walks around this place with his nose up in the air, mocking the time he has to spend in the Guard like the rest of us. And then, the son of a bitch has the audacity to challenge the handful of people who organized this whole place."

The next man in line, a grizzled, wiry man who had obviously been a physical laborer, nodded his head in agreement. His gravelly voice sounded like he munched on barbed wire for his breakfast every morning. "Way it looks, he was either a politician or a union boss before the war. Either way, he doesn't know what he's talking about. This is war we're in. This is no time for messing around to build yourself up for some political popularity contest."

"Yeah, but," another man interjected, "this is America. Free speech and such. If we run things like a dictatorship, we're no better than the invaders."

Derrick shook his head as he stepped up further with the line. "Here's something you all need to understand if you want to support Treadmore's way. Every army that runs itself by elected committees and popularity games will be beaten by the one that is organized by leadership with a goal. What do you think got us in this situation in the first place?"

"You're saying that our American system is what got us here?"

"No, that is not what I'm saying." The line moved forward another step. "What I *am* saying is that lazy people who misunderstood our system got us here. Like de Tocqueville said way back when, if I can paraphrase, 'once the people realize they can vote themselves government money, it's all over' and that's what made us fall."

"Yeah but," the third man said, "de Tocqueville never said that; that was an internet myth."

"Well somebody said it," Derrick replied.

"Yeah but, not until the 1950s. It wasn't one of the founding fathers or any one from that era."

"Does that make it any less true?" Harold said as the line took another step. "The statement can stand on its own merits. It is pretty obviously true even if no one ever said it in the past. History has a ton of examples."

"Yeah but, misquoting people makes everyone else doubt what you have to say."

"By the way you're speaking, you sound like one of them liberal pseudo history professors or something."

"Yeah but, while I was a history professor at the University of Alaska in Anchorage, it was not 'pseudo history' as you call it and I am not a liberal. I am a registered Alaska Independence Conservative Party member."

Derrick reached the counter and held out his hand to give Farley with his ration coupons.

"Farley, you know Treadmore more than a lot of us. You came in with him. Help me out here."

Farley took the coupons and reached behind him to grab the weighted packages of meat that matched his allotment.

"I don't really know him," he said. "He was a tagalong from Valdez that joined our Glennallen party just a couple days before we got here. But so far, since I met him, he has done nothing but complain. Which is what the people behind you will be doing if you hold up the line."

Derrick shot him a look, took his packages, and turned to leave.

When the professor reached the counter a moment later, he handed over his coupons and Farley handed him the matching weighted packages.

"So, is this moose or caribou?" he asked.

"Moose," Farley answered, pointing to one package, then pointed to the other and added, "and this is caribou."

The professor glanced at them with a look of uncertainty then back up to Farley. "Are they a particular cut of roasts?"

Farley glanced at the labels then grinned back up at the professor and replied, "Yeah, butt."

20

Mai

Mai had arrived at ten to begin her shift sifting through the remaining DMV records, marriage certificates, and property ownership records. Two of the other officers assigned to the duty were already there, and the rest arrived a few minutes after her. Throughout the day, there had been no opportune moment to sneak the folder from her bag and slip it between documents destined for the shredder without the other soldiers seeing, and instantly drawing suspicious looks from the whole group. An electronic beep sounded across the room to signal the end of their regular shift.

"Oh my back!" one of the male lieutenants said as he rose to his feet and stretched, a rapid succession of muted pops rattled his spine as he twisted to one side then the other. "Just in time, I am done with my section."

"Me too," said one of the females.

Another nodded.

The second male lieutenant pushed back from his table, closed his last folder, and logged out of his computer. "I think it is time for a beer. Ladies, want to join us?"

"I do," said Lieutenant Lee Ming Ling. Her name meant "bright and dainty." Mai thought she was anything but bright and dainty. Lt. Lee was the tallest female in the division. For that matter, at 180 centimeters (just under six feet tall), she was taller most of the men in the battalion, and likely taller than most of the men in the Chinese People's Liberation Army as a whole. While extremely tall for a woman, her figure was of very obvious feminine proportions, large breasts, wide hips, and curves in all the right places. Many of the men in her unit and others openly lusted for her. "Bright and dainty" Ming Ling also had the rough hands of a farm girl, broad, thick shoulders, and a face that while not unattractive had obviously been in weather all her life. She was a tough, physically strong woman, and many, both men and women, assumed she was probably a lesbian, although no one had seen proof either way.

"Two beers is even better than one," replied Lt. Ho Dong Fa, a short, thickly mustachioed officer from northern China, Mongolian ancestry evident in his genes. "Can we call this a date, Ming Ling?"

"Only if I can call you my sex slave, Dong Fa," she replied.

"Ooh...kinky," Dong Fa gave a wink and a smile, "you're on!"

"You're buying!"

"If Dong Fa's buying, then I'm coming too," said Na Fenfang. She was pretty, but known to be wild. A good time girl. She was well liked by most of the men, but considered not to be one for marrying according to the many soldiers who'd pillowed with her.

The rest of the group joined in the plans as they put away their file folders and stacked their responses in the proper basket for the special police to investigate those individuals.

"What about you, Mai?" said Ming Ling. "Will you join us?"

Mai shook her head. "No, you go have fun. Ping has me doing regular shift work as well as this project."

"Oh, he is such an awful man," Fenfang said, her lips curled in a hateful grimace.

"He's not so bad," said Chao Dai, the other male lieutenant. His name meant "surpassingly great swordsman," according to Fenfang and some of the other ladies, his skill lay with a different sword than his parents had probably envisioned at his naming.

"He works us hard, but at least he does not beat us or get physical like Major Zhang. I've heard *he's* a real prick when it comes to order."

An uncomfortable silence fell among the group as Chao Dai realized he'd just insulted Mai's older brother. Several held breaths passed before Mai responded.

"You are right, Lieutenant Chao, but I would not say that out loud very often. If any superior officers heard you, you'd likely find yourself transferred to his unit."

Chao Dai let out an uncomfortable laugh.

"Mai's brother is at least very handsome, and the son of the general," said Ming Ling. "You only think Ping is okay because you are a man. I don't think there is a woman here he has not tried to touch in an inappropriate manner."

"Yeah, he is a pervert." Fenfang turned after placing her stack of papers in the correct tray. "Every time he is near me, he tries to brush up against my breasts. It's gross."

"How about when I try to brush up against your breasts," said Dong Fa.

"You are a pervert too, Dong Fa. But at least you are not older than my father. That's just gross."

"Mai," Ming Ling said, "if you get done in time, come join us."

"I will," Mai said. Ming Ling gave her a nod and a look that said she knew Mai would not be joining them. She never did. One of the downsides of being the general's daughter was that she was not free to party with the other officers during her time off. Anything she did in public immediately became associated with her father, so she had little choice but to keep her nose extremely clean. Tonight, she had other plans anyway.

"Have fun, guys," she said as they walked out. She finished the last two data sheets in her folder, both of whom seemed to be likely suspects as both were 'concealed carry' permit holders and members of the Republican party according to their state records. When she was sure she was alone, she pulled the Stone's datasheet from her bag and slid it into the stack of other papers she was taking to the shredder.

She got up and walked across the room, nerves rattling beneath her skin. She listened intently to the constant tap of footsteps in the hall outside the door. None came closer. She turned on the shredder and pulled a small handful of papers from the stack, about twenty pages, and fed it into the slot. The blades inside the machine turned the pages into thousands of one-millimeter squares in seconds. She grabbed the next handful and fed it into the top of the shredder as well. This included Brad and Youngmi Stone's datasheets. The pages made it half way through, then jammed with a high-pitched screech.

Mai hit the button to back the pages up. The machine ground in reverse for a moment, then screeched again. She pushed forward and backward several times, but each time it only moved a few centimeters then jammed at the same spot. Brad Stone's picture was on top, staring up at her, accusing her of destroying his marriage. She tugged at the pages to try and pull them up. They tore and the sudden release flung them out of her hand, scattering the pages across the floor.

She rushed to grab them, stuffing them in her arms as fast as she could. The door suddenly crashed opened and Colonel Ping walked in.

"What are you doing, Lieutenant Zhang?"

She let out a yelp of surprise. "Sir, sorry, sir." Flustered, she rose, papers falling from her hands. "I...uh...the shredder jammed and these flew out while I was—"

"Clean up this mess and get back to your cubicle." His voice was angry, frustrated sounding. "The others said you were done, and we have urgent data that needs analyzed."

She started to answer and some pages slipped out of her hands to the floor. She glanced down and saw Youngmi's image staring up at her. She surreptitiously stepped forward, sliding her foot over the image of her Ayi.

"I will be right over as soon as I clean this up."

"Five minutes," he said. "I want you at your desk in five minutes."

"Yes, sir." She stood there, waiting for him to leave.

"Well?" he stared at her, eyebrows raised expectantly.

"Sir?"

"Get moving!"

Startled by his shout, she took a step back, quickly realized she'd exposed the picture and pretended to accidentally drop several more pages on top of the one with Youngmi's picture.

"You are the clumsiest girl I have ever seen," Ping shouted at her. "Get this mess cleaned up and get to work! NOW!"

"Yes, sir," she replied, cringing. Nearly in tears, she reached down and lifted the stacks of pages.

"Give them to me," he said. "You pick up the others and I will shred them."

"No, sir," her heart was racing, "you don't need to do that, I can do it."

"Give me the Goddamned papers, Lieutenant! I don't often offer to help a junior officer with their work! Especially a lazy one like you, but I need you in the analyst room ASAP!"

She handed the stack in her hand to Ping; he snatched them away and walked to the shredder. She did not know how far down Youngmi's page was, or if her husband's page was still in that stack as well. Ping stood at the shredder, glaring at her over the machine as he fed the pages in a few at a time.

The third handful he fed in, Mai looked up and saw Youngmi's picture looking back at her. She forced her face not to register the terror that had her heart pounding so hard she was certain Ping could hear it as stared at her, anger seething in his eyes and lips.

"What are you looking at? Get to work! Hurry up."

The image slowly descended into the blades and Mai's heart started again. She walked the last few pages over to him. As he fed them in, she listened with relief as the millimeter-sized bits of paper dropped in the receptacle like flakes of snow beneath the spinning blades.

"That's it?" he demanded.

"Yes, sir," she replied, still trembling.

"Then get moving, woman!"

She hustled out of the room ahead of him and scurried down the hall to her regular office.

"The work is on your desk," he called after her. "Three binders with drone images and HUMINT data."

HUMINT referred to Human Intelligence, as in data physically collected by agents on the ground rather than digital images or space born spy satellites.

"I want a summary report on my desk no later than six AM."

"Yes, sir," she replied breathlessly. "Six AM, sir."

She hurried down the hall.

21

Brad

Gunnar drew circles with a dry erase marker on the sheet of plastic that covered the large topological map of south-central Alaska that hung on one wall in Brad's office. The map had been taken from a Department of Transportation equipment depot on the highway and provided excellent detail of the region from Anchorage to Valdez, over one hundred thousand square miles of territory with only three major roadways connecting the cities, towns, and villages on the highway system.

"The blue circles mark out the locations where we had visual surveillance teams observing enemy movement," Gunnar said. "The red circles are where we had hard contact with enemy forces, and killed most or all of them. The hair-ball will give the details."

"Hair-ball indeed, you are just jealous of my highly regarded coiffure, and self-insulating chest blanket," Kharzai said.

"Whatever," said Gunnar. "The carpet on your back is pretty gross though."

Kharzai waved off the giant and rose from his chair to give the oral debrief on their long-range patrol. Happy and Penny stood at either side of him, necks craned to look up at their master as he spoke, as if they too were preparing their own tactical plan of battle.

"In addition to static two-man observation posts at these four locations," he pointed to four small blue circles on the map, "we put two larger hunter-killer teams out with more than a dozen mean and nasty men each, one east, and the other west. Those teams went as far as we could in thirty days or until major contact. The west team reported back that they were able to get visuals on large Chinese movements along the Glenn Highway as far as just past Palmer but not extending all the way to Sutton."

He waved his hand over the large area the scouts had reconnoitered. "Not sure why they don't come further, other than that it seems they are mainly working to keep control of their fortifications in Palmer and Wasilla, where bands of small private insurgent groups are wreaking God-blessed havoc on them like what the Taliban used to do to our guys in the day."

John shot a glance at him. "The Taliban were not blessed by God. I do hope you don't mean our peers in town are donning suicide vests."

"No, no, no." Kharzai shook his head vigorously. "Our guys have much better fashion sense and considerably more staying power than the martyrdom groupies. What I mean is IEDs, sniper nests, booby traps, ambushes, and one of the groups has managed to get somewhat adept at officer assassination via poisoning of all things. From what they could gather, our team said that since organized resistance stood up a few months after the invasion several thousand soldiers and a 'large number,'" he used air quotes, "of officers have been sent to Comrade Mao's vacation retreat in the sky."

John nodded.

Kharzai did a quick double take, suddenly noticing the new silver star on John's uniform shirt and added, "Uh…sir."

John gave him an uncomfortable look and acknowledged him.

Gunnar glanced over from the map. "Oh yeah, boss. Congratulations on your promotion…General. How'd you skip three ranks so fast?"

"It was necessary to impose the right image on his actual responsibilities here," Brad said. "He isn't in the US Army anymore. This is the Alaska Defense Force, and he's in charge of the whole thing. One of the guys in town is a silver smith and made the stars for him."

"Indeed he is," Kharzai smiled, "our own Wendell Fertig."

"Huh?"

"Wendell Fertig was an engineer living in the Philippines in the nineteen-thirties and forties. He was a Lieutenant Colonel in the Army Reserve when dub-dub-two broke out and the Japanese invaded the Philippines. He refused to surrender, ran into the jungle, and started his own guerilla army that wreaked absolute havoc on the Japanese Imperial Army for years until the Americans came back with the regular army. To make himself authoritative enough to the local Filipino population to get them to follow him in the fight, he unofficially promoted himself to brigadier general. It worked; in the end, he had nearly forty-thousand guerillas working for him."

"That's a lot of apes," said Gunnar.

"Uh...not GO-rillas, GERR-illas." Kharzai gave the Swedish a school teacher look. "Fertig was the leader of one of, if not *the*, most successful guerilla armies in history." He paused then added, "Of course, promoting himself like that really pissed off the Supreme Prima Donna General Douglas McArthur. Good ol' DJ Dougie-Mac not only refused to recognize the promotion, but he severely reprimanded Fertig for doing it and came close to giving him a court martial for insinuating he was at an almost equal level as the glorious emperor, even though it is almost certain that McArthur could not have invaded the Philippines so successfully were it not for Fertig's work beforehand."

Gunnar grunted and nodded at John. "Don't expect me to salute you any more smartly than I already do, General."

"It's only a title," John said.

"I'm sure you're not complaining about the pay raise though." Kharzai smiled.

"Yeah, twenty percent increase on my Defense Force captain's pay."

"Uh, General," Gunnar muttered. "You weren't getting paid as a Defense Force captain."

"Oh yeah," John grinned back, "twenty percent of nothing is still a raise though, right?"

"Okay, back on track," Brad said. "What about your easterly patrol? What did they discover?"

"That's the one me and Gunnar were on, and we made some interesting discoveries as we roamed about." Kharzai moved to the map where Gunnar was circling the location of their firefight with the Russian patrol. "We stayed north of the Glenn Highway and just kind of snooped around toward the general direction of Glennallen." He pointed to the circle. "We ran into our good old friends from across the Bering Sea here." He pointed to the area on the map where they'd met the bear chasing soldiers. "Russians." He pronounced the country's name with a Boris and Natasha Sovietish accent. "They are seriously entrenched in and around Glennallen. And these are staying there kind of troops, like a full-time garrison of regular infantry with a couple of Spetsnaz companies operating out of the town as well."

"Russian special forces teams?"

"Yup." Kharzai acknowledged the Russian version of America's Green Beret/Ranger/Navy SEAL force. He pointed to a place on the map near the town of Glennallen. "They have taken over the old State Trooper's barracks there as a command post and have locked the whole highway down hard. The Spetsnaz guys look like they are doing anti-guerilla ops and pipeline security. While we didn't get hot contact with any of them specifically, we did get into a firefight with a few dozen regular infantry types out on a long-range patrol like we were. We killed most of them. I got the impression they felt like it was a vacation in Easytown."

Brad stared at the map locations then back up at Kharzai. "Why do you think that?"

"Apparently, they were not aware of any potential enemy presence in the area because they were way too chill for a combat patrol."

"Just sloppy soldiers?"

"No, fresh, confident soldiers. Well fed, and not nervous."

"Which means?"

"Which means," John put in, "they feel like they've got enough manpower to put down whatever comes their way. And they've got a good working supply chain that is not meeting much of a fight."

"I doubt the Russians had it as hard as the Chinese in the fighting last summer and winter," Kharzai said. "Anchorage, Kenai, and Mat-Su areas accounted for nearly seventy percent of the population before the war. Fort Wainright and Eielson Air Force Base are relatively small bases. And Fort Greely is a missile base with mostly techno-geeks and contractors protected by a handful of infantry and contract security forces. All of those locations had more National Guard than full-time regular troops. While National Guard troops are just are usually equally good soldiers as active duty regulars, they're not usually all in one place at one time."

Gunnar agreed. "Just like me and the general."

"Yup."

Brad walked over to the map and studied the circles and lines Gunnar had drawn.

"General Charles, get a tactical plan together. We need to change their attitude."

"Yes, sir."

"Oh and we also got you a birthday gift, Brad." Kharzai grinned in a more mischievous way than normal. The look in his eyes hinted at serious mischief afoot.

Brad cocked an eyebrow. "A birthday gift?"

"Him and not me?" John acted hurt.

"He'll probably share it with you if you ask nice," Kharzai said.

"What is it?"

"Giant warrior of Swedish extraction," Kharzai said with a flourish, "would you do the honors?"

"Of course, little hairy man of dubious talent." Gunnar bowed in reply. "I would be happy to. This way, gentlemen."

He led them out of the command office and past several other buildings to the edge of the settlement. A large, blocky thing stood just within the tree line, covered by a camouflaged tarp. Nearby, a similarly sized cube was identically covered. The two covered objects were ringed about by guards.

"What in the world...?" Brad muttered.

Gunnar and Kharzai jogged up to the largest one, posed briefly like game show models, then yanked the tarp off the object with a Broadway style flourish.

"Tadaaaa!"

Brad and John's eyes both went wide as they stared at a full-sized, armored Humvee with a pair of blocky-looking, swivel-mounted missile launchers on top.

"Gentlemen," Kharzai was smiling like a child on Christmas morning, "I present to you a fully functional Avenger Surface to Air Missile System and," he waved toward the covered cube, "several dozen stinger missiles to go with it."

Brad flashed a look of utter incredulity to the two men. Kharzai yanked the cover off the other cube to reveal a trailer loaded down with boxes of gear and ammunition.

John sputtered, "Where the hell did you find this?" He walked toward the vehicle, hands out, as if to make sure he wasn't seeing things.

"It looks like a unit mostly escaped the main battle with this stuff," Gunnar said. "Far as we could tell, they ran it into the woods with the Humvee pulling the trailer, followed by a deuce and a half truck that had the missiles on it. The cab of the truck was shot to pieces and non-drivable. There were about a half-dozen long dead bodies in and around it, last summer's casualties by the look of them. They were probably strafed before they could get set up to return fire. We topped off the Humvee from the truck's gas tank, put most of the missiles in it, and the rest had to be hand carried, but we managed to drive it all the way here without being detected."

Kharzai danced excitedly around the cased missiles, reached under the tarp, and pulled out a long tube.

"There's three handheld launchers too." He looked like a puppy shaking its tail so hard he was about to break in half. "Three!"

"And check this out, bosses." Gunnar reached into the back seat of the Humvee and pulled out two chunky-looking weapons that seemed like a cross between a cowboy six-shooter and a mortar tube. "M32 Multiple Grenade Launcher."

John walked over and took one from the giant. The massive Swede had a grin that stretched across his face from ear to ear.

"You look like a man who just found his long-lost puppy," John said as he opened the breech of the weapon and inspected it. "Gunnar carried one of these through most of our last couple tours in Afghanistan."

"Yes, sir. Her name was Olga, and she was beautiful. She also kicked a whole hell of a lot of Taliban butt."

"You named your grenade launcher Olga," Brad asked.

"Of course."

"And it was a female?"

"Yes, best girl I've ever known. Always faithful, and never once complained when I gave the world a good healthy Olafson fart," Gunnar added emphasis to his thought by releasing an explosion of gas from his rear end.

"Jeeze, man," John stepped back several feet from his friend, "give a brother a bit of warning."

Kharzai danced around the stacks of lethal equipment, his face stretched in a smile so tight it seemed about to split. "Oh!

Wait! Wait! Wait! There's moooore!" he sang out like the host of Price is Right.

He reached into the Humvee and pulled out yet another item, a green metal tube.

"LAW Rockets! It's the M7A5 1980s versions, yes, but still in working order AND we have a dozen of them new in boxes as well as a couple more SAW machine guns and a bunch of full-sized M16 rifles some with M203 grenade launchers of their own. Whatever these soldiers were intending to do, they were ready for anything!"

Kharzai paused for a moment then spoke in a lower tone. "Well, ready for anything except 20mm cannon fire strafing them from a fast-moving helicopter that caught them in the open it would seem."

He quickly gained back his excitement, eyes sparkling with mischief. "You realize what this means?"

"Uh..." Brad was unsure how to answer.

"YES! We can kill more of them faster! Doesn't that make you want to sing, and dance, and shout and run naked through fields of daisies?"

"Oookaaay," John said, "do we have people who can use the missiles?"

"Of course, boss," said Gunnar, indicating himself and Kharzai, "for the Avengers we both know how, and we have three other Rangers who are trained on the handheld system. And Franklin figured out the vehicle borne system as we came back. As for the LAWs and other stuff, easy to train the rest of the Rangers and Patrol on that. We're good to go, General."

Brad stared at the stack of missiles and the vehicle, then put his hands on his head in a gesture of awed realization.

"Thank you, Jesus," he muttered. "This is a complete game changer."

22

Youngmi

The Friday morning food distribution had been smooth and uneventful so far. Blue skies and a warm summer sun were a welcome energizer. The constant gray clouds and non-stop rain over the previous few days had dampened many moods. Youngmi stood behind one of the distribution tables handing out bags of vegetables to mostly grateful citizens whose card swipe flashed authorized on the reader.

A woman with her daughter came to the table and swiped her card. The green light flashed and the display read "Carlson, Megan – M0 F1 C2," the number of mouths to feed, zero adult males, one adult female, and two children. She and her daughter held up their wrists to display their ID tags. Youngmi scanned the bracelets, the matching numbers confirming they were mother and child. Youngmi looked at the woman and child, glancing around looking for the other child listed on her card. There was only the one. She handed the woman one bag marked "female" and one bag marked "child."

"Excuse me," said the woman, "but I have two children, not just one."

"I am sorry, ma'am," she said, "but I can only give you rations for yourself and the children you have with you. Is your other child here?"

"He is at home, very sick." The woman reached into her purse and removed another ID bracelet. "I have his tag though."

"I am sorry, but each person must be here to receive their rations."

"He is too sick to come out here," the woman said. "Can you just give me his food?"

"No, Mrs. Carlson," Youngmi shook her head, "I cannot. If your child is too sick to be brought for his rations, you can request to have a social worker come to your house. They can verify if the child needs medical care, and if necessary, bring the required food to you. But we cannot give rations out here unless the person is present."

"My son is too sick," the woman insisted, an edge creeping into her voice. "He is too weak to come; please just give me food to take to him."

"I am sorry, please step over to the social work area and we can assign a worker to—"

"Look, you collaborator bitch!" she hissed, spittle flecking her lips as a hateful glare filled her eyes. "You are starving us. Give me the Goddamned food for my son."

A soldier started toward the table. Youngmi waved him off. He stopped, but stayed attentive.

"I realize your son is sick, as you say. But because people have been trying to cheat the system, he must be here to receive food, or have a social wor—"

"My little brother is very sick," the little girl's voice was pleading, tears streaming from her eyes. "Please let him have food. He has not woke up since three days, and his face is blue. If you give him food, he will wake up and his skin will be normal color again."

Youngmi stared sympathetically at the child. Rage burned in the mother's expression as she turned and shot a fiery stare at her daughter. Youngmi's heart sank as she digested what the girl had said. She turned back to the mother, hardening her expression.

"Yes," the mother growled, "you and your traitor kind killed my son. You starved him to death. I am only trying to get food for my daughter to live."

"You have your proper rations then. Please take care of your son's body before it brings disease to the rest of your household."

"You robotic, bitch. You communist traitor. You and your type don't go hungry, do you? Party members don't starve, do they?"

"We all get the same rations, ma'am."

"NO! No, you don't! We all know who you are! You are the general's whore! You spread your legs to the enemy and get all the food you want, you selfish traitor whore!"

The soldier stepped close, rifle still slung, but ready to move. The woman snapped her gaze at him, eyes burning.

"Ma'am, you need to leave, please," Youngmi said, forcing calm in her voice.

"I will go," she said, "but you will pay!"

With a flash, her hand came up with a long fillet knife, slashing up toward Youngmi. But the soldier was faster and the butt of his rifle connected with the side of her head, sending the woman sprawling to the ground, out cold. Her daughter screamed.

Other guards lifted the woman onto a stretcher, strapped her arms down, and carried her away. The soldier who'd hit the woman picked up the child with surprising tenderness, and followed. Youngmi was left standing behind the table; the rest of the crowd instantly carried on as if nothing had happened.

She let out a breath and before she could fully process the event, the next person in line was at the table, a man with another young girl at his side. He smiled sympathetically at her. "Don't let it bother you. We know most of you are not really traitors."

She glanced up at him as he swiped his card and recognition flashed in her eyes. He had a slightly crooked nose, like it had been broken and badly set, and a gold Christian cross in his ear lobe.

"Anthony's Pizza, ninety-one," he said.

The code word Captain Chi had said would be presented by the man to whom she was to give the micro-SD card. She handed him his bags, then reached into her pocket and pulled out a small candy which she handed to the father.

"This is for your daughter."

The little girl smiled in surprise at her, then looked at her father expectantly.

"When we get home, little one," he said. "You can share it with grandfather."

The little girl nodded happily and took the bag her father handed her. They turned and left, the little girl looking back to Youngmi with a delightful smile.

The crowd of uniformed party workers opened up behind her, growing quieter. She turned, and saw General Zhang approaching.

"Carry on everyone," Zhang said in unaccented English. "These people look hungry; we must feed them."

Youngmi glanced back and saw that the man with the broken nose had vanished. She turned toward Zhang as he came up behind her.

"My general," she said, "it is good to see you here."

"It seems your work is going smoothly." He glanced around at the crowd. They averted their eyes from his gaze and carried on with their business. No one dared try to cheat the system while the general and his body guards were there.

"It goes as well as can be expected," Youngmi said. "I wish we could give more food to them, this is so little."

"Hrm," he sucked in a breath, "I will see what we can do." Zhang stepped up to the table and looked over it. "Let me help you for a little while."

He smiled up at the waiting family in front of her table and motioned for them to swipe their card. They did and held up their wrists, which he scanned with the reader and then handed them the bags that matched their allowance.

"Thank you, sir," said the father. "We truly appreciate your kindness."

"I am happy to see families being fed, now that the suffering is over."

After half a dozen customers received their packets of food directly from the general, he smiled and backed away from the table. She followed him, two other workers taking their place.

"Youngmi, I must return to work."

"Yes, my general."

"Please do be careful," he said, concern on his face when he looked into her eyes. "I heard there was trouble earlier."

"It was nothing." She smiled demurely. "Some people are still hungry with the meager amounts we supply. But most of them understand what is happening, and are willing to work harder for their families."

"Perhaps you should have a larger security detail."

"Oh no, sir, I…"

An explosion boomed in the distance, the shock wave rumbling through their bodies even from so far off. Screams and cries of surprise erupted in the crowd, as everyone turned and stared at the column of black smoke rising to the east, closer to downtown.

"Close it up," cried the security chief, a white man wearing the uniform of the newly formed gendarmerie, a military police force made up of locals who signed a commitment to serve the new rulers.

"But we have not gotten our food yet," shouted a woman in the crowd.

"Yeah, we need our food, we've waited all day!" called another man.

General Zhang raised his hand to calm the crowd and shouted, "The distribution center will not be closed until everyone here has received their ration. Captain." He motioned for the security chief to come over; the man ran to the general and saluted. "That was one bomb, a mile away, at an army guard post, not a food center. You will feed these people and make sure you keep your security alert."

Then he lowered his voice and gave the young officer a stern look, "If you close this distribution center, these people will panic, and riot, and then they will come after you and your family. And I will let them. Do you understand?"

The captain's eyes grew wide with terror. He stood at stiff attention and saluted the general. "Yes, sir! I understand, sir."

"Carry on."

"Yes, sir!"

He turned and called back to his men and the workers, "Continue to distribute the food. Do not waste time."

23

Treadmore

Terry O'Dell was fifteen, one year away from being old enough to join the Tactical Patrol Force. His ultimate goal, as soon as he turned eighteen, was to be a Ranger. He had watched his parents get murdered by the Chinese soldiers that had come into their neighborhood in Palmer and rounded up every man and every woman who had the slightest defiance in their eyes. He had been hidden in the trees at the edge of their several-acre property, more than fifty yards from the house. He'd been frozen in place, watching through the cheap binoculars his father had given him for his birthday. Eyes wide, he stared across the open yard, too terrified to run out and help them.

The soldiers forced his father and mother to the end of their driveway and, when they refused to drop to their knees, one of them raised his pistol right to his father's head and pulled the trigger. He heard his mother's scream as his father collapsed. The Chinese soldier said something to her. She turned an angry face to him and screamed an obscenity he'd never heard his mother use before.

The soldier shook his head slightly, almost as if he felt remorse for his actions, then raised his pistol and put a bullet in her forehead. Terry remembered the misty pink cloud that burst from her silky brown hair, and watching her stand there, wavering on her feet for a moment in time, as if wondering what to do next, then falling straight backward, landing with a crunch on the gravel drive. The soldier silently turned and walked away, his men following close behind.

Terry waited until he heard their vehicle rumble off down the country road before he ran out of his cover toward his parents. The dull-eyed looks in their faces had been frozen in his head for more than a year now. But when he thought about them, he could almost hear them calling to him.

"Avenge us, son, avenge us."

Terry O'Dell wanted nothing more than to take the fight back to the enemy. To find that soldier who had shot his parents and to put a bullet into his head just like he had done to them. To that end, he spent countless hours drilling with the guard. He took every class on stalking, fighting, and weapons he could get into outside of his scheduled chores.

Only a few days earlier, Ranger Commander Kharzai had commented that he was surprisingly good at most of the military skills they were learning, especially for such a young man.

They had been learning about the OODA Loop. A type of military thinking process that helps a soldier decide what actions to take in a rapidly changing combat scenario, OODA stood for Observe, Orient, Decide, and Act. The actual process, especially once the practitioner understood their very lives depended on its outcome, only took fractions of a second to run through. Terry had shown himself to be a surprisingly fast thinker in simulated life and death scenarios during training.

He had performed so well in that class, that Kharzai had even taken extra time to work with him personally at hand-to-hand combat skills that could be very useful for him if he found himself in unexpectedly bad situations. Bladed weapons, something the funny-looking, hairy man seemed especially good at, was a skill that Kharzai took special care to teach him over the last few weeks. Terry had become quite proficient with his hand-made tomahawk and knife.

His next best skill was stalking, which was what he decided to work on today on his own time. He had seen Treadmore and Weasel walk into the woods and decided they would be a good subject to spy on for the day. He didn't like either one of them. Mr. Treadmore seemed mean, and maybe even a pervert of some kind. He rubbed most of the people, kids and adults, the wrong way. Weasel was just plain creepy. He reminded Terry of the Child Catcher from the movie Chitty Chitty Bang Bang he'd seen as a kid. As much as he loved every other part of that movie, the Child Catcher scene had actually given him nightmares. Weasel brought that bad memory to life. He followed them into the woods. Maybe he could catch them plotting something and Ice Hammer would kick them out of the town, and even let him join the TPF sooner as a reward.

He crawled through the dense undergrowth, inhaling the odor of the decaying foliage, feeling himself one with the forest. He continued until he was very close to his prey, barely more than ten feet from the two men as they leaned against a large rock. Concealed in a grassy space behind a tangled mass of weeds growing around a fallen tree, he was invisible, the camouflage he'd chosen blending in perfectly with the surroundings. As long as he controlled his breathing and did not move, he would remain undetected to even the most observant eye.

"You were not supposed to kill anyone," Treadmore's voice said. "You were supposed to steal the harvest and hide it, that's it."

"Yeah, well when the idiot harvesters saw us, what was I supposed to do? Make them promise not to tell?"

"I…you were not supposed to kill them. There were plenty of other ways it could have been dealt with. And those kids in the woods, that should never have happened at all."

"Too late," Weasel said. "What's done is done. Besides, harvest is over and your elections are coming up soon. All you have to do is keep people doubting Stone's ability to maintain control and you will very soon find yourself taking over his job as head honcho of this whole place. That's what you wanted, right?"

"Are your men trustworthy enough to remain silent?"

"My men are professionals; they never talk about work with anyone outside the team."

Weasel stood up and moved away from Treadmore. His feet crunched on dead leaves and twigs as he walked closer to Terry's hiding place. He stopped beside the fallen tree and Terry heard the sound of his zipper opening.

"You have nothing to worry about, boss," Weasel said, his voice full of confidence. "You will be the next leader of Chiknik very soon."

Terry looked up just as the stream of urine started above his head. Without thinking, he instinctively rolled to the side to avoid being pissed on, instantly regretting the impulsive reaction.

"Hey!" Weasel shouted. Unable to stop the stream, he held onto his penis with one hand and turned with a more than awkward movement to grab Terry with the other. "What are you doing here?"

He yanked Terry to his feet then looked down at his own.

"Dammit, kid! You made me piss on my shoes!"

Treadmore rushed over.

"Shit, kid! What did you hear? Tell me what you heard us talking about."

Terry said nothing, looking back and forth, defiance and terror mixed in his glaring eyes.

"What did you hear?" Weasel demanded. Still no reply. "Shit, he heard everything we said."

"Boy, if you tell anyone..." Treadmore started.

"He won't tell anyone," Weasel said as he pulled a small pistol out of his waistband. "Will you, kid?"

Terry looked into Weasel's eyes, sped through the OODA Loop, and instantly realized that one of them was about to die. He just as quickly decided that it was not going to be him and snapped into action, snatching the tomahawk and knife from his belt. Weasel raised the pistol to put a bullet into the boy's forehead. Terry's arms were a blur as his hands flashed up. The knife blade slashed across Weasel's gun arm, slicing through muscle and tendon as his other hand swung the razor sharp tomahawk into Weasel's thigh with a thunk as it stopped in the bone. The blade went in deep, bright red blood sprayed from the wounds as the man fell, the pistol flying from his grasp without a shot.

Terry yanked the tomahawk back, another spray of arterial blood erupted as the blade released from the wound, arcing in an almost unnaturally bright red color. The boy spun around and ran towards the village as fast as his legs would carry him.

He glanced back and saw Treadmore raising the pistol Weasel had dropped. A crack sounded, no louder than a fire cracker. Terry felt a fiery stab in his back, between his shoulder blade and his spine. He tripped and fell face first into the ground. His limbs barely seemed able to move, as if they were suddenly a hundred times their mass, becoming too heavy to support him.

He pushed through the fog of pain and terror and continued toward the forest edge. A cold panic set in as the expectation of death grew in his young mind. He could hear the voices of his parents calling, urging him on toward the edge of the wood.

Treadmore ran to where he had seen the boy fall, the gun still in his hand in case he had to deliver the coup de gras. The boy was not there. He followed the blood trail for a distance but lost it in a boggy spot. The boy would not last long enough to get back to the town, he was sure of that. He had almost certainly hit him in a lung, and the kid was losing a lot of blood.

He went back to Weasel. His body lay on the ground, where he had bled out from the sliced femoral artery. His eyes stared up, dull and dead, looking for the most part as unintelligent as they had always been, but missing the animal cunning that the man had in life. The body lay still, not breathing, pale as a faded linen sheet, a pool of coagulating blood mingled with the brown, grassy vegetation between his legs.

Weasel was very dead.

24

Sammi

The bright light of the early autumn sun gave a glow to Sammi's face that Brad could not help but enjoy. She seemed positively beautiful, as though living in Chiknik had caused her to look more alive than ever before. She smiled as she noticed the look he was giving her.

"What?" She gave a coy sidewise glance.

"Just enjoying the view," he said.

She wrapped her arm in his and drew closer.

"And what do you see?"

"Beauty," he said. "You are absolutely radiant."

"Trick of the sunlight," she said, blushing.

"I don't know." Brad stopped, took in her face, gazed into her dark brown eyes. "It is as if the sun is glowing from inside you."

"Well," she said, taking a deep breath, her smile stretching even further, "that is the kind of thing that happens…when a woman is pregnant."

Brad froze, his expression taking that deer-in-the-headlights look of shock that billions of men throughout history have experienced.

"I am surprised you didn't notice already," Sammi said with a laugh. "I mean, you've been through this a few times before. I thought you'd recognize the condition a little quicker."

"Uh…I…Not for nearly seventeen years." A sheepish grin spread over his features. "How long, I mean, how far along are you?"

"Well, we just got married a little more than two months ago," she spoke like a teacher instructing a slow student, "and you may have noticed I have not had a period since we've been married."

"So, since the wedding night?"

"Or within a few days after that."

"Holy cow!"

"No, I hope not," Sammi giggled, "just a normal boy or girl would be fine."

"I mean..."

"Mr. Brad! Mr. Brad!"

The shout came from behind him. Jung's voice called his name as she ran toward him.

"Come quick to the hospital," she demanded between panting breaths. "A boy has been shot and he says he has important news for you."

Brad looked back at Sammi. "We'll talk more later." He turned and followed Jung across the town to the building where Dr. Garner, a former veterinary surgeon, a nurse practitioner named Susan and two paramedics had setup shop as the makeshift Chiknik hospital.

The boy on the table was pale, foamy blood bubbled at the corners of his mouth. He struggled to maintain the breaths that rasped between his teeth. Although his features were twisted with pain, Brad recognized him as the boy Kharzai had pointed out a few weeks earlier, one who had shown a lot of promise as a fighter.

"He's been demanding to talk to you since they found him crawling in from the woods at the edge of town," the doctor said.

"How long ago was that?" Brad asked.

"Maybe twenty minutes," Jung said. "We found him by the trees where we were picking raspberries. He crawled out and called your name, Ice Hammer, right away."

Brad went to the boy and bent close to him.

"What did you want to tell me, son?"

Between wheezy gasps, Terry said, "Treadmore...and We...Weasel. They killed...the people...in...the fields."

"What?"

"To hurt you..."

"How do you know this?"

"I heard them...talking...and...Weasel caught me...in the...bushes."

Terry closed his eyes and struggled to catch his breath. The doctor pushed Brad back and put a suction device into the boy's mouth, a gurgling sound curled up the tube as blood was sucked out of his throat before choking him.

Terry pushed him away and continued gasping between words.

"Weasel tried to...shoot me...but I...cut him...with my tomahawk...Treadmore..." he sucked hard for air, his teeth clamped together, lips spread in a tight grimace. He tried to form a word, "sh..." a hiss of breath came out with a tiny squeak.

He coughed, and a splash of blood exploded upwards and spattered Brad's clothes. Terry's Adam's apple was to be twisted off center in his throat. His eyes were wide and the veins in his neck started to bulge. The doctor pushed Brad aside.

"Tension pneumothorax," he declared authoritatively, motioning to one of the paramedics. "16 gauge needle."

The medic was already grabbing for the item on the shelf. He ripped open the sterile plastic wrapper and handed over a needle the size of a coffee stirring straw. The doctor quickly counted up from the bottom to Terry's fourth rib and shoved the needle into his chest cavity just above it. Instantly, a high-pitched hiss sounded through the needle, and within seconds, the boy's expression calmed, the veins in his neck receded and his demeanor relaxed. Before his speech could return, Terry faded out of consciousness.

25

Ping

"The long-range drones are down," People's Air Force Colonel Quai said to General Zhang and the gathered officers, "and we have no way of getting them back up unless central command can put more satellites in space."

"What happened to the ones we've been using all year?" Colonel Chong asked. "Alien attack?"

"Of course not," Quai grunted. "It is believed a solar flare last week damaged the two we used until now."

"When will it be fixed?" Zhang asked.

"It will not be fixed for many months, sir."

Ping looked at Quai with an expression as if he'd just eaten his own bile. "So how are we to gather intel now? Are you going to send manned aircraft up with cameras?"

Quai ignored him. Facing Zhang, he said, "That brings me to the other problem we have. Since the American Air element was effectively wiped out during the initial months and we have no truly major ground operations continuing here, central command does not believe we need more jet fuel than it takes for minimal security operations. When last I spoke to my commanders in Beijing, I was told that they need the fuel elsewhere and we will be getting a bare minimum ration of it here."

Zhang looked at his notes. "So, they are drip feeding us with the minimums, eh? They think we've got everything under control here and trust we need nothing else now. Well, in one sense that is good, they believe we have completed our objectives, which we have, to a degree. On the other hand, they do not understand the volatility of the local situation. But I suppose that is always the case with frontier locations; they are always the last considered for supplies and support, being on the edge of the world like this."

"Yes, general," Quai said. "This is usually the case."

"But do they not know," Ping said, "that most rebellions that bring down great empires begin in the frontiers? That is where the insurgents gain their first strength and victories!"

"That is true, Comrade Ping," said Zhang, "but with that truth in mind, we need to make sure we are fully cognizant of what must be done here and use what resources we have most diligently, so we do not get caught with our pants down."

Ping went silent, unusual for him. Colonel Quai continued.

"We have enough fuel for two or three recon sorties per day for the next three months, and rocket or missile attacks only once or twice per month, so we need to save those for serious and solidly verified targets only. No guessing on those missile targets. I would request that missile targets be authorized by me alone."

"Granted," said Zhang. "Missile and rocket attacks will only be authorized by Colonel Quai from today forward."

The colonels in the room nodded their assent to the order and wrote in their various notepads.

"Are there any other discussion items, gentlemen?" The general glanced around at the officers. After none of them added anything more to the conversation, he said, "Return to your duties and keep me informed via email in your daily status reports. If important or urgent issues come up, do not rely solely on email though. Come see me personally. Use your own judgment for that. I trust you all, as none of you are young junior officers. Just make sure you and your men do nothing to make me question the leniency with which I am managing your operations."

"Yes, sir," they all called out in unison as they rose, a group of fifty-year-old men acting as if they were seventeen-year-old recruits trying to impress him.

As the other colonels filed out of the room, Ping hung behind until they were gone.

"Yes, my friend," Zhang said. "What would you like to add to the meeting, Colonel Ping?"

"It is only, well...erm..." Ping drew out his sentence as if he was leery of broaching the subject he was about to bring up. "I just wanted to bring up a recent discovery I have become aware of that did not seem fitting for me to address with the rest of the officers."

"Oh?" Zhang leaned back in his chair and raised his eyebrows. "Tell me what is in your heart, Colonel Ping."

"According to what I have heard among my younger officers," Ping said, "particularly the younger female officers, there has been an uptick in sexual assaults right here in our command staff recently. Even some of the young female officers have reported untoward advances, as well as the occasional stalker that make them fear for their own safety, especially when working a late shift."

"Is that so? I have not heard this rumor." Zhang had a serious look of concern. Sexual assault was an unforgiveable sin in his mind. "And what do you propose to solve this problem, Colonel Ping?"

"I would like increase night patrols in any area where female soldiers or other civilian personnel are known to frequent."

"You know my stance on sexual assault, Colonel."

"Yes, sir, exactly that."

"Then act accordingly, Colonel Ping," Zhang said matter-of-factly. "Make it happen."

26

Treadmore

Treadmore walked halfway around the town before entering back in between a couple of low-built mound cabins. The style of architecture that had become most common in Chiknik reminded him of Hobbit homes from the Tolkien novels he'd read as a child. And just like the novels, he felt like this whole existence was one completely unrealistic fantasy that he'd gotten himself wrapped up in somehow. What he'd thought would be easy pickings was getting harder and harder as dealing with so many bumpkins and fools threw up road blocks at every turn.

He went to his own cabin, a regular wood house that, while comfortable enough, was barely larger than the smallest bedroom of his home before the war. One of the few single occupant homes, he'd taken it over after the previous occupant had suffered heart failure or something, his body discovered by a neighbor when he went to check on him after not showing up for work. The dead man, a union construction worker type before the war, had been an early supporter of Treadmore, but turned coat and started plotting against him after only a few weeks.

"Amazing what the wrong kind of mushrooms will do to a fella," Treadmore muttered under his breath at the thought of the man as he changed his clothes. He laid the pistol on the night stand by the bed. Then he picked it back up, reloaded a bullet into the magazine to replace the one he'd shot the kid with, and quickly ran a cleaning rod down the barrel to remove traces of having been recently fired. "Now, to find out what happened to the kid. Need to make sure he can't talk."

As he walked out of his home, he found himself immediately accosted by several men of the TPF.

"Treadmore," their captain said, "you will be coming with us."

"Excuse me?"

"You will be coming with us, right now."

His heart raced, but he kept a calm appearance, showing nothing but indignation.

"What is this all about?"

"I believe you know."

"I most certainly do not!"

"Well then, start guessing, and think .22 caliber, and 15-year-old kid."

"Twenty two…what? I have no idea what you're talking about!"

"Yeah, sure," replied the captain. "Look, you can choose to come with us of your own volition, or we can beat the shit out of your ass and drag you across the commons feet first and face down, your choice."

"Is this what this nation has become?" Treadmore raised his visible indignation meter to the red zone as he straightened his body and jutted his chin. "Nothing more than a bunch of militant thugs?"

The captain gave him a blank look.

"You have to the count of one to decide, asshole."

Treadmore quickly realized that his bluster was gaining him no points at all with Stone's enforcement gorillas. He took a deep breath and motioned with his hands for them to lead the way.

"Sure you don't want to resist?" the captain asked. "I was actually kind of hoping you'd want to resist."

"I will not give you young ruffians the satisfaction. I know my rights. Take me in."

The captain and his men grunted derisive laughs. A man moved to each side, grasping an arm. Two others walked behind, while the captain led the way to the Chiknik jail house.

* * *

Four men carried the body on a makeshift stretcher to the cemetery at the edge of town. It had been dead for a day or two, but there was no mistaking the identity. Weasel Davis looked equally weasel-ish in death as he had in life. The only difference was that now his eyes had been eaten out by ravens and his right pants leg was dark brown with old dried blood. The residents of Chiknik had agreed not to waste materials on coffins, since so many people died from either sickness, injury, or starvation. For burials of the general population, the corpse was wrapped in a cloth if the family had one, or simply laid flat on their back in a shallow grave and covered with three feet of soil, into which their decaying bodies would assimilate. Ashes to ashes, dust to dust.

They made an exception for Weasel. His posthumous trial had been short and quick. Brad submitted the testimony Terry had given with Dr. Garner and his staff verifying as witnesses, as well as the women who had found him at the edge of town.

It had been easy to verify the wound on his right thigh had been caused by Terry's tomahawk. The boy had made the weapon himself with help from the town blacksmith. At the tip of the steel blade, Terry had cut in his parents initials in millimeter high block letters, tiny but easily legible. FO for Frank O'Dell. BO for Becca O'Dell. The basic autopsy of Weasel's body showed the clear imprint of the letters on his femur, perfectly matching the tomahawk. The gun was recovered from Treadmore's quarters and a crude test was done with homemade ballistic gel and a high school microscope. The results were not only impressive, but repeatable. Weasel's firearm, his ownership was verified by multiple witnesses, had been the one used to shoot Terry. The men carried Weasel's body to the grave and, as townspeople watched, unceremoniously dumped him into the hole, face down.

The fact that the weapon was in Treadmore's possession created a number of other issues. He claimed that he had found it in the weeds near his cabin and picked it up rather than leave such a dangerous item for a child to find. He cleaned it out of habit when he got home. Few believed him, no one had ever seen him handle a firearm, but no one could prove his statement otherwise. Treadmore sat in the jail awaiting his sentencing.

"The boy was strong, but he could not win against the infection in his body," Dr. Garner said. "He apparently dragged himself through a lot of debris and ground the dirt into the wounds."

"Wounds?" Kharzai asked. "I thought he was only shot once."

"He was. But it looks like when he fell, the tomahawk cut into his leg and opened a doorway for every kind of ground-based organism to enter. There were a number of other scrapes and cuts that swelled up pretty badly as well. We are very low on penicillin so he had to fight most of this on his own."

"Did he say anything more?" Brad asked.

"No. The fever had him delirious most of the time when he was awake. What he did manage to say after your first visit did not make sense very often anyway."

Brad sat behind his desk, elbows on its surface, and rubbed his face with both hands. "So now it is a murder investigation."

"Looks that way," said Dr. Garner as he headed to the door. "By the way, Sammi's checkup this morning looked really good. Too bad we don't have an ultrasound machine to see which model you're getting, but the baby sounds really healthy."

"Thanks, Doc. I'll just be happy with ten fingers and ten toes."

At least he had that bit of positive information to dwell on.

*　*　*

"Merrill Treadmore, please rise for the court's judgment," Justice Arlen Coolidge said in the court session. He was a former lower court judge from Wasilla who found it sad that he still had a place even in this mini-utopia they were cutting out of the wilderness. "You have been found guilty as an accomplice to murder in the first degree. This court sentences you to banishment from Chiknik."

"Banishment?" Treadmore said, barely masking a sneer. "What is this? The Middle Ages?"

The judge stared down at him with no emotion, cold and blank. Treadmore looked defiantly up, his countenance darkening. He scanned the crowd that filled the open-air court room and judging by the stares shooting back at him, he realized no one was taking his side anymore.

"Your sentence begins at sunrise tomorrow. You may choose which side of town that we release you on: north, east, south or west. You will be released five miles beyond the edge of our settlement and if you are seen anywhere within a five-mile radius of Chiknik at any time after your release, you will be instantly subject to the death penalty without any chance for discussion or appeal. Do you have any questions?"

"How can you banish me? You have not proved I killed that boy!"

"That is why we are banishing you instead of executing you by our own hands," Justice Coolidge replied. "We're giving you the benefit of the doubt. Otherwise, you would be sharing a cold hole in the dirt with Weasel."

Treadmore's voice shook with panic. "It is September. In a few weeks, everything will be frozen. I will die out there."

"You should have thought about that before you started stirring up trouble."

"What kind of barbaric society have you all become? This is still America, isn't it? Don't we still run ourselves by the rule of law, and by democratic principles? Don't we still show mercy and give the benefit of the doubt?"

"Regarding your first question: No, sir, it is not America anymore," the judge said. "America was destroyed by its enemies a little over a year ago and we have no time for political foolishness right now. As to your question about mercy, too many lives are at stake to show mercy to your kind, Treadmore, actual real lives, not statistics, budgets, salaries, or jobs, and certainly not political reputations. At stake are actual people who depend on a smooth working community, and on the harvest you plotted to damage, to survive day to day. You and your associates messed with the ability for us all to eat over the winter. Why should we feed you one scrap of food, or provide a single degree of heat to your cell, when your followers destroyed enough food for several families to make it through the winter? You literally stole food from the mouths of babes. No one has time for the kind of bullshit you brought to our town. No one. Go see if the Chinese or Russians are interested."

"But..."

The judge glanced at the bailiff.

"If he utters another word, the sentence will be changed to execution to be meted out immediately."

Treadmore's lips slapped shut.

Merrill Treadmore moved through the cold autumn forest with all the woodsman skills of a small-town shyster politician with big office dreams. That is to say, he swore and tripped over roots a lot.

He sipped at the recycled one-liter water bottle they had given him, refilled from a partly frozen stream that morning as he headed east, the direction he'd chosen to be released. The water bottle and half a pound of moose jerky he'd had in his room were the only sustenance they let him take. Beyond those, he had the clothes on his back and a small ruck sack with a few of his personal belongings. No weapons or ammo, and no map.

He did not know how far he'd walked. His stomach grumbled. It had been nearly a week. The moose jerky was long gone and he'd had nothing but water for the past couple days. The cold was sucking the energy right out of him. Nights dipped well below freezing he knew, because his water was a chunk of ice every morning. Luckily, he'd been allowed to grab his coat and gloves but hadn't thought to take long underwear. They had not given him time to plan for anything. Five minutes was all he'd been allowed.

Bastards.

His stomach gurgled, protests echoing from its cavernous emptiness. He'd have to find something to eat soon, or he would be too weak to continue on.

When they kicked him out, he had chosen east because that had been the way from which he had come. He figured he might run into other refugees who would help him out, maybe. Worst case, he would come to the Russians and surrender himself. They and he were more likely to be of a similar type of thinking, he told himself. And it would be much better, in his opinion, to be captured by white men than the Chinese. He'd heard too many horror stories about mass killings, and the torture of prisoners among the Chinese.

"I might stand a better chance with the Russians," he mumbled aloud. "At least they eat bread and potatoes instead of rice and fish heads. Their prisoner camps would be better in that regard, if nothing else."

On the eighth day, the fourth with no food, after a bitterly cold night where he lay awake shivering beneath the low-hanging branches of a spruce tree to protect him from the light snow flurries that had started to drift down, he found a camp. Its occupants had apparently succumbed to the elements. A man, two women, and three children, all locked in an icy embrace. They had a tent set up and had huddled inside for warmth, the children in the middle. Now they were frozen solid, entwined in a blue-skinned death grip. He searched through their belongings, found some food, and immediately ate the dry items, washing them down with his water. The rest, the majority of what they had, was canned goods. But there was no normal can opener he could find, just a small piece of metal with a hooked blade on one end. He had no idea how it worked. He'd have to figure something out. Among the soups, vegetables, and chili, there was a half empty can of baby formula and some coffee, as well as a matchbook with five matches left in it. He put the items in his own bag then glanced back inside the tent at the pale frozen bodies.

The dead man was about his size and wore a pair of baggy sweat pants over what looked like long underwear. His own legs quivered with chill. He reached in to try and remove the sweatpants from the corpse to add the layer to his own clothes. Treadmore tugged at the waistband and they started to come down, but the man's hip was frozen to the ground, catching the pants. He rocked the body, trying to free it. The mass of dead flesh, five frozen bodies intertwined, shook as a whole with the motion. His heart gave a sickening lurch as a sound came from inside the huddle of corpses. A high-pitched plea, like a crying breath. He stared, eyes wide, then dismissed it as the sound of gasses escaping the bodies and continued his grisly work.

He tugged harder. The pants gave a couple inches, then the sound came again. This time, it was clearly a word in a tiny child's voice.

"Water," the small voice said. "Please."

Treadmore backed up and stared into the pile. A cloudy pair of brown eyes stared back.

"Please," the child whimpered, "help me."

Treadmore scrambled to his feet. The eyes remained locked on his. He stared at the child, then hesitated.

She can't survive. I can't take care of her.

"Please," the child rasped.

Treadmore backed out of the tent in a rush, picked up the bag of canned food, and scurried away. The child's mournful sobs followed him until he disappeared into the forest.

✳ ✳ ✳

Treadmore woke with a start, a painful jab in his side driving him from his shivering sleep.

"Who are you?" a voice demanded.

"Roger," Treadmore said, using a pseudonym in case they'd heard of him somehow. He chose the name of the reporter in Valdez who had been about to expose him before the war. "Roger Anderson."

"How long have you been out here?"

"I came up from Valdez a few months ago, been hiding out since spring."

"By yourself the whole time?"

The person talking to him was a young man with a very serious expression. He was armed with an assortment of weapons, and looked like he knew how to use all of them with a high level of skill.

"No," replied Treadmore. "I was with a group when I started, but we got separated."

"When was that?"

"When was what?"

"When did you get separated?"

"Back in June."

"You've been alone out here since June?" The young man ran a wary eye up and down him, his rifle remained trained on his chest. "You look pretty well fed for roaming around the woods for four months."

"I found a stash at a cabin," Treadmore said, indicating the backpack. "This is the last of it."

"What was your telephone number before the war?"

"Huh?"

"Your telephone number." The man glared at him with a cold stare that told him the question was serious.

He gave a number with the Alaska nine-oh-seven area code.

"Alright," the man said, "you pass that test."

"Test?"

"Yeah, a surprising number of Russians don't know the right sequence of numbers in our phone system."

"Oh," Treadmore said.

"So, what is your plan?"

"My plan?"

"Yeah," the young man said, "your plan. Are you intending to stay here alone? Or do you have a specific place you were going?"

"Neither," Treadmore said.

"You can come with us if you like."

"Sounds good." Treadmore grabbed his pack. "Anything is better than being alone out here, especially with winter coming."

"My name is Ben." The young man gave only his first name. He waved an arm and a dozen more young men and boys came out of the woods, carrying weapons, and hard expressions. "We're the Alaska Scouts."

27

Brad

Snow drifted lazily earthward in large, fluffy clusters of flakes. It was mid-October and the white stuff was a week or so early. The good thing about the drop in temperatures, was that the ground was mostly frozen solid, strong enough to easily support the M-973 Small Unit Support Vehicles, shortened to SUSV and pronounced *Sus-Vee*. They had commandeered the wilderness transports from a nearby National Guard Armory along with all the fuel they could carry. The vehicles had little problem moving over most types of terrain, but made much better time when they didn't have to contend with swamps and marshy bogs.

With the wall map and pages of intel on the table in front of them, Brad and John pored over potential winter mission plans, organizing where and when they would attack. Gunnar fed them details of the information the Rangers had collected through the summer.

Months before bringing Brad to Chiknik, John had formed a link with a spy inside Chinese operations. That link had not only let John know where Ice Hammer was, but had become a valuable asset gathering information from the intelligence command and passing it on to a resistance group in the city, who then passed it on to a couple of major groups outside the city, including John's then gradually forming militia, now one of the largest in the state. The information they'd been receiving from that source so far had been very accurate thus far. While there was always the knowledge it might turn out to be a trap, the intel had cost a lot of Chinese lives, and none of it had backfired so far.

Kharzai stepped into the room, pulled up a chair and joined them at the table. His typically crazy smile was both wider and brighter than normal. His entire body seemed to buzz with an electric energy barely contained, threatening to burst from his body in bright blue lightning bolts at any second.

"So," he started, eyes glittering with the overflow of information that seemed about to bubble over the edges if he didn't get it out first, "you wanna know why I am smiling?"

"Jung let you kiss her?" Brad asked.

"No, silly," Kharzai said, "although that would definitely be very nice too."

"You had a good bowel movement," Gunnar said.

"Uh, no."

"That always makes me happy," the Swede said in an almost wistful tone.

"Yeah, but that's not…no."

John looked up from a map he had been marking. "You figured out a way to single-handedly end this war?"

"Close."

"Tell us," Brad said, rubbing the creases between his eyebrows. "The suspense is killing me."

"I found out that General Zhang has a mistress from the local population. Apparently, she's a real looker too. He's put her in charge of setting up food distribution in Anchorage."

"So, how is this information helpful to us?" Brad asked, a look of frustration growing on his face.

"Because he is totally smitten with her," Kharzai replied in an exasperated tone, "and takes her out to restaurants in town on a pretty regular basis, as in once or twice every week."

"So, what?" Brad was not in the mood for comic relief. "You want to go have dinner with them?"

Kharzai let out sigh. "Okay, you're not seeing what I am try-ing to communicate are you?"

"No," Brad said. "Obviously, I'm not seeing it, bro."

"They go out to dinner," Kharzai illustrated the words with hand motions, "in a small motorcade, with limited security, on the streets of Anchorage."

"You want to plan a hit," Gunnar blurted.

"BINGO!!"

"Do you have access to the dates and routes they take?" John asked. "Or their restaurant choices?"

"Would you believe, yes?"

"Is this the same inside source we've been working with?" John asked, leaning forward.

"You got it."

"Are you sure this is not disinformation?"

"Not only is this the same source inside that told you where to find us," Kharzai said, "I actually got to meet him in person. The mysterious man is a Korean American who passes as native Chinese who, would you believe it, I'd met before. He is a CIA plant I worked with on an anti-Al Qaeda operation in western China during the Afghan war many years back. We both recog-nized each other instantly. He is from good American stock, his real father is a retired US Marine, and I'd say we can trust him with no reservations."

"Let's plan it then," Brad said. "When can we take it to them?"

"Full winter is the best time," John said. "We can use the SUSVs to get a full platoon almost all the way to Anchorage, and from there, we can probably hike in the rest of the way and hook up with the local resistance group to get into place."

A knock on the door drew their attention.

"Enter," John called out.

A soldier came in with another man following him, someone Brad, John, and Gunnar had never seen before. The new man was tall and fit, a light-skinned black man with almost Asian features. Kharzai's expression told a different story though. He seemed to recognize the new man right off the bat.

"Sir, this man showed up at the gate this morning with a dozen others and insisted on seeing you."

Kharzai and the new guy stared at each other, their mouths hung open for several seconds before either spoke.

"Mojo?" asked Kharzai, his face twisted in disbelief.

"Al Gul?"

They looked at each other, equally befuddled.

"No one's called me that in a long time," Kharzai said.

"What are you doing here? I saw you die."

"Well, I got better," Kharzai said. "And…now I live here."

He turned to the other three men, sucked in a breath, looked back and forth, then hesitatingly introduced the visitor. "Gentlemen, may I present to you Marcus Orlando Johnson, aka Mojo, retired Master Sergeant USMC. We served in the same theater on a few occasions, in a couple of past life times."

"Welcome, Marcus," Brad said, confused about the 'saw you die' comment, but not wanting to inquire at the moment. "You here to join us?"

"No, sir," Mojo said, "at least not in the manner you're probably thinking. I am the commander of the recon arm of the Fairbanks resistance. We're here to link up with your people and return with a report to Fairbanks on how the situation is down here."

"How many men have you got up there?" asked John.

"About as big as your operation, few thousand including families."

Kharzai offered a chair to Mojo. "How is your wife and the child you had right after our last, uh…encounter?"

"Don't know," Mojo grunted, his face turned hard as granite at the mention. "I was guiding a hunt when it started. Took me a week to get home on foot during the initial invasion. Haven't been able to locate Lonnie and our daughter since."

"I'm so sorry," Kharzai said, his face drew tight, tears welling up in a very uncharacteristic display of emotion. Mojo caught the sincerity, and gave a slow nod of acceptance.

"How are you guys holding out?" John asked in a low voice.

"Decent, but nothing spectacular," Mojo said. "We've been running patrols and ambushes since spring and might be able to get through the winter with the supplies we have, but it'll be hard. A lot of folks won't make it."

"Same here," Brad said. "How big is the enemy force in your area?"

"About ten thousand divided up between the City of Fairbanks, Fort Wainright, Eielson Air Force Base and the Fort Greely Missile Defense Base," Marcus said. "They are mostly Russians, and Russian Federation troops, some Khazakis and Turkmenis. No Chinese up there."

Brad and John described the situation in their area.

"Chinese to the west, Russians to the east," Brad finished. "It's like we're the meat and cheese in a crap sandwich."

"Pretty much," said Mojo. "The thing I can't figure out is how the hell the Russians and Chinese agreed to team up on this. Historically, they have always hated each other with a passion."

"Stranger things have happened," Kharzai said. "But in the end, if we don't kick them both out, they'll start into each other like Hitler and Stalin did way back when."

"So Marcus," Brad said, "you staying a while or passing through?"

"We're going to be passing through pretty soon, but I'd like to stay a week or so and let my men rest up for a bit if you don't mind. We've got our own supplies so we won't have to dig into your stores of food or anything."

"No problem if you do," Brad said. "We've done well enough this year, despite some bad stuff happening. I think we could take care of your guys for a few weeks."

"I really don't want to impose," said Mojo.

"Really, it is the least we can do for our brothers to the north," Brad said.

"When you came in you called Kharzai, Al Gul," Gunnar said. "Why did you call him that?"

"Can I tell him?" Mojo glanced at Kharzai.

"Yeah, I suppose so," Kharzai said, "not like the national secrets thing really makes a difference anymore."

"That was his nom de guerre back in the war on terror," Mojo said, "when he was a CIA asset in deep cover all over the Middle East. Seirim Al Gul."

"The Hairy Demon," John said bluntly.

"Uh, yeah?" Kharzai turned to John, then noticed the hard look on Gunnar's face. "Uh…do I know you guys from something more than here? I don't owe you money or anything, do I?"

"I don't think so, little hairy man," said Gunnar, "and that is probably a good thing for you."

"Seirim Al Gul was the name of one of the top terrorist assassins we were hunting in Afghanistan when we were there," John said. "Slipperiest bastard we never caught."

"Also had a list of war crimes he was wanted for that was more than a mile long," Gunnar said. "They said he was a CIA turncoat who went rogue and killed his handler. Then burned a couple of villages full of civilians and became a terrorist."

"Well, you guys might not have got the full story on that," Kharzai said, physically shrinking into himself as he sat in the chair. "I definitely did not kill my handler, just broke his nose and made a mess of a bar table with his bodily fluids. And maybe kinda cracked his jaw…and possibly a few fingers. But he was definitely alive when I left him. As far as that supposed village burning, it was a Taliban stronghold, and the serious terrorist type of stronghold at that, no love for America in any way, shape, or form in there. The terrorist title they put on me really only held if you were Al Qaeda and I was looking for you, or if you were a CIA agent trying to find me."

Mojo held up a hand. "Trust me guys, I was with him for his last action before this war. He's cool."

"We know," John said. "The CIA asshole who briefed us on the hit for him was a bit too Moto-Moto for the situation, so we always figured it was an internal thing."

Moto-Moto meant unrealistically motivated, or super-fake.

"So," Kharzai tentatively put in, "you guys aren't going to try and collect a bounty on me then?"

"Nah," said Gunnar. "I'll just wait till you piss me off and put a slug into your head from behind one day in the field."

"Oh...uh...cool." Kharzai gave the giant an uneasy grin. The latter reached over and patted his shoulder with a heavy hand.

"Don't worry, crazy man, you've done a good job today, very impressed," Gunnar said, then quoted Dread Pirate Roberts from the classic movie *Princess Bride*. "We'll probably kill you in the morning, though."

"Uh...okay...cool," Kharzai said, giving a portion of his typical smile, although this one nervous and uneasy-ish.

"If we get a vote, I say we come up with some kind of Monty Pythonesque death for him," Mojo said.

"Yeah," said Kharzai, instantly snapping back to his quirky self, "like a bunch of naked women chasing me to the edge of a river then slowly pushing me in with their big squishy breasts?"

"I'm telling Jung," Brad said.

"Oh, no...erase my last statement," Kharzai exclaimed. "Make that Jung slowly pushing me in with her breasts...no, wait...just drop that whole idea, she'd probably do it."

"Okay, back to real life," Gunnar said. "Once you guys are rested up, would you be willing to go on a mission with us?"

"I was kind of hoping you'd ask," Mojo said.

28

Youngmi

Youngmi sat in a large, comfortable chair she had arranged by the south-facing window of the apartment. Steam from the cup of tea in her hands formed billowing white clouds illuminated by the bright beam of sunlight that lit up the room, caressing her face and continuing on to cast a rainbow of color on the far wall as it streamed through the crystal chandelier that hung above the dining table. The piece of perfect blue sky through which the sun peeked was merely a break in the slab of low, heavy clouds from which floated fluffy clusters of snowflakes. She stared out at the early appearance of winter, and wondered if Brad or her sons saw the same snow falling wherever they were.

A wave of emotion knotted her throat and squeezed out a tear from her eye that ran down her cheek before she realized it was there. She closed her eyes and pictured them, her husband and their boys. She could still see every detail of their faces from the last time they'd been together. She remembered the phone conversation with her husband that they'd had moments before the bombs started falling. It hung in her mind word for word.

She thought of her sons. How Jay had looked the last time they'd spoken. How she'd admonished him to lose weight, while quietly thinking how handsome he was with his dark skin, thick black goatee, and handlebar mustache. His easy smile and sparkling eyes were like jewels in her memory's treasure box. Always ready with a joke, a riff on his guitar, or a song that drifted from his beautiful voice. His natural friendliness drew people to him as if they were moths circling his light.

Benjamin had similar dark skin, but usually wore the most serious expressions compared to his brothers. Never severe or cruel, he just always looked like his mind was hard at work grasping the meaning of the universe around him, or grinding away at his beloved math problems. MIT had offered him an early scholarship if he was willing to forego the rest of high school and start right away. Instead, he opted to finish high school so that he could do the last two years of swim team and break the state record in the mile swim. She had been so proud of his restraint.

Ian was the tri-polar opposite of both of his brothers. He was the tallest of the three, nearly six feet before he was even fourteen. Broad shouldered and deep voiced, he was just as likely to get into a fist fight as he was to smile and joke. He was the only one of the three that regularly challenged his mother's authority, and sometimes even his father's, although the occasions were few once he realized his father's seeming meekness was just a veneer that covered a true skill at causing physical pain when necessary. Even with all his macho bluster, when he was feeling down or sick, her rough and tumble youngest son melted into her arms in private, always willing to cuddle, or receive a massage for his tired, aching muscles after a hard swim practice. He was also the best of the three at giving her a foot massage whenever she asked.

Brad. Her husband for nearly three decades. She recalled the thin, muscular Marine corporal she had met in her sophomore year in college. She'd been at a bar with her girlfriends in Korea Town in Los Angeles. They were singing popular tunes to the tinny sounding accompaniment of a karaoke machine, the new fad of the late-eighties, and the last thing she expected in an almost entirely Korean club was to see a white guy with the ubiquitous US Marine Corps high and tight hair staring at her from a stool at the bar.

He was there with a Korean man who had a similar haircut and a mile-wide smile and who was staring at her best friend, Myongju. Myongju saw them staring and, less inhibited than Youngmi, strolled over toward the pair of Marines and told them that if they were brave enough to sing a couple songs with the girls, they would let the men buy them a round of drinks. A year later, Youngmi and Myongju were both pregnant with sons from their respective husbands.

And now while Youngmi had no idea what had happened to Jay, or her other sons, she was passing potentially deadly information from Myongju's first born son to the Alaska resistance, and possibly even to her own husband, Brad, the Ice Hammer.

A knock at the door to the apartment made her jump. The sunlight slowly faded as she pushed the memories into their secret place in her mind, both sun and past obscured by their respective clouds. The room drifted to a dull gray as fresh snow continued to cover the ground inch by inch. It was time for her morning English lessons for the junior officers.

29

Marcus 'Mojo' Johnson

They parked the SUSV below the top of the hill out of sight of whoever may be on the other side. While taking the vehicles risked noise from the diesel engines, it also cut travelling time through the snow to a fraction of what was required to walk the distance. They could also carry a lot more ammo and food, not to mention stay warm on their way to the battle space. They dismounted and clambered up the hill, cresting the top to look down at the city of Palmer where the Chinese had set up their forward operating base, taking over the Matanuska Susitna Borough Building, the seat of government for the region since colonial days in the 1930s.

The city of Palmer, Alaska, was the United States' one and only true colony project, bringing up scores of families from Minnesota, Wisconsin, and Michigan who had lost everything in the Great Depression and granting them forty-acre homesteads as a sub-arctic farming experiment.

Most only lasted a few years and left behind the brutal winters to try and settle elsewhere further south in Alaska, but enough stayed that the town gradually flourished as the bread-basket, or more accurately the potato-and-cabbage basket, of Alaska. From those long past years of experimentation, Palmer remained the seat of government for the Matanuska Susitna Borough, an area roughly the size of West Virginia.

At its peak before the current war, the Mat-Su Valley had over one hundred thousand residents. Now the Chinese Army controlled a wide swath of the area and had set up their largest forward base in Palmer to mount operations against the guerrillas that plagued their hold on the highway system.

Kharzai and Mojo lay side by side at the edge of a rock outcrop beneath a cluster of spruce trees, white over-clothes concealing them against the snow. They stared down into the compound through high-powered binoculars. Guard positions rotated shifts. Patrols moved through the trees just outside the general area. Anti-aircraft and anti-personnel rocket emplacements spiked areas of the grounds of the main building as well as the fields behind and around the land of the United Presbyterian Church. Berms had been built up using their version of Hesco-units, huge steel mesh reinforced plastic bags filled with dirt and stones. These were a lot more than just shopping bags in chicken wire though. Hesco units are huge sacks of very thick plastic, and bomb-resistant steel mesh capable of building walls forty feet high and however many however feet thick one wanted. They could withstand a whole lot of rockets and grenades.

They had already walled off about a quarter of what had been three baseball fields and a soccer pitch. The area looked as if it were being developed in the same style the U.S. military had done at their forward operating bases in Afghanistan and Iraq. About one-third of the space behind the barriers was filled with large wall tents. Columns of wispy blue smoke rose from black metal chimneys jutting from the tent roofs, the heavy canvas shelters were most likely temporary structures until more permanent barracks could be built on the location.

Kharzai knew that many of the original settlers in the area nearly a hundred years previous had spent several winters in barely warm structures just like the ones he was looking at. Spending a winter or two at negative twenty degrees in a canvas tent may well have been why more than half of the original colonists had left within the first five years. To the south of the compound, across the street, the log-walled Presbyterian Church building, a large cross-shaped structure that had stood since colonial days in nineteen-thirty-seven, lay in ruins, a jumble of shattered logs scattered like a lost game of Jenga.

"Here comes someone," Gunnar's deep voice rumbled from behind them. He pointed toward the highway south of the compound then briefly touched the thing at his chest as he had before.

Kharzai noted the gesture then turned to watch a column of Chinese Humvees rolled up, a black suburban in the middle.

"Must be someone big, riding all presidential like that."

The column rolled up to the gate of the base and was quickly waved through, the soldiers snapping to attention, their sergeant threw up a salute the men on the hill could almost hear click across the distance.

"Hrm...could it be the big boss?" Kharzai raised an eyebrow.

The suburban slowed and came to a stop in front of the main building. The Humvees circled it forming a cordon as if to protect the VIP against his own people. They focused their binoculars on the black SUV as the driver opened the rear door. A tall man in his fifties stepped out, general's rank glittered on his shoulder. The general turned back toward the vehicle and reached a hand inside. A moment later a woman stepped out, holding on to his hand. Kharzai studied her. Shapely features, and a well-defined face, she was a very attractive woman, not Chinese though, she looked more like Korean. She smiled at the general as he helped her up and held her arm as they crossed the icy sidewalk and went into the building.

"Ah, the Dragon Lady in the flesh."

"Dragon lady?" Mojo asked.

"Turncoat," Kharzai said. "She's an Anchorage local that was captured by General Zhang's son. Apparently, he thought she looked so much like his dead mom he took her to daddy rather than give her a bullet like all the other middle-aged women."

"That was nice of him," Mojo said.

"Yeah, the son is commander of one of their Special Forces units, and well known for blasting civilians wholesale," Kharzai said. "Otherwise, I hear he enjoys long walks on the beach and bouquets of roses and eating SPAM and drinking cheap wine by the fire."

"Lovely," muttered Mojo. "Sounds like a match made in the stars."

"I hear the son sleeps with a teddy bear," said Gunnar, "and eats crullers while listening to Karen Carpenter when he is alone."

"That's really detailed intel," Mojo said.

"We have a really good mole." Kharzai smiled.

"I made up the teddy bear part," Gunnar said.

"You're just trying to justify your teddy bear, big guy," Kharzai said.

"What, it's cuddly," replied Gunnar.

"You guys planning a hit here?" Mojo asked.

"Eventually," Kharzai said. "Firebombs, mortars, something like that. Problem is we are short on the good armaments for that kind of op. We have tons of explosives and can do IEDs all day long, but other than bows and arrows, we are somewhat limited on our targeted munitions, at least in regards to a big attack. So, we want to make sure we pick the right target. Our strategy right now is to hit convoys and infantry patrols and take their stuff for stockpiling."

"Looks like you could do some good sniping ops from up here."

"We tried, but we don't have the talent for a two-thousand-meter shot. Wherever that guy goes, they have really sophisticated anti-sniper tech running. So far, that tech has taken out three guys who missed their first shot, before they could reload."

"That sucks."

"You were pretty good in the day, Mojo," Kharzai said. "You wanna give it a go?"

"I am just an observer on this mission," Mojo said. "Besides, I don't have my Barrett fifty-cal with me. But maybe next time."

"Alright, I'll hold you to that," Kharzai said. "Seen enough?"

"Yeah."

"Time to head east and check out the Russkies." Kharzai gave that famous shiny smile.

✳ ✳ ✳

"Man, a guy could get used to this riding stuff," Mojo said.

"No kidding," said his team sergeant. "I think this is the longest time I have not had to hump a ruck since the war started."

"Don't you guys have SUSVs up there?" asked Gunnar.

"Oh yeah, we have SUSVs," the sergeant said, "and we have Argos, snow machines, and even plenty of bloody tanks, MRAPs," Mine Resistant Ambush Protected vehicles, "and Humvees, but not a drop of fuel for any them."

"Oh."

"Yeah," said Mojo, "some of our Army guys had managed to protect a huge fuel reserve and held it against the Russians. They held out for several days, but then the Russians took the North Pole refinery and decided they could make new stuff, so they bombed the crap out of the existing dump. Over six hundred soldiers died, as well as a couple hundred civilians caught in the blast wave. You could see the mushroom cloud from fifty miles away. Biggest explosion I have ever witnessed, and I've seen some big ones. Looked like a nuke."

"Wow," said Kharzai.

"Yeah, wow," said Mojo. "We've been straight leg infantry ever since. Don't think I ever walked this much in twenty plus years in the Corps combined."

The vehicles pulled to a stop amid a stand of birch trees. The white shell of the SUSVs blended in with the newly fallen snow and paper-white birch bark. The men inside rolled out of the vehicles and set a perimeter, crouching in the shin deep snow, nearly invisible in their white smocks as they listened for any indication that their approach had been detected.

The sounds of the forest quickly returned to normal once the wild inhabitants were satisfied that the recent arrivals probably meant them no harm. As the humans came to accept that there was no impending firefight about to erupt, they rose and moved east on foot, toward Glennallen, the heart of which was twenty miles distant, well within absolute Russian control.

According to their map and compass bearings, they were nearly at the halfway point to the small town when the sound of a convoy moving slowly westward on the highway rattled through the trees a few hundred yards ahead on the curving Glen Highway. They turned toward the sound.

Kharzai raised an eyebrow as he again saw Gunnar touch something at his chest as they made their way towards the enemy.

Soon, they were at the edge of the forest. They took positions high on a ridge that overlooked the highway. The men lay in wait, watching from behind cover. After a few minutes of staring at an empty road, a vehicle patrol came into view. It consisted of a collection of half a dozen TIGR recon vehicles, similar to the American Humvee, with a Ural Typhoon MRAP, *Mine Resistant, Ambush Protected* vehicle, at each end. Mojo could see the soldiers joking and smiling inside the lead vehicles and let out a short, exasperated sigh.

"Damn," he grunted, "they look well fed and confident. Apparently, we've not disrupted their supply lines well enough."

"We hit a group a couple months ago that was actually playing around in the woods," Gunnar said, "actual boyish frolicking, as if there wasn't even a war on. Until we killed most of them."

"Looks like they are feeling pretty confident that they have the upper hand," Mojo said. A movement in the woods a hundred yards ahead of the Russians snatched at the corner of Mojo's eye.

He slid his binoculars that direction and caught sight of another man in a position similarly camouflaged to theirs, watching the column through binoculars of his own. The man was Caucasian, dark hair, sharp nose, square featured, and looked like he'd lived in the forest for a long time. The glint in his eyes and granite-like expression had professional soldier written all over it, probably a special forces operator before the war. Or maybe a merc, short for mercenary.

The man made a hand gesture to someone out of view. The way the gesture was made answered Mojo's question. The man was definitely a merc, probably Brit or Irish.

The merc turned as another person drew near. A grubby-looking young man, with a muscular jaw and a scar running up his arm crouched beside him. The man, boy actually as he was not much more than seventeen or eighteen, leaned in and listened to what the merc said, then crept across the hill through the snow with wolf-like stealth.

"Hey, guys," Mojo whispered to the others and pointed. "Southwest hill, two o'clock high."

"Got it," hissed Kharzai. "Ooooh…ambush?"

"Looks like it."

"Want to join?" Mojo's sergeant asked.

"No," said Mojo, "they don't know we're here. We'd most likely get ourselves shot up."

"We can always be the cavalry if they get into trouble though," Gunnar said.

"They don't look like they'll need much help," replied Mojo.

He followed the line of sight from the man high up on the hill to the convoy, passing over what looked like several very well-camouflaged positions with cleared lanes of fire through the trees toward the highway.

"Those guys have seriously prepped this road," Mojo said. "This is like textbook Special Forces work."

"Holy cow," muttered Kharzai gazing intently through his own binoculars, "they've got claymores in the trees and det-cord all over the place."

The convoy continued forward until they reached a point in the road where the forest grew directly beside the narrow shoulder. The whispery silence of the winter afternoon exploded with a body-slamming percussive symphony of massive proportions.

Several huge trees from both sides of the road crashed down onto both ends and the middle of the convoy.

Something splashed across the windscreens of both MRAPs.

The occupants reacted in an instant panic, doors flying open only to find themselves engulfed in the bright flash of gasoline flame. The high-pitched squeals of men on fire reached all the way up to their observation point. Mojo and the others cringed at the pain in their screams. Even though they were the enemy, it was hard to watch and listen to another man burn to death.

Soldiers in the other vehicles quickly dismounted while being covered by the mounted heavy machine guns and grenade launchers. A dozen or more men fell in a fusillade of automatic weapons crossfire. The Russians returned fire, tearing up the woods, faces grimaced in rage and fear as they poured thousands of rounds into the forest in the direction of the resistance fire.

Thirty seconds later, utter silence.

The kind of silence only heard after a hell-storm.

After a quick inventory of vehicles and men, two squads of Russian soldiers rushed into the forest, one on either side of the highway. The remainder set about with chainsaws to remove the trees that blocked their way.

Their medics worked on the wounded.

They pushed one vehicle that was damaged beyond repair onto the shoulder.

Fifteen minutes later, the soldiers from the group that had run off into the trees to the south of the road returned. The strolled up out of the forest, spreading out as they drew near. A burly sergeant stepped out from beside a TIGR and pointed his finger in a manner anyone who ever served in the military would recognize. The soldier he berated tilted the muzzle of his rifle upwards and shot his face off.

The column erupted in more gunfire as the returning soldiers opened fire on their mates. Mojo looked closer. The men who had returned, were not the same who'd left. They wore only the jacket and helmets of the Russians, and carried their weapons. They wore an odd assortment of trousers and foot gear. The rest of the rebel force charged in. Russian turret gunners falling prey to relentless and accurate sniper fire. The squad of Russian soldiers who'd gone north of the highway came back to aid their comrades only to be cut down in the confusion, both by their own men and the rebel fighters.

Within minutes, the Russians were finished, annihilated almost to a man. A handful of wounded tried to crawl into the trees to find a hiding place, perhaps hoping for rescue. One of the young rebels slid a nasty-looking hatchet out of his belt, something that looked like a Viking's fantasy weapon. Rather than end these wounded men with a precious bullet, he played Whack-A-Mole on their heads with his blade. A frightening smile stretched from ear to ear each time he split a skull. Several times, he had to put his boot on the dead man's head to hold it down so as to extract his blade when it became lodged in their skulls.

Moments later, the bulk of the rebels ran into the forest laden with new rifles, cases of ammunition, grenades, and Russian MRE meals. Two of the older men used some of the enemy's explosives to set charges on the fuel tanks of the vehicles before vanishing into the wilderness.

Eight minutes after the rebels had vanished, explosions rocked the ground on which Mojo and the others lay hidden.

When the dust settled and silence had returned to the highway, they scanned the destruction left in the middle of the road.

"Umm, wow," Kharzai muttered. "That was kind of impressive."

"No kidding," replied Mojo. "I believe they will be my next rendezvous."

30

Kharzai

"**S**ure you don't want to come with us to meet these guys?" Mojo asked. "We should be able to link up with them in a week or so, maybe share some intel."

"No, not this time," Kharzai said. "By the time we get back to Chiknik, we'll already be a week or more past our scheduled return. I've got an idea of their area and we'll come looking for them later in the season. If you connect with them, let them know about us though. Maybe they can initiate contact if they're in our AO (area of operations)."

The two groups parted company and moved in their opposite directions. Kharzai felt an unsettling guilt in his belly. These were Brad's sons. He knew it. The hatchet man's bodily movements looked uncannily like Brad's own. The body shape, the charming smile, the slope of his back and shoulders as he swung his hatchet into the enemy's skull, all looked like a thirty-year-younger version of Brad. Add in the dark hair, skin tone, almond eyes, and generally half-Asian features, and there was no mistaking him.

The young leader, the one who'd spoken with the merc commander, was also almost definitely Brad's son, the one they'd seen more than a year earlier in a field escaping from the Chinese platoons near the Knik glacier, at the battle that made Brad infamous. He'd gotten a clear look at the boy's face then, and although he looked a lot different now, harder, changed by the violence of war, he was certainly Brad's son Ben.

Kharzai had made a relatively long living in a very bloody profession in deep cover within tribal warlord organizations of the Middle East and Central Asia, where sons and cousins were the extensions of their fathers and uncles by being able to identify not only immediate relatives but even general accomplices by sight in order to avoid getting a not-so-proverbial knife in the back. He'd be willing to bet his life that these were definitely Brad Stone's missing sons.

If I tell him that I found his sons, will he try to leave? Will Sammi and their baby be enough to make him stay with Chiknik? Or should I just keep it to myself until a more stable time? Dang, I wish I had psychic fortune teller prophetic powers to know what was best for the future.

"These guys were not only hard core, they were cold blooded," Gunnar said as they broke down the long mission to Brad and John.

"Men after my own heart," Kharzai said, a wistful look on his face.

"But some of them were only children," Gunnar added. "Thirteen or fourteen years old maybe. That kid with the hatchet was tall, but could not have been over fifteen maybe, looked like he'd never taken a razor to his face."

He paused and took a breath, the others waited as it was clear the big man had more to say.

"I have to say," his voice rumbled like it was coming from a deep cave, "there are few things in life that really scare me, but that kid is one of them. He's going to have to be put down like a rabid dog when this thing is over."

"Yeah well, that's what gets the job done in this environment," Kharzai said. "Besides, my former employers would always have a nice job with a cushy salary and generous retirement package for guys like him. Trust me, I know such things from experience."

"Any idea who they actually are?" John asked.

"Hard to say." Gunnar refilled his glass and the glasses of the others at the table with the homemade birch sap and barley beer the village brewers had recently perfected. He took a sip and smacked his lips in satisfaction then went on. "The one adult I saw looked like he was in his middle to late forties. Probably retired SF or a Merc or something."

Kharzai glanced at Brad, pursed his lips, screwed up his eyes, then hissed out a breath and said, "They might be your boys, the scouts that escaped."

"What?" Brad sputtered.

"They were unusually young, as a group that is. And they were pretty well disciplined, as one would expect Boy Scouts to be."

Brad's face fell slack, numb-looking.

"No guarantees, Kemosabe. I'm just saying they fit the description and possible location."

"Boy Scouts." John's eyebrow's knitted as he set his own beer glass down.

"Two of my sons were at the Scout camp in Chugiak when the war started," Brad said. "Me and Kharzai came upon the bodies of several dozen boys and men at the camp a week later, but my boys as well as their troop members and scout masters were not there. We caught up to them at the Knik glacier a couple days after that, but a recon drone had spotted them and a pair of choppers full of Chinese soldiers showed up not long after. We drew them off, but a bunch more boys died fighting off one of the helicopters as they ran. I figured they were heading toward the eastern wilderness, maybe Glennallen. But I don't know if they even survived that day, let alone made it to where you saw this group."

"Hard to say." Kharzai nodded. A silence grew in the room, not mournful as much as respectful.

"You want to tell them the other news?" Gunnar said after a few seconds.

"Other news?"

"Palmer? Zhang? Dragon Lady?"

"Oh! That news," Kharzai said, the sparkle returning to his eyes immediately, glad to not have to divulge his true thoughts about the boys he'd seen. "We may have a great opportunity here."

"Oh?" said John.

"Okay," said Kharzai, "remember how I was telling you that General Zhang has a mistress handing out goody bags to the people of Anchorage?"

"Yeah."

"Well, we discovered two things about her." He paused as if building anticipation. The mood was all wrong and it just became awkward.

"And...?" Brad said, his mind still on the hope of his boys being alive.

"Right," Kharzai continued, dropping a note in his tone. "One: She's seriously smokin' hot! I mean...man, was she hot!"

"Confirmed," put in Gunnar. "I'm not into the Asian look in general, no offense to your wife Brad, but she was definitely a ten plus."

"General Zhang's preference in women," John said, "does not exactly provide a tactical advantage for us."

"Well, in this case it does, with this specific woman," Kharzai said. "He apparently is so enamored with her that he actually takes her to forward operating bases, like their Palmer Ops center."

"Still not seeing it," Brad said.

"In an executive suburban," Kharzai added, eyebrows stretching farther.

Brad gave him a blank stare.

"Which means he probably does the same around town." His eyebrows stretched further yet, looking like thick black caterpillars arching their backs.

"Get to the point."

"I am," Kharzai said. "You're just not listening!"

Brad twisted his face in confusion. "Tell me what I am missing."

"Like I mentioned when we first learned about her, psychological warfare," exclaimed Kharzai. "We find a time and place to hit him while he's with her. Even if the suburban is armored, we can hurt them bad enough to maybe take them both out of operation."

"Why do we want to take her out?" Brad asked. "You said all she does is run the food distribution program."

"Because she is making him look legit to the people they are doling out the food to, that's why."

"Makes sense," John said. "Hit the pretty face for the collaborator she is, slow down the food distro, and that makes them look bad."

"It could backfire on us though," Brad said. "If she is liked among the common people, then hurting her may turn them against the resistance."

"If nothing else, we can seriously shake up their security by hitting him," Gunnar said, "with or without her."

"True that," John said. "If he is comfortable enough to bring his mistress with him that close to the front lines, then he thinks he is secure anywhere. I think the best thing would be if we can find a way to hit him in the city, on his own turf, where his guard is likely to be down. Even if we failed to kill him, we'd still force them to provide massive security upgrades to his own entourage."

"Alright," Brad said. "Putting it that way, I see the sense of it. Start planning and get the opportune time figured out with your contact inside his HQ."

31

Ping

"Sir," said the captain, "we have no available drones at this time. We are waiting for an ammo shipment. And without clear video from the satellites as to what is down there and authorization from Colonel Quai, I am not authorized to fire a missile. Perhaps you can get assistance from the Air Force with a fighter jet or a drone."

"I have already been to Colonel Quai's office and the only thing they had to say was that all of their craft are either on missions already or in maintenance." Colonel Ping ran his hand through his hair in an effort to control his patience. He held up a piece of paper clenched tightly in his hand and pointed with the other hand toward the window past the two enlisted technicians sitting at the launch console. Outside stood a pair of multi-rocket launchers, each loaded with four large surface-to-surface missiles, "I have coordinates, you have missiles. You must launch on these now."

"I am sorry, sir, I cannot," replied the captain, his stern expression seeming to take a personal edge of defiance toward Ping. "General Zhang explicitly said that we are not to launch without a visual on the target, either satellite or human eyes via radio."

Ping glared at the missile commander, ice forming in his voice. "I am the general's oldest comrade, his right-hand man. Are you refusing my order, Captain?"

The atmosphere in the room sizzled with tension; hairs prickled on the younger soldier's necks as they listened to the exchange. The technicians turned in their chairs to stare wide-eyed as their captain stood his ground.

"Sir, I am simply following the required protocol that orders us to have visual on target before any launch, to make sure there is no waste of munitions."

"I have, in my hand, solid intelligence that the enemy is in that valley, and with that evidence in mind, I am ordering you to fire on these coordinates right now, Captain."

"Sir, no disrespect, but even you are required to go through the chain of command to request a fire mission. You cannot come in here directly and order me to fire," the captain replied with a firm tone, holding his ground against the infamous Colonel Ping, commander of the Intelligence Command. He was damned if he was going to burn for this asshole's bad judgment. "Put in the request for a fire mission to the operations center. Colonel Quai will approve or disapprove it and send it to me to fire once we have visual."

Ping sucked in a breath, then growled with barely controlled anger, "This is time sensitive and must be done now."

"I am sorry, sir, you must follow the chain of command. I am not willing to be punished for your sake for breaking protocol."

The skin on Ping's face boiled to a deep shade of purple.

"Captain," he hissed, "I could have you shot for disobeying my direct order."

"No, sir, you cannot. You are not in my direct chain of command."

Ping shouted over the captain's shoulder to the young soldier at the console. "Corporal, launch your missile at these coordinates."

He started past the captain's desk toward the technician. The captain raised a hand and pushed back against Ping's chest, calling back to his men in response, "If either of you fires a missile,

178

I will have you shot, which *I* can legally do, as I am your direct commander."

Ping's eyes twisted in rage as he looked down at the younger man's hand on his chest.

"Colonel, you must leave now or I will call security to have you escorted out under arms."

Ping slapped the captain's arm away from his chest then smacked him across the face so hard it instantly raised a finger-shaped welt on the officer's cheek and sent him spinning.

"You do not give me orders!"

The captain regained his balance and moved for his desk, reaching for the panic button beneath the lip. Before he could summon the armed security patrol from their guard house a hundred yards away, Ping snatched up a heavy paper weight from the desk surface and struck him on the head, dropping him like a sack of rocks.

The colonel turned to the two young soldiers at the console. The corporals, neither more than twenty years old, stared back, cowed and shivering.

"Load these coordinates and fire four missiles on them."

The men gaped, turned toward their commander, then back at Ping.

"Do I need to kill you as well?"

"No, sir!" said one of the corporals, his voice shaking with terror.

The colonel stepped up and handed him the grid coordinates. The tech put them into the system and armed the launcher. Then got up and moved toward the captain.

"What are you doing?" Ping demanded. "Sit down and fire the missile!"

"Yes, sir, I need the captain's launch key for it to work. It takes all three of our keys to authorize a launch so there are no mistakes."

"Hurry up!"

The corporal squatted beside the captain and pulled the key chain from his neck, lifting it around his head. The captain let out a light moan as the soldier gently lowered his head back to the floor. He moved back to his console, sat in the chair, and inserted the captain's key into the center panel, then turned it to the armed position. He put his own key in the system and motioned for his partner to do the same. The two of them counted down and turned their keys at the same time. The console beeped and red lights glowed bright at all three panels, indicating the warheads were armed. The corporal flipped up the cover over the commander's firing button, put his finger over the red cube, and with a moment's hesitation, sucked in a deep breath, then pressed.

With a whoosh, one missile fired off vanishing into the air trailing a white vapor trail.

"Only one launched!" Ping raged. "I told you to fire four!"

"Yes, sir, Colonel. On this model, we have to re-arm for each rocket. It can only fire one at a time."

Ping rolled his eyes. "Incompetent idiots!"

In a blur of motion behind Ping, the semi-conscious captain's hand shot up and hit the alarm button under the desk, then dropped back to the floor as if the effort to move sucked every last ounce of energy out of him. An alarm sounded outside the building and the panel suddenly locked, refusing to respond to anything the corporals did. Ping spun around and kicked the captain in the ribs, sending his eyes wide as the pain of breaking bones shocked his system into momentary consciousness. Ping hustled out the door and marched off before the guards crossed the space to the fire control shed.

32

Sammi

School had been in session for more than two months. One would think that the children of Chiknik would have loved being free from school all year long, but the reality, as most parents know as the end of summer vacation draws near, was that they yearned to be doing something, especially as the weather got colder and fewer games could be played outside. The smiles of the children, both in class and out, were an absolute treasure, raising the spirits of everyone who watched their classes. As Sammi's belly showed obvious signs of her pregnancy, the children had gotten into the habit of saying hello to the baby every morning, and goodbye every afternoon as they went home. At the end of the school day, which ran from ten AM to four PM to take advantage of the most sunlight for the children to walk in when winter came fully upon them, the children came out of their classes and walked to the door of the small school house, where she and senior principal Anders stood to say good day. As they passed, most of them rubbed Sammi's belly with a hand, or put their faces close to her soccer ball-sized six-month baby house and speak directly to the child inside.

"Bye, bye Mrs. Sammi's baby," some said.

"Can't wait to play with you, little baby," others called out to her baby bump.

The children ran outside and hustled toward their waiting parents or directly to their homes. Steam puffed over their heads in the cold air like tiny train engines. A dusting of what was probably the first permanent snow of the season had settled on the ground, the temperatures outside indicating it was not going to thaw again until spring. As the mercury dropped, the heating stoves in each classroom, converted fifty-five-gallon drums with a chimney that rose through the ceiling, had quickly become the favorite places. Students would rush to class to be the first ones there so they could get a desk near the heat. Eventually, the teachers had to make a roster to make sure everyone who wanted it got their day in the warm spot every week. The presence of the Chiknik Coal Mine just a few miles north of the town made the area mostly self-sufficient. Massive piles of coal had been dug up and bunkered in huge warehouse-like buildings equipped with conveyor belts to feed the coal chutes for dumping it into train cars or dump trucks, or even personal pickup trucks for resale shortly before the war began. It had gotten the town through last winter, and would definitely be sufficient for this winter, and probably most of next. If this war lasted longer than that, which seemed likely, they would need to get people into the mines to bring up new coal. For this year though, between wood and coal, they should be able to keep everybody warm enough.

Sammi looked back into the building as the last of the students filed out of the school on their way home. One of the parents waiting outside to pick up their child signaled to the principal.

"I am going to take off, Sammi," Principal Anders called to her as she waved back. "Maxine's mom had asked me to come over for dinner tonight. Can you lock up?"

"Sure, no problem," Sammi said.

As the principal walked off with her friend, a lone student came straggling out of the bathroom. Little Luke Thomas, a first grader, always seemed to be running to catch up to the rest of the kids. He wasn't slow by any means, his intelligence was probably well above average, he was just always distracted. Luke was one of those kids who spent his class time with his mind in another universe, only to have to spend his playtime doing the work he neglected during class. He reminded Sammi of the kid in the old Bugs Bunny cartoon that spent all his time day dreaming, looking out the window and imagining himself as a bird or a super hero or whatever struck his fancy at the moment.

"Hope you don't make her hiccup too much," Luke shouted to Sammi's belly as he bolted out of the school, his loud voice made the baby jump inside her womb. "'Cuz she looks funny when she hiccups."

The little boy stepped out the front door, a big smile spread across his face as the last rays of the early winter sun shone across the schoolyard.

The next things that registered in her mind were a flash of light and catching Luke in her arms mid-air. A blink later, she was staring up at faces above her own. Deep lines creased the foreheads, and pushed their lips into a rictus of terror. Mouths moved but no sound came out. She stared wide eyed. Panic spread through her, sending a painful tingle down her limbs as she realized her lungs were not expanding. The panic stretched time to an infinitesimally slow sequence of events. Faces talking but she could not hear anything they were saying. Shadows of movement like a stop motion video from the early nineteen hundreds flashed around her in a nonsensical blur. Suddenly, bells started clanging in her head and every joint pulsed with an ache as if someone had shoved a sliver of ice cold steel between each of her bones. Her belly constricted in tight bands that threatened to choke off her blood supply. It felt as if her abdomen had transformed into stone.

"The baby," she gasped as she sucked in a breath.

"It's alright," Jung said, her voice distant, barely audible even though she was only inches away, "you're not bleeding, you should be fine."

"Please let the baby be okay," Sammi said, choking sobs back. She felt a tug against her arms and she realized she was no longer holding Luke to her chest. "Oh God! Luke, Lukey! Is Lukey okay!?"

"He's breathing," a voice said.

"Keep it that way," said another.

"Someone get Ice Hammer," said a third voice.

"He's on the way," said the first.

Sammi suddenly let out a cry as her belly grew even harder. The pain was unlike anything she'd ever felt before, like a blacksmith were slowly hammering abdomen flat, folding it over, then hammering flat again. She grabbed Jung's hand and squeezed as the air pressed out of her lungs, unable to inhale or exhale.

"Oh no," the older woman insisted. "You're not having the baby now Sammi, not now."

She twisted her head, eyes wide with panic as she tried to find Luke, to catch sight of him. Her belly constricted again.

"Please, God, no," Sammi grunted.

The pain subsided, but her muscles quivered with a tension that told her it would not stay gone long. She breathed as though the air was only a temporary commodity, that she had to stock up on for the next shortage. That shortage came abruptly a few minutes later as another wave of contractions washed her in a tsunami of pain that seemed ready to overcome her. It rose to a crescendo that had her fearing her heart would explode at any moment, only to suddenly subside. She gasped a lung full of air as she fell into the abyss between waves.

"Look here, young lady," Jung ordered, her voice stern like a scolding mother, "you are not having this baby for another four months. It is as simple as that. Your mother would not allow it, so neither can I. You have to hold it in and bake it all the way through, or she will be so mad at me when I see her in heaven."

Sammi responded by way of a grunt as another wave of contractions washed over her with pain that seemed exponentially more intense, nearly surpassing her assumed ability to cope every time it struck. Sweat poured from her brow as the air escaped her lungs. Her heart swelled to double size, breath jamming in her chest.

"Where is she!" Brad's voice called out from the distance.

"Over there," someone replied.

He was by her side in an instant, holding her hand and whispering unintelligible words against her belly. She could feel the rumble of his voice against her abdominal muscles. Instantly, the baby in her womb calmed, the contractions stopped, and her breathing relaxed.

"You're okay, Sammi," Brad breathed into her ear. "You're okay, my love. Baby's okay, too. Just relax. All is good."

A tiny voice called out from across the room, "Mrs. Sammi, I'm alright. Is your baby hurt?"

"No, Luke," she panted in reply, "the baby is good. Its daddy is here to take care of us. Are you okay, Luke?"

"I am okay," the boy replied, his voice barely audible from across the hall.

"Let's go, Luke," said a soothing voice. "Let's go see the doctor; he needs to patch up your scratches."

Sammi sat up with help from Brad and leaned against the wall. The contractions were over. Her baby was not going to come now.

She glanced over in Luke's direction. A man was lifting him up. Another man stood nearby holding his pants up with one hand while he reached down to pick something up, a denim-colored object with what looked like a dirty shoe hanging from one end, like a tiny odd-shaped hockey stick. Sammi suddenly noticed the man's belt was missing. Then she saw the brown leather band squeezed tightly around the stump of Luke's thigh.

"I'll be okay, Mrs. Sammi," Luke said as the men carried him out of the school, his voice growing weaker by the moment. "The doctor will patch me up just fine."

* * *

"So, what was it? A drone strike? Artillery?" Brad paced the office. Anger seethed visibly through veins that pulsed in his neck as if he had serpents swimming in his blood. "How the hell did we have no warning, with your source supposedly being so well connected?"

"Had to be a drone or rocket," said John. "There is no artillery within range of us, even their best stuff is ten miles too far back."

"I don't know how we got no word, boss," Kharzai said apologetically. "I really don't know, except to say that sometimes things get past even the most diligent spy, as I can well attest. More than likely there was no advanced planning. Just a last-minute order."

"Do they actually know where we are," Brad demanded, "or was this just a fluke?"

"No idea," Kharzai said, "but we need to get some defenses up ASAP."

"We can get the missile system up for air defense and start having someone watch it full time," Gunnar said. "But that would leave us open to them sensing that system's radar array, and they'd be on us for sure after that."

"That blast was lucky," John said. "If they knew what they were aiming at, they could've easily caused serious damage, which tells me two things."

"Talk to me, General," Brad said.

"First, that shot was based on intel that they only know *approximately* where we are."

"Obviously."

"Second, it was less than accurate thanks to the surrounding mountains and likely had poor or no satellite coverage."

Kharzai spoke up. "Satellites usually work pretty well." He'd had his own experience with satellite-guided missiles and their all-too-perfect accuracy when the CIA hit the building his fiancé had been in.

"Yes," John said, "but the Chinese intentionally screwed up our satellites, some of which were shared with their own. If the virus they put in ours somehow got into theirs by the various spyware they've always had running, that might screw up their own stuff, right?"

"Another option," said Gunnar, "is that they are out of fuel for their drones and fighters and are relying on guess work. Maybe one of their officers had something to prove and just forced a single launch on an 'almost target' just to check off a box on a list. Our guys used to do stuff like that in Afghanistan to expend ammunition when a unit was rotating out or a base was closing just so the Hajjis wouldn't get their hands on it."

"Hrm…" Kharzai rubbed his fingers on his chin. "Maybe so."

"Whatever it was," John continued, "if their satellites and drones are having a hard go of it, maybe our eighties technology missile defense system which relies on ground-based radar instead of satellites might actually be accurate enough to blow their arrows out of the sky before they hit their mark."

"I want to do more than just defend ourselves," Brad said in low, almost growling, voice. "That bastard wants to hit us when we've done nothing but try to survive. He killed my first wife, and maybe my sons, and now he wants to kill my new wife and child. I want to take a missile straight to him and blast him and his turncoat bitch to kingdom come."

"Well," said Kharzai, "that's certainly an admirable objective."

"Make it happen."

"Aye, aye, sir," said Gunnar.

33

Winter preparations had been completed just as the real snow started in. Those more permanent flakes of the white stuff took residence a few weeks earlier than normal. Fish, moose, caribou, and bear meat hung in cellars below the various buildings, most was smoked and dried, but some had been salt cured using what salt was available for such things. Since Alaska had no inland salt mines and could only rely on sea salt, Chiknik, nearly one hundred miles inland, was very low on that commodity.

They had canned as many of the vegetables and fruits as they could with the limited number of mason jars and new tin cans available. Much of the rest of what they had for storage was dehydrated. Some of the cellars had been dug deep enough into the permafrost, the layer of soil several feet beneath the surface where the ground never thawed out on its own, that items could be kept frozen in them year round. Some of the vegetables were also pickled in homemade vinegars. Many berries were preserved as jellies, but a significant amount was also bottled as wine and spirits for the long winter nights.

As Brad pored over the records and inventory lists, he felt like they were as ready as they could be, but they were nowhere near ready as they needed to be for the number of people the camp had swollen to over the summer, not to mention those who added to the population on a weekly basis. They simply did not have enough to survive the whole winter if people kept coming in. And no one had the heart to turn people away.

He racked his brain, as well as the minds of the village council members, three men and three women who'd been elected to serve the three districts of the fast-growing settlement. As the debates went back and forth, they ranged from refusing more refugees, to culling Chiknik of all the old, sick, and handicapped since they were a burden to the community. The individual that had that particular brainstorm got a 'come to Jesus' moment from a couple of the other council members.

Before any solid ideas were presented by the council, one of the Ranger patrols returned from a long-distance recon mission that had taken them all the way to the Palmer base of the Chinese army for a status update. As the group was debriefed and were told about the potential serious food shortage before winter was out, a very sharp sergeant who'd been halfway through chiropractic school before the war stood up in the rear and raised his hand. Daryl Chalifour qualified to be an officer due to his education or to have a professional exemption and serve on the clinic staff as a doctor with his medical background. But the tall muscular former competitive powerlifter with the constantly positive attitude convinced Kharzai and Gunnar that he would be better able to serve as a Ranger medic, who could perform advanced medical procedures in remote locations far from home. With much cajoling and lobbying, he convinced them and was assigned as one of the senior medics with the Rangers where he taught the others many advanced techniques in both combat medicine and physical therapy and spinal manipulation.

Kharzai motioned to Daryl's raised hand, "Yes, Doc D., whatcha got?"

"We saw a massive stock pile of supplies in Palmer, all around the borough building. More than what we saw on the patrol with Mojo and his guys, much more. And the way it is laid out, it looks like they've a bunch more coming too," he said. "The way I see it, it seemed like they're prepping to significantly enlarge the base in there. They've got a bunch more Hesco units going up than they did in October with huge piles of empties waiting to be filled. It's like they're building a fortress over there. And like I said, we saw stock piles of what looks like pallets of food and water. It was all laying, barely guarded, out in the wide open on the baseball fields, waiting for us to snatch it right up."

"How are their defenses?" asked Brad.

"Minimal," said the captain next to Daryl, the Ranger commander who went only by the nom-de-guerre Jephthah, from the Old Testament story of Jephthah the Warrior from the book of Judges. When he spoke, his voice came out low and dark, like wisps of black smoke curling from a chimney, gliding its way to the listener's ears in the most intimidating way imaginable, even when he was in a jovial mood. Between voice and demeanor, and his brutal skill as a leader of Rangers, most of the other men assumed Jephthah had been some type of Special Operations soldier or perhaps a contract mercenary with the Army. Whatever his past, Jephthah inspired his men and was always successful in his missions and fierce to his enemies. "I was kind of surprised actually. We first saw their construction more than a month ago, and they're just now adding to the buildup. It looked as if they thought there was nobody to worry about. They're too confident. Like Daryl said, they had their supplies practically in the open."

"Could it be a trap?" asked John.

"I don't know, sir," said Captain Jephthah. "It could possibly be a trap, but to be honest it looked more like a supply line FUBAR *(fouled up beyond all repair or recognition, most often starting with a different f-word in known mature audiences)* where they sent the supplies before the troops even got there. I've seen it happen with multiple armies and in multiple war zones, where they do too much preparation ahead of time and the supply guys ended up feeding the enemy instead of their own troops."

"Might be," said Kharzai. "It could be a risk worth taking to get a closer look."

"Definitely worth checking out," Gunnar said. "Never hurts to try and steal the bully's lunch money before he gets ours."

John nodded. "Let's send a company of Rangers out and do just that, Top."

"On it," Gunnar grunted in reply.

34

Major Po Zhang

Sergeant Lung raised a fist, held it in the air ten seconds, then slowly lowered it as he slowly dropped his own body into forest undergrowth. The signal was repeated back along the line of men, each fire team forming a small perimeter, facing their pre-assigned directions until the whole company was bristling like a fifty-meter-long, fat, poisonous centipede on the eastern side of the Talkcetna Mountains, looking over the Matanuska Valley.

Smoke rose in the distance in a quantity that made an unmistakable sign pointing like an arrow in the bright blue sky, straight down to a very large village. Rising into the air like a hazy pillar, there was far too much smoke to camouflage. By its density, Major Zhang thought that it looked more like coal smoke than wood smoke. An established settlement for sure. Just as had been reported in the intel briefing two weeks earlier, it marked the rebel's position like a giant arrow pointing to the top of their heads.

Zhang did not understand exactly how satellite imagery worked; he'd always assumed it was just pictures of what was actually there. Therefore, he could not understand how the scientists and analysts that worked with his sister at headquarters could not decipher their imagery for what it obviously was from his perspective here on the ground. A huge village, no…a city.

From the distance, he could smell the wood and coal fires that heated the buildings and cooked their food. Other than the smoke though, he could make out no actual buildings through the trees. They probably had few, if any, buildings over one story, or perhaps they were living underground or in earthen shelters like the hobbit holes from the fantasy movies he'd seen before the war.

Zhang whispered into his radio, "Sergeant Lung, what is the holdup?"

"Sorry, sir," the sergeant whispered back, "thought I saw movement to our right. Looked like a man, but may have been a bear."

"A man bear," said Zhang.

"Maybe it was bigfoot," muttered the soldier next to him. Zhang glared at the young man, who immediately shrank into himself, then resumed his watch outside the line.

"If you cannot still see this, man, or bear...or bigfoot...then I suggest, Sergeant, you get up and keep moving."

There was a pause, then after a beat, "Yes, Major, must have been a bear that has run away."

Sergeant Lung raised an arm and gave the hand sign to resume. The company rose like ghosts from the forest floor and continued through the trees, making their way toward the smoke.

The cold, hard ground forced them to move painstakingly slow as it resisted their attempts to move without sound. Brittle, dry twigs lay strewn underfoot everywhere as if someone had intentionally sprinkled pallet loads of Rice Krispies along all potential paths while the few inches of recent snow squeaked like Styrofoam packing peanuts with every step.

"What was that?" Zhang's lieutenant hissed as a distant crack sounded. He flung his hand up to halt the column.

They stopped, crouched, and listened. Eyes scanned the forest around them in silence. Puffs of steamy breaths drifted up in shallow streams to keep both visible steam and audible noise to a minimum. Zhang could hear his own heartbeat above the whisper of the arctic wind that crawled through the trees. An odor floated toward them, something of this arctic wilderness, but familiar, not alien to his senses. Fresh. Wild. With a tang of violence.

A crackle of gunshots erupted to their left and in front of them. Half a dozen men dropped like meat sacks to the forest floor, muffled cries of pain rang out on the frigid air as the company collectively dropped behind cover, then returned fire. The air split with the violence of thousands of rounds of five-point-eight-millimeter lead ripping the forest to pieces.

"Cease fire!"

The call repeated down the line.

"Cease fire!"

Men lowered their rifles, dropped their spent or partially spent magazines out of their weapons, and slapped fresh ones in. Several shadows erupted from the nearby trees. Moving like spirits, they pounced on the line, set men screaming in agony, then vanished into the forest before anyone could react.

The fire teams blasted away into the trees where they'd seen the shadows run, rising panic barely contained by their well-trained reflexes. Silence once again fell upon them like a leaden weight. A chill wind blew across the snow-dusted ground, wafting the coppery scent of blood and the acrid sting of gun powder and bodily fluids across their senses. Within less than one minute of contact, they'd used nearly a third of their ammo, and half of his men were down, dead, or injured.

Several seconds passed. The lieutenant slowly rose from his crouched position, and turned back to the men to observe the damage done. A single shot rang out and he collapsed in a heap beside Zhang, the back of his skull opened like a cracked coconut, eyes wide, exposed brain still pulsing as his last moments of life leaked onto the frozen soil.

"Hi there," a voice called out across the empty space before them. "Um, you might not want to come any further this direction, unless you all want to die, that is."

"Who are you?" Zhang shouted back.

"The spirits of the forest, oooooooooh," the voice called back with a comic ghostly sound. "And we're kinda not happy with you guys being here and stuff, ya know?…And will in all likelihood be really not nice to the rest of your men if you don't leave very soon…oooooooooo."

"We will come back with more men and crush you," Zhang shouted.

"No," said the voice, "you won't. Because if you do, we will kill all of them, too. We're only letting you live so you can warn the others."

"Tell Ice Hammer we know where he is now, and we will be back!"

"Ice Hammer?"

"You know who I am talking about!"

"Yes, being the spirits of the forest, we know everything," the voice sounded bored, "but Ice Hammer is not worth your time. He is just a man, kind of a dork actually, computer nerd who got lucky with a few shots, I think. I am the one you should worry about."

"Who are you?" Zhang was curious now.

"I am Seirim Al Ghul." Suddenly, the voice switched to speaking fluently native Mandarin Chinese. "And if you or any of your people return to this place, I will peel your skin off to wear as my clothes. I will take your eyes out and eat them so I can see your families and haunt them. Then I will cut your tiny little Chinese peepees off to use as toys for my dogs and send pictures of your mutilated bodies back to your mothers to mourn over."

Zhang was struck dumb. In more than ten years as a combat experienced officer, he had never experienced anything like this.

"You are Arab?" Zhang signaled to one of his men to find the source of the voice and shoot it.

"Arab? Are you crazy?" the voice shouted back.

The soldier raised his head briefly to look through his rifle scope in the direction of the voice. A crack of glass and metal was followed by the grunt of the soldier as he collapsed, a bullet fired through his eye.

"I am a Persian Djinn, my silly little Chinese friend," the voice continued, in Mandarin, with a Persian accent, "and if you persist in questioning me, you and your remaining men will all fail to return home to your base with my message save that which I shall burn into your skin with my fingers of hell fire."

Another shot cracked the afternoon light and a man behind Zhang in the column cried out in pain.

"Alright!" Zhang called back. "Let us go and we will not bother you further."

"Liar!" replied the voice in a demonic growl that sent the heebee geebees through the company.

"I am not lying," said Zhang. "I cannot guarantee if others will come. But me and my men will not."

"Well, if the others are as blind as you, Major Zhang," the voice suddenly sounded like it was behind him, "I will not be worried."

"How do you know my name?"

"Because I am the spirit of the forest," the voice replied. "I know you Major Zhang Po Bai, oooooo, and your father, oooooo, and his whore, ooh ooh ooh lala."

The men with Zhang looked at each other in amazement.

"I know you all," continued the voice, "and I will avenge the people whose blood you have spilled. I am the spirit that watches every step you take."

✳ ✳ ✳

Zhang's remaining men scuttled away in the controlled, organized manner of a group of professional warriors who'd just had all possible crap scared out of themselves for the rest of their lives. The Rangers lay silent and still in the cold forest. Once they were gone and the Rangers could move again, Kharzai stood up and moved close to Gunnar.

"What'd you think of my act? I've been working on it for years!"

"Hollywood quality. You should put in to be a wood sprite in the next Lord of the Rings movie."

"Lord of the Rings?" Kharzai gave his friend a look. "That was so pre-2010."

"I have not watched movies since then, had there been something more recent?"

"Well, no, not really anything good," Kharzai said. "So I guess that's okay."

"I do think you kind of freaked him out by calling his name," Gunnar said.

"Yeah," Kharzai replied, "apparently our inside contact has it nailed down pretty well."

"Apparently."

35

Jung

Jung handed the tortilla filled with moose steak and vegetables to Kharzai. She only recently stopped spiking his food with extra spices, not so much because she was being merciful to him, but because she didn't want to use up the spices they had for everyone.

"Thank you, m'lady," he said as he accepted it.

"Your lady?" she replied with an indignant smirk. "Are you already declaring ownership?"

"Ownership? Are you offering to become my sex slave?"

She slapped him hard across the shoulder. After decades as a mechanic shop owner, her hands were as hard as rocks.

"Ow!"

"Tough love." She grinned at him. "You need to rethink the wording of that last statement hairball, or you'll wake up with your head shaved and duct tape all over your back and chest."

"Sheesh! Straight to the death penalty, why not!"

"No, you're too cute to kill," she said. "I'd just torture you for rest of your life."

"So you do want to be with me for the rest of our lives!"

"What? No," she waved him off, "just the rest of your life, which once the torture starts probably won't be long. I know things that could put any twenty-year-old vixen to shame."

His eyes stretched wide. "Oh wait...that kind of torture. Oh Jung, I'm...where are the furry handcuffs? I'm willing to get started, now even."

She slapped him again, but this time he leaned in.

"Gimme more of that tough love, baby," he grunted.

"You really are crazy, you know." She gave him a playful punch to the chest then leaned into him. He wrapped his arm around her shoulder and squeezed.

As much as she played rough with him, she truly enjoyed when he just took her in his arms and held her. As a man, she had a hard time comparing him to her ex-husband. While the ex eventually found Jung's physical strength and tomboyish-demeanor challenging to his own masculinity, Kharzai seemed to not only accept her for what she was, but was able to see the feminine tenderness just beneath the surface and coax it out of her. He made her feel like a woman in every way, without stealing her individuality. Crazy as it was at their age, she just beyond fifty and he about ten years younger, she found herself willing to accept that they were in love.

"Hey, Kharzai! Mrs. Kharzai!" Franklin ran toward them from across the commons shouting for their attention. "Come over here, you gotta see this!"

They turned toward the noise and he caught up with them a moment later.

"You guys have got to see this kid...well, maybe not really a kid, he's like in his twenties maybe, but a kid to me anyway. Anyhow, dude has some crazy mad archery skills. I mean, like Genghis Khan would be staring like, 'Damn, dat some crazy shit! Yo?'"

They jogged across the town and just beyond to one of the weapons training ranges where a row of targets of various shapes and sizes had been setup up in a scattered pattern ranging from five to fifty yards. A young man whom Kharzai recognized as one of the recent refugees to join the camp was standing at one corner of the firing line with a bow in one hand and a quiver full of arrows strapped tightly at an angle across the small of his back.

He took four of the arrows from the quiver with his ungloved right hand, holding one between each finger and pinching one between forefinger and thumb. He nocked the first arrow, then took off at a sprint parallel to the targets, feet crunching in the packed snow with a rapid crack-crack-crack like an insane metronome. In the space of a second or two, the sound of the bowstring twanged four times in rapid succession, immediately followed by the dull thunk of the arrows planting themselves into the wood targets, each at dead center. The man continued without stopping, grabbed four more arrows, and throwing his body to the ground fired the arrows again just as fast, the 'ping-thunk' of string and target like a short burst from a machine gun. He rolled back to his feet, reloaded, changed directions, and fired at the previous four targets again, planting his arrows a hair's breadth from the first ones.

Someone brought a horse to the range, a small, fast quarter horse, the type bred for flying through race courses. He ran back to the starting line and with a swift leap was on the horse's bare back, guiding it with only his knees as his hands reloaded the bow. The horse turned toward the targets, quickly skirting between the ones with arrows already in them and advancing on the more distant fresh targets. The man leaned sideways in the saddle until he was parallel to the ground, gripping the horse's flank with his legs and fired two more rapid bursts of arrows, all landing with a solid thump into their targets.

He brought the horse back to the starting point, to a crowd of cheering onlookers who'd watched the spectacle. He dismounted, bowed politely, and patted his horse on the neck, whispering something into its ear that elicited a nod and a quick nuzzle against the man's cheek. Kharzai and the others approached him. A sergeant of the Rangers was beside the young man, shaking his hand.

"Dude," the sergeant exclaimed, "you were not kidding you are good at archery. I have never seen anything like that in my life, and I've been a military man since longer than you've been alive."

"Thank you," the young man said with an eastern European accent Kharzai found familiar. "It is skill whole family has since days of Genghis Khan, maybe before. They say maybe this is reason why Khan never crossed Danube."

Kharzai glanced at his bow. Scores of fine notches were carved along its face in perfectly straight lines.

"What are the notches on your bow?" he asked.

"One for each of Russian or Chinese communist pig I kill since war start."

Kharzai raised his eyebrows and gave an approving smile. "Can you teach this to others?"

"Of course. I am master instructor of archery and martial arts in home country before I come Alaska to fishing trip and war happens."

"What is your name, son?" Kharzai asked. "And where are you from?"

"Ivan Czyrgiczlicz, from Romania. My father is Yanut Czyrgiczlicz, owner of YC Military Academy in Romania."

"I thought you looked familiar. Your father trained Chechen resistance fighters in the 90s."

"Yes, you are Chechen?"

"No, no, no, but some of my best friends are Chechen."

"Wow, is small world, eh?"

"Indeed." Kharzai turned to the Ranger. "Sergeant, see to it this man is kitted out for the Rangers as a lieutenant; he will be a training officer and commander of the archery cavalry company."

"Uh, sir?"

"Yes, Sergeant," Kharzai replied.

"We don't have an archery cavalry company," the sergeant pointed out.

"Oh yes, well," Kharzai muttered. Then he shouted, "Sergeant!"

"Yes, sir!"

"Find the lieutenant that's in charge of creating stuff on paper and tell him I said to make us an archery cavalry company," Kharzai said imperiously, "and to put its new commander, Lieutenant Criggfoshizzlelix, in charge of training some of our people to kill the bad guys with pointy sticks while riding horsies. This could be a really cool thing when the circus comes to town."

Kharzai turned to Jung, took her by the arm, and lead her away.

"Come, my darling," he said loud enough for everyone nearby to hear, "you must demonstrate for me these fuzzy handcuffs you mentioned earlier. I believe I've been a very bad boy, very violent urges, I seem to be in need of much discipline."

As they walked away, Ivan turned to the sergeant.

"Torture? Circus? I am not circus freak show act. I just am not liking communist pigs. Who is crazy man with big hair?"

"He is the ring leader, and you just became the star attraction," the sergeant said. Ivan gave him a look of total confusion. "That man is Kharzai. He's a little weird, but one of the best and most hard-assed warriors I've ever met. And he's also the commander of the Rangers. You, my man, have been fast-tracked to the top of the food chain."

36

Youngmi

Youngmi was more than surprised: she was shocked. Her female officer's English class, with Mai's assistance, had arranged the birthday party in the classroom. The cut-out letters forming the words HAPPY BIRTHDAY AYI and WE LOVE YOU, reminded her of the baby shower her Sunday school staff had given her fifteen years earlier when she was carrying her youngest son. The current party had been almost as fun, too, since back then she could not have any wine like she could today. These women, most young enough to be her daughters, had become the next best thing to family since her captivity.

The high-pitched chatter and laughter sounded like that of women in any culture, in any part of the world. After a couple of hours of enjoying each other's company, the party gradually wound down and the girls all made their way back to their own rooms to sleep it off. Most of them had duty the next morning. Youngmi took the gifts they had brought for her and headed back to her own room in General Zhang's quarters. She walked along the hall, her heels clicking a rhythm to the tune she hummed from the last song the girls had sung to her. It had been a barely adequate version of an eighties American party song they had learned in China. While their performance had been all X's on the America's Got Talent scale, the beat of the music still made her feel good, nostalgic. As she passed the ladies restroom, she felt like she should stop to relieve herself before going all the way back to the apartment. Having imbibed two full glasses of wine during the party, there was a definite uncomfortable pressure she did not want to try and hold if the general decided he wanted to chat after she walked into their shared space.

She dropped the bag of gifts outside the door and entered, quickly chose a stall, and sat down. The winter sky outside was dark, but bright lamps atop poles lighted the walkway just beyond the window, bathing the room in a soft yellow glow. Combined with the single fluorescent light that always stayed on at the back, she'd not felt a need to flip the switch to make the whole room bright white.

The outer door opened, causing her to start at the light tap of footsteps, military-issue dress shoes that clicked with each step. The door to another opened and swung shut. As soon as the pressure on her bladder was released, she wiped, then rose and fixed her skirt, flushed the toilet, then moved out of the stall to the sink to wash her hands.

She finished, dried her hands on a paper towel, and started toward the door when the other occupied stall burst open with a loud bang.

A figure jumped out, cloaked in half-lit shadows.

Startled, she spun only to be met with a massive crash that sent bright white lights across her vision and blasted a shockwave of pain through the side of her head.

She fell back against the sink, grasping to stay upright, blinded by the blow.

The shadowy form rose above her, cocked back an arm, and drove a fist into her belly, causing her to double over.

She collapsed, gasping as the air refused to refill in her lungs. Strong hands grabbed her and spun her over onto her belly, her face pressed into the cold tile floor.

She sucked enough breath back into her lungs that she managed to push out a feeble scream.

The assailant, a man she was sure, yanked her skirt up over her hips and pressed something hard into her backside. His hands scrabbled at the waist band of her panties.

Youngmi sucked in a deep breath, recognizing the odor of the man's sweat, sour and hateful.

She gulped the toxic air and screamed, this time her will driving it to full volume. The shrill sound echoed off the tiles, causing her eardrums to rattle.

The man slapped her across the back of the head.

The restroom door suddenly flew open.

The attacker leaped to his feet.

She heard a zipper run up and quick footsteps tapping across the tile floor toward the back of the room.

A click, a swish, and a grunt and the man was out the window, the sound of running feet quickly silenced by the snow outside.

Po Zhang, the general's son, knelt before her. He was dirty like he'd just returned from a patrol.

"Are you okay, Ayi?"

His voice was the most tender she had ever heard from him. It was the first time he'd called her Ayi.

"Yes," she sobbed. "He didn't get what he wanted."

The young warrior rose, his body tense with rage as he strode to the back of the room.

"Get up, and go to my father," Po grunted back to her as he jogged to the back window. He stopped at the sill and looked down to the parade ground. He let out a low curse. A moment later, he returned to find her washing her face in the sink.

"The bastard got away," Po said. He paused, then said with a voice that seemed to drip with contempt, "Was it Ping?"

"I think so," she replied, staring down into the sink, grateful the son of a whore had been caught before he'd gotten any further.

"Say nothing to father," Po grunted. "I will take care of this myself."

37

Rangers

The Mat-Su Borough building in Palmer was by all appearances a half-built fortification. The three-story structure stood in a wide-open field several acres in size with few other buildings around it. The snow-covered baseball diamonds to the east had become the staging grounds for supplies, surrounded by an incomplete ring of Hesco units and dirt berms, which only amplified the fact that the entire space was practically open to the public and way undermanned.

It was the perfect combination of full of supplies and hard to secure.

Perfect, that is, for someone who wanted to cause mischief with the Chinese Army.

Barbed wire and concertina lay in large spools stacked and waiting for someone to roll it out to impede intruders. Pallets of food and dry goods were stacked in orderly rows covering several acres of snow-covered baseball fields in front of the building that originally housed the offices of the Palmer Colonial Government decades prior.

A handful of nervous-looking guards stood sentry duty, staring out into the darkness from large, generator-powered electric lamps that lit the snowy grounds in front of them with a blinding white light.

"Someone in logistics is going to get seriously spanked for having the gear here before the guards," Gunnar whispered into his radio as the troop slow crawled through the calf-deep snow. He reached up and touched the thing on his chest, not breaking stride.

The white smocks they wore over their insulated clothes rendered them nearly invisible, more so given that the guards were standing within the lighted compound, screwing their night vision all to hell.

The problem with the layout of Palmer, and maybe the one smart reason the Chinese chose to put a major outpost there, was that there was no high ground around it close enough for anyone to snipe from for a mission like this. The nearest elevated location that could overlook the general area was more than two miles east, well out of range of even the best shooters with the best equipment.

Therefore, Kharzai's second troop could only advance with what ground support Gunnar could put in place and a couple of men who managed to get on the roofs of nearby houses giving them a slight, barely measurable, advantage. If the Chinese had men on top of the Borough building itself, they would have their pick of targets to the north, east, and south.

Ivan, the Rangers preferred to call him Ivan the Terrible, led his platoon of trained archers into range of the posted sentries. Making enough bows and arrows for the men had been fairly easy, although the available timber was not as good for the purpose as that which Ivan had been accustomed to at home.

To ensure the power required for a fatal shot, and that the bow wouldn't snap in the middle of a fight, Ivan had the men reinforce their staves with moose or caribou hide sinews. The resulting bows stored sixty pounds of tension in the string when pull back two feet. It took a strong man to fire one, but the results were lethal. They were even able to penetrate military body armor from distance of up to one hundred yards.

Like a Jedi's lightsaber, each of his archers was required to make their own bow staves. They performed every part of the process with their own hands. From selecting the wood for the stave, carving it to shape and size, heat tempering it, shaping it, cutting and wrapping the sinews, and making their own bowstrings.

The only thing they were allowed to have someone else make was the arrows, as making and fletching enough arrows for a battle was very time-consuming. A carpenter in town had devised a way to easily make straight and true arrows out of birch, poplar, and tamarack, each type of wood used for different purposes and styles of arrow. Likewise, a metal worker used scrap metal from old vehicles and other metal scrap to form razor-sharp arrowheads. He made hunting points, razor blades, and barbed spikes. Each of them could penetrate the best of body armor.

Ivan's team was swift, silent, and absolutely deadly.

Kharzai made the signal and a dozen shadows slowly rose, just above the snow.

The four pairs of Chinese soldiers sitting in listening posts, foxholes situated a hundred yards out from the edge of the quasi-fortress discovered the hard way, that they should have been listening just a little bit harder. It was too late as knife blades slid through the soft flesh of their throats. The death rattle of those guards was barely audible against the still night air, muffled in their snowy graves.

Ivan's men rose from the corpses in those foxholes and drew near the compound itself.

A series of soft 'twang-thud' sounds signaled the felling of the guards inside the wire.

Gunnar's troop trained their rifles on the doors and windows of the borough building and the thick-walled winter tents on the lawn that surrounded the building.

"Sentries down," Ivan whispered into his radio.

"Team 2, go in," Kharzai replied as he rose from his own position and trotted into the compound, keeping to shadows between the piles of gear. He spoke into his radio, "We've got maybe ten minutes max, but don't count on it. Take what you can carry and set bombs and booby traps on what you leave behind."

The men rushed in and did exactly that, placing mines, bombs, and trip wires wherever they could, and snatching the better items they could find among the stacks.

Two pairs of Rangers dashed to a row of vehicles parked at one side the compound. They peeked into the beds of one, then another. If satisfied there was nothing they could take, they planted timed explosives on the gas tank and ran to the next.

"Hey, check this out!" hissed Phil Staley to his younger brother Martin. They'd been with Brad and Kharzai since shortly after the invasion. Martin came to him and they stared into the bed of the five-ton truck.

It was filled, top to bottom, with hundreds of ramen noodles. An entire truckload of one of the world's most popular comfort foods.

A moment later, the other team jogged up beside them.

"There's two whole truckloads of 5.8mm ammo for the Chinese rifles we've got so many of," said one man. "Would you believe they left the keys in the ignition?"

"We just found two truckloads of freeze-dried apocalypse food," called another team over the radio.

"That is some seriously stupid, once in a lifetime, arrogance on their part."

Phil smiled a wide toothy grin that would've made Kharzai proud.

"We have a five-ton packed with ramen noodles."

Silence hung in the air.

No one breathed.

Then someone let out a low whistle.

"Holeeeeeeeeee sheeeeeeeeyat!"

"I think, we need to commandeer these trucks," said one of the Rangers.

"I second the motion," said Martin.

"Agreed," said Phil. "Let's booby trap the rest of these vehicles, then Martin you take the gun mounted on the noodle truck. I'll drive." He motioned to the other pairs of Rangers. "You guys take the other trucks. We'll cover you from behind."

When the engines started, Kharzai called over the radio. "What's going on over there?"

"Sorry, chief, could not pass up taking these bad boys," Phil replied. "Four tons of rifle ammo, two truckloads of freeze dried food, and an entire truck load of ramen noodles."

"Ramen noodles! Holy schmoley! Go, go, go!"

Kharzai motioned for the rest of the men to beat a fast retreat before the soldiers inside reacted to the engines starting up. He snapped the radio back on, "How're you going to get them back?"

"We'll take Highway Three," Phil replied, referring to a mining road just wide enough for the large trucks. Halfway to Chiknik, the road became barely traceable in heavy thickets of trees. The Happy Eagle Mine road, as it was named, was the kind of road that after nearly fifty years of disuse only someone who knew it intimately could maneuver to its end without becoming entangled, or dropping off a cliff. If somehow that driver managed to survive to the end, they'd find themselves in a hidden cove, behind massive rocks, which concealed a series of large caves left from the decades old Happy Eagle Mining Camp, where they could hide the trucks, unload the gear on to the SUSVs, then transport it all back to Chiknik.

Phil and Martin both happened to know that road like that the veins in the back of their hands. The older signaled to his brother, they put the rigs in gear, and they rolled out of the camp, taking back roads out of the city.

Kharzai and Gunnar's teams tensed, waiting for the firefight that would surely ensue, but nothing came.

They signaled the retreat and pulled back, making their way back towards the SUSVs. Just as they ducked into the deeper woods half a mile from the borough building, the thump of a dozen massive explosions rocked the night.

The timed bombs set under the trucks.

From where they were, Kharzai and his men could not see it, but their ears heard the story. Half-a-minute after the huge explosions, a series of loud pops went off, sounding like pull-string party poppers in contrast to the roaring fire among the larger trucks. Claymores and booby traps the teams had left behind to keep the enemy from chasing them too soon. The screams of men shredded by shrapnel or burning in the gasoline fires provided an eerie musical score to the imagined scene.

Kharzai paused and glanced back at the bright orange mushroom cloud that built over the camp. He sucked in a breath, put the tips of the first two fingers of his right hand to his mouth and whispered, "I am the harbinger of death, for all who dare stand against me."

"Come on, hairy man," hissed Gunnar.

Several miles away, Martin stood in the gun turret in the ramen truck, eyes glittering in the reflection of the bright orange blaze as fireballs roiled into the sky over the city of Palmer. He wiped sweat from his brow, sweat that ran into his eyes in spite of the below-freezing temperature. The hand came back smeared red.

He scrunched his eyes as he processed what he was looking at.

He glanced down toward his brother in the driver's seat and saw what was probably a nearly identical spatter of blood across his cheek.

It was the blood of the sentries they'd taken out by slitting their throats. Just as the event started to replay in his mind, the sky lit up with another massive rolling fireball as if a larger fuel container had been caught in the blaze.

"Wow," he muttered, his blood-smeared face glowing in the brilliant light of the miniature sun. "That is beautiful."

38

General Zhang

The general slammed his fist onto the table. "You lost not only the food, but the rebels also either stole or destroyed nearly all of the weapons and ammunition for the Palmer mission!"

Zhang paced the room as if looking for someone to devour with the flames that seemed about to burst from his mouth. The logistics officer stared at the floor.

"Well?"

"Sir," the officer stammered, "we were ordered to send the materials out there, how could I have known there would not be sufficient security at the base?"

"How could you not know?" Zhang bore into him with laser eyes. "You could have known by verifying with the base commander if troops were there to protect it! That's how!"

"Yes, sir," replied the officer. "I will make sure to verify there is ample security in the future before executing requests."

"That is correct, Major," he said, his voice rumbling in a low tone that amplified his anger to a level of physical threat. He waved his hand toward the door. "Leave me."

"Yes, sir!" The major stiffened, took a step back, and executed a smart about face, then marched out the door.

Zhang pressed the button on his phone for the secretary. She answered immediately.

"Yes, General?"

"Send in Colonel Feng."

"Yes, General."

A moment later, the door opened and a tall, thin man stepped in. His uniform was well tailored, and his demeanor intense. Zhang always thought Colonel Feng looked like a Chinese version of Peter Cushing in the first Star Wars movie from the seventies. He could picture the man striding along the decks of the Death Star. Today, he could also picture the man being "force choked," feet dangling off the floor in the grip of his rage.

Feng snapped a salute. "Sir!"

"Colonel Feng," Zhang said, "how long have you been in my command?"

"Ten years, sir."

"In those ten years, how many combat operations bases have you coordinated or commanded, Colonel Feng?"

"Sir, I have commanded four bases in active combat zones, and coordinated the setup and security for seven others since I've been under your command."

"Correct, Colonel." Zhang stretched his hands flat on the top of his desk. One of his knuckles shifted with a pop that elicited a tiny twitch at the corner of the colonel's mouth. "And you have been in the People's Army nearly thirty years, yes?"

"Yes, sir. Twenty-nine years and eight months, sir."

"Those facts, and my knowledge that you have always served the People's Republic wholeheartedly in the past, are the only reason you are and will continue to be breathing the air of this mortal life, for the time being."

"Thank you, sir." A barely visible sigh of relief flushed the colonel's face.

"Why were those supplies sent to the Palmer operations base without proper security being in place, Colonel Feng?"

"Sir, I had ordered the special service group to be sent to provide security on a short-term basis until the third battalion could be organized and delivered in a week or two. I did not know until after the supplies had already been sent that my order had been rescinded by Colonel Ping, who sent Major Zhang's team on a different mission of higher priority. I was unaware of this until the night of the attack."

"You were unaware that someone else had taken the soldiers you had requested, and put them on a different mission? How can this happen? Did none of your people call your office to let you know they did not arrive? Did no one from Colonel Ping's command inform you or your office of the change in orders?"

"No, General." Feng stiffened again. This was dangerous ground. Ping was one of General Zhang's lifelong compatriots, a friend even. The fact that the bastard had stolen troops that had been committed to another mission and said nothing to him meant little if the general did not believe it. "I received no communications regarding the change in orders from Colonel Ping's office. Captain Kwang at the Palmer base did call when the supplies arrived with only basic security. I assured him that they were on the way, then I started calling around to find out where they were. By the time I discovered the change in orders, the attack was already underway."

Zhang was quiet for a long time. He stared at Feng who stood ramrod straight, eyes boring into the wall behind him like a recruit before a drill sergeant. The general took in a long, deep breath then slowly let it out with a hiss.

"Colonel Feng," he rose from his chair and stood behind the desk, rising to his full height, matching Feng eye to eye, "return to your duties. But be warned, another error like this and you will find yourself back in a line unit leading men in direct combat against the insurgents."

"Yes, sir!"

"Get out."

Colonel Feng made an exit identical to that of the previous guest in Zhang's office and wasted no time in getting out of there. Zhang pressed the intercom button again.

"Have Colonel Ping come to my office as soon as possible," he ordered.

"Yes, sir."

He walked over to the west-facing windows, looking out toward the northern edge of the Pacific Ocean just beyond the treeline that blocked the horizon. He gazed over the massive parade field that stretched several hundred yards in each direction.

A formation of soldiers stood in ranks in the mid-distance, an officer giving them some kind of speech. The officer pointed north, his arm like the needle of a compass, as if pointing to the place his men would soon be attacking. Zhang tried to read their unit guidon, the flag that designated their battalion, company, and platoon. From the distance, he could see the flag that fluttered at the end of the pole was green with gold lettering, but his eyes were not what they used to be and he could not make out the writing on it. He cursed middle age, and briefly wondered if he would lose his sight entirely when he got old.

"If I were blind," he muttered to himself, "I could never see Youngmi's face again." He let out a sigh and added, "That would be a shame."

The unit on the parade field snapped to attention. A shouted cheer resounded on the crisp air.

"She certainly does look very much like Xiu Ying," he continued aloud, "but Youngmi's heart burns with a totally different kind of fire."

The troop on the parade field did a smart right face, then marched in formation toward the barracks.

Memories of being a young officer flooded Zhang's mind.

The power of knowing your words commanded the lives of men, that their lives were lived by your direction, good or bad, their very existence was in your hands. The power of a lieutenant or a captain was so far removed from that of a general that they were incomparable.

The general makes orders and sends men by the thousands to their deaths or worse, but he never has to see the look of terror in their eyes as they charge into the field at his command. They are all just chess pieces, little plastic toys being flicked around a board.

The junior officers though, they had to look directly into those terrified eyes and give them confidence, as they are thrown into the maw of combat, the terror of torn flesh, and the full realization of their own mortality.

Those young leaders had to hide the same terror from their own eyes. They had to bury their fears. Force down their nightmares of running into the bullets and blades of their foe. They had to bury their own desire to scream and puke and run home to their mothers, and had to lead their men into the grinder of war.

A memory of himself and Ping as young captains in western China, as they crushed the Muslim Uyghur rebellion, passed through his mind.

The energy they felt.

The power.

The immortality of youth.

Hundreds of men under their command, forcing the rebels to bow the knee to the one truth of Maoist Communism. They were so motivated. So young. So naïve to the realities of the world.

But they had power.

Real power.

Men willingly laid down their lives for their captains, because they worshipped them as real heroes.

In those days, he and Ping would rush into the face of the enemy, bayonets fixed, with no trace of fear.

They exhilarated in the bloodlust. Alive in the grip of battle.

Or maybe they were just insane.

So many young men laid their lives down, their blood draining into the dust of a land not their own, dying at the command of the two young hero captains. So many enemies killed. Families decimated. Entire towns and villages burned to the ground.

No mercy.

The mantra of the People's Army.

No mercy. No quarter. No survivors to rise up and take revenge.

Ping loved it all, every moment of it. Even the dead civilians, women, children, none of it ever bothered him.

But for Zhang, the longer they fought, the less he enjoyed the slaughter. As he grew older and the lusts of his youth were sated, even to the point of nausea, he determined to make it less brutal. To stop the killing of civilians, but still to win the wars.

That's what he wrote his Master's thesis on.

A Merciful War.

His theory of war with less civilian casualties was attractive to the world political market of the day, when he was up for promotion to colonel, more than a decade earlier.

The further distillation of his concepts earned him his first star. By forty-two, he was a general who was able to carry on with the traditional Chinese communist method of warfare, but whose stated theories, and the way he carried himself before the cameras, looked good to the western world. His perceived merciful attitude got him one star then another.

As for his friend Ping, who had saved Zhang's life on more than one occasion, his honest brutality stuck him as a permanent colonel.

But Zhang's ideas of limited warfare were never fully adopted by the established leadership. They were little more than a veneer slathered over the shining steel of the bayonets, to make them look more appetizing to those about to eat them.

Ping's style of kill them all and let, what he considered as, their non-existent gods sort them out, still ruled the PLA psyche.

Zhang wasn't so sure about the God thing himself; he often felt like there had been a guiding hand in his own life. But as he watched the world around him continually spiral into never-ending violence and anarchy, he often doubted his own thoughts and understanding of everything. After the pain-filled death of his beloved Xiu Ying, he felt as though no matter how good or bad you were, fate kicked you in the teeth anyway, and you might as well go for the biggest win, because what you did personally made no difference in the end.

We all die, so maybe we should just kill them all and let their gods sort them out…if there even is a God to sort them out.

And then his son brought Youngmi to his office and everything changed again. He sucked in a deep breath, then let it out with a sigh.

"You are getting old and lonely, General Zhang," he muttered to himself. "You have nothing to attract such a woman again, not an honorable woman at least. And Youngmi, while she is such an honorable woman, is not looking for a 'sugar daddy' as these Americans would say."

The sound of a throat clearing snapped his attention back into the moment. He whirled around ready to pounce. Ping stood at attention two feet in front of his desk.

"Colonel Ping," Zhang said, "I did not hear you come in."

"I'm sorry, sir," Ping stayed at attention, staring at the back wall of the office, "I did not intend to overhear you."

Zhang let out a short laugh. "Don't worry, my old friend. You have always been swift, silent, and deadly, and since I did request your presence, I should have been listening for you to come in."

"Thank you, sir," Ping said. "I have indeed enjoyed a long and lethal career."

"Sit, please." Zhang motioned to one of the chairs in front of his desk.

Ping lowered himself into the chair and let himself look somewhat relaxed as his lifelong friend calmly took his own seat.

"Do you remember Uyghur?"

"Uyghur?" Ping nodded as the images of that war flooded his mind. The thought of the death and destruction they had caused, the violence, the killing, and the rape, caused his manhood to pulse and slowly stiffen. "Yes, General, how could I forget?"

"I was just thinking about our young careers. How different they were before we got old, and…"

"…full of responsibility?" Ping finished for him.

"Yes, before we were actually in charge of the whole shit-parade."

"It was so much easier to be a young captain, who only had to lead men into the fight, than to be a senior officer who ordered them to their deaths by the hundreds."

"Yes, it was." Zhang's melancholy mood instantly dropped several degrees at the assessment of his friend. He took a breath, seemed to don his command persona, then said, "Colonel Ping, why did you take the soldiers away from Colonel Feng's mission? Your actions cost the lives of more than two dozen of our soldiers at the Palmer base as well as the loss of several truckloads of food, weapons, ammunition, and other equipment."

Ping sat forward in his chair. "Sir," he said in a carefully modulated, conciliatory tone, "when I ordered Major Zhang to do the recon mission, I had no idea he was already devoted to another mission at the same time. If I had, I certainly would not have asked his unit to be reassigned."

"He did not tell you he had other orders?"

"No, General," Ping asserted. "If he had, I certainly would not have taken him from it."

Zhang contemplated this. Would his son do such a thing? They had once been so close, but in recent years, since his son became an officer under his own command, they had grown so far apart he felt he no longer knew the younger Zhang's way of thinking or his intentions.

"I see." General Zhang said after a long pause. "I will deal with him then directly, then."

Zhang reached into a cabinet behind his desk and pulled out a bottle of Jim Beam whisky. He poured two fingers of the famous American liquor into a couple of glasses, then handed one to Ping.

"I feel like reminiscing," he said. "Let's talk about days gone by."

The clock spun slowly until the wee hours as their blood-paved past unraveled between them with a type of nostalgia only a lifelong warrior could understand.

39

Sammi

Sammi slurped the noodles in a most unladylike fashion, holding her long hair back with one hand to keep it out of the broth as she lifted the noodles to her mouth with homemade chopsticks. She spoke with her mouth still half full.

"This is the best booty you could ever take, Kharzai."

"It wasn't me," Kharzai replied as he sucked up a mouthful of the famous spicy, freeze-dried comfort food. Happy the black lab sat tall on his left, while Penny the golden retriever squeezed in between his and Jung's chairs. Both dog's tails wagged in anticipation as their master gave each of them a bite for every one of his own. "It was the Staley boys. They found it, snatched it, and delivered it on their own initiative."

"God bless them," Sammi muttered between mouthfuls, closing her eyes in ecstasy as the noodles slithered down her throat, the burn of the red pepper as powerful a drug as any narcotic.

"Three meals of ramen noodles for each person in the village," Kharzai said. "Who knew a two-ton truck could hold that much."

"Well, the noodle packs are pretty light weight," Brad said as he sucked down his own food.

Jung Ah slurped back a wad of noodles, let out a breath, turned to Kharzai and said, "The boys may have got it, but you led the mission, therefore you are my hero tonight, Kharzai."

She leaned in and nuzzled his chin. As he turned to give her a kiss, she flicked his nose, a hard snap resounding from her mechanic-lady fingernail. She sat back up straight, leaving Kharzai's lips smacking at empty air as she turned away.

"Not in front of the kids," she said.

"Imo," Sammi raised an eyebrow toward Jung whom she addressed as "Auntie," "please keep your sex maniac boyfriend under control, there are children in the room." She rubbed her belly then made as if she were averting the baby's eyes.

The room exploded with laughter. Even the dogs joined in the cacophony of noise. It was several minutes before they caught their breath and were able to resume eating their noodles.

"The best thing with this find is that these are actual, real life Shin Ramyun," Sammi put in, "the most popular of Korean noodles, not even a Chinese knock off."

"How do you know it's not a Chinese knock off?" Kharzai asked. "They're pretty good counterfeiters."

She pointed to the lower left corner of the package.

"See this 'No MSG' label with the black background?"

The men glanced at it.

"That is only on the original packaging made in Korea. The Chinese version of the package was almost identical but the fake ones had a weird green/brown MSG label. If you didn't know to be looking for it, you'd miss it."

Brad gave her a look. "Yeah, but they could've changed their labelling by now."

"Maybe, but I don't think so. There is a distinct difference in quality and taste between theirs and the real thing," Sammi said. She gripped a cluster of steaming noodles in her chopsticks, slurping it loudly through her lips. Red broth dripped from the corner of her mouth. The sound she made would have been considered very unladylike in most European cultures, but in Korea, and most other North Asian cultures, slurping noodles showed you liked the food, and to eat noodles quietly was in some places considered rude. "Yes, this is definitely Korean. Ours don't need MSG to make them taste good. The Chinese version of the noodles they use a kind that are barely better quality than the ten for a dollar American Top Ramen kind. They taste almost plastic, where these are chewy and taste like actual noodles."

The child in her belly suddenly stretched, forcing her to make a noise somewhere between a hiccup and a burp.

Brad started. "You okay?"

She sucked in a breath, stretched, arching her back to give the baby room and then let the breath out in a rush.

"Whew! Baby got really excited about the noodles," she huffed out.

After a few seconds of stares in Sammi's direction, they all resumed eating their noodles, savoring the deliciousness of the broth, the freeze-dried vegetables, and tiny crispy shrimp.

"Yup," said Kharzai as he emptied his bowl into his mouth, tongue stretching toward the last few drops of red liquid, "this was definitely worth the effort."

"Definitely," replied Sammi. She slurped down the last of the salty broth in her bowl, then leaned against her husband. She rubbed her very round belly. The baby pressed back against her hand for a moment, then relaxed back as if the hot broth were putting it to sleep. The baby seemed to have been completely calmed by the heat of what momma had just eaten. Sammi let out a soft breath and muttered into Brad's chest.

"The world is at peace again."

40

Mojo

Mojo and his men lay in the snow, snuffling the air and listening for movement.

Relatively fresh human footprints were obvious all around the area. Someone had been gathering water from breaks in the ice near the edge of the nearby lake on a very regular basis, including within the past twenty-four hours.

By six o'clock in the morning, with the sky still dark as night, the presence of the local inhabitants was verified. A pair of young men came ambling out of the woods carrying several large animal skin bladders, with rifles slung across their backs.

They went to the water's edge where they knelt down beside the lake and pushed the containers into it, the fresh water instantly started bubbling into them. On deeper observation, it became clear that these were not grown men, but teenage boys.

Young ones at that.

One of them was a native Yupik boy, fourteen or fifteen maybe; the other was a couple of years older of mixed race, white combined with either Asian or Alaska native. Mojo himself was half-black/half-Athabaskan, but he could not tell the second boy's ethnicity. An almost imperceptible movement at the woods edge drew his attention and Mojo barely made out the shape of two well-concealed persons providing over watch. They lay silent, scanning the area around the water gatherers through their weapon sights.

Were it not for more than twenty years as a Marine sniper, Mojo probably would not have even seen them himself. They were alert and observant, trained warriors.

As the boys rose from their water gathering task, Mojo called out, "Hello at the lake."

The boys instantly dropped the ground, the water skins hitting the surface with a splat. The air rang with the high speed 'shlick' sound of leather and wood against flesh as they unslung their weapons indicating the level of training they had been through. They lay invisible in the grass.

"We mean you no harm!" Mojo said loud enough for the overwatch to hear. "We're from the Fairbanks resistance, looking for friends out here."

"How can we know that?" said a young man's voice.

"I will stand up, without my weapon," Mojo replied. "If you think I am Russian, you can shoot me. I am from Salt Jacket, outside of Fairbanks. I am the senior NCO of the Alaska Defense Force up there."

"Okay," said the young man. "Stand up slowly."

Mojo laid his rifle on the ground and slowly rose to his feet, hands in the air.

"How many others are with you?" asked the young man.

"I have twenty men with me," Mojo said. "We just came from Ice Hammer's camp and meeting his people."

"Who?"

"Ice Hammer," he replied. "He's the leader of the resistance around Anchorage."

"Never heard of him," replied the young man. "Step forward and prove you are an Alaskan."

"How do you want me to prove that?"

"Sing the first line of the Alaska Song."

"Okay." Mojo scanned his memory for the words to the song all Alaskan kids had learned in elementary school. "Eight stars of gold on a field of blue, Alaska's flag what's it mean to you?"

"Good enough," said the voice. "What's the best pizza in Anchorage?"

"Moose's Tooth," he said immediately.

"Okay, you at least know our stuff," the young man said as he stood up. Like Mojo, he had an Asian or Native look about him. He stood about five-foot-nine and had the broad shoulders and thick back of a competitive swimmer. How he'd kept that shape a year into the war was a mystery to Marcus.

"What's your name?" the youth said.

"Marcus Johnson, but my friends call me Mojo."

"Alright, Mojo, you and your men can get your stuff and come with us." The young man made a signal with his hands. Others rose from their positions as well. "I'm Ben, sergeant in Bravo Company Troop 104, Alaska Defense Force. Please don't mention your last name to anyone else. We make a habit of only using first names or nicknames; mine is Snake," he showed him the scar running the length of this arm, "for obvious reasons. I will introduce you as Mojo to our leaders. We do this so that if anyone is captured they will not know our full names, and be able to retaliate against our families if they have managed to survive."

"Smart policy," replied Mojo.

Ten minutes later, they were sitting beside a fire built beneath a shelter of timbers and a thatched roof made of spruce boughs and grass to dissipate the smoke column and keep their position less visible. Tommie and Mike sat across from them, sipping on cups of a hot beverage.

Mojo glanced up as a group of boys entered the camp, apparently returning from a patrol. Faces dirt smeared, dark-rimmed eyes, sunken with exhaustion. They scanned the newcomers warily as they trudged past them toward their own lodgings.

The men that made up the patrol looked young, and very dangerous, like dogs trained to kill at their master's order. Mere adolescents trained for nothing but the fight, waiting for the signal to leap. A violent rage rested, barely contained, within their jaws, as if humanity were a disguise they wore uncomfortably.

Among them, he recognized some of the faces he'd seen at the ambush several days earlier with Tommie, including the boy who'd gleefully dispatched the wounded with a tomahawk.

That young man was the only one who did not look completely worn out. His expression seemed to express angry frustration. Mojo wondered if he was upset that he found no one to kill today. He'd had seen that look before on Marines and soldiers who'd grown too used to combat as a way of life. Men who were more than dangerous, they were a threat to everything in their path.

"We saw you and your boys in action a couple weeks back," he said to Tommie, "when you took out the Russian column. That was pretty hardcore for a bunch of kids."

"Most of these boys are that, kids. Tough mind you, but kids nonetheless." Tommie took a sip of his tea. "But some of them," he let out a steamy breath, "some of them, they are beasts."

He handed Mojo a cup of tea he'd made from the local Labrador leaves. They weren't real tea, and they had no caffeine, but since he'd run out of his own blended Assam and Lapsang Souchong leaves several months earlier, the taste was as close as he was going to get, until they could steal more of the real thing from the Russians.

"Those two for instance," he pointed to Ian and Ben. "Brothers, but as different as night and day, or perhaps I should say the light and the dark."

Mojo recognized them both as the leader and the killer from the ambush.

"Yeah? How so?"

"Well, Ben, the older one, is the squad leader. Got a good solid leadership mindset. Very smart head on his shoulders. But will avoid a kill any chance he gets. Does not enjoy the killing even a little, although when pressed he's quite good at it."

He took another sip of his tea.

"His younger brother on the other hand, that lad is stone cold. He is fine among the boys, and is a really nice kid when talking one on one. Put him among the enemy with a rifle though, or even better with his knife and tomahawk, and God help those poor souls that are trapped in there with him. I lost count of his kills after a hundred."

They watched Ian sit by a fire, a wide, still boyish, grin spread on his face as he chatted with the others. He said something funny, and they laughed. As one of the others started a monologue that got everyone's attention, he slipped his tomahawk from its sheath and started absentmindedly sharping it on a whetstone he'd pulled from his backpack.

Mojo's eyes fell on the blade and realized that Ian was grinding out blood stains that had colored the steel blade a dark brown.

"I was a soldier of the IRA at sixteen, then changed allegiances and became a mercenary before I was twenty-one. I am almost fifty now. And that boy, a year younger than when I started off, has a higher kill ratio than my entire career."

"I've met kids like him," Mojo said, "as a Marine NCO. Guys who went off and did what you did after their military service. Not too many lived to be as old as you."

"Yeah," Tommie sipped his tea, "I would not have lived to this age were it not for my Ebony Angel." He sucked in a breath, pretending to inhale the scent of the tea a cover for the hitch in his throat.

"Ebony Angel?"

"My wife." Tommie closed his eyes for a moment, sucked in a breath and continued. "She was a Somali woman, black as ebony. Would you believe that, looking at shiny white-boy me?"

Mojo grinned. "As a half-Athabaskan, half-black man married to a Korean woman with white parents, I can picture it."

"I imagine you can then," said Tommie. He continued, "Well, we married and she took me out of direct action for a decade. I always figured she saved my life by convincing me to become a contract trainer instead of a contract killer."

"Sounds like a smart woman."

"Indeed, very smart."

"Is she here in camp?"

"No." Tommie took a long slurp, draining the tea from his cup. "The bastard goat-lovers I'd been fighting before I married her caught up with me, and killed her and our child. That's why I was here when the war started, training young Yankee Army grunts to go kill them back."

"Sorry to hear that."

"Your wife up in Fairbanks, Mojo?" Mike asked.

"I don't know," Mojo said. "I have not seen her since the war started. We had a year-old child too, a daughter. Lonnie was a fighter, an Alaska State Trooper actually. I pray they're still alive, but I don't know where they are."

A short silence followed that statement as each man in the circle thought of his own missing family members.

"So, Mojo," Ron said. "You met this Ice Hammer fellow?"

"Yes."

"What's he like?"

"Just a guy," Mojo said. "I'd say 'like the rest of us' but he's not from the same background as me and Tommie and Mike. He was in the Marines a long time ago, force recon even, but only one tour. Then was a computer nerd for the past twenty years, according to what he says."

"But he's leading the largest militia in the state."

"Yeah, he claims he has no idea how that happened, but he's got some pretty hard-core support. He has some pretty serious leadership too. Guys who know their stuff and have set up Ranger teams and long-range recon patrols."

"So," Steve said, stepping up to the fire pit and entering the conversation, "what's it like in the rest of the state?"

"Well," Mojo took another long sip of the tea, then said, "basically, we've lost."

"Like, totally lost?" said Ron.

"Pretty much." Mojo put his cup down. "The Russians control the north and eastern part of the state and the panhandle. The Chinese the west and south, and the Aleutians. Their control is fairly complete in a general sense. That said, the resistance is giving them a hard time in a major way everywhere we can. Fairbanks has about three thousand fighters holding out still, and Ice Hammer has about five thousand at his main base plus another couple thousand in cells in Anchorage and the Mat-Su Valley. But the Kenai recently surrendered to the authority of the Chinese and the oil pipeline is totally under Russian control."

"Shit," said Steve. "They've got the whole pipeline?"

"Well," said Mojo's sergeant, "they may have the pipeline itself, but not a whole lot of oil has passed through that pipe since the war started. Amazing how easy it is to disrupt with so many potential single points of failure."

The other men nodded in understanding. Over eight hundred miles of pipeline was almost impossible to protect from every possible attack. Russia certainly was not planning to bankrupt themselves doing so in this least populated state while trying to gain control over massive areas of Canada and the US Mainland as well.

Another middle-aged man strode toward the group of leaders. At a distance of twenty yards or so, his expression changed for a brief moment, then regained the painted look of a politician. The look in his eyes made Mojo stare at him for several seconds as he passed. The man smiled, waved, and then abruptly changed directions, heading toward the latrines at the edge of the camp.

"Who was that?" Mojo asked.

"Say's his name is Roger Anderson," Mike said. "One of our patrols found him sleeping in the woods about a month ago, just as things were freezing up. He claims he'd escaped from Valdez and spent a couple months at a trapper's cabin that was stocked with plenty of food, then was living off the land for a month when our boys stumbled on him. But I don't know. He seemed pretty healthy for someone who'd been foraging for a month in early winter."

"And he definitely does not have the air of one who would travel alone through the forest and mountains from Valdez to fifty miles past Glennallen," Steve said. "He didn't even know how to dress and cook the grouse some of the boys brought in from a hunt."

"I recognize him," Mojo said. "But his name doesn't match the face."

"Yeah?" Ron shifted in his seat. "He gives a lot of the boys the creeps when he is around."

"And," injected Steve, "he definitely has not deigned to carry his fair share of work around here."

"Claims he was a school teacher," Tommie said, "which I can imagine. He's like the kind that'd be a mean, bully of a school teacher."

"I can't remember all the details," said Mojo, "but I don't think that is his name. Roger Anderson was the name of a political reporter for Anchorage Dispatch News. I read his articles all the time. Last I recall before the war, he was working on something shady in Valdez, some kind of embezzlement thing I think."

"You think this guy is that reporter?" said Mike.

"I don't think a reporter would go around telling folks he was a school teacher," said Mojo.

"Roger Anderson is kind of a generic name though," said Ron. "There's got to be a whole page or more of them in the phone book for Anchorage."

"Yeah well," said Steve, "the Valdez phone book is less than an inch thick, including the yellow pages. Not too likely there are very many."

41

Merrill Treadmore

Merrill Treadmore walked back into camp after a trip to the woods to relieve himself in peace without the stench of the shared latrines. As he strolled back into camp, he passed the group of leaders sitting around the fire kept burning in front of the commander's huts, the three dugout buildings that housed the senior commanders, and their adult staff. He smiled and gave a perfunctory military-ish salute toward the group around the fire. As he drew nearer, he noticed several new men sitting around the fire. The looks they cast in his direction were not comforting. In the weeks since he'd joined this ragtag band of Boy Scouts and men, he had found himself growing increasingly more uneasy than he'd ever felt with Brad Stone's camp.

These men and boys were not refugees; they were fighters, very dangerous fighters. Every action they did made them targets for the Russians. Their days were limited and Treadmore wanted nothing to do with a group headed toward their own massacre.

These new visitors looked even harder than the boys. They were all grown men of the same breed as Mike and Tommie: professional warriors. This could mean nothing good. He had to find a way out of here. It would be better to live under Russian rule than to die with these fools.

42

Mojo

Marcus and his men were packing up for their trip back north to Fairbanks when Mike approached him with an offer to have him and his men join them on a patrol. Mr. Tatum, the professional spy turned Alaska bushman, had left a message for them via a system they'd arranged on one of his many trap lines. The Russians were moving a large amount of food and ammunition to their troops at various points along the Richardson Highway.

"Time for some grocery shopping, boys," Tommie said.

"We'd love to come along as working observers if you're cool with it," Marcus said. "We've got some good snipers with us."

"Grazi," said Mike. "We could always use the help."

Ben spoke up. "You guys ever see that movie Red Dawn? Where the Russians put transmitters in the food the Wolverines find?"

"We've got that taken care of. At the Ice Hammer camp, there was this nerdy little ex-Navy SIGINT guy named Franklin," Marcus reached into his ruck sack and pulled out the small scanning device, "who made a couple of these babies, and was kind enough to give us one."

"What is SIGINT again?" asked Ron.

"It's a military acronym for Signals Intelligence," Steve said. "Electronic warfare is another name for it. Basically, they are the combat computer nerds."

"This little thing Franklin made is the love child of a GPS and a barcode scanner or something like that." Marcus held it up for all to see. "It scans for passive signals from RFID chips. They found chips a plenty in the gear they took, but were able to disable them all."

"Sounds like a good deal," said Mike. "I imagine that might be what got our last base blown up."

"Just took them some time to find us," Tommie smiled, "since we tend to go for the total annihilation ploy when we pull an ambush."

"Best kind." Marcus smiled back, hefting his ruck and turning to signal his men to come in for a chat about their new mission.

It was a two-day march to the point where they would hit the enemy. Twenty boys, half a dozen men, and three reindeer made their way over thirty miles of wintry landscape pulling contraptions that looked like large dogsleds they had made from polished birch boards. On the way to the ambush site, one person at a time could take a turn riding in each sled, along with the heavy gear to conserve energy and rest up. On the return though, if all went well, there would be no rides back, as the sleds would be full of loot they took from the enemy.

After nearly a year and a half using their legs as their sole mode of transportation, the boys and young men were hardened and strong; like the Dall sheep that roamed the mountains, they could run and leap up nearly vertical climbs with barely a trace of effort. The half-dozen older men, ranging from dad to grandpa, had to put in a lot more work, but they tried their best to never let the boys see that their knees ached and their backs groaned under the strain. As the patrol came to the top of a hill a mile from the highway, the point man signaled for the rest of the team to stop. They took a knee, or squatted in the snow.

Mike and Marcus crouch-ran to the crest, crawling on their bellies the last few yards so as not to highlight themselves against the clear afternoon skyline. From their perch, they could see a ten-mile-long, relatively straight stretch of the Richardson Highway.

"Get your snipers to those two points," Mike said to Marcus, pointing to two areas overlooking the road. "Open up on the drivers and anyone you see with a radio or cell phone once they are near the end of that point." He pointed to a bridge where the trucks would be concentrated in a narrow space with no way to turn around.

"On it," Marcus replied. He slithered back to his men and relayed the orders.

As the sniper teams moved into position, the scouts and other men crept down the face of the hill making their way closer to the road in preparation for the up close and personal assault. They staged the sleds at the edge of the forest, camouflaged them from view.

Half the boys crossed to the other side of the road, setting up a crossfire for the oncoming Russian convoy.

Ben held his rifle close to his chest, finger stretched across the trigger guard in anticipation of the coming action. Ian stroked the handle of his tomahawk, his expression a terrifying hunger for the blood it would soon be bathed in.

"Hey, Ian," Charlie whispered as he held his captured Russian rocket launcher close. "You think we could order some Taco King Lengua Burritos after this?"

Ian turned to his friend, grinning ear to ear like a maniac. "Anything you want, brother," he said, licking his lips. "Lengua Burritos and chicken hearts sounds good to me."

"Chicken hearts?" asked Charlie. "Taco King don't do chicken hearts."

"No, but my mom did," Ian replied. "Dad used to order Taco King delivery, then he would mix whatever weird left-overs we had in with the stuff we ordered. Best combo ever was my mom's spicy Korean chicken hearts mixed with kimchi, black olives, carne asada, beans, rice, and sharp cheddar cheese."

"Stop talking," Ben hissed. "Listen for the enemy coming."

The patrol fell quiet. The only sound was the whispery breeze that sifted through the spruce needles and dry twigs of the paper birch.

It was more than an hour before the first sound of the convoy came to their ears. Several minutes after first hearing them, the large green painted tractor-trailers and six-wheeled trucks appeared in the distance.

Marcus and his men stared down their scopes, watching as the first of the vehicles moved slowly onto the bridge and into their cross hairs.

As the lead trucks came over the threshold of the bridge and back onto the asphalt highway, the shooters opened up on the drivers of each of the dozen vehicles in the convoy. Red mist sprayed onto the windshields as their shots found their targets.

Charlie let loose with the rocket launcher on the front of the first vehicle, blowing its tires apart and sending the engine cowling flying. Oil and diesel fuel ignited and soon was blazing. The engine compartment of the rear-most vehicle also erupted in an explosion, as another boy did the same. Some of the vehicles had better glass than others, but the drivers only lived a very short time longer, as the snipers quickly took their second shots.

The guard detail on the convoy opened fire into the brush where the shots had come from, but distance and good camouflage saved the shooters, who continued their accurate rain of death.

The boys on the far side of the road lay quietly in their snowy hides, frozen in a deathlike stillness. Harvesting angels making ready for their day's work. They remained immobile until soldiers started to dismount and take cover right in front of them.

Before the Russians on the ground could return the sniper's fire, Ian's team opened up from less than two meters away, ripping a dozen men to shreds in seconds.

As the fire died down, both teams of boys switched the battle from trading shots, to close quarters "edged" combat in a heartbeat.

They rushed onto the vehicles and ripped up the remaining Russian soldiers in short order with knives, machetes, and tomahawks.

In less than five minutes, the enemy had lost thirty soldiers, an entire platoon, and the boys, none.

Ian and his friends kept their blades out, strolling up and down the line of vehicles, systematically ensuring there would be no survivors to tell the tale of their encounter with Alaska Defense Force Troop 104.

The rest of the patrol ran up to the vehicles, cracking open each container and ascertaining what they would be able to carry back to their camp to be useful. As Ben's team approached the back of one of the trucks, an explosion of screams and terrified sounding voices burst from inside the metal box, making his heart slam a half dozen Bruce Lee kicks against his ribs. As he caught his breath and regained his composure, he realized the voices inside the cargo container sounded unmistakably, female.

Ben stood at the end of the trailer and motioned for his men to not open fire. He reached up, gripped the handle on the Connex container, flipped it up, and twisted the lock open. The door swung instantly open and Ben was knocked backward, his butt slammed the pavement, knocking the wind out of him as a sudden flood of screaming bodies burst out of the dark space, and ran wailing past him onto the road several meters away.

"Who are you?" he demanded as he sucked air into his semi-collapsed lungs and struggled to his feet.

"The Russian soldiers were forcing us to be prostitutes for their regiment," replied a woman old enough to be Ben's mother. "Thank you for saving us!"

Ben stared at them wide eyed, then reached for the radio handset strapped to his shoulder and called out, "Uh...Mike... we have a situation."

"What's up?" Mike's voice crackled through the radio's speaker.

"Sir, there's a bunch of women here who say the Russians were making them prostitutes. What do we do with them?"

"How many?"

Ben glanced at the group huddled nearby.

"At least twenty, sir, maybe a few more."

"I see them. Bring them back to us, we'll figure out what to do next."

"Hey!" Ben shouted above the tumult of the women scrambling and the young soldiers trying to keep their wits about them in the confusion.

"Everyone grab as much food or ammo as you can carry," Ben called out as they settled down. "Take whatever you can carry, stuff that could be of use, preferably. You have two minutes to grab as much as you can and hustle it back to the sleds and get out of here."

The women stared in confusion, unsure what to do with their sudden freedom.

"What about us?" asked the older woman.

"You too, ma'am," Ben replied. "You and the rest of your group grab as much as you can carry and put it on those sleds," he pointed to the sleds being pulled up onto the roadway, "and come with us."

"Where?"

Several of the girls looked at him and the other dirty-looking warriors with trepidation.

"We have a base camp in the forest about thirty miles from here; our commander said to bring you with us." Ben noticed the expressions on their faces. "Don't worry, ladies, we're Boy Scouts. You'll be safe with us."

They gave him a look, then glanced around at the bodies of the Russian soldiers lying in pools of blood. Ian walked up at that moment and one of the girls let out a terrified shriek. The rest stared, aghast. His face and hands glistened with slowly freezing blood.

"Hello," he said to the girls and let out a shy smile, some of the dried blood cracking and flaking off his face.

Ben turned and looked at his brother, saw the grotesque mask, and made a motion with his eyes and a hand for him to go wash his face off in the snow.

"Don't mind my younger brother, it's not his blood," Ben said, then realizing the awkwardness of that sentence added, "Uh...I can explain later, but unless you want to be shot to pieces by a Russian helicopter, we need to get moving. We've got a very long hike ahead of us."

The women joined the looting of the trucks. Once the sleds and their arms were full, they followed the raiding party into the deep forest. Loads of heavy ammunition boxes and cases of Russian MREs and other boxes came back with them.

In addition to the mass of food, weapons, and ammo, they took whatever among the clothing wasn't too bloody such as boots and gloves from the dead, and the men's ruck sacks. They checked everything they took, looking for the RFID tags that could lead the Russians back to their base.

They worked fast, and in barely more than ten minutes, it felt like less than the two minutes Ben had commanded, they had every sled packed, the loads covered with furs and tied down with rope. They set charges on the trucks, and scuttled into the forest, rejoined the overwatch and commanders and hustled across the snow-covered landscape in a round-about path toward camp.

A light snow began to fall, soon becoming a steady cascade that would cover their tracks nicely.

✷ ✷ ✷

The party of nearly sixty people moved quietly through the forest, focusing on not falling behind or getting injured tripping over a hidden log or root mound buried beneath the knee-deep snow.

Between the treasure trove of supplies they'd captured and the unexpected extra living bodies, they only made less than half the distance per day on the return as they had coming out. No one talked, because no one had the energy to form the extra muscular movements required to get their vocal chords vibrating. The group moved in a sullen snow-drizzled mass, the members of Troop 104 heading home, while the females headed into the unknown.

With the cloud cover to hold the heat close to the surface of the earth, and the snowfall to insulate the ground, the temperature stayed relatively warm for winter, typically in the high twenties. While that may not seem warm to those uninitiated to the arctic, the reason Alaskans and other Arctic dwellers consider it warm becomes very evident, when the snow stops and the clouds clear out, leaving a nice blue sky and starry night. When the sky cleared and there was no ceiling of clouds to hold what heat there was near the surface, the warm air at the surface rises into that beautiful blue sky until it is a long-forgotten memory and the temperature drops to deep negative digits, sometimes getting as low as negative fifty degrees below zero, a temperature so cold that boiling water tossed into the air instantly freezes with an audible snap, falling to the earth like so many ice BBs.

For the moment, at least, they did not have that fear to deal with. When they finally stopped to make camp, the boys dug the snow out from under each of the sleds until they were down to the hard ground. They cleared a large area around sides and rear of the sleds, then leaned long branches and fallen birch poles onto the sleds and covered them with spruce boughs. They built several other similar shelters using trees rather than sleds.

Once they were done, they had dry and relatively warm shelters, large enough for everyone to get out of the snow. They put extra furs they had brought onto the ground under the makeshift lean-tos.

"Ladies," Mike said, "you get two of the shelters. Ten of you per shelter. Put the smallest or weakest in the center, sleep close together to stay warm. Sorry we don't have enough furs to use as blankets, but we weren't expecting guests."

One of the women replied, "Can't we just use the bottom one as a blanket?"

"Trust me, you'd rather have it under you," Mike said. "The frozen ground will suck the heat out of your body a whole faster than the air above you."

"Can we build a fire to warm up?" one of the younger women asked.

"No," said Marcus. "It won't provide as much warmth as snuggling together, and it will make us visible to any patrols flying overhead looking for us. We're still too close to the scene of the fight for any fires."

"Here," Steve handed the women several of the Russian MREs, "split one of these between two of you. There is a chemical heater in each packet with which you can warm the food and a small heat tablet that can boil a cup or two of water to make tea or coffee with, whatever is in the bag. That is the only external heat source you'll get."

Tommie looked at the expressions on some of their faces.

"Do you need one of us to show you how to use it?" he asked.

"No," said the leader, "my husband and I were hunters and used to eat the U.S. version of these meals. I think I can figure it out."

"Okay good," Mike said. "You've got your setup, and we've got to get the men scheduled for watch rotations. We will be up and on our way before the sun. We need to try and make up for the shortage in miles if possible so the pace tomorrow will be a bit more intense. Try to get as much sleep as possible."

"Thank you...um..."

"Mike, my name is Mike."

"And I am Linda."

"We'll get a lot of chances to talk and get to know details later, Linda. I hate to be curt, but everyone really does need to get as much sleep as possible and we've got stuff to do."

With that, Mike and the others turned to the work of securing the camp, and getting the boys fed and assigned to their tasks.

"Are we going to be okay, now?" one of the young girls in the group turned to Linda and whispered, her tiny frightened voice sent puffs of wispy steam into the night air.

"Yes, honey," Linda whispered back, "I think it will be alright."

43

In the end, it took six days to get their treasures back to the Troop 104 encampment. The addition of the women and girls to the group was met with mixed emotion from both boys and men. Some of the boys resented the fact that they had to give up their quarters and pack tighter in the already cramped spaces of the dugout cabins they had hastily built months earlier just before winter.

Others were mesmerized by the presence of the first females they had seen in a year and a half. Yet others, particularly the younger boys, wept at the sight of a mother figure walking among them. Some of the men were more pragmatic.

"How the hell are we going to feed them?" said Ron. "I can understand the need to help them out and rescue them, but realistically, Mike, we're barely making it here just with the boys and us. I mean," he put his hand to his forehead, "we don't have the supplies for an extra twenty mouths to feed."

Mike started to speak, but Tommie put a hand up and stepped forward.

"God will take care of it," the Irishman said.

"Really? He's just gonna what? Give us manna from heaven?"

"No, not likely," Tommie said, "but he will take care of it. He always does."

"Oh really," Ron said. "Since when are you, the Irish mercenary, such a devout believer in divine providence?"

"Since I was very young actually," Tommie replied. "Don't forget, I grew up in later part of the Troubles in my homeland;

I survived in the most violent parts of it all not by my own wits, but by God's will. My wife was a Somali refugee whose entire village was massacred when she was a child, yet she survived to meet me and give me a few years of peace until her time came and she was taken. I survived until now to be able to help Mike and all of you to bring this troop of boys to this point, all of us alive and kicking Russian ass. And we all survived and won this fight, because God willed for us to save these women for something greater than being abused to death as sexual playthings. If he allowed all of those things to happen, he most definitely will take us to the point where we can faithfully trust that he has not done it all in vain."

There was silence between the men, tension neither fading nor growing.

"Does anyone really believe that stuff? That is no kind of real logic," Treadmore put in. "Just a bunch of Christian religious bullshit."

"While I did grow up Christian, Presbyterian to be precise," Tommie gave him a look that could've curdled milk, "I can assure you everything I just mentioned was not taught me by the church, and certainly is no bullshit. It was what I lived for real, therefore it is the purest logic."

Treadmore started to puff up his chest, but something in Tommie's expression left him with the distinct impression that this was the wrong alpha-dog to cross, regardless of the perception of gross intellectual inferiority.

"The women stay," Mike said, breaking the tense moment. "We will find a way to make sure everyone is fed and secure. They can help lighten the load of many camp chores as well as aid in gathering and hunting."

He glanced at the group of them going through the looted baggage with Ben and the young leaders. Some of the girls seemed unsure of what they were doing, but a few seemed to have no doubts. They were confident and sure of themselves, refusing to accept assistance from any of the boys and young men.

"Some may even be useful on patrols."

They moved the gear out of the sleds, spreading it in a semi-organized state across tarps and skins laid on a cleared space on the ground. They stacked them into similarity-based groups to more efficiently make an inventory of what they had captured. After what they had eaten from the supplies, they still had several hundred pounds of food both in MRE format and canned and other preserved foods that were likely intended for mess sergeants at some remote bases to make "fancy" meals with.

There were two twenty-pound cases of what Mr. Tatum said was canned beef stew. They wrote the English names of the contents on each can with a sharpie as he translated the Russian labels. Vegetables, smoked fish or soups. A few cans of jelly and marmalade. Several cases of canned salmon from the cannery in Valdez, actual almost fresh salmon. They also had several containers of freeze dried foods, including a case of powdered eggs and freeze-dried ham chunks that the cook quickly stole from the pile to hide in the mess hut for a special occasion.

Weapons-wise, they took more than a dozen AK-12 rifles with ammo vests packed with loaded magazines, as well as ammo boxes accounting for about fifteen thousand rounds of ammunition for them. Many of the rifles were equipped with small grenade launchers, for which they found four cases of grenades. Two cases of traditional hand grenades found their way into the payload, as well as two of the more potent PKP general purpose machine guns and a couple of thousand rounds of belted 7.62x54 ammo.

The treasure of it all, at least in the grown men's eyes, were the two cases of Russian vodka. Twenty-four bottles of Russian white-lightning. They didn't recognize the brand, it was labeled in Russian of course, but it brought smiles to their faces nonetheless. Mike, a devout Mormon, was not willing to partake of the alcohol. Tommie, Ron, Steve, and the others though, being of various other denominational persuasions, were each willing to drink up their share as they cracked open a bottle to pass around.

Tommie took a big swig and made a face that looked like a fire had erupted in his chest. He coughed out a curse and passed it to Ron. Ron took a mouthful and quickly passed it to Steve who raised it to his lips just as Ron swallowed and suddenly gasped for air with a loud inhalation.

"Oh dear God," Ron squeaked. "That is like drinking kerosene that's already been lit!"

Tommie grinned as his eyes twisted in a royal effort retain his composure at the pain of the sinfully cheap alcohol. Steve got half a swallow down and spewed it right back up.

"GAAAAH!" he erupted, "this is poison!"

"No," said Tommie, "this is legitimate Russian vodka, albeit..." he sucked in a breath and quickly blew it out his mouth, "not from the higher shelves in the liquor store."

The woman Linda who had come in with the patrol strode over to them and snatched the bottle from Steve's hand. She sucked down a mouthful, paused, then guzzled another, swallowing with little effect other than briefly squeezing her eyes shut then popping them open again and letting out a flammable sigh.

"That, boys," she said, her face showing no signs of shock other than a slight reddening as the warmth crept into it, "is real vodka! Just like my husband used to make in our still!"

The whole crowd burst into laughter.

Ben smiled as the "adults" were laughing it up over the vodka. The scene reminded him of his dad, who used to imbibe from time to time and liked to try different types of alcohol, sometimes landing on a label that apparently focused more on value than quality and suffering like the folks in front of him.

A movement in the corner of his eye caught his attention and he glanced over at a freckled red-headed girl about his age. She had come in with the others but seemed to stand apart from them. She worked hard, never complained, and during the journey home had never fallen behind the pace of the main party.

During that march back, there had been neither time nor energy to strike up a conversation and get to know any of the women. Twice, the sound of helicopters in the distance had them huddling under their shelters, praying thermal scanners would not detect them and shred them to pieces. Somehow, they had made it back to the relative safety of their base. And now that they were able to relax a little, conversation could begin. He worked his way toward her until he was near enough to comfortably talk with her.

"Hi," he said. "I'm Ben."

"Hm," she replied.

"You're a hard worker," he said.

"Yeah."

He looked at the box in front of him, opened it, and started pulling out cans of something heavy that might have been food, but he couldn't read the Russian on the labels.

"Boy," he said, "I wish I could tell what this stuff was. I mean, is it food or is it axle grease?"

"It is smoked fish in oil."

"You read Russian?"

"Yes," she replied.

"Did you take Russian in high school?"

"No."

"Then how…"

"Are you Eskimo?" she asked.

"Uh…no."

"Then why do you look Yupik?"

"I'm not," he said, stunned by the sudden change of direction in the conversation.

"Then what are you?"

"My mother is Korean," he said. "My dad is white."

"Mixed breed," she grunted.

"Yeah," he replied, feeling insulted, "is there a problem with that?"

"Only if you have a problem with it." She picked up an ammo can, and walked several yards over to a stack of similar cans.

He snatched one in each hand from the same stack and followed her. The unexpected weight of his cans nearly pulled his arms out of their sockets. He covered the sudden discomfort both at the jolt on his shoulders and the realization that she had lifted the same sized can one handed with no effect.

"Why would I have a problem with my DNA?" Ben asked, trying to hide the strain in his voice.

"You wouldn't, unless you were a weakling looking for an excuse to hide from your weaknesses."

Ben put the cans down and tried to ignore the pain in his shoulders. He couldn't. He felt like a wimp as his shoulders and upper back throbbed. She went back to the stack of ammo cans and stood there staring at him. He stared back, trying to work the strain out of his joints and arms.

"Well," she said. "What are you waiting for?"

"What?" he shot back at her.

"Are you going to come over here and help a damsel in distress, or what?"

"What?" He gave an incredulous look. "You just effortlessly carried something over here that nearly took my shoulders out of joint. Why do you need my help?"

She gave him a look. He gave it back to her.

"What?" he said.

She pointed to the cans they had carried. His had the numbers 7.62x54 but the rest of the writing was in Russian. Hers just had words in Russian, no numbers.

"You just carried two thousand rounds of 7.62x54 ammo, a thousand in each hand mind you, to the wrong stack," she said with a condescending smile.

"Then so did you," he grunted, shaking out his shoulder.

"No," she replied, "I carried a can full of maps and documents."

He glanced at the cans, then back to her, a look of confusion on his face.

"Hi Ben, I am Katarina, and I speak and read Russian... natively."

✳ ✳ ✳

Once the larger gear was sorted and organized, they put those items in storage and began the much more detailed job of going through the backpacks and personal items of the men they had killed. From within that gear, they collected and sorted toiletries, paper pads, ink pens, chewing gum, candy, and other sundries. There were some books and magazines, nearly all in Russian and most of the latter being pornographic in nature. They also found more personal effects, like family pictures, letters written in Cyrillic script most of them could not decipher, even diaries.

"So, Katarina," Ben said, "anyone else in your group speak Russian?"

"I don't really know. A lot of us didn't know each other until a couple days ago when we were all taken from Valdez."

"Valdez is a pretty small town, how did you all not know each other?"

"I didn't say all, I said a lot," she corrected. "The other girls my age, late teens, do mostly know each other, but I don't know them. When the war started, I was just in town with my family for a fishing trip with some friends."

She removed the contents of a soldier's wallet that had been in his coat pocket. There were a few hundred rubles in cash, an ID card that looked like a civilian driving license, and a number of pictures in a clear plastic accordion pack. She lifted the pictures and the packet unfolded revealing images of what was likely his mother and father, other relatives, and what may have been his sister or girlfriend. She glanced up and saw Ben's face go beet red. She looked back at the pictures then flipped the stack over to view the other side.

The picture of the young woman on the first side had definitely been his girlfriend. Unless this guy had a highly immoral relationship with his sister. She shook her head, folded it back up, and tossed into the trash pile.

"I come from a traditional Old Believer Russian village near Homer," she continued, barely missing a beat. "My family has been there longer than Alaska has been part of America. We speak Russian and English both. Because my ancestor's Orthodox religion is slightly different than traditional Russian Orthodox from way back when, back in the eighteen-hundreds, they found it easier to come and stay over here, since Alaska was part of Russia back then."

"What was so different about the religions?"

"Fingers."

"Fingers?"

"Yup," she took a deep breath and said in a sarcastic tone, "the main difference was whether you crossed yourself with two straight fingers and your thumb, or with just your pointer finger straight, your middle finger slightly bent and no thumb."

"Wow," Ben said, a befuddled look on his face, "that's a kind of minor point to move to an entirely different continent over."

"Yeah, well," Katarina said, "it was important enough to the folks back in the sixteen-hundreds to persecute and even kill my ancestors."

"That sucks."

"And that suckiness is how my family ended up here on the Kenai Peninsula several decades before the U.S. bought Alaska from Russia."

"Do you think it still should be part of Russia?"

"No. Way," she said, emphasizing each word solid stop. "We are Americans, who happen to speak Russian. We like to be free, and want to do everything we can to kick these invaders out." She moved several items to the stacks matching the subject they fell under. "The uncle we were staying with in Valdez most of last winter was actively involved in the resistance, picking up information that he could pass on to other guerillas, like you guys, but down in that area."

"Really?" Ben said. "Maybe you could get him in contact with Mike and Tommie and we could share information."

Katarina took a long pause, her eyes glazing over as if she saw something she wished she hadn't.

"Not likely," she said.

"No? Why not?"

"He and his entire family were killed a couple weeks ago, along with both my younger brothers and my little five-year-old sister when someone turned him in to the soldiers. I was the only one who escaped." Her voice caught in her throat for a moment. "And that was only because they intended to rape me to death."

Ben reached out to take her hand, but she pulled back.

"I don't need your sympathy," she grunted. "I need you to help me get vengeance."

Ben stared at the ground for a while, took in a deep breath, and let it out with a slow hiss.

"That seems to be something we're getting very good at here," he whispered. "Vengeance."

44

Chinese Base

Captain Fang jogged up to the line of a half-dozen trucks that were almost fully loaded with food, bedding, and toiletry supplies, as well as mail for the men at the Palmer FOB (Forward Operating Base). Their security team consisted of a single thirty-man platoon of infantry.

The young lieutenant in charge of the convoy snapped to attention and saluted as the captain came up to him.

"Good morning, sir, what can I do for you?"

"I am going to add several vehicles to your convoy. A company of new special scout troops who are assigned to Palmer arrived a couple days ahead of schedule. We have no billets for them here, but the bedding material in your trucks is for them at their new location."

"No problem, sir." The lieutenant looked at the line of trucks then added, "They have their own vehicles, I assume? We've got no room where a whole company of combat soldiers and their gear can ride with us."

"Yes," Fang replied, "they have several Tiger four by fours, as well as a number of armored Humvees."

"Excellent, when can they be ready to go?"

"Their gear is already loaded; it will only take moments for the men to get in."

"We'll be ready to leave in fifteen minutes. The bridge over the Knik River is still out of commission after insurgents blew it up last month, so just before we get to Palmer, we'll turn off and take the Old Glenn highway through Butte. It is a much narrower road, so tell those men to stay about five minutes behind me. That way if something happens, we don't get all jammed up on the road."

"Are you expecting contact on the way?" asked the captain.

"There have not been any attacks there recently, since we have pretty solid control of the area, but it's better to be safe than sorry. Tell them that they will be close enough to be a quick reaction force if we get hit."

"I will let them know."

The lieutenant snapped a salute, Fang responded in kind, and they went back to work.

Fifteen minutes later, the convoy pulled out of the main gate of Ft. Richardson heading northeast on the Glenn Highway. Five minutes after that, the company of special scouts followed.

45

Butte
Near U-Pick Farm

The Ranger patrol had been out four days when they arrived at the site of the ambush. It had taken them that long to sneak far enough behind enemy lines that the invaders would have no idea where they had come from.

The rule for ambush patrols was that they almost never performed an ambush within fifty miles of Chiknik, to avoid leading the enemy back to their base. It made it hard when they wanted to steal supplies, as they could only take as much as twenty or thirty men could carry in a single trip to their vehicles, usually a SUSV or four-wheel ATVs which would be parked a mile or more from the actual attack site.

This ambush, though, was primarily a psychological one. Hit a food supply run, kill everyone, and destroy the contents of the containers. Spies inside the Chinese army had passed the information on the convoy. Another militia group had blown up the bridges over the Knik River a month earlier, forcing all traffic north toward Palmer and Wasilla to use the more narrow Old Glenn Highway. It was the perfect setup, and they acted instantly.

"Mills," called out the team sergeant, "get the LAWs set up over there in that defilade." He pointed to a depression in the ground twenty yards away. "Blow the engine block of the first two vehicles."

Mills nodded and ran to the indicated location, three LAW rocket tubes hanging from his shoulder.

"Staley brothers," the sergeant pointed to a cluster of trees on the other side of the two-lane highway, "set the M-32 over there, use armor-piercing grenades to take out the rear vehicles, then blow the cabs of the vehicles stuck in the middle. Phil, cover your brother with the Stoner."

The brothers moved to the spot indicated, packed the snow down beneath them, and began the prep work for the killing to come. Phil quickly setup the M63 light machine gun, sweeping it side to side, visualizing his field of fire to ensure no natural objects blocked his view.

The fifty-year-old weapon, also called a Stoner after its inventor, had been favored by Navy SEALs from Vietnam thru the late eighties. This particular weapon had been donated to the Rangers by a seventy-year-old man, who'd brought it to Chiknik earlier in the year. The Vietnam veteran, being too old himself to join their long-range patrols and assaults, figured it'd be best put to use by the men who were the age he had been when he first carried an earlier model of the weapon against Viet Cong guerrillas, back when the Staley boys' dad was just a sparkle in his parent's eyes.

Beside him, Paul stood the M-32 against a tree and flipped back the cover of a bag full of 40mm grenades. He cracked open the cylinder of the grenade launcher. It opened much like his father's old .357 caliber revolver did, except that it was just about twenty times bigger. Once open, he primed the cylinder with a twist until it locked into position, and loaded it with the HELLHOUNDS rounds the sergeant had instructed.

The HOUNDS of HELLHOUNDS stood for, "High Order Unbelievably Nasty Destructive Series," literally, that is the official name of the grenade. The HELL was tacked onto the front for additional coolness factor. They truly were an unbelievably nasty destructive weapon too.

Upon impact with a target, a firing pin inside the grenade's warhead is driven into the detonator, which in turn initiates a spit-back charge, producing a jet of molten metal that instantly penetrates up to one centimeter thick steel, or several inch thick wooden doors or brick walls, and then explodes inside showering any occupants with a fiery rain of steel shrapnel, killing everything within a ten-meter radius.

While it lacked the specific punch of the LAW rockets Mills was preparing, the fact that Paul could put six rounds down range in a matter of three seconds and reload in only ten more seconds to repeat the act increased the M-32's lethality exponentially.

The remainder of the twenty-man patrol set up in a pattern to provide deadly crossfire and booby traps using rifles, machine guns, and homemade claymore mines. The whole ambush should take less than ten minutes, including finishing the wounded. Then they would disappear into the forest, back to their vehicles to lay low in the wilderness for a few days before heading home.

"Doc," called the sergeant, "you stay with me in the middle, that way you can deploy either direction as needed."

"Yes, sergeant," replied the young medic.

William Henry was twenty-four and had just finished paramedic school a few months before the invasion. He'd been on an internship with the Anchorage Fire Department before returning to his home town in Salt Jacket where he would work with the Salt Jacket Fire and Rescue Service covering nearly sixty miles of highway between the cities of North Pole and Big Delta. Now, instead of being lead medic in an ambulance picking up injured victims of automobile and snow machine accidents or making house calls for medical emergencies, he was a combat medic with an elite paramilitary team fighting off invaders that had ransacked his country. Not only could he patch up the men that were injured or wounded in a fight, he could, and had, deliver babies, give inoculations, treat hemorrhoids, and kill the enemy with his bare hands. The latter of which he justified by telling himself that unlike a doctor, paramedics did not take the Hippocratic Oath.

Thirty minutes after setting up and camouflaging their positions, the rumble of trucks could be heard; a few minutes later, a slow-moving convoy appeared at the far end of a long straight stretch of road. The attackers were spread far enough that they could completely envelop the trucks, pinning them in the middle between dead vehicles, and make quick work of them.

As the last vehicle came across from the Staley brother's position, they opened fire. The Hummer's cab dissolved in a bright flash, as the armor-piercing grenade burst through the window and exploded just beneath the turret.

The upper half of the soldier manning the machine gun spun into the air, landing with a thud on the road a few meters away, his skewed helmet covering his face that no doubt stared in wide-eyed confusion by his sudden death.

Paul corrected his aim and blew the thin-skinned cab of the tractor trailer completely apart. At the same time, two explosions erupted in succession at the other end of the column. The rapid fire of rifles and machine guns burst from the woods on all sides.

Trailers and truck beds full of food and materials for the barracks in Palmer were systematically shredded, the cabs of the vehicles sprayed with bullets and grenades.

Anyone trying to dismount and fight back was either shot or cut in half by hundreds of steel balls and nails blasted from the homemade claymores. Half the men in the convoy were dead or dying in a matter of moments.

Before the slaughter could be completed though, Paul heard a new sound. His heart leapt in his chest as he saw another column of vehicles speeding toward the scene.

These were not on the list of vehicle types their spies had mentioned. The vehicles headed their way were heavily shielded Tiger Armored Personnel Carriers, and up-armored Humvees, all of which had either 12.7mm heavy machine guns or 30mm grenade cannons mounted in their turrets and ten armed men inside.

Paul instantly counted at least ten of the Tigers and four Humvees. That was over a hundred regular infantry coming their way, guns blazing.

Paul clicked on his radio to alert the patrol sergeant.

"We've got company, lots of company!"

"Where?"

"Coming up the road from the rear, at least a full infantry company, with big guns."

Just as Paul finished those words, the trees around him splintered at the impact of the 12.7mm bullets, the Chinese equivalent of a .50cal, bullets the size of a man's index finger.

He tapped Phil on the back with the signal they'd practiced to initiate a fighting retreat. Paul fast-crawled deeper into the woods then turned to give covering fire to his brother Phil. As the younger brother scurried back, the elder put rounds out of his machine gun towards the oncoming troops. The pinging sound they made confirmed the thickness of the armor on the Tigers; they were not going to be easy targets.

Suddenly, the amount of fire coming from the armored vehicles rose to a cacophonous storm and the very earth erupted around them. The Rangers attempted to return fire but those who did quickly found themselves the subjects of intense Chinese attention.

The call was made for everyone to evacuate on their own and make their way back to the rendezvous at the vehicles hidden deep in the woods.

Giving the order was one thing, actually evacuating was another.

The special scout company was a very highly disciplined and well-trained group, and they had five times more men that laid down a seriously heavy rain of lead and explosives.

As the men leapfrogged back into the woods, melting into the deep brush, William Henry heard the call that sends every combat medic into impulsive action.

"Medic!"

William sprinted toward the sound of the pained voice, and found a soldier kneeling beside the team sergeant who lay in a pool of blood on the frozen ground, the snow stained crimson like a blood-slushy. The sergeant's eyes were wide open, staring skyward in a look of surprise. William could see the ground through the cavity in his chest.

"He's gone," he shouted to the other soldier. "Get out of here!"

The man hesitated.

"Now!"

He grabbed the soldier by the arm and dragged him in a crouching run toward the trees. The sound of bullets zipped past their ears like scores of angry bees.

William felt a slap on his back, like someone had whacked him with canoe paddle. He tumbled headfirst, the soldier he was leading falling with him. The other man rose back up to continue running then realized Doc wasn't getting up. He turned back to the medic, but was waved away.

"Go! Get out of here," William gasped, gripping his assault rifle to cover the other man's escape.

The soldier hesitated.

"Get the hell out of here!"

The man sprinted into the trees as William shimmied his back up against a Birch stump and reached into his breast pocket. He felt the life draining out of him, punctured lungs slowly filling with blood. He stared at the picture in his hand, taken at the clinic in Chiknik. He and his wife with the doctor, Brad "Ice Hammer" Stone and his wife Sammi. Both women six months pregnant, glowing in the late autumn sunlight. Beautiful. He wished he could have met his child. He wished he could have held his wife one more time. A shadowy figure moved toward him. He saw the small red star on the soldier's helmet. His finger twitched on the trigger of his rifle. The shadow was gone. Then the impact of a dozen more canoe paddles pounded his chest. He felt a brief, sharp impact on his forehead, and his thoughts drained into darkness.

* * *

Paul and Phil made it back to their four-wheeler to find a handful of other men already there. Of their original group of twenty, only nine had made it back to the vehicles. Several were being patched up, blood oozing from wounds they'd received during the retreat. One man lay dead, his skin pale white, almost indiscernible from the snow around him.

"Should we wait for the others?" asked one of them.

"I counted at least eight definitely dead back there," said another soldier. "That leaves three that may still be heading this direction."

"No," said Paul, "we all know the rendezvous point. Get out of here now before the Chinese come after us. The more of us that can get home, the more that can tell the story."

"I agree, if we go back to get them, we're all dead," said Phil. "Live to fight another day."

"Leave one of the four-wheelers for them," said one of the others.

"Okay," Paul said, "but we have to go now."

With that, the Staley brothers hopped onto their four-wheeler and took off toward the first meeting point. They would each take different routes to meet up at the first point, then follow the same procedure for four more rendezvous until they were far enough out of Chinese-controlled territory to safely head straight to Chiknik.

46

Chinese HQ

Youngmi stared out the window, watching fresh snow falling in large, lazy clusters of flakes. A knock on the door pulled her out of her reverie. She walked across the main room of the quarters she shared with General Zhang and opened the door.

"Mai," she said with a smile. Their relationship over the past year and a half had grown very close. Mai even called her Ayi. As the young woman stepped into the apartment, though, tension sizzled around her.

"Mai," Youngmi said, her voice dropping to a worried tone. "Is everything okay?"

Mai closed the door behind her, and turned the lock.

"Ayi, we have to talk," Mai said, "where no one can hear us."

"There is no one here but me right now," Youngmi said. "The general's staff are all out of the house at the moment."

Mai went to a couch across the room and sat down on the edge of it, her body stiff, knees together, back straight, hands closed in white-knuckled fists. She seemed unable to look Youngmi in the eye. The older woman joined her on the couch, concern etched on her face.

"Mai, what is it? You seem very upset."

"Yes, I have learned some very difficult news, and I don't know what to do about it."

"What is it? Is it about your father?"

Youngmi put a hand on Mai's knee. The young woman flinched and Youngmi pulled it back.

"Mai?"

"I know who you are…Mrs. Stone."

"Yes, yes you have known me since I was brought here more than a year ago." It took a moment for Youngmi to realize that Mai had called her by her married name rather than Mrs. Ma. Her heart stuttered. It missed several beats.

"I now also know the identity of the one called Ice Hammer."

"Ice Hammer?" Youngmi said, a slight quiver in her voice.

"Yes, he is one of the most wanted men in the resistance," Mai said. "His name is Brad Stone. Your husband."

Youngmi's heart lurched in her chest. What else did Mai know? Did she know that Youngmi was actively passing intelligence to the resistance? Did she know about the other spies inside the Chinese army?

"My husband is alive?" she said, playing it for more information.

Mai looked up at her, misery written in her tear-filled eyes. "I found out when we were collecting records of people who were suspected of being in the resistance. I found both of your records and put them together."

"What are you going to do with me then?"

"Nothing." Mai quickly wiped tears from her eyes with her sleeve, forcing a stoic expression. "I shredded the paper evidence and altered the electronic records. No one will ever find out."

Youngmi stared at her in shock.

"Why did you do that?"

"Because I know you, and I know how much my father cares about you. If word of this got out, everyone would question your loyalty, and my father's heart would be broken and his reputation would be destroyed."

"But, if someone does find out what you have done, you will be in terrible danger," Youngmi said, fear causing a tremor in her voice as the thought materialized. "You could be shot."

"No one will find out," Mai said. "I was very thorough."

"I don't know what to say." Youngmi struggled for a moment to find something, but nothing came.

"You don't need to say anything. For that matter, you must not ever say anything."

"But if my husband is still alive, I mean, he is my husband."

Mai let out a sigh, then hesitantly continued, "Recent intelligence indicates he probably thinks you are dead."

"Why do you say that?" Youngmi whispered.

Mai handed her a piece of paper, an eight and a half by eleven color picture on it.

"He has apparently remarried, to a much younger woman. She is pregnant with his child."

Youngmi stared at the picture in stunned silence, instantly recognizing Brad. He wore a huge smile on his face, surrounded by a group of happy-looking people, one of whom had a stethoscope around his neck, like a doctor. Brad's hand was on the belly of a very pregnant woman, a woman Youngmi also recognized. Sammi Park's face beamed with that glow that only pregnancy can give. She sucked in a deep breath.

"How did you get this picture?"

"We found it on the body of one of the other men in the picture." Mai pointed to the man. He was standing on the other side of Sammi, medic scissors and a stethoscope stuffed into his breast pocket. The young man's arm was around the waist of another woman dressed likewise but just as round with child as Sammi. "He was killed during a small battle near Palmer."

"Do your people know where Brad is?"

"No," Mai said. "His soldiers were preparing an ambush of one of our supply convoys, but were caught in the open before they were ready. They seemed to have walked very far judging by what they carried."

"So, you don't know where Brad and his people are?"

"Not exactly."

They went silent again as Youngmi stared back at the picture in her hand.

"Ayi," Mai said, reaching up and touching her forearm, "I have told you more than I should have. I did not want to hurt you. Only to let you know what I know, and that I will say nothing to anyone."

Youngmi wiped a tear from her eyes, and quietly nodded.

"But Ayi," Mai continued, "I cannot protect your husband or his people when they are discovered."

"I know, Mai." Youngmi sucked in a sharp breath, then let it out in a long sigh. "Their fate is in their own hands."

47

Chiknik

News of the failed ambush hit Brad and the others of the Chiknik community hard. By the time everyone had returned, nearly two weeks after the attack, they realized they'd lost thirteen men, more than half the patrol. Of those who had initially managed to escape, four had died of their injuries on the way home. Their frozen bodies were carried all the way back by their teammates for burial by their families and friends.

The blow hit hard. It was the single biggest loss the Rangers had experienced on an ambush, which usually ended up with few or no losses to their numbers. The only larger loss of life had been during the rescue of Brad and his people from the relative luxury of the house they had spent the previous winter in. That fight had taken fifteen dead, and two dozen wounded.

But that was a rescue mission based on intel that a large force was heading his way.

This ambush, this loss was based on faulty, maybe even fabricated, intelligence handed them by spies within the Chinese army.

Had they been lied to? Set up?

"I do not think it was a setup," said Gunnar. "If it had been, they would not have allowed the supply convoy to be shot up so easily."

Kharzai nodded his head. "I'm inclined to agree. I think it was fate, just a coincidence that those crack soldiers were a couple minutes behind the main convoy."

"Fate or failure, doesn't make a difference for the wives and children of those men that lost their lives," Brad said. "Doc Henry's wife is close friends with Sammi; their babies are due the same day. And now he will never see his child, and that baby will never know its father."

"Happens in this business all the time, sir," said John. "It's why they say, 'war is hell' you know."

Brad slumped, elbows on his desk, face in his hands. "I just want it all to go away. To wake up and realize it is all just a bad dream, and everything is back to what it was."

"Yeah, well," Kharzai walked across the room, popped open a bottle of scotch whiskey that had been scrounged from a cabin recently, and poured four glasses, taking out half the bottle, "it won't, it ain't, and it…uh…it won't."

He handed the glasses to the other three men, keeping one for himself.

"Those soldiers that hit our men," said Gunnar after taking a sip from his glass, "they were heading to be deployed at the Palmer base. That means they are most likely going to be looking for us."

"There are also about half a dozen other groups causing havoc out there," Brad said.

"Yeah but we're the biggest by far," Kharzai put in, squeezing his face as he swallowed a sip of the very strong liquor. "Gah! This is not one of the finer scotch brands I am thinking."

"Only the best for Ice Hammer." John raised his glass. "Which means that while there are other groups out there, only we have the Ice Hammer, the figure head for the resistance."

"Why do I have to have a crosshair painted on my head? Why can't someone else get their attention for a while?"

"Because you're loved," said Kharzai. "You're all the paparazzi talk about, you know?"

"Like we said before," Gunnar sipped his drink and made a face like Kharzai's, "we need to take the fight to them."

"We just did that and it backfired massively." Brad gulped his scotch down like it was water.

"Dude," said Kharzai, "did that not burn at all? You got an iron stomach?"

"Huh?" Brad looked at the empty glass, gave a smirk, then put it down.

John let out a breath, then said, "We recently got intel that gives us a couple of dates for the Chinese commandant's schedule over the next month. We can put a hit on him personally."

"That could be a serious game changer," said Kharzai.

"Kill the man who has lead this whole invasion?" asked Brad.

"At least the Alaska part of it," said John. "Won't make difference in the big picture, but at least it would be significant for us."

"That it would," said Brad. "Get it planned. And I want to be in on it."

48

Scouts

"So, how long have you and these boys been out here?" Linda asked.

"Pretty much since day one of the invasion," Ron said. "Not this site exactly; we've only been specifically here since mid-June. The last camp we'd built was discovered and the Russians sent a couple missiles into it."

"Oh my, did you lose a lot of men?"

"None in that bombing actually." He put his foot up on a stump used for splitting firewood, and leaned his elbows over his knee. "Some of the boys had spotted the Spetsnaz troopers and killed them, we think before they'd reported their findings. When they didn't perform their scheduled check-in later that night, the Russians did what they like to do, and obliterated the camp. By then, we were more than ten miles south and heading this way."

"Where was your original camp?"

Ron pointed generally north. "Up by Tazlina Lake. It was a real nice village too. Much more work had been put into it than we've got in this one."

"You guys walked all the way from Tazlina?" Linda gaped in awe. "That's like twenty miles or more, with all this stuff."

"Twenty miles as the crow flies," said Ron. "It turned into over sixty miles with going around the natural obstacles, mountains, and avoiding giving the Russians an idea of where we were heading."

"How long did it take?"

"A little over a week. But that was nothing compared to the hundred and eighty or so miles we hiked the first summer to get to Tazlina. At least from that camp to here, the reindeer really helped. They carried a lot of the load."

"I was wondering about those reindeer," Linda said. "Where did you get them?"

"From the herd out there." He nodded toward the mountains.

"They were wild?"

"Yup." He pointed toward a grizzled man that was brushing down one of the animals. "Walt there was a hostler back before. Trained horses from the ground up. He made it look pretty easy, but I think he's got magic or something. The boys call him the 'caribou whisperer.'"

She watched as Walt cared for one of the animals and could see where the boys got the idea for the name. As he brushed its neck, he spoke softly, getting a nuzzle in response. He smiled at the animal and scratched behind its ears. Two others noticed the attention and ambled over for their share.

"He really does seem to have a knack with them," Linda said. She sucked in a breath, then it out. "How long do you think this will go on?"

Ron's brow scrunched in confusion.

"The reindeer? Well, Walt's teaching a couple of the boys, so I don't see an end to it."

Linda gave him a sideways look, "Uh, no. I mean this." She motioned toward the camp as a whole. "This camping out in the woods, fighting Russians and Chinese."

Ron pursed his lips and drew a long breath through his nose. He glanced down at the ground, out toward the camp, then to Linda.

"As long as it takes."

"Takes to what? Kick them out? For us to win?"

"For whatever the future will bring."

"You are forty some odd boys and men, and now you have another twenty or so girls and women added in. The invaders have tens of thousands of soldiers and fresh ones coming all the time."

Ron nodded quietly as she continued.

"How long can you guys, how long can we, stay out here, poking fingers into the eyes of the Russian army and then running back to this little hideout?"

He looked up, inhaled a deep breath, and let it out with a sigh.

"You smell that?" he said.

"What?"

"The smell of the forest. The spruce and alder. The clean scent of the snow. Not a bit of pollution in this air."

A pause.

"And listen to the sounds."

He stepped over the stump he'd been leaning on and sat down. She sat on one next to his.

The life of the camp rose around them. Fires crackled and popped with the sounds of old-fashioned warmth. A woodpecker rattled against the side of a tree in the distance. Reindeer snuffled at the ground as they rooted for food. A gentle breeze whistled softly in the tops of the trees and the scents of smoke, sweat, and food mingled in the air around them as fresh snow fell in fat clusters of flakes.

She looked at him, took a deep breath, and said, "Those sounds and smells are why I live here, and have lived here for my whole life. But things have changed; the whole place has turned upside down."

"Yes, it has," Ron said. "I have lived here my whole life too. I have been hunting and fishing in the Alaska bush since before I could even walk. My dad fished for salmon in the Kenai carrying me in a baby-carrier with a huge .44 Ruger Redhawk in a chest rig right next to my little body. When I was four, I shot my first rabbit with a tiny little .22 rifle I could barely hold up. My dad made me skin and clean it, and we roasted it over a fire in camp that night. The sounds and smell of the forest, and its creatures, is so deeply embedded in me I cannot imagine a world that's not like that."

He picked up a stick and traced a circle in the snow.

"Several times in my adult life, I had to go outside of Alaska for work related stuff. Seattle, Portland, even Los Angeles. Those huge cities, fifteen or twenty times bigger than Anchorage. Millions of people. Massive sprawling urban and suburban areas packed so tightly you can't tell when you've passed from one city to the next except some green sign says 'Welcome to Pasadena.'"

"I felt like I was stuck in an anthill. Surrounded by noise and the stink of exhaust, constant lights blaring everywhere. Cars playing loud music at all hours of the night. When I was there, I could not even smell the trees if I was standing right under them. I could not hear the birds or the water in the creeks, or chirp of the squirrels over the sound of constant traffic and people talking nonstop."

He drew an X in the snow.

"Now here we have the Chinese invading, trying to find room for their billion plus people by taking our land so they can turn it into yet more sprawling waste. The Russians are the same, except they're not here for the land, but to take our resources, even though they've got plenty at home. Siberia is three times bigger than Alaska."

He let out a sigh. Linda watched him intently.

"I guess what I am trying to say is, we lived in paradise. And they are trying to take away the very essence of our lives, the life of all Alaskans. So, when you ask when will it end, I say it will end when I and everyone like me is dead."

A scream shattered the air.

They bolted to their feet and rushed to the sound of a young girl in agony. When they arrived, several of the others were comforting a thirteen-year-old named Katie. She looked like she'd seen a demon or something. Her typically rosy face was deathly pale, lips stretched in a terrified grimace exposing her teeth.

"What happened," demanded Mike as he burst into the group.

"It's him, it's him," the little girl kept saying.

"Who's him?"

"The man who…he…" her body trembled so hard she couldn't speak.

Fearing she would go into a seizure, Mike ordered the women to take Katie back to her room and get her to calm down.

"Then find out what happened and get back to me as soon as possible."

They lead Katie away, her sobs choking out between terrified gasps of breath.

"What could she possibly have seen that could have gotten her that riled up?" Steve asked.

"Whatever, or whoever, it was, we need to get it figured out," Mike said. "We definitely do not need her flipping out like that again; it could end up causing a major panic that we don't have time for."

An hour later, as lunch was being served, Linda and one of the other women came to meet with Mike just as he was about to get into the chow line. He stepped out and signaled for Tommie, Steve, and Ron to follow suit. They entered Mike's cabin, Linda shutting the door behind them.

"She is calmed down now," Linda said just above a whisper. "And we got her to talk."

"And," Mike said.

"Apparently, someone she saw here, a man, looks very much like a man who molested her a year or so back."

"What?"

"And she is terrified he is here to get her back for telling on him."

"Did she say who it was?"

"She said his name is Merrill Treadmore," Linda said. "I never saw the man in person, but do know that there was some kind of corruption scandal going on in the city government, and that name was tied to it."

"We don't have anyone here by that name," said Steve.

"Who of the men may have come from Valdez?"

"Anderson," muttered Tommie. "Mojo said he had a strange feeling about him."

"Anderson," Linda asked. "Who is that?"

"One of our patrols found him in the woods just as winter was starting," Mike said. "He said his name was Roger Anderson, and that he was a newspaper reporter from Valdez."

"Really? My husband was friends with a Roger Anderson at the paper. I haven't seen him around here since we arrived."

"If I pointed him out to you, would you recognize him?" said Mike.

"Of course," replied Linda. "He ate dinner at our house once or twice a month. And while a name like that is not exactly uncommon, I only knew of one in Valdez."

"Let's get some food and see if you can point him out," Mike said.

The group went back out of the cabin and rejoined at the end of the food line. They filled their bowls with steaming hot hare and wild herb soup, with the added blessing of black pepper, salt, and bay leaves snatched from the convoy.

Sadly, the raiders had not grabbed any flour or yeast, so the bread they had with their soup was stomach filling, yet weirdly chalky, birch bread. It was made from the inner layer of bark from the paper-birch trees that were plentiful all over most of Alaska. As long as one gave it a good soaking in the broth, it wasn't too bad.

Once they had their food, they headed to the leader's benches at one side of the dining area.

As they sat, Tommie noticed two boys get up and move to another bench with their still-full bowls, joining some other boys rather than sit with the adult who had approached them. He whispered to Linda, "The man sitting alone to your left, that's Anderson."

She gave a surreptitious glance that direction and immediately said, "That is not the Roger Anderson I know. No resemblance whatsoever."

"Like you said though," Mike whispered, "the name is kind of common."

"But there was only one I knew in Valdez, and that is not him."

At that moment, Mike saw Katie come out of her hut with a couple of the other girls and start towards the food line. She looked up, glanced over at the others where they ate sitting on benches or rounds of unsplit firewood. She suddenly froze, stumbled back several steps, then quickly turned and sprinted back into the hut, her face a rictus of terror. Mike traced the direction she'd been looking a moment earlier. Roger Anderson had vanished.

* * *

"Most of his stuff is gone from his cabin," Ron said. "He left in a hurry looks like, just grabbed the essentials and ran."

"Well, that proves some kind of guilt," Tommie said.

"Send a patrol after him," Mike said.

"What do we do if we find him?" Steve asked. "We've only got the testimony of one girl, which serious as it is, he would likely refute."

"The fact that he ran when he saw her tells me he is guilty as hell," Tommie said. "And running in itself is bad for a guy like him, because if the Russians catch him, you can be damn sure it won't be long before he talks."

Ron nodded then added, "That's assuming he makes it far in the open forest. He's not exactly a mighty woodsman. I give him less than twenty percent chance of even surviving to get to the

Russians, especially in this weather. Even if he does, I doubt he'd be able to point us out on a map."

The snow fall had increased significantly; tracking him would be difficult, as would his own journey.

"But there is that chance he might make it," Mike said. "Let's send out a patrol and see what they can find."

Several hours later, as the sun dropped below the trees, and dark shadows stretched across the landscape, Ben's patrol made their way back to camp.

"We were able to track him about two miles out," he told the leaders when they arrived back, "but then lost his trail near a hillside where there'd been a little avalanche that destroyed any sign."

"Think he was buried in the avalanche?" asked Ron.

"It wasn't very big of an avalanche; it could have knocked him down or not, might have buried him if he was weak enough, but it was definitely enough to wipe out his tracks. We went around it but between moose tracks and the new snow, it was impossible to read."

"Well," said Mike, "like Ron said, he most likely won't survive."

Tommie shook his head slowly. "We can only hope."

49

Merrill Treadmore

The snow was getting deeper and he was having a hard to keep his bearings with the low clouds blocking out the sun. Merrill had no doubt he that he had to keep moving though. As long as he kept the mountains behind him and to his left, he would eventually reach the highway. Part of him wished he'd gone on that ambush with the others, just so he'd know the way out. But then, had he been there that little bitch would've discovered him even quicker.

How she happened to show up in that remote, middle of nowhere camp astounded him. She'd been the niece of one of the businessmen in Valdez with whom he had been doing under the table deals.

The girl had only recently moved in with her uncle after her parents had been killed in a car accident.

The uncle had offered her up as a willing virgin he'd caught looking at his porn collection. She insisted she'd merely stumbled upon it in the bathroom and didn't know what it was. The men knew otherwise and decided to teach her what it was all about. The only problem was that the girl had been taught to be a tattle-tale, and first chance she got to escape, she ran and told the police. A few days later, the invasion started and all those cops were dead or running to the hills. He soon found himself running as well.

"And now, after almost a year and a half that little bitch had to show up here! With these goody-two-shoes, fricking boy scouts of all things." He gave a shudder. "They make my skin crawl!"

He tripped and fell onto his face in the snow. He cursed and pushed himself back up, struggling to stand with the heavy pack. Once on his feet, he brushed the snow off his face and clothes, and trudged on toward what he hoped was east.

"The girl claimed she wanted to know what it was she was looking at and we showed her," he muttered, as he lifted his leg over fallen tree, "that is all. She was never hurt. From the look on her face, she even enjoyed it then." His mood picked up briefly as vivid memories of the experience flashed through his mind. "There is no doubt in my mind that the same things will soon be going on with those so-called 'honorable' scouts in no time."

Treadmore ate the last of his food on the morning of the sixth day, just as he reached the Richardson Highway. He waited under cover, unsure of how long it might be before anyone came down the road. His heart leapt in his chest at the sound of a convoy approaching in the distance only a few hours later. When they were half a mile down the road, he crawled out of his shelter beneath a wide-branched spruce tree and clambered up the bank of the highway.

He stepped out onto the pavement and waved his arms high over his head, pleading for assistance.

The convoy of several armored trucks and troop carriers slowed to a stop, many guns pointed at him, a lot more pointed all directions. This did not look like a supply convoy. These vehicles were heavily armed, even more heavily armored, and full of angry-looking infantry.

A soldier in a machine gun turret shouted in Russian at Treadmore. He raised his hands to show he was unarmed and shook his head, indicating he did not understand. The soldier said something into a radio, and a number of other men dismounted from two vehicles a dozen yards back in the column.

They strode towards him, weapons pointed directly at him, fingers curled around their triggers.

"I am unarmed! Please, I am trying to escape from a terrible gang of guerrillas that had taken me against my will!"

The leader of the group, an officer who carried himself with confidence, glared at him, his sharp features projecting an intensity that burned into Treadmore's eyes. He motioned with his hand and said something in Russian.

Two of his men rushed forward and roughly frisked Treadmore. They pulled a small 9mm pistol from a pocket inside his parka, as well as a knife from a sheath on his waist.

"Unarmed?" asked the officer in English his accent giving the word a sinister sound.

"Shit…I…forgot about those," Treadmore stammered. "Really, I didn't think about those. I mean who would come against a convoy this big, with just a little pea shooter and a knife?"

The officer said something in Russian again and one of the soldiers standing beside Treadmore grabbed his shoulder and rammed a fist into his gut, doubling him over. The soldier cocked his arm back and drove his fist into the side of Treadmore's head.

The pavement reached up and slapped him on the other side, and the lights went out.

✶　✶　✶

Treadmore felt like someone had driven an iron spike into his temple. He was at least relieved that he was warm. He slowly cracked his eyes open only to squeeze them shut against an intense bright light that suddenly flashed on, searing his retinas.

A sudden blast of ice cold pain washed over him eliciting a gasp, his testicles retreating protectively deep inside his body. He glanced down, and realized that he was completely naked. Each arm and both legs had been secured to a chair with by thick leather straps.

"So, Mr. Merrill Treadmore," the voice of the officer who'd had him knocked out sounded in front of him. The man himself was a distorted skeletal shadow floating in a painfully bright light. "Did you have a nice rest?"

Treadmore sputtered, and trembled out the words, "How... how do you know my name?"

"You were a famous man in Valdez, as I recall."

He opened his eyes and looked up at his tormentor. "I don't remember seeing you there."

"Ah, but you did not need to see me. My friend in the FSB in Valdez was able to identify you from a picture I sent to him."

The officer drew closer, put a hand on Treadmore's shoulder, and circled around his chair from one side to the other. He leaned down and whispered into his ear, "Mr. Treadmore, you are a very naughty boy. Under investigation for political corruption, accusations of child molestation, accomplice in the murder of your fellow refugees."

"You must be mistaken. I've never done things like that."

"Ah, but Mr. Treadmore, while we did change out the police force in Valdez, we did not destroy the records, most of which included pictures. And we hear rumors of other things."

Treadmore's mind raced. The first two he could understand them getting from records, the last one though. How could he have learned of those killings? Had they captured Chiknik? Or was it the ones on the trail.

"I can see your mind is working hard to process this information, particularly the latter."

Treadmore's gaze followed the officer as he walked slowly around the room, boot steps echoing against the cement walls until he gradually returned to him in the center. He squatted to eye level with Treadmore, and smiled.

"You are not a very efficient killer, I am afraid." The officer clapped him several times on the shoulder, then rose and stepped in front of him. "Two of your victims survived and were...rescued…by my men. They were very willing to share your name, and those of your friends, who thought it wise to join you in murdering the others in your party to take their supplies for yourselves."

Treadmore tried to mask his guilt with an expressionless face.

"It is much harder to kill a man than you might think, isn't it? You can hit them in the head, their skull can even crack, but they may hold on for weeks, or maybe even fully recover. As was the case with one Mr. John Jones and one Mr. Karl Rexer, both very resilient men. Both of them, as it would happen, let me know in no uncertain terms, that they hate you with a passion."

Treadmore said nothing. He could see the faces of those two men, insisting they help other refugees they come up against. Treadmore and Katie's uncle had disagreed and bashed their heads with rocks. Then they'd gone through the camp and killed the half dozen other refugees with the knives they'd taken from the first two. They'd gone back and stabbed Jones and Rexer in the back to make sure they'd finished them off. They left the camp for dead, taking their combined supplies and heading off. A few days later, they'd hooked up with another, larger group of refugees just before reaching Chiknik.

"Mr. Treadmore, I feel badly," said the officer apologetically. "I have not introduced myself. My name is Colonel Khristofor Ilyich Grall, commander of Spetsnaz Detachment 32. My job is to find out everything any refugees or prisoners know, or things they have seen that may help us detect potential threats to our authority. That, and the safety of my men."

"I will tell you anything you want," Treadmore said through trembling lips.

"Oh, I know you will," Colonel Grall replied. "There is no doubt in my mind you will tell me everything you know. And not only that, you will tell me with utter honesty. Because you do not seem like a man who likes to endure pain."

He glared down at Treadmore. The former school teacher's knees were literally knocking together. His whole body shivered, eliciting a tiny whimper from the wooden chair he was strapped to.

"Well, truth be told, some men I have worked with turned out to have an amazing tolerance to pain and mental coercion, but most others not so much. That said, some men, especially the weaker ones, will lie to stop the pain, which is highly unacceptable, in every way you can imagine," he said, as if he were talking down to a child. "Therefore, you will answer all my questions with complete honesty, or things will not be very pleasant for you." He held a contemplative expression and let out a commiserative sigh. "No…Not. Pleasant. At. All."

Grall lifted a small device, like a remote control, and motioned with an index finger for Treadmore to look down. He did and for the first time noticed two wires taped to his genitals that lead to a small box between his feet.

"You will answer my questions, and if we discover you are lying…"

Grall pressed a button on the remote, and Treadmore's entire world filled with blue lightning that ripped canyons across the inside his skull. He tried to scream, but his vocal chords clenched as if he were being strangled. All he could force out was an extended high-pitched squeak.

The barrage of pain exploded to a sudden halt.

Treadmore slumped in the chair, urine dripping off his thighs. He had vomited what little contents he had in his stomach, sputum running down his chest.

"Now you have a more practical understanding of our methods, as well as an idea of your capacity to withstand it."

Treadmore nodded exhaustedly, a whimper sounding in his throat.

"Oh, and so you know, that was the lowest setting." Grall smiled. "One, on a scale of ten."

Treadmore let out another whimper.

Grall leaned closer, predatory grin on his face. "Sorry, say that again?"

"Please, I'll tell you whatever you want to know."

"Yes, you will." Grall smiled like a kindergarten teacher, proud that her student remembered not to eat his paste in class.

"You can start with who led the ambush on my supply trucks last month?"

Treadmore hesitated.

Grall's finger slid over the button.

Treadmore started to speak.

Grall pressed the button.

Five seconds of utter agony coursed through Treadmore's body, the release abruptly slammed him back to mere misery.

He slumped forward against the restraints. Strings of snot mingled with saliva stretched from his face to the floor.

"I want your answers to be that instantaneous, Merrill. When I ask, you simply start talking. When you hesitate, I fear you may be trying to think of a good lie. And that would be no good for either of us."

He raised his eyebrows, waiting until Treadmore grunted a response in the affirmative.

"Now, let's ask that question again. Who ambushed my supply convoy last month?"

This time, Treadmore did not hesitate.

50

Youngmi

ood distribution had opened up more, allowing everyone, regardless of party membership, to receive the same basic ration. Party membership was still rewarded with more than the general population, mostly with items, in addition to basic food, such as spices not generally available. They also got extended hours on electricity, additional fuel coupons, and free tickets to concerts and arts shows at museums.

In a similar vein, only party members were allowed to perform music publicly, or display their art in museums or restaurants.

Party members were also allowed to pick berries in the prime spots in the mountains several days before the general population, and were allowed to participate in communal gardening plots throughout the city.

Non-members were only allowed to use windows boxes or gardens on their own property. They had to wait until members had cleared out the berry-picking areas, before they were allowed to enter a week later, often to find only meager remaining harvests.

Youngmi continuously worked toward gaining more benefits for the general population, but the going was slow. She was working within an unfamiliar cultural mindset, ingrained with a strong connection to party membership, and being part of the state system.

The Chinese generally looked down on those who refused to join, or were rejected by, the communist party for whatever reason. Non-party members were considered inferior citizens who had either proved untrustworthy to be counted among the enlightened, or had rebelliously chosen to stand against the party to their own doom. The party was regarded as their god, and non-party members were thought of as heathens and infidels.

Youngmi was gradually trying to change that attitude by making things as even as possible, as much as her position allowed. Gradually, her concept was working, even though it was slow. Because of her position with the general, her teachings among the officers in her English classes were not suppressed to the level that many others in the public system had been. So, while she did not blatantly spread the concepts of western democracy, the little bits and pieces she put into what she used in her English classes for the officers and NCOs, seemed to be slowly, bit by bit, making a difference.

Those successes also lessened her stigma with the population in general. Rather than a traitorous bitch, as she'd first been labeled, she had over time become known as a type of Florence Nightingale among the American population. She often found herself inundated with requests for people who wanted to volunteer for public service with her projects. They did it willingly, and not because they had been 'volunteered' by the new police force.

General Zhang also found himself enjoying a much higher regard on the part of the population at large, mostly as a byproduct of her actions. Of course, that regard for him did not carry through to the resistance, who did everything they could to discredit his mercies as merely a slick way to gain more control by the communists.

"You have been doing a wonderful job, Youngmi." Zhang beamed at her as they sat at dinner inside the quarters he shared with her. "You know that in my position I do not get to heap praise on many people. My subordinates are merely following orders; few are very creative beyond that. On the other hand, you have taken a small project of your own making, and turned it into a major success that has reduced fighting in the city by a significant margin, as well as allowed a way for us to broker peace with many factions. I cannot tell you how happy I am."

"It is only a small work, my general," Youngmi said, a slight blush on her cheeks. The food and benefits distribution was indeed a large work worthy of praise. If only he realized how she used it as a conduit to pass intelligence to the very rebels she kept at bay with the free food and medical assistance, he would certainly retract any praise he had for her. "I believe there is so much more that can be done, and your leadership will gain even more acceptability by the population."

"Seriously, Youngmi," he said, his voice growing more intense, "what you have done here for your people is something that has happened under no other Chinese army on this continent. To bring peace, and encourage the population to cooperate is no small thing. Our nation's general tactic over the centuries has been, and continues to be, crushing the conquered nation, and decimating its people, rather than attempting to share the land in relative peace. You have done something new here, and I am happy for it."

She smiled demurely, a blush on her cheeks spreading slowly, enhancing her complexion.

"I have to be out of the house for a few days for some meetings in the other parts of the state," he said. "When I return, would you be willing to accompany me to dinner at the Crow's Nest?"

The Crow's Nest restaurant had been, before the war, the premiere fine dining restaurant in Alaska. Situated atop the twenty-two story Captain Cook Hotel in downtown Anchorage, it boasted fine French cuisine prepared by European trained chefs and served by a highly trained wait staff worthy of any New York coat and tie mandatory restaurant.

"I would certainly enjoy dining with you, when you return," she said. With the success of the food program and her name being publicly tied to it, she got far fewer cold stares when they went out these days. People often recognized her from the distribution tables, where her smile brought a cheer to an otherwise dismal existence for many.

"Good," Zhang said. "I will make sure all arrangements are made for when I return. In the meantime, I hear your English classes are doing very well. All the officers praise you; they truly enjoy your style and the conversation you bring to the classroom."

"I am sure whatever you have heard is exaggerated," she said.

"Even Colonel Ping, who is seldom gratuitous toward anyone, has nothing but good things to say about you."

Youngmi held her gentle smile as best she could, but the sound of Ping's name brought an icy shiver down her spine. Every time she saw, or even imagined, his face, a quiver of disgust rattled her body with a desire to lash out in defense, or to vomit.

Zhang's face twisted with an inquisitive look. "Is everything okay between you and Ping?"

"Yes, my general," she said, "everything is fine."

"The look that just came over your face tells me otherwise." Zhang picked up his glass and sipped at the lemon water, ice cubes tinkling as he set it back down. "When I mentioned his name, it was as if I had stabbed your palm with a needle."

"It is nothing," she said, attempting to force a change in her own expression.

"Tell me," he said. "I cannot bear to leave if there is something I must fear for you."

There was a long silence. He allowed her to collect her thoughts. The fact that he thought she was afraid of Ping made her wonder if he really did know about his attack. At length, she took a breath, held it for a moment then let it out in a long sigh.

"I think Colonel Ping resents me being his English tutor," she said, the image of the attempted rape in the ladies' room months earlier crisp in her mind, as she struggled to maintain a professional aura. "He seems to feel that it is beneath him to be subject to the instruction of a Korean/American woman."

"Yes, well, from his perspective I guess that is a 'three strikes and you're out' scenario," Zhang said, the totally American colloquialism seemed to come naturally to him.

"I am sure that is what it is and I just need to deal with it," she hesitated, "but can he perhaps be exempted from the classes, my general?" She paused again, fidgeting with her fingers as she tried to force her nerves up to say the next line, "He just... makes the entire classroom very tense, even among the other colonels and majors near his own age. It is a very difficult learning environment."

"Would you prefer to tutor him independently?"

Youngmi gasped, her eyes wide with fear.

"I am joking! Only joking, Youngmi," Zhang laughed aloud. "I understand your feelings, truly I do. Believe it or not, I have heard of the way he treats women, especially those he finds attractive. Don't forget, I have been his friend for over thirty years."

Youngmi gave him a wary look, as if he might turn her over to his friend Ping.

"He might be my friend," Zhang said, "but that is only because he saved my life on multiple occasions. He is still very much an asshole, please excuse the English expression."

Youngmi could not cover her surprise at his statement; she barely caught a softly snorted laugh before it fully erupted.

Zhang noticed and grinned at her. "That of course is highly confidential, need to know, eyes only information, you realize."

"Of course, my general." She smiled back at him conspiratorially, and ran her thumb and finger across her mouth. "My lips are sealed."

51

Scouts

The depths of winter had come and gone in a blur, surviving long, dark days and deep sub-zero temperatures. The focus from December through February had boiled down to simply trying not to die from the freezing cold, a force that had hovered around negative fifty degrees Fahrenheit for nearly five weeks from Christmas to almost the end of January.

By mid-February, the temperatures rose back up to the relatively balmy teens and twenties until the sun started coming back in force in March and temperatures quickly made their way closer to the "not going to kill you overnight" range.

The leadership had managed to keep the boys and girls at the camp mostly separated, or at least under supervision, for the majority of the winter. Several of the youth did get to know each other nonetheless, especially the heartier ones that had no fear of hard work, or being out in the cold.

Ian finished his weekly range time and stood at the makeshift shooting bench, cleaning his weapons and reloading his magazines.

He glanced up as Ben and Katarina walked up to the bench next to him to start another session.

"So is this where you two go for a date?" He said it as an obvious jibe to embarrass his brother in front of Katarina. Ever since they were little, he frequently went out of his way to poke his older sibling. Sometimes it worked, but this time it fell on mostly deaf ears.

"We tried the restaurant but they're booked till next October," Ben replied, using a phrase he and his brother had long ago made up to mean beyond the foreseeable future.

Ian let the corner of his mouth turn up in half a smile, something that happened with less and less frequency of late.

He was actually glad his brother had found a girlfriend. What that may mean for the future he had no idea, but he was happy to see his brother enjoying her company. The lines on Ben's forehead combined with the tiny wrinkles around his eyes, belied the stress of leading a platoon of boys.

The toll of the combat and strain of ensuring everyone was fed and medically cared for visibly weighed on his brother. Unlike himself, Ben could not just let pain roll off his back. He seemed to deposit it somewhere inside of himself. No matter how hard he tried to hide it, he was like a man who ate too much garlic. It slowly seeped through his pores.

It was as if this new life had cut something out of him. Their oldest sibling, Jay, had been the consummate comedian, always ready with a joke or witty retort, usually delivered just at the right time to soothe the discomfort of the listener. Ian often pictured his 'keun-hyung,' Korean for eldest brother, as something like a pastor or priest with a twisted sense of humor, who managed to get most of his parishioners to smile by the end of a counseling session.

Ian, the youngest, saw himself as more of a hands-on, building and making things type, who enjoyed playing physical sports. He knew he could be brash, and often regretted the words that sometimes burst from his mouth. But he also knew how to look into other people's hearts and sense their inner thoughts. Sometimes, he clearly read the things that terrified them.

He understood that many of the others in Troop 104, boys and men alike, were terrified of him on a very real and personal level.

They had seen him mercilessly dispatch dozens of Russian soldiers, some in single combat, but most with the cold-blooded precision and robotic ruthlessness of a serial killer.

But they did not see what was really in his heart.

They could not hear the silent words his lips shaped as he drove his tomahawk into the skulls of the men who'd tried to kill him minutes earlier.

They did not realize the love he felt for every man that met their fate by his hand.

They would not understand if he told them that every time he put a wounded enemy out of his misery, he prayed for them. He begged God to accept their soul into heaven. To let them see his grace and ask for his mercy in the moment before their soul departed their body.

He asked God to make them realize they needed to repent and surrender to Him. That they needed to be just like the thief on the cross beside Jesus, as his Sunday School teacher had taught it, the one that asked to be received in God's kingdom.

Whether or not his friends understood his motives didn't matter.

Who he was and how he lived was between him and God, and that is all that would ever make a difference to him.

As long as he could stand before God with the knowledge that he served his Lord, honored his parents, and loved his fellow man, he would have no qualms about the blood on his hands taken in this war. There was no pain that could stick to him anymore.

His brother Ben on the other hand, 'cha-keun-hyung,' next brother in Korean, was not one to let it all roll off of him. Ben was the most bookish and heady of the trio, always coming up with philosophical questions or what Jay referred to as "Deep Space Jibber Jabber."

Now Ben was in charge of the lives of a bunch of others, boys who could live or die at his command. None of this war was rolling off of him as far as Ian could see. He was holding on to every terror yet leading with an amazing amount of skill, even in his younger brother's eyes.

Ian thought about their situations, where the Lord had put their feet. What had been set before them was their defining life's work. Jay was missing. It was unlikely they'd ever see him again. His fate was his own, if he was even still alive. Ben was a sergeant in charge of a dozen boys whose lives were committed to violence.

Ian had morphed into the personification of a young grim reaper as far as the others were concerned.

He let out a barely audible chuckle as he packed up his cleaning kit then slung the new AK-12 over his shoulder, holstered the Russian made Glock 34, and hefted a Dragunov sniper rifle, all items he'd acquired during their last raid.

"You guys have fun," he said to them as he walked off the range back to camp. "Remember, sound travels toward camp from here, so keep the smoochy noises to a minimum."

Ben started to raise his hand as if to flip off his brother, only to have the action interrupted as Katarina tugged him in, planting a quick kiss on his cheek. Ben's expression changed to one of pleasant surprise and he lowered his hand to her waist.

"Excuse me." Ian rolled his eyes. "I've got to go before the puke I'm about to spew from my gut actually lands on you guys."

"Don't worry," Katarina called after him, "you brother is probably safe with me."

The younger Stone walked away, shaking his head.

Ben turned to Katarina and said, "Uh...okay...let's shoot stuff then."

Katarina picked up the AK-12 they'd brought to the range, and picked up a magazine loaded with ten rounds of 7.62x39. She looked at the two as if they were completely unrelated, like the rifle was a square hole and the magazine a hexagon or something.

Ben put his hand around hers and guided the magazine to the feed well on the rifle.

"Turn the magazine this way," he whispered to her as if instructing a first-time shooter. "Insert it into the space like this, the curved end of the crescent points to the front of the rifle."

He guided her hand until the magazine connected with a satisfying click.

"Thanks," she said, a sheepish expression on her face.

"Okay," Ben continued the instruction, "with the magazine fully inserted, reach up with your finger and snap the safety down." A satisfying metallic *snack* signaled the operation's completion. "Okay, now pull the charging handle back all the way, then let it go."

Katarina pulled the charging handle back, then opened her fingers and let it slam back home, driving a round into the chamber with another satisfying slap.

"As my dad used to say," Ben paused then dropped his voice to a forced baritone, "you are now ready to kill."

"Really?" Katarina turned a skeptical eye to him. "Your dad really said that to you?"

"Yes, actually," Ben replied. "He was kinda given to the dramatic side of life sometimes."

"Sounds like a guy I'd like to meet," she said.

"Let's hope that happens," Ben whispered as he leaned in and showed her how to position the rifle and get the target image lined up in the sights. "As you focus on the target, you'll see the sight post at the end of the rifle…"

"The pointy thing on top of the tower?"

"Uh…yeah" Ben grinned, trying to keep a serious look on his face. "The pointy thing on top of the tower. As you line that up with the bullseye and the rear sight, you will notice that it moves in something like a sideways figure eight."

"An infinity symbol," she said.

"Yeah, an infinity symbol," he said. "So you just watch that movement, which is caused by your own heart beating in your chest, by the way, that's why it is so rhythmic, and as the sight comes back to the middle of the X in the infinity symbol, you fire."

"Will it kick hard?"

"No, AKs are really kinda easy on the kickback."

Katarina took a deep breath, sighted along the rifle toward the target, a disk of wood sawed off of a log and painted in charcoal with concentric rings around a bullseye, one hundred meters down range. She released the breath.

"Slowly squeeze the trigger as you exhale," Ben whispered to her.

The crack of the shot was much quieter than she seemed to have expected. She barely flinched at all. Ben looked through the 10x scope on his rifle and let out a breath. The bullet punctured the target dead-center. Literally dead-center, as in she had shot the tiny 'x' that'd been carved out of the center of the black dot.

"Hrm...can you do that again?" he asked.

"Of course," she said.

"Put five more shots into the target," he said. "Let's make sure the sights are zeroed."

She squeezed the trigger five times in so many seconds.

"Uh," Ben said as he stared through the scope. All five rounds were not only within the small black bullseye, they evenly circled the first hole she'd put in the target.

Ben was reminded of the movie Lethal Weapon, which he watched on cable before the war, where the main character shot two eyes, a nose, and a smiley face onto the head of a paper target at long range.

"You are, if I remember the pre-war slang of the urbanite population, a pool shark aren't you."

"Me? I don't know what you mean?"

"You'd told me you didn't do much shooting before."

"Well, compared to my brothers and father," she smiled innocently, "I didn't do much at all. Maybe only a couple hundred rounds a month. Dad made his own ammo so we always had a nearly endless supply."

"You are something." Ben smiled back at her and slowly shook his head. "Multi-lingual, crack shot, and still smiling."

"Yes," Katarina leaned close to him, "I am something."

She gave him a flirty wink, then a quick kiss on the mouth.

"What was that for?" he gasped, cheeks turning red.

"What, you don't want it? Fine," she said, "I'll take it back." Then quickly leaned in and kissed him again, "There, I undid it."

"No, give it back," he blurted then stretched toward her and took the kiss back. The quick peck turned into a full-blown kiss as they wrapped their arms around each other, the rifles pushed aside.

She started to say something but was cut off by a sudden shout from camp.

"HELICOPTERS!"

Pots and pans clanged in alarm.

Everyone ran to their assigned defensive positions.

Ben and Katarina snatched the weapons they'd had with them and ran back to camp. As they approached, the not-so-distant sound of rotor blades thundered to the east. They both snatched up an ammo vest with six extra magazines, giving each of them two hundred ten rounds apiece including what was already in the rifle.

"Let's hope we don't need all this," Ben huffed as they ran to their position a hundred yards into the trees at the eastern side of the camp.

Mike and Tommie had laid out a trench system that connected multiple fire holes with interlocking fields of fire. The mountains to their rear were mostly barren of trees, and generally too steep for soldiers to assault from.

While the lake to their north was solidly frozen enough for helicopters to land and disgorge troops, it was a wide-open, uncovered stretch of several hundred yards before the enemy would have any sort of cover. They would find that cover mined with homemade claymore mines and booby traps of every sort imaginable.

The only direction from which the enemy could bring an attack was directly east. Those that were about to do so were going to find themselves running against a phalanx of machine gun and rifle fire. They would also find more homemade claymore mines raining a deadly hail of super high-speed metal, gravel, and wood shards at them before they even reached the lines.

The helicopters rose back to the sky and fled back toward the highway, the sound of their rotors faded to a deafening silence that blanketed the forest.

Ben glanced to his left. Ian and Charlie manned a PKM medium machine gun with several boxes of ammunition in a row beside it. Ian had his hand on the grip, finger straddling the trigger guard in expectation, his tomahawk was stuffed in his belt next to the ammo pouch holding extra magazines for the QBZ that stood against the trench wall at his knee.

Ian turned and gave a quick look to his brother. His eyes were huge and his face stretched in a smile as wide as if he was expecting to have the time of his life any minute.

Boots crunched in the snow behind him, he twisted toward the sound, rifle at the ready only to relax as he saw Tommie crouch run up to the position he and Katarina shared alongside the other members of his platoon.

"You lovebirds got all your ammo and grenades?"

"Yes, sir," Ben said, cheeks blushing again.

"Lovebirds," Katarina replied, "whoever said…"

"Yeah well, you'd best give each other one more kiss, for luck. This shit's gonna get real in a few heartbeats kiddos." Tommie moved on to Ian's position, then down the line to the next just as fast.

Ben put two of his four grenades on the rim of their foxhole for easy access if needed. The other two stayed in their pouches on either side of his vest.

Somewhere down the line, he heard the sound of a boy puking, and Tommie's voice.

"Get it out now, and get focused. It's us or them, boyo."

Katarina turned towards him. "Well?"

"Well, what?" Ben asked, looking nervously into the forest, his face pale, lips tight in a rictus of fear.

She stared at him until he looked back into her eyes.

Beautiful green eyes.

Set in pale white skin flecked with a smattering of freckles, beneath soft auburn hair.

"Good luck kiss," she asked.

He leaned forward and gave her a quick kiss. She pressed her hands on his face and held him there for several seconds, mouths pressed together, as if they may never have another moment to share. A crack in the trees snapped their attention back to the front.

"That should give us a lot of luck," he said, a slight smile breaking through the fear.

"You have to survive," she said, "so I won't be lonely."

An explosion shattered the tension, causing the line to cringe simultaneously.

Screams of agony quickly rose to a fevered pitch from several men in front of them. Men hit by the wild shrapnel from the devices in the trees.

Russian curses echoed on the air, followed a moment later by two more rapid blasts as the second line of booby traps did their job on the advancing men.

The white coveralls of the oncoming Russian soldiers rendered them nearly invisible against the backdrop of the snow as they closed ranks and continued toward the enemy.

They advanced with no more booby traps or mines blasting them, drawing closer every step to the well-concealed lines of Troop 104.

The cries of the wounded still rang in the forest behind. Then every noise in that valley was drowned out by the sudden, violent, cacophony of gunfire that erupted all down the line.

Ian's machine chattered a regular beat as he fired three- and four-round bursts directed at targets he saw in the trees.

Ben and Katarina both leaned into their rifles, scanning through their scopes, waiting for targets to present themselves.

A grayish white mass moved in the distance, a hundred meters away.

Ben squeezed the trigger and watched as a pink mist burst skyward and the mass collapsed into the snow.

Then, in a heartbeat, the tempo of the fight erupted into a frenzy unlike anything he'd seen so far in nearly two years of war. Return gunfire poured from the front in sheets of flame and steel, drowning out the screams of boys and men trying to return an equal amount of fire.

Shapes moved in every direction, rushing toward his hole.

He had to fight.

He had to protect Katarina.

Out of the corner of his eye, he saw his brother's best friend, Charlie Charles, the Athabaskan native who'd grown up in the bush, but loved Taco King and cable TV, crumple in their hole.

Ian's rage ramped up multi-fold and he sent endless streams of lead into the attackers. As the last round of ammo chinked out of the belt, he slammed the box off the gun and slapped another one into its place, continuing the rhythm with barely a break. Tracers illuminated the forest like an army of hornets, fanning side to side, ensuring every soldier on the other side got their fair share of stinger.

The machine gun jammed, but he quickly moved through the clearing drill Mike and Tommie had taught him then resumed fire. The second box of ammo was soon depleted and he slapped in a new one, resuming the constant stream of fire. Ben's rifle kept popping off rounds as the shapes in the distance kept coming, like ghosts from a nightmare.

Steam rose around his brother. The barrel of the machine gun glowed cherry red as burst after burst cleared the field in front of him like a reaper's scythe.

Ben fired a burst of his own into the bark of a tree behind which a Russian soldier had taken cover. The bark exploded and there was a yelp as it slashed the face of the soldier. He saw the man's shadow as he dropped back further, then watched the telltale wiggle of a willow branch as he crawled past it in the snow. Ben put two more rounds a couple feet in front of the willow and movement stopped.

A resounding bang that sounded like no gunshot he'd ever hear snapped his attention to his brother's direction. The end of the PKM's barrel was splayed out like a demon flower. A round had exploded in the overheated tube, rendering the gun useless. Ian instantly picked up the Chinese QBZ from its place on the trench wall and started picking targets.

A cluster of shapes charged towards Ben and Katarina. Ben grabbed a grenade from the shelf in front of him, yanked the pin, and hurled it out. The baseball-sized device burst in a globe of shrapnel that dropped the beasts charging his position. Several of them got back up though and he and Katarina fired their rifles into them until they too stayed down like their comrades.

Yet more men came at them.

A whistle sounded, shrill and piercing to his left, past Ian's position.

Two short blasts followed by one long and three very short.

The call to tighten the lines.

Mike and Tommie had taught the group several prearranged whistle signals to give orders over the chaos of battle.

Ian took off down the trench line, toward the sound of the whistle, grabbing Charlie's rifle and ammo pouch as he moved firing one handed toward the attackers. Ben tossed his second grenade toward the forms coming their way, then he and Katarina followed, maintaining fire as they moved.

Fifty meters down the trench line, the surviving scouts and leaders condensed into a tighter fighting group. From the slope of the nearby hillside, deadly accurate sniper fell among the oncoming Russians.

From within the trench, sheets of hot lead withered the trees and the men among them. Most of them were regular infantry soldiers of the type the scouts had so often ambushed in convoys. But among them, visible by their different uniforms, was a cadre of Spetsnaz.

Russian Special Forces.

They knew their tactics.

After the initial few dead in the first moments of the fight, they quickly ascertained their enemy and their training took over. Seventy highly trained warriors face to face against the sixty or so men, women, and children of Troop 104 Alaska Defense Force. The training Mike and Tommie had been providing the past two years showed, but against these young warriors in their physical prime, the difference was obvious.

Ben ran along the trench behind Katarina, firing his rifle one handed over the lip. A dozen yards ahead, a man suddenly landed in the pit in front of his brother. Ian's arm moved in a blur, a primal roar on his lips as his tomahawk flashed into view and a spray of bright red arterial blood erupted skyward from the soldier's neck, his head flapping sideways, nearly decapitated. Ian kicked him in the chest and stepped over his body, flipping the tomahawk into his left hand and raising the AK slung across his chest to fire one handed into two more soldiers rushing the trench.

Eyes wide with rage, his teeth were bared in a bestial grimace.

He spun and for a second Ben feared his brother, blinded by blood lust, had forgotten who he and Katarina were. The barrel of Ian's rifle stopped before passing over them and returned to face the enemy.

Katarina tossed another hand grenade toward the rushing soldiers. The explosion was muffled in the snow. Ben did not dare look up to see if it had an effect, just pushed her on and kept running.

Moments later, they were beside Mike. He signaled for them to turn and keep firing.

Ben raised his rifle over the side of the trench and saw a Russian trooper point a pistol of some sort toward their position as he spoke into a radio.

Mike pointed to the man, "GET HIM! That's a laser spotter for a guided missile!"

Ben snapped his rifle to his shoulder and fired several shots, the man crumpled, the laser pistol pointing downward as he fell into a heap in the snow. Seconds later, a tearing sound ripped across the sky, above the sound of battle.

"DOWN!" screamed Mike. He suddenly lurched back against the trench wall, his head snapping at a crazy angle, then dropped to the frozen dirt floor.

Those who heard the warning crunched into fetal positions, deep into the trench just as the world was engulfed by with a roar that sounded like the end of all things. Those who did not drop to the bottom of the trench were instantly shredded above ground level.

The bulk of the explosion ripped the Russian teams to pieces. The laser designator had pointed straight down, marking his own position instead of the scouts.

The Russian missile landed smack in the middle of their own men.

A dull silence followed the explosion. Ben could hear his pulse in his ears, but nothing else. He reached forward and touched Katarina's back; she turned to face him, terror etched in her face.

Her lips moved, but he could not hear what she was saying.

He saw the shape of his brother leap up out of the trench, pistol in one hand, tomahawk in the other, and stride into the enemy positions.

Several other boys joined him.

There were not many Russians left to dispatch. The massive bomb had decimated their own ranks.

The dozen men left gave little fight as the murder boys descended upon them, ensuring none would leave to tell the tale.

✳ ✳ ✳

"Grab your go bag, and as much ammo and food we can put behind the reindeer," Tommie shouted as he strode through the camp. "Walt, get those beasts harnessed. We've got to get out of here as fast as possible before they realize their mistake and come piling in on us again."

"What about the wounded?" Ron argued.

"If they can walk, they can come with us. A couple can ride in the sleds pulled by the reindeer," Tommie said, then his face turned grim. "The rest stay. We give them each a grenade and pray for a quick death."

Ron stared at him in disbelief.

"You can stay and die with them if you like," the mercenary said, "because that's what'll happen to anyone who is still here in an hour.

Ben rushed back one more time to check for any survivors. Too many of his friends and leaders lay dead at the bottom of the gash in the land.

Charlie's body lay crumpled in a fetal position, as if he'd fallen asleep. The pool of black blood puddled around his head formed a halo, as if verifying he was no longer among them. Further down, Mike lay flat on his back, his son Todd weeping over him. There was a neat bullet hole in his father's forehead like a third eye. The back of his skull was an open flap of skin.

"Todd," Ben called, "c'mon, we've got to go, man."

"My dad," he sobbed, "my dad is dead. He's not supposed to die, he's a Green Beret."

Ben jumped down into the hole and pulled Todd to his feet. He gave a firm hug and let him sob on his shoulder for a count of ten and was about to tug Todd up to his feet when Tommie appeared over the lip of trench and looked down on his old friend's body, a hint of sorrow briefly melted his face. Ben caught a glimpse as the Irish mercenary squeezed back a wave of painful sorrow. The man sucked in a deep, shuddering breath and composed himself.

"Move it, you two! Get out of there now!"

Todd looked up with a fierce glare. "We have to bury my dad!"

"There is no time," Tommie replied with a steely hardness. "We have to leave him and all the rest."

"How can you say that?" Todd shouted back. "He was your friend."

"Yes," Tommie's eyes blazed, "he was a very good friend that I knew since before you were born, boyo! And I am also your godfather, Todd. I swore to him that if something like this happened, I would take care of you., Now get out of the feckin' hole and move your arse."

"But..." Todd started.

"But nothing. We're leaving in two minutes. The Russians will be sending more troops, or more missiles, or both here anytime, and we need to be miles away, or we're all dead."

Ben clambered up out of the hole then he and Tommie both reached arms down to help Todd up.

"Don't worry, son," Tommie said in a more soothing voice, "you know your dad always said he wanted to be laid out for nature to take him. Remember, it's only his body. His spirit is with his God, and watching you now. Let's make him proud, by surviving to fight another day. Avenge his death on the invaders."

A look of resolve transformed Todd's face. He gave a quiet nod.

"Now go get your go-bag and whatever gear you can carry." Tommie patted him on the back. "We really are leaving in two minutes."

In the end, there were only two of the surviving wounded who could not walk. They put them onto the sleds, booby trapped the bodies of the Russians, and within an hour of the initial helicopter sighting, were headed north. Two hours and just more than eight miles later, several small explosions echoed from the distance.

The thirty-five survivors picked up their pace as they drove north, towards the village Mojo had told them about.

Ice Hammer's town of Chiknik.

5 2

Brad

The months that were typically considered spring in the Lower-48, March and April, were in Alaska more like the last gasps of winter. March often saw the last foot or two of snowfall. April could be spring like or winterish, depending on the mood of the weather gods, it seemed. By May, though, the twenty-four-hour sun brought on an almost instant summery feeling.

May sat in the near distant future. April's mud was yet a few weeks away. March's snow and still hard, frozen ground provided Brad and his men with the opportunity they needed for one last strike against the Chinese enemy a hundred miles away. Ten Rangers headed by Kharzai and accompanied by Brad himself had piled into the pair of SUSVs for the dangerous trek across the back country towards Anchorage.

Three days later, they left the vehicles just north east of Chugiak with a five-man guard, not far from the Gorsuch Scout Camp that Brad's boys had escaped from in the early days of the war.

The remaining men made their way on foot into the city of Anchorage proper, spreading out through the suburbs to accomplish two separate missions. One to gather intelligence on internal resistance they could assist with.

The other, to assassinate the general.

Brad, Kharzai, and three of the Rangers were tasked with the latter of those missions. Brad stopped to take in a lungful of Anchorage air, and reminisced briefly about his former home and life.

"I haven't seen papayas since the war started," came a voice from the woods where the group had stopped at the foot of the mountains east of the Muldoon neighborhood of Anchorage. It was a deep, gravelly voice. One that had breathed plenty of fresh Alaskan air, swirled generously in a tobacco haze and bathed in regularly scheduled soakings of Jack Daniels.

"Yeah, but you should try the chili," Kharzai replied.

Several shadows emerged from the woods and approached the Chiknik team.

"Who the hell comes up with your pass-phrases?" Brad asked the burly man who stepped near, presumably the leader of the men that came up behind him. The man looked like an old-school Alaskan trapper.

"You know," the trapper had a full beard and long dark hair that jutted thickly from beneath a fox fur cap that looked home-made. The fox's head was still attached, staring down from empty eye sockets, "I have no idea who comes up with these things; compartmentalization is our motto, you know. But this one was nothing. Last time, it was something about Southeast-Asian jungle horticulture and 'The Time Traveler's Uncle,' whatever the hell that means. Those HQ guys must be eating the wrong kind of wild mushrooms to come up with some of these."

The old trapper stretched out his hand in greeting. "I'm Jared, Anchorage resistance."

"I'm Brad, Chiknik Rangers." He reached out his hand and found it grasped in a vice-like grip within Jared's massive paw.

"You're the Ice Hammer fella' everybody talks about," Jared said as he released the iron grip with only seconds to spare before Brad's metacarpal bones would've succumbed, shattering to pieces. "There's some pretty good pictures of you out there. Very recognizable if you're seen on the street."

"How does anyone have my picture?"

"Chinese put a most wanted poster out for the public a few months back," Jared said.

He handed Brad a mobile phone. The screen was filled with a picture that Brad was certain had been either his driver's license or Costco membership card photo.

"Chinese masters didn't want you to be coming in and doing just what you're about to do, so they spread your face all over with a pretty spiffy reward for news leading to your arrest."

"Well, that sucks, boss," said Gunnar.

Kharzai looked at Brad, then back to Jared and asked, "Just how much reward we talking about here?"

"One year double ration coupons for the whole family," Jared answered.

"Oh, that's not bad," Gunnar said.

"Hrm," said Kharzai.

"But wait," Jared held up a finger, "there's more. The person who turns Ice Hammer in also gets deluxe housing for life."

"Ooooh…this is tempting," said Kharzai.

"Look out, boss," Gunnar nudged Brad.

"And, as an added bonus," Jared continued, "if they turn in his faithful sidekick too," he pointed at Kharzai, "they get free gas and electric for life."

"Wait, what?" Kharzai said indignantly.

"Interesting," said Brad. "So I am worth a house to my betrayer, but Kharzai just gives them gas. Sounds about right."

"Hey! I'm right here, you know!"

"Not to worry, gents," Jared said. "No one will be betraying either of you today. Because we can get you on site and ready with barely even poking your pretty little faces above ground level."

The local resistance group had full access to the city, regardless of Chinese military presence, via a series of tunnels that meandered under the tiny metropolis. Some had been built for the purpose of transporting jet fuel from ships at the Port of Anchorage to Ted Stevens International Airport. Others had been under the city since as far back as World War Two as a manner of reorganizing if the Japanese invaded the mainland. After two hours meandering beneath the city proper, with only a few snaps of fresh air as they crossed above ground between unconnected tunnels, they made their way into a position on the top floor in the building that had previously housed the Canadian Consulate. The position looked down on 4th Avenue and the entrance plaza to the Captain Cook hotel.

On the top floor of the Captain Cook was Anchorage's most exclusive restaurant, the Crow's Nest. Brad had taken Youngmi there several times in the past for special occasions, but only after he'd been promoted to a senior position in the government. The vast majority of customers at the Crow's Nest made well into the six-figure income range back in the day. Which is typically what it took to cover the more than one to two hundred dollars per person for dinner, wine, and dessert. He had always been judicious about what those occasions were that brought them there.

Now it was almost exclusively for high-ranking Chinese officers and those local party members who demonstrated the absolute best form at kissing their master's behinds.

Their intel source had sent General Zhang's itinerary for the week. He was scheduled to take his mistress to the Crow's Nest for dinner tonight. They would be arriving at the restaurant just before six o'clock in a large, black, armored, suburban SUV, two medium-armored Humvees providing security. The armor-piercing rounds for the LAW should be able to take out the vehicle or at least damage it enough to kill or severely injure the passengers.

Snipers set their hides up in nearby offices to take out the guard vehicles expected to be in front and behind the general. The windows in the building were among the few in the city that slid all the way open rather than tilting partially. This way, just as the targets came into the view, they could slide them wide enough to fire through without having to break or shoot through the glass.

By four o'clock, they were all set up. In two hours, it would be judgment day for General Zhang and his collaborator mistress.

53

Youngmi

Youngmi climbed into the suburban, General Zhang right behind her. They laughed as Zhang repeated a humorous story one of the officers had told after the mid-day meeting. The day itself had been pleasant.

Youngmi felt very peaceful after good classroom sessions with both the Junior and Senior officer's English classes, as well as a fun time chatting with and teaching Mai. It had been a beautiful sunny April day, winter's deep chill long faded into memory.

While still below freezing at night, the fifty-degree spring air felt nearly balmy compared to the sub-zero ranges of a month earlier. With the days being back to nearly twelve hours of sunlight, nearly everyone was in good spirits as the long dark winter drew to a close, opening up their world for the bright and cheerful summer midnight sun in this second year of occupation.

General Zhang was taking her to the classiest restaurant in the city as a reward for her hard work on the food distribution system. The time they spent together now, after nearly two years, had begun to feel natural, no longer forced or strained. She enjoyed his company most of the past two years and more. Youngmi looked forward to private moments they could spend with each other, chatting about his work day.

Was it a case of Stockholm syndrome?

She'd thought about that often, but if she honestly admitted to herself, she no longer cared if it was Stockholm syndrome or not.

Zhang had been, and still was, not only honorable and kind toward her, but he was a real gentleman. Part of her sometimes regretted passing information to Captain Chi, the spy in Ping's intelligence unit, fearing that something she gave him might end up causing personal harm to General Zhang.

Since the revelation of her husband's remarriage, something had broken in her.

No...something had been freed in her.

He thought she was dead, so she considered her old self to be just that.

Dead.

All those years of marriage, tied to one man, committing herself to him with unwavering devotion, had been snuffed out in a single day.

Brad had not even waited to find out what happened to her. He had never come to rescue his wife, as he'd always promised he would if something like this happened.

Instead, he'd gotten a much younger woman pregnant, one who had been his student when she was a teenager and he was in his thirties.

When she had learned of his faithlessness, her heart had ached with a sorrow that nearly killed her. She had contemplated taking her own life, but could not follow through with the knowledge that her sons may still be out there looking for her.

Then something changed inside her.

Why should she be the only one in misery? She decided she would not sit in the shadows of a past that had been ripped apart and chose instead to open her heart and let the wind take her where it may.

"Youngmi," Zhang said, "you are absolutely radiant tonight."

The young porter who opened the door to the suburban handed a medium-sized box to him.

"Sir, Colonel Ping said to give this gift to you. It arrived in the mail this morning from your old friend General Han, mistakenly delivered to the colonel. It was apparently intended for Christmas but arrived late on the ship."

"Thank you, Corporal," Zhang said taking the gift. The corporal saluted and pushed the door to the SUV shut.

The small convoy took off toward the restaurant. An armored Humvee in front and back, 12.7mm machine guns scanning the buildings around them, they rolled through the streets of downtown Anchorage. They turned onto 4th Avenue for the last couple of blocks, sentries increasingly wary as the buildings grew higher and closer together. Even though the city had been mostly secure and few attacks occurred in the downtown area, there was still a threat of the terrorists striking any time the general went out in public.

Zhang untied the ribbon that held wrapping paper around the box the soldier had handed him. He folded the paper neatly and set it on the seat between himself and Youngmi. He studied the plain brown wooden box sealed around its seam with clear tape, then smiled over to Youngmi.

"You don't think it is a bomb, do you?"

"Knowing Colonel Ping, you might want to be careful," she replied.

"Here goes nothing." He pulled the lid off the tightly sealed box. A stench instantly filled the cabin. The smell was horrible. It almost immediately had them both gagging. "Oh my God," Zhang shouted, "what kind of friend would send a box of fish for Christmas?"

What had probably been shipped in dry ice four months earlier, had long ago thawed and completely rotted in its airtight container. The stench threatened to ruin both their appetites. Youngmi hit the button to roll down the passenger window for fresh air, and Zhang did the same on his side then tossed the box outside. The rotted fish splattered next to a dumpster in an alley.

"Driver! Turn the AC on full blast back here immediately!" Zhang ordered.

"Oh," Youngmi gasped, "that was awful!"

"Think happy thoughts, Youngmi," Zhang coughed. "Happy thoughts! Happy thoughts to wash away the stench!"

They burst into laughter at the absurdity, as the SUV rolled toward dinner.

54

Brad

The first vehicle of the convoy nosed into sight as it passed 4th and H. They slid open the windows on the top floor, keeping well inside the dark shadows of the room. Remaining out of view of the guards in their turrets with the big guns. The team snipers readied to take out the guard vehicle gunners from different rooms in the consulate building.

The LAW man prepared to launch his rocket, a backup unit lay opened on the floor next to him, ready for a fast change over in case of a miss. Brad held the range finding binoculars to his eyes, watching the behemoth vehicle roll into range.

"Ready," he whispered.

The rocketeer, a Knik Ranger who had been an anti-tank gunner in the Army during the War on Terror, put his hand on the firing lever and started the slow squeeze.

Brad gave a count down, "Three...two...o..."

The passenger side window of the SUV suddenly rolled down. Dark hair flowed out on the breeze and a woman seemed to be trying to suck in fresh air as she laughed, coughed, and gagged. A box of something flew out the opposite side of the vehicle, splattering on the pavement in an alley next to a dumpster.

The woman on the passenger seat turned toward the window for another whiff of air, her attractive Asian face smiled widely at something the other person in the back said.

Brad caught a full view of the general's mistress and his heart suddenly stopped beating.

He stared at the face of his wife, Youngmi.

"Wait," he started, but the Ranger took it as part of the count, his fingers depressing the firing lever, the click of the launch button ringing loud in Brad's ears as it pressed home.

The hiss of the rocket leaving the tube a split second later silenced him. His eyes grew wide as he watched the rocket's contrail draw a direct line to the SUV. A straight line to Youngmi's smiling face.

A scream tried to form in his chest but was drowned out by the blasts of the sniper's rifles as they killed the convoy gunners. A half count later, the rocket impacted the side of the suburban, striking the passenger side front door.

A ball of flame engulfed the massive black vehicle, obscuring it from view. As the blast of white light dissipated, Brad looked down to see the flaming SUV on its side in front of the Hotel Captain Cook.

No one crawled out of it.

"C'mon!" shouted Kharzai. "We gotta do the beat the baddie boogie or the baddies will be on us in no time!"

He grabbed Brad by the arm and pulled him out of the room. They raced down the stairs, past the basement, and into a sub-basement. Then from there through a door that led into the underground tunnel system.

They ran until it felt like their hearts would burst.

The dank musty smell of the subterranean corridors clung to Brad's every breath, threatening to suffocate him, as he stumbled, dazed, through a kaleidoscope of tunnels, light, and darkness.

Images of Youngmi being killed a second time kept flashing in his mind. But this time, he was the one who had killed her.

Kharzai dragged, pulled, cajoled, and supported his friend as they fled through the tunnel complex.

Eventually, Brad lost track of time in the emotional melee that battled in his soul. They climbed a set of stairs and cautiously opened a door.

Weapons ready, they entered the space. It was dark in the room, a dull strip of barely visible light coming from beneath a door ahead. The room was cold, almost as cold as the outdoors.

One of the local resistance fighters turned on a small mag light, illuminating the space. He stepped to the door, putting his ear against it.

It was quiet on the other side.

He opened it slowly, and the group made their way through, weapons at the ready.

"All clear," whispered the leader.

They gathered in the main room of what turned out to be a fifties era salt box house set in a quiet, mostly abandoned-looking neighborhood. Cars stood in driveways covered in snow that was piled so high they had obviously sat unused all winter. Those that were under carports were blanketed in thick layers of dust.

Several of the houses showed scars of a battle in the past, unrepaired bullet holes and broken glass. Two houses side by side half a block down had been burned to their foundations.

Other than a couple of forlorn chimneys with smoke curling out of them, the neighborhood looked completely deserted.

One of the local resistance fighters saw Brad looking at the area and said, "We call it 'Fallout Town,' 'cuz it looks like one of the abandoned post-apocalyptic towns in the old video game, *Fallout*."

"Where'd all the people go?" Brad asked.

"As you can see, there was some fighting here," the man replied, pointing towards the burned-out skeletons of the houses. "A pocket of resistance was found here, before we discovered the tunnel exit in this house. The People's Liberation Army came in last summer and promptly 'liberated' the fighters to death. Then they killed or imprisoned everyone on this street and one street over in every direction for not having reported the presence of the rebels."

"Who lives there now?" Kharzai asked, pointing to the smoke rising from a few houses.

"Some of the original owners moved back after being 're-educated,'" he said. "A handful of other houses where the owners were dead or otherwise unaccounted for were taken over by squatters, including some of our own who act as watchers."

"After all that," Brad said, "you still have a base here?"

"Nothing left to worry about since they purged the place the first time." The rebel pointed to the door they'd come in from. "Besides, that tunnel has come in handy more than once and they've yet to discover it."

"How could they not know about the tunnel?" Kharzai asked. "I seem to recall there was a terrorist attack here a couple years ago that tried to blow up the president or something; the thing was world news."

Not only was it world news, but Kharzai had been one of the operators who had managed to foil the attack...mostly. A dozen civilians still died, but not the hundreds the terrorists had intended.

"Oh, they know about the main channel of the tunnel alright. They just don't know the extent of its branches, nor do they know the private connections like this one that were illegal *before* the war. This house was built in the fifties, and it was probably just a root cellar, until an owner way back when discovered he was close to the access tunnel and bored into it."

"Why would they do that?"

"Who knows? They might've been up to something shady. Some parts of the tunnels had been used by gangs and drug smugglers prior to the war. Others were just secret hiding places carved out in the cold war. Or they might have just wanted a way to get downtown without going out in the cold. Either way, we knew about the entrance under the Canadian Consulate, and by exploration discovered this Shangri-La."

The sound of a vehicle drew his attention to the window.

"There's your ride."

"Ride?"

"Yeah, ride."

"We're not taking the tunnels back?"

"Nope. I got a message just as we were packing up at the consulate. The tunnel exit we planned to use currently has a PLA tank sitting right beside it. And we can't go back the same way we came in, as that is never a wise move. So that," he pointed to the delivery truck outside, "will get you as far as the south side of the park you came in from; you'll have to walk out from there."

"You're not coming back with us?" Brad asked.

"No, we've got other egress routes in the tunnels that go the wrong direction for what you need." He reached out his hand and shook Brad's, then Kharzai's, then the rest of the team. "It was a pleasure working with you. Hopefully, we made a difference. And I hope to not see you again until the war is over, unless we're killing Chinese together again that is."

Brad's face grew pale. He replied with a solemn nod.

"You fellas need to go; he can't sit out there like that for long."

The vehicle was a medium-sized delivery truck with a stylized logo on the side crying out in bold letters, *Tomasi! Freshest Vegetables in Alaska!*

The truck and the logo looked they'd seen better days. The driver slid the back door up and they climbed into the compartment among empty palettes and a single box of beets that just past their end of life cycle. They were probably last summer's harvest, having spent the winter in someone's larder.

The driver said nothing to them, simply slamming the door shut the instant the last man was inside. The cold metal clanked as the locking bar was twisted into position. Sealing the team into whatever fate lay ahead.

Kharzai watched Brad's face, the latter staring into space as the driver's door slammed shut, and the truck jostled to life then rolled out of the neighborhood. They were all silent for several minutes. Brad looked very unlike the triumphant leader who had just witnessed the assumed death of his mortal enemy.

"Hey, Kemosabe." Kharzai nudged his friend. "What's with the sour look? You're not exactly motivating the troops here."

Brad gave him a look that was full in equal measures with sorrow, pain, and anger. He looked like he wanted to wipe out all of the empty spaces in his body, to condense every molecule into a tiny mass and implode like a black hole.

"Dude," Kharzai whispered, "what is going on? He was the enemy."

"The woman," Brad started but choked on the words. He sucked in a shaky breath and tried to continue, "his…mistress. She," he closed his eyes and leaned his head back against the cold metal of the side wall, "it was Youngmi. She was my wife." A tear rolled down his cheek.

Kharzai's mouth fell open, his expression truly shocked. For the first time in his life, as far back as he could remember, he literally had nothing to say.

"I don't know how it could be," Brad said. "I saw her body, in her car, wearing her favorite shirt. But the face was completely blown away. I…when I looked through the binoculars and the window rolled down on the SUV, there was no mistaking it. That was my wife, Youngmi, in the back seat of General Zhang's vehicle."

Kharzai finally managed to get his voice back. "Maybe it was just someone who looked a lot like her, maybe—"

"No," Brad cut him off. "It was her. I was her husband for most of three decades. We got married when I was barely twenty years old. I know my wife. I don't know who was in the car where I saw her dead body. Maybe…maybe that was her sister or someone else, but there is no mistaking what I saw today. The woman with the general was definitely Youngmi." He paused and choked again. "And I just ordered her killed."

"Look, Brad." Kharzai ran a hand through his curls, trying to find something to say that would ease his friend's pain. Something to make sense of it all. "We don't know the circumstances of how she ended up there. She was probably captured and forced to be with him. Not only that, we don't know if she was killed. The way that SUV rolled instead of just blowing up tells me it was seriously up-armored. They may have survived after all."

"It doesn't matter, Kharzai." Brad leaned forward onto his knees, letting his head droop. "If she is dead, then it is over. If she is not, then she is still with the general. I have remarried and have a new baby on the way. Everything old is gone."

55

Youngmi

The blast had hit the driver's compartment on the passenger side of the SUV. The armor-piercing rocket penetrated the three-inch-thick armor plating and exploding with such force inside the compartment that the vehicle went airborne for a moment then flipped onto its side.

The blast vaporized the driver and bodyguard instantly. The passenger compartment fared much better, thanks to the second layer of thick shielding that enclosed that space a second time, essentially creating an armored room inside an armored vehicle. That fact alone saved Youngmi and General Zhang from being turned into blood jelly.

Survival for either of them had still been tenuous. The occupants of the guard vehicles who'd not been killed rushed to put out the fire and get the general and Youngmi out of the wreck.

Zhang was bruised and banged up with a couple broken fingers and a pain in his ribs that announced itself with every breath, but he was still conscious.

Youngmi lay inert on top of him, heartbeat and breaths barely discernable.

A third Humvee arrived, set up as an ambulance, and both Zhang and Youngmi were quickly moved into it and rushed to the hospital. Zhang's injuries, while definitely painful, were not, as it turned out, life threatening.

Other than his head ringing for a few days, a dislocated shoulder, and a couple of cracked ribs that would bar him from laughing at funny stories or gifts of stinky fish, he seemed to be no worse for the wear and was quickly out of the doctor's immediate care.

Such was not the case for Youngmi.

Zhang sat on a chair next to her bed in the hospital, his left arm in a sling after the doctor had reset the dislocated joint and his ribs taped up. His head ached with concussion and in spite of the tape, the cracked ribs stabbed him with every breath. Youngmi lay silent in the bed, unconscious since the attack. Lights on various monitors flashed. Her pulse and respirations displayed in big yellow numbers. A nearly empty IV bag suspended above her bed dripped life-giving fluid and medication into her system. A blood pressure cuff on the opposite arm automatically ran every fifteen minutes and an oxygen tube at her nostrils emitted a constant hiss. The door to the room opened and a nurse entered, accompanied by a military doctor.

The general started to rise, but the doctor waved a hand at him. "General Zhang, please do not try to stand too quickly; your concussion needs more time to heal, sir."

The general felt the dizziness already swirling in his head and dropped back into the chair.

"What is the prognosis for Ms. Ma, Doctor Feng?"

"She needs to stay in this induced coma for another day or two until the swelling around her brain goes down," the nurse handed Feng her chart, "but things are going well, it seems. She is a very strong woman to survive a blast like that. Other than the severe concussive blow to the head from the explosion's blast wave, the rest of her injuries are relatively minor. A broken finger that will give her arthritic pain one day, and some significant bruising, but nothing else that will last. Once the swelling is settled inside her skull, she will be fine."

"Thank you, Doctor," General Zhang said. "Make sure you give her the best care possible. You must care for her as you would for me personally."

"Yes, General," Doctor Feng said. "Of course, she will receive the highest level of care we have to offer. And now, sir, if we may be excused, we have other patients to attend to."

The general nodded and they left the room.

Zhang took her hand in his and gently squeezed it.

"Please do not leave me, Youngmi," he whispered. "I cannot bear such pain a second time."

56

The SUSVs rolled back into Chiknik almost a week after the attack. Brad walked slowly to his house. Sammi came out onto the porch and gave him a look of relief. He climbed the steps and took her in his arms as best he could with her more than nine-month pregnant belly between them.

"We are so happy to see you," Sammi said, tears welling in her eyes. "I was very worried while you were gone. Kept having bad dreams."

"I am here for you, baby." He kissed her long and deep, then leaned down to her belly. "And for you too, baby." He kissed her belly.

She suddenly gave a little grunt.

"You okay?"

"It seems like you came back just in time," she said. "I've been having contractions all morning, about every ten minutes now."

"What? We've got to get to the clinic." Brad's misery partially dissipated.

"No, it's okay," Sammi said, "the midwife is on the way and Doc is on call if needed." She suddenly gritted her teeth and squeezed his arm hard. "Oh my, that was a lot faster. Less than five minutes."

The midwife turned the corner of the house, took one look at Sammi, and said, "Alright, young lady, you need to get to bed right now. Dad, come with me, you've got some work to do as well."

* * *

At four minutes after eight PM, Sammi released a scream that abruptly turned into relief, and the midwife, a broad smile on her face, handed Brad his new baby daughter.

"Have you already picked a name?" she asked as she cut and tied the umbilical cord.

"Victoria," he said, "because she will bring us victory."

ACKNOWLEDGMENTS

This book is dedicated to my wife and sons.
I would climb mountains and ford rivers to keep you from harm
I would face the fires of hell to rescue you

These are some of the folks who made this book possible.
Among them are fellow writers, experienced mil-
itary, engineering, and explosives experts as
well as philosophers and woodsmen.
John Gilstrap, best-selling author and explosives expert
Chris Grall, US Army Special Forces,
Weapons & Explosives, RET
Glen Craig, US Army Special Forces Medic, RET
Jeremy Price, US Air Force EOD, RET
Brad Alexander, US Army Paratrooper, FMR
Jim Amundsen, US Army Combat Engineer Officer, FMR
Michelle Paugh, Grammar Enforcer
Wally, the Master Carpenter whose last name I never knew
Daryl Chalifour, Chiropractor/Power Lifter
Alex Tatum, Scoutmaster, Bush Philosopher
Steve Gebert, Scoutmaster, US Navy Fighter Pilot, RET
Ron Mattfield, Scoutmaster, Alaska Bushman
and
The Scouts and Leaders of the real BSA Troop 104
with whom I have floated rivers, paddled among
whales, and hiked over mountains
you guys are the real thing.

ABOUT THE AUTHOR

Basil does not just write stories, he has lived a lot of what they contain. The backdrop for his writing started with his birth in rural Alaska. He spent his school years among the only slightly less rural, yet somehow slower moving, corn fields of Ohio, where he wished to be anywhere else, as long as it was exciting. He has lived in Fairbanks, Palmer, and Anchorage, Alaska, Camp Pendleton and San Diego, California. Washington DC, Baltimore, MD, and Baltimore, Ohio. He tried a career in the Marines, but injuries sent him home way too early. After that he waited tables, managed a family diner, worked at the NSA, owned a computer shop, was a carpenter, farmer, intelligence operative, actor, lumberjack, voice actor, EMT, network admin, helpdesk supervisor, Boy Scout leader, IT trainer, radio talk host, youth minister, and a sergeant in the Alaska Defense Force Coastal Scouts. Until a ski injury in 2008 he was an avid weight lifter and could bench press over 420 lbs. Now he's limited to a brisk walk each afternoon, hefting his laptop to his lap whilst sitting in his comfy chair, and curling a pint or three of stout each night. He lives in Anchorage, Alaska with his wife and sons, and Heimdall the Norse Dog.

PERMUTED PRESS
needs *you* to help

SPREAD (THE) INFECTION

FOLLOW US!

f | Facebook.com/PermutedPress
🐦 | Twitter.com/PermutedPress

REVIEW US!

Wherever you buy our book, they can be reviewed! We want to know what you like!

GET INFECTED!

Sign up for our mailing list at
PermutedPress.com

PERMUTED PRESS

KING ARTHUR AND THE KNIGHTS OF THE ROUND TABLE HAVE BEEN REBORN TO SAVE THE WORLD FROM THE CLUTCHES OF MORGANA WHILE SHE PROPELS OUR MODERN WORLD INTO THE MIDDLE AGES.

EAN 9781618685018 $15.99   **EAN** 9781682611562 $15.99

Morgana's first attack came in a red fog that wiped out all modern technology. The entire planet was pushed back into the middle ages. The world descended into chaos.

But hope is not yet lost— King Arthur, Merlin, and the Knights of the Round Table have been reborn.

THE ULTIMATE PREPPER'S ADVENTURE.
THE JOURNEY BEGINS HERE!

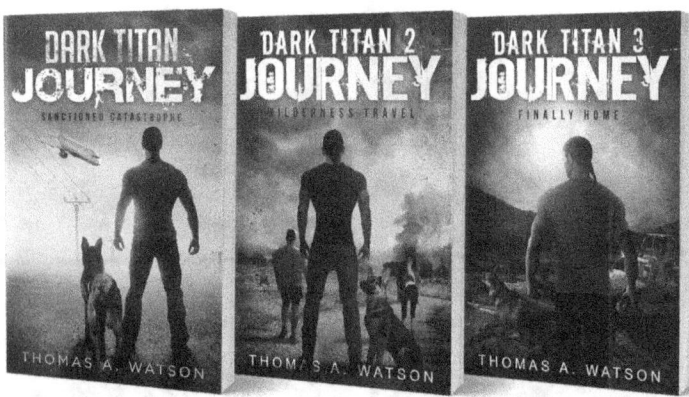

The long-predicted Coronal Mass Ejection has finally hit the Earth, virtually destroying civilization. Nathan Owens has been prepping for a disaster like this for years, but now he's a thousand miles away from his family and his refuge. He'll have to employ all his hard-won survivalist skills to save his current community, before he begins his long journey through doomsday to get back home.

PERMUTED
PRESS

THE MORNINGSTAR STRAIN HAS BEEN LET LOOSE—IS THERE ANY WAY TO STOP IT?

EAN 9781618686497 $16.00

An industrial accident unleashes some of the Morningstar Strain. The doctor who discovered the strain and her assistant will have to fight their way through Sprinters and Shamblers to save themselves, the vaccine, and the base. Then they discover that it wasn't an accident at all—somebody inside the facility did it on purpose. The war with the RSA and the infected is far from over.

This is the fourth book in Z.A. Recht's The Morningstar Strain series, written by Brad Munson.

PERMUTED
PRESS

GATHERED TOGETHER AT LAST, THREE TALES OF FANTASY CENTERING AROUND THE MYSTERIOUS CITY OF SHADOWS…ALSO KNOWN AS CHICAGO.

EAN 9781682612286 $9.99   **EAN** 9781618684639 $5.99   **EAN** 9781618684899 $5.99

From *The New York Times* and *USA Today* bestselling author Richard A. Knaak comes three tales from Chicago, the City of Shadows. Enter the world of the Grey–the creatures that live at the edge of our imagination and seek to be real. Follow the quest of a wizard seeking escape from the centuries-long haunting of a gargoyle. Behold the coming of the end of the world as the Dutchman arrives.

Enter the City of Shadows.

PERMUTED
PRESS

WE CAN'T GUARANTEE
THIS GUIDE WILL SAVE
YOUR LIFE. BUT WE CAN
GUARANTEE IT WILL
KEEP YOU SMILING
WHILE THE LIVING
DEAD ARE CHOWING
DOWN ON YOU.

EAN 9781618686695 $9.99

This is the only tool you need to survive the zombie apocalypse.

OK, that's not really true. But when the SHTF, you're going to want a survival guide that's not just geared toward day-to-day survival. You'll need one that addresses the essential skills for true nourishment of the human spirit. Living through the end of the world isn't worth a damn unless you can enjoy yourself in any way you want. (Except, of course, for anything having to do with abuse. We could never condone such things. At least the publisher's lawyers say we can't.)

PERMUTED
PRESS